CW00551009

One Girl Began

ONE GIRL BEGAN

Kate Murray-Browne

PHOENIX

First published in Great Britain in 2024 by Phoenix Books,
an imprint of The Orion Publishing Group Ltd
Carmelite House, 50 Victoria Embankment
London EC4Y 0DZ

An Hachette UK Company

1 3 5 7 9 10 8 6 4 2

A CIP catalogue record for this book is
available from the British Library.

ISBN (Hardback) 978 1 3996 1365 1
ISBN (Export Trade Paperback) 978 1 3996 1366 8
ISBN (eBook) 978 1 3996 1368 2
ISBN (Audio) 978 1 3996 1369 9

Typeset by Input Data Services Ltd, Bridgwater, Somerset

Printed in Great Britain by Clays Ltd, Elcograf S.p.A.

MIX
Paper | Supporting
responsible forestry
FSC
www.fsc.org   FSC® C104740

www.orionbooks.co.uk

For Florence and Nancy

'It just went like tinder; one girl began, the rest said "yes" and out we all went.'

Account of the Matchwomen's Strike, 1888

'I too shall marry, have children, but *not like her*. I shall find a way of doing it all differently.'

Adrienne Rich, *Of Woman Born*

I

I

Ellen

1909

There are pleasant streets in Hackney, yellow-brick houses with green curtains and closed front doors, and sometimes, walking down them, looking at the fresh flowers in the windows, I feel an ache for how things were before, in the days when we were respectable. But the streets near the factory, the cluster of houses between our lodgings and the high street, are not like that. Everything that should be inside is out, as if the seams of the houses have burst and they've spilt their guts out onto the road. Every front door is open. Women hang about in doorways, squat on front steps or lean out of windows. Washing is strung across the narrow street. Children run around in circles or climb on front walls, lost in odd, formless games.

The day before we moved in to the new rooms, I went to see the factory building, picking my way through litter, passing cracked panes and torn curtains. I came out on the high street and walked past workshops and small factories that I had never noticed before. They made the sorts of things – chairs, soap, glue, hats – that I had once used without thinking about where they came from. When I got to Simpson & Fields, Card and Box Manufacturers, I crossed to the other side of the road to look at it.

From Monday, I would be working indoors. I'd been doing piecework for them for months, making cigarette boxes at the kitchen table and dropping them round the back – but I had never been inside the building, never thought about what went on in there. I tried to imagine what was happening there now, behind the smooth red walls and the glinting windows bigger than doorways.

It must have been dinner-time because the doors opened and the front yard filled with workers – some men, a few boys, a few women, but most of them girls. The girls were my age, and dressed like me, in straw hats, plain skirts and shirts. But they were not like me. They were loud and fast, jostling and shoving, calling and shouting to each other across the yard. My mother would have called them 'rough' or 'coarse'. My father would have called them 'whores'.

I sometimes wonder what would have happened to me if we hadn't had to leave our old house, if I'd stayed on the other side of Hackney, if I'd never heard of the factory. Perhaps I might have managed a bare, comfortable sort of life after all. But the truth is, comfort never suited me, even in my old existence of schoolwork, needlework and polishing the aspidistra leaves with milk every Saturday. I could never leave things alone; I was always picking at my skin or seeing how long I could hold my finger in the candle flame. Looking up at the building, the crowd of girls in front of it, I felt scared, but also a familiar restless excitement.

The smell set it apart, a mix of card and dust, which, after the fried fish, rotting vegetables and canal scum, smelt like lavender to me. I didn't know then about the animal smell of the glue. I didn't know about the girls, about Mary or Eliza or Mags. I did not know what was about to begin.

On my first day at the factory, I got up at half past five, though I'd been awake earlier. I crept between the furniture to the passageway, still unused to how little space there was in the new, cramped rooms. In the passageway, there was a crescent of inky-blue light above the front door, the glass framed by the arch above the doorway. I went through the scullery to the back yard, used the water closet and filled a jug from the tap.

Back in the parlour, I washed my face, pinned my hair back, filled the kettle and laid the grate. I put away the sewing machine and the work basket, spooned tea in the pot, put out the bread and crockery for breakfast. I gently lifted my blanket off the sofa, folded it and put it away in the orange crate by the fireplace, covering my nightdress and pillow. At six, I looked over the room, running through everything that would go on there that day, trying to work out if I had everything ready, and it felt impossible to imagine it all happening without me. I stood for a long time in the doorway, stuck, until I forced myself into the street, shutting the door softly behind me.

By the time I reached the high street, I felt a little better: the sky was getting lighter, the smell from the coffee house as I passed was enlivening, and the doors of the public house were opening. I got to Simpson & Fields early, and went in through the gate to wait in the cobbled yard, where there was already a crowd forming. That was when I saw Mary's gang for the first time.

I noticed their hats first. Most of the girls wore straw

hats, like mine, a few were bare-headed and some of the women covered their heads with shawls. But this group, four or five girls, wore peaked caps, like the ones the men had on, but puffed up like loaves of bread. They'd done their hair nicely too, tucked under the hats and curled around their faces. Their jackets were smart and their boots looked new, even though they couldn't have been earning more than fourteen shillings a week. I thought that everyone must have been right about factory girls after all: vain, foolish things.

But I made my way across the cobbles, sidling past the other clusters of workers, so I could stand just beside these girls and watch them, as they jumped on each other, punched and wrestled – *Betty, you never, you stupid cow, oh, fuck yourself.* They didn't notice me. Then a bell rang, the doors opened and we all began to move.

I had never met Mr Simpson before, and when I knocked gently on the door of his office on the ground floor, a man in a dark suit looked up from behind a large desk with a deep-green surface. I explained why I was there and he seemed not to know who I was. For a moment I thought I'd made a mistake – perhaps there was no job after all – and I felt stupid, but also relieved, despite myself. I knew that we couldn't do without my wage and if there was nothing for me here, we'd be in an even worse mess than we were already, but still, the thought of walking out felt sweet and comforting, as if it would somehow lead me back to my old life.

But he must have remembered because he told me to follow him up to the top floor. He took the stairs two at a time and I struggled to keep up with him, embarrassed at how short my breath was. At the top of the stairwell, there was a window reaching from the ceiling to the floor, and I stopped for a moment, just to see what the streets looked like from up here, the messy string of miniature back yards, with their tiny water closets and washing lines, the collapsing roof tiles and smashed windows. A train track cut across the sky above them.

I followed Mr Simpson through a door to the left, into a vast room, each wall lined with huge domed windows. Slanting squares of sunlight fell on the clean brick walls and wooden floors, and three long benches lined the room. The girls standing at them looked up when we came in, but their fingers did not stop moving. A man in a waistcoat walked between them, making marks in a notebook, and as soon as he saw Mr Simpson he came towards us.

'Mr Clifford,' Mr Simpson said. 'This is Eleanor. She's starting today.'

'Very good. I'll stick her with Mary,' Mr Clifford said. 'Mary!'

One of the girls I had noticed outside joined us. She had taken off her hat and jacket, rolled up her sleeves and put on cotton overalls. She was tall and very thin; beneath her shirt, I noticed the gap where her slight body did not meet the stiff top of her corset. Her eyes burst out of her face. She looked at me as if she was trying to see beneath my skin.

'Yes?'

'You can have the apprentice,' he said. He turned to me. 'Mary will show you what to do and take your wage at first. If it all goes well, after three months, you can start getting the wages.'

I started to panic. It would be impossible for me to work

without wages for three months; we couldn't manage. I was struggling to find the words to say it, that I couldn't be an apprentice, that I would have to go back to working from home, but Mary spoke first. 'I've seen you before. Have you moved in to Digby Street?'

I nodded.

'Enough chatter, please, girls,' Mr Clifford said. 'It's breakfast-time in half an hour, you can gossip to your hearts' content then.'

'Didn't you do boxing-up at home?' Mary asked.

'She's new. She's an apprentice,' Mr Clifford said, and Mr Simpson nodded, although I could tell he was already tired of the conversation, looking towards the door.

'She ain't an apprentice. She already knows how to do it.'

'She makes the cigarette boxes,' Mr Clifford said. 'She'll need to do all sorts here. The hat boxes are a different matter altogether. Besides, we don't know how quick she is.'

'She'll be as quick as me in a couple of days.'

'Oh?' said Mr Clifford. 'Well, if the work's easy, we'll adjust *your* wage.'

'She can be my apprentice for a week. After that, she should get her own wage.'

'All right, settle down, will you, Mary!' Mr Simpson said distractedly.

Mary's face set into an expression – eyes narrow, mouth firm – that made me shrink, but the men were not looking at her. She cocked her head towards the back of the room, and I followed her.

'You have to fight for everything here,' she said. 'I'll give you the money for this week and then you make sure you get your own wage. Just watch me do a few. It won't be that different to what you're doing at home.'

She took me to her space at the bench, where she had laid out piles of cardboard and paper, a board and a pot of liquid glue. I watched her take a brush and spread the glue evenly on the board, bend the sides of a piece of card, draw a sheet of paper across the glue, and cover the box with it in one motion. Then she began on the lid. She was working slowly, to show me, but each movement – the dipping of the brush, the folding of the card, the tucking and smoothing of the paper – was easy and exact.

I must have made hundreds of boxes at home, but – I now understood – in a much less practised manner. I did my best, but I was horribly slow. Mary took my first attempt out of my hands and threw it on the floor. 'Too much glue. Don't worry, you can chuck the odd one before you start getting fined for them.' She was getting quicker and quicker, the boxes piling up in the crate. 'Don't ever be late, though. If you're even a minute late, you'll have to work an extra half-hour.' I kept watching her hands, which seemed no longer connected to her, her fingers moving without her even knowing. 'That's how they make their money. All those unpaid half-hours.'

We had worked together for a few minutes before she said, 'Do you have a name?'

'Ellen,' I said.

'Ellen,' she said, as if she was considering it. 'Number twelve, is it? Below Mrs Atkins?'

I nodded, still having to concentrate on my slow, clumsy hands.

'I live at number six,' she said.

'Is it a good street?' I said, and then felt a sudden burst

of pain in the arch of my back, which left me panting. I turned round and saw Mr Clifford, his hand curled in a fist. 'No talking, girls,' he said as he walked past. Mary gave me an apologetic look.

A bell rang and the girls stopped abruptly, their hands now busy in their skirts, producing little parcels of paper and unwrapping them as they drew stools out to sit on or gathered on the floor. I stared stupidly, not sure what to do, but Mary said, 'Here, come on.' She pulled on her jacket and hat, and took off down the stairs. I went after her, and out the front she was greeted by the same handful of girls I'd seen that morning. They went round the back of the building to the yard where I'd queued so many times to hand over the work I did at home.

Mary took a parcel of newspaper out of her pocket and unwrapped two slices of bread and dripping.

'This is Ellen,' she said. 'It's her first day. She's on my floor, she lives on Digby Street.' She told me their names and I forgot them at once. The girls smiled or said hello but they were busy with their breakfast, tearing into sweet white buns, licking treacle off their fingers. One girl was lazily peeling a boiled egg, bits of shell falling to the ground with clumps of delicious white flesh still clinging to them.

I was suddenly overcome with hunger. I hadn't thought at all about what I'd eat at work; I'd hoped perhaps that I just wouldn't want food. It would have been easier not to, saving the time, the money, the thought, for something else. But the smell of Mary's bread and dripping was sending me deranged. The dents in the soft wet crumb, the brown stains on her fingers, the small dribble of gravy that ran down the side of her mouth. I could taste it; the dark, savoury, salty tang was on my tongue, in my head, blotting out all thought. It was half past eight.

Mary turned to me and asked, 'Do you not have breakfast?'

I shook my head. 'I forgot.'

She paused and in those seconds of hesitation I could see on her face what it cost her, but she still held out half a slice of bread. I could barely manage to shake my head. She turned her face away and pushed it towards me. I grabbed it, then bolted it so fast I barely tasted it.

'I'll show you where you can get a bun for your lunch,' she said, licking her fingers, pressing them on the crumbs on her jacket, and licking them again.

After breakfast, I got faster. I still wasn't as good as Mary, but the movements were beginning to feel more natural, and I was making fewer mistakes, marvelling at how smoothly the paper clung to the card and how precisely the edges lined up. I had even started to let in other thoughts, judging how far I could let my mind wander before the work started getting sloppy. 'I knew you didn't need to be an apprentice!' Mary said, and I felt happier than I had in a long time.

When the dinner bell rang, I followed Mary down the stairs again, and this time, she and the other girls went out of the gate and started walking down the high street, turning into the smaller street of shops where they held the market on Saturdays, past the forbidding brick wall of the fever hospital, a public house and a butcher's.

'Let's go to the fish shop,' the girl who'd had the egg said. She was fair with a flat, freckled face, shorter than me but stout; she already had the body of a woman. Her jacket creased at the front where it strained to meet, one button already missing.

'I ain't going in there, Mags, it fucking stinks,' another girl said. She was also fair, but dainty, the smallest of the four of them and the smartest: the velvet of her hat looked new and her hair was elaborately rolled round the brim.

'Well, you can wait outside then, can't you?' Mags said.

'I ain't going in,' Mary said. 'Last time I did, some bloke knocked the eel bucket over.'

'Oh, he didn't!' the small girl said.

'He did. They was everywhere, the little bastards. The bloke behind the counter was running about with the net, some other lad was down on the floor trying to grab 'em, but they kept slipping out of his hands. I swear I saw two of them go out the door. Probably went down the drain.'

'They'll come out somebody's plughole,' the fourth girl said, and they all yelled.

'I wouldn't touch one now,' Mary said. 'It's the way they move. They're sly. I don't trust 'em.'

'Good in a pie, though,' said Mags.

The fish shop was in the middle of the street, at the crest of the hill, with dark-green tiles surrounding the windows and doorway. I saw the lettering on the glass advertising 'Live Eels' and shuddered. Fish were heaped on a marble counter in the window, blank black eyes and limp shimmering bodies. The smaller girl was right: the smell was awful. I waited outside with her and Mary, while Mags and the other girl went in.

They wandered down the hill, going in and out of shops, and I was shocked by the ease with which they bought things, coming out with kippers, bloaters, meat pies. I spent a penny on a bun and swore that I would bring bread with me every day from then on.

But as we walked down towards the park at the bottom of the hill, I realised I was beginning to enjoy it: the children playing out and women buying groceries, the swooping coloured awnings, the gold lettering on shopfronts, offering confectionary, bread, fine ales, good meat, dentistry, cigarettes, low prices. And most of all, the girls, the careless way they spoke and behaved, walking through it all as if it belonged to them.

'Did you see Eliza and Ruth at it last week?' the smaller girl, who I'd learnt was called Lou, said, taking a bite out of her pie and brushing the flakes of pastry off her jacket.

'I didn't see it,' Mags said, throwing a ball of greasy newspaper in the gutter. 'But I saw the hair. Eliza tore a chunk off.'

'You lying bitch!' Lou said with her mouth full.

'She did! She's got the lock. She was waving it around before we went in the other day.'

'I don't believe you. She'll have got a hairpiece from somewhere,' Lou said.

'You ask her. She'll show it you.'

'You're talking out your arse, Mags,' Mary said, and Mags grabbed her from behind, trying to climb on her back.

'Oh, get *off*, will you, you daft bitch,' Mary said, pulling at Mags's arms, which were round her neck.

A group of boys laughed and a woman drew away from us in a showy manner. A man coming out of the tobacconist's said, 'Bloody factory girls,' to his mate and looked straight at me. I stared back, startled. I felt an urge to tell him that he was mistaken, that I was not one of them.

But there was no way to explain: I was now a factory girl after all, only not in the way he meant it.

The girls did not seem to care that they had been noticed. Mags let go of Mary and Mary adjusted her jacket and hairpins. 'Stop frightening Ellen,' she said. 'She's not from the East End.'

They turned towards me, interested for the first time.

'Where are you from then?' Lou asked.

'I was born in Clerkenwell,' I said. 'But we moved out here when I was six.'

Mary looked at me. 'A nice little house opposite the park, I heard.'

'Oh, fancy!' Mags said.

'How did you end up here then?' Lou asked, curiously.

In that moment, I didn't know. How had I ended up here – the kind of girl that women disapproved of and men swore at in the street?

'Her dad died so they lost his wage, and her ma was in the family way so she lost her job too,' Mary said. I supposed she'd heard about it from Mrs Atkins above us, or any other bored woman on the street, intrigued by the spectacle of new neighbours. The others nodded; it was an ordinary story, the kind of common bad luck – the broken leg or the visit from the inspectors – that made everything collapse all at once. I heard these stories all the time. We'd never lived more than two or three streets away from the rough neighbourhoods after all. But even though I'd known it, I hadn't expected it. I hadn't expected it to happen like this.

By the time I turned into Digby Street at six o'clock, I felt soaked in experience, as if I'd seen more in that day than I had in my first fifteen years. As I said goodbye to Mary, I saw that Miss Povey, our landlady, was standing in front of our house, with a lady I'd never seen before.

Miss Povey was around forty, with small round glasses and a straw hat. Her friend was younger and much taller, holding a sheaf of papers, with light-brown hair badly pinned under her hat. I noticed that her nose and chin were pointed and slightly lopsided, as if her face had had a knock when it was setting. Neither of them were good-looking or even particularly nicely dressed (I'd been told ladies who did this kind of work never married), but the way they spoke, the way they gestured, the weight of their skirts, the softness of their gloves – they stood out like a couple of pelicans.

'Ah, Ellen!' Miss Povey said. 'I was hoping I'd catch you home from work.'

'Have you come for the rent?' I asked. 'Only I thought it was Sunday.'

'Oh no,' she said. 'I'm here for a different reason today.'

Mrs Atkins from upstairs was sitting on the step outside the front door, which it seemed was never closed, peeling potatoes into the apron on her lap. She stood up to let us pass, holding her apron up to keep the peelings, and we went into the narrow passageway, which curved like a dog's leg around the staircase. I showed them into the parlour. Mother was sitting at the machine and she looked up, startled.

'Oh, it's rather charming!' Miss Povey's friend said.

'Yes, the houses were in good condition when we took them on,' Miss Povey said. 'Very little repair work needed. One imagines they would have been the homes of a rather different class of person not so long ago.'

A few genteel touches remained: the dark stone mantel and the decorated tiles, purple curling petals on a pale-yellow background, surrounding the fireplace. The wallpaper had a delicate print of pink flowers set against cream, although the paper was starting to peel and the cream was turning brown in patches and at the edges. The hearthstone was cracked and so were the frilled gas lamps on the wall. Still, I could sometimes imagine how the room would once have looked – I could see a chair by the fire, antimacassars on the arms, velvet curtains, a house plant, a rug. I imagined the kind of people who would have lived here – a clerk or a policeman, his kind wife and serene children – and then the vision would fade and the room looked like a senseless jumble again.

The day we moved in, I spent hours rearranging our belongings, like a maddening puzzle, thinking that if I could just set the sofa like that or the table like this, I could make the rooms pleasant and proper. But nothing worked, we still had too many things: a sofa, an armchair, a dining table, a sewing machine, cutlery, work baskets, knives, linens, blankets and tea tins, all crammed in together. The worst part was that our nicest things, the ones we could not bear to sell or pawn – the dark-framed oval mirror above the mantel, the fringed oil lamp, the stuffed bird under a glass dome – looked absurd in these dark, overfull rooms. Our finest tablecloth was folded in an orange crate. Our Sunday dresses hung on a hook inside the door.

'This family have the two downstairs rooms,' Miss Povey said to her friend, 'and the Atkinses have the upstairs. The scullery and water closet are shared.'

Her friend nodded and looked down at the papers in her hands. I saw our family name at the top, handwritten in blue ink, with the words 'Case Notes' below it.

I was the one who'd found us the lodgings on Digby Street – a girl in the piecework queue had told me about rooms going nearby, managed by ladies who did good works. She said the rent was cheap, but you had to be in need and look respectable. I dressed carefully for the interview – clothes that were old but clean and mended. I chose my second pair of boots, the ones with the cracked, greying leather; it was raining and my stockings got damp, but I didn't want to look as if we could afford new boots. I told Miss Povey our story and she made notes, and we were offered two rooms in number twelve. The girl had been right: the rent was cheap.

'May I introduce you to Miss Morton?' Miss Povey said, gesturing to her friend. 'She's just arrived in the East End, a volunteer at the St Edward's Settlement. She'll be acting as my superintendent on Digby Street while she's here, collecting your rent, managing repairs and so on.'

She turned to Miss Morton and told her a little of our family story – my mother, recently widowed and her confinement drawing near, two young boys in school, a daughter aged fifteen, out at work, getting by on less than a pound a week. While she spoke, Miss Morton looked at me as if I was a sort of sad exhibit, a dog with lion's feet or a bearded lady. She pitied me, I could tell, but also found me curious, something kept behind a pane of glass. It was almost worse than not being seen at all.

'Would you like tea, Miss Povey? Miss Morton?' Mother said, and I hoped they would say no, because I couldn't remember how much tea was in the tin or whether we had sugar, but Miss Povey said, 'How kind of you to offer! Only if it's no trouble,' and sat down at the table.

Miss Morton did the same. I picked up the kettle and took it into the scullery.

When I came back in, the sewing machine had been cleared away, a cloth and cups had been put on the table and Mother was spooning tea into the pot in our kitchen corner. The fire was lit and I put the kettle on the grate.

'And where are your boys?' Miss Povey asked. 'George and . . . ?'

'David,' Mother said. 'Playing out.' She looked unhappy. 'I used to keep them in, but here, well—' She gestured at the room.

Miss Povey smiled sympathetically. 'Of course. And at least they're getting God's good air. Well, what passes for it in the East End. Miss Morton was thinking she might organise some proper games for the children on Sunday – cricket and so on. Something with structure. Much better than the dreadful, repetitive things they come up with themselves.'

'That sounds nice,' Mother said, smiling faintly.

'It was actually Ellen I wished to speak to,' Miss Povey said, and I took Mother's work basket off a stool so I could bring it over and join them at the table. 'I believe you work at the box factory? With Mary Cunningham?'

'That's right.' I nodded.

'How nice to have a friend at work.' She turned to Mother. 'Mary's a nice girl. Irish family but very decent. Now, the reason I called, Ellen, is that as your circumstances change' – she nodded at Mother, who put a hand on her belly – 'as they are bound to, I fear things may be very difficult on your factory wages—'

'We've put money aside for the confinement,' Mother said.

'Oh, how clever you are! I'm sure you have. But we do

try to improve the lives of our tenants, if we can, and one of the ways we do this is by finding little jobs, something to rely on if work is irregular or some sort of accident happens . . .' She nodded at Mother again. 'And Miss Morton had a rather clever idea.' Miss Morton reddened and looked down, placing her hands on her lap and spreading her fingers out. 'She suggested that Ellen come and whiten her step at the settlement on Saturdays. Perhaps scrub the passageway as well.'

I did not look at Mother. We'd never had servants, but we once had a step girl, a neighbour's daughter, who came on Saturdays.

'I'll be needed at home,' I said. 'When I'm not at the factory.'

'You can go on Saturdays when you finish at the factory. You'll get sixpence, which you can put aside. Then you need never be late with the rent!'

'I've never once been late with the rent,' Mother said. 'And if you'd spoken to our landlord on Victoria Park Road, you would know that.'

Miss Povey took a deep breath. 'It would be excellent preparation for a job in service,' she said.

'Ellen won't be getting a job in service,' Mother said.

'But you surely can't wish her to be a factory girl forever.' Miss Povey leant forward in her chair.

'She can go back to school,' Mother said, 'when we're back on our feet. She was going to be a schoolteacher.'

There was a horrible quiet. Miss Morton looked distressed, anxiously turning her head from Miss Povey to Mother. I saw the steam coming from the kettle and got up to make tea, but by the time I reached the fireplace Miss Povey was also on her feet.

'You must do what you think is best,' she said courteously.

'I'll come this Saturday,' I said. 'You're right, it'll be good to have something put aside.' Miss Morton gave a delighted gasp and Miss Povey sat down with a small smile. I poured the tea while Miss Morton wrote down her address, and nodded as she eagerly told me the route I should take, how I would recognise the house, the size of the step and the length of the passageway compared to ours. Then Miss Povey talked at length about the rent, repairs, how she would not tolerate drunkenness or debt, or the misuse of dustbins, and then finally they stood up to go. As Miss Povey said goodbye, she clasped my hand tightly and smiled with such unexpected warmth, it was almost alarming.

'I do hope I can make your lives a little better,' she said. 'And that one day you may consider me a friend.'

We began to clear the tea things away before we even heard the front door shut. I inspected the cloth for stains, folded it and put it back in the crate. The ladies were still in our front garden and I could hear Miss Povey speaking to Mrs Atkins about a woman who'd come to look at some rooms. Mrs Atkins had heard that the woman went to fetch beer for her husband, bought two jugs and only returned with one, 'if you get my meaning'.

'I do,' said Miss Povey. 'That's most helpful, Mrs Atkins.'

After we'd got the boys in, given them bread and jam and sent them to bed, Mother got out her work basket and set up her machine on the kitchen table. As it started to get dark, I pinned an old sheet up over the parlour window.

'Take it down, Ellen, it looks awful,' she said. 'I'll make some curtains.'

'I'm the one who has to sleep in here,' I said.

She shook her head but didn't say anything else about it. I took out the sewing box and sat in the easy chair, darning a pair of Davey's socks. We worked in silence, listening to the noise going on outdoors. The children's voices were as loud and close as if they'd been in the parlour with us. *Grandmother, grandmother, tell me no lie, how many years before I die?*

'These children don't go to bed, I suppose,' Mother remarked, taking another pair of trousers out of the crate. 'It's like trying to sleep in the Roman Road market.'

'We'll get used to it,' I said. Perhaps I was annoyed with her, because I said, 'Imagine if Dad had been here.'

She didn't look up. 'If he was still with us, we wouldn't be in this place.'

'He wouldn't have made it easy,' I said.

'No,' she murmured. She stood up and fiddled with the thread on top of the machine. 'He never laid a finger on me, your father.'

I had heard that many times before. It was true, but it did not make the other things untrue.

It was hard to sleep that night. I couldn't stop trying to place each noise – the creaks, footsteps, muffled cries and shouts – trying to work out if it came from upstairs or next door or the street. As I drifted in and out of sleep, the noises seemed to come closer until it felt like the man was shouting at the foot of my bed, the child wailing next to my face.

When I did drop off, I dreamt about the house. I dreamt that beyond the back room was another room, and another, and another, more rooms than I could count, all empty, clean and light. I wandered through them, amazed that I had not seen them before. I hadn't needed to worry. We had room for everything after all.

When I heard a small insistent voice calling my name, I thought I was still dreaming, but then I saw Davey standing by the sofa, twitching anxiously. I was barely awake, heavy and confused, and I turned over and pulled back the blanket. He climbed in and put his arm round me, his ice-cold feet squeezing between my legs to warm up. His pyjamas were wet and the smell was strong. I tried not to think about it and to think instead about how lovely it was to feel his tiny warm chest pressed into my back. I wondered when we would have our first wash day.

By Friday, I had got almost as quick at boxing-up as Mary and she told me I could expect twelve shillings a week – 'easy' – if I carried on like this. It *was* easy – or at least it was in the mornings. I relished the light coming through the windows, the space of the room, the feeling of being surrounded by other girls, all of us silently working at the same thing. We made boxes for soap, for candles, for hats and artificial flowers. Mary showed me how to strengthen the corners of the larger boxes with little strips of calico. We took it in turns to fetch the hot water to make glue, collect the card from the cutters two floors below and take the finished boxes away, but otherwise it was the same movements again and again and again, and it felt marvellously simple, so unlike doing it at home, where I was always interrupted by the boys or the teeming, breeding demands of the house. I could let my mind go completely now while my fingers worked relentlessly.

It was in the mid-afternoon, when dinner was over

and the light began to fade, that time slowed until it was almost intolerable and I was struck by a maddening restlessness. My legs ached from standing, and I had to gently stamp my feet, rock on my heels, stretch my neck, while not drawing attention to myself. Sometimes I thought we all felt it. I imagined it as a mist or a fog, settling in the space between the bricks. It was too much, this great store of unused energy. I fantasised about crushing the boxes underneath my feet or smashing my body against a wall.

And yet, every morning, I woke up excited because I'd get to see the girls again. They were better than any performance I could have paid to see. Every breakfast and every dinnertime, I followed Mary out, running down the stairs to meet the others in the back yard. As I wrapped four slices of bread and put them in my pocket in the mornings, Mother said she didn't see why I couldn't come home and have dinner with her and the boys. I told her I didn't have time. In fact, I wanted every moment of the girls' company.

That Friday of the first week, we strolled down the high street to the fish shop and everyone went in. Tables and benches in dark wood lined the white-tiled walls, a large mirror above each one. I noticed two silver entwined eels wrought in the bottom of the frame. As I joined the queue at the counter, I saw the metal bucket by the door – thick, black, wriggling ropes squirming in water – and a large green mesh net.

The next morning I would collect my first wage. I had spent hours working out little pencil sums on waste paper, planning how I'd make the money last the week. It was gone already, really – on rent, funeral insurance, loaves, tea, coal, soap and herrings. We couldn't afford fish for lunch. I knew that, and yet tomorrow I would be handed an envelope of coins that would briefly be mine. And I was hungry again.

The bread in my pocket felt heavy, reproaching me as I asked for fried fish and potatoes. I took the bottle of vinegar as the other girls did and vigorously shook it over the food, drops spurting out of the rubber stopper with a hole in it.

I tried to save it, but when I unwrapped the paper, just to smell it, I started taking quick, furtive bites. It was magnificent: so salty, so sharp, so comforting. All at once it was gone, and I had stomach pains, but I could have eaten more, and more, and more.

When we got back to the factory, there was something going on in the yard: shouting and a flurry of movement, like a disturbed bees' nest. A small group of girls had gathered, shouting things like 'Go it, Liza!' or 'Stop it, Sal!' A few men, cutters, were watching too and laughing.

As we got closer, I saw two girls in the middle of the crowd, gripping each other's shirts, yelling at each other. Their hats had come off and one of the girls' hair had come loose, dark and tangled. The other girl's shirt ripped. 'Eliza, you bitch,' she howled, and tried to grab her face, but Eliza turned away in time and then she punched the other girl, hard, in the face. There were gasps and an older woman grabbed Eliza round the waist and pulled her away, holding her back as she leant forward, panting and shouting. The other girl had blood coming out of her mouth, running down her shirt.

There were more gasps, and murmurs, and the woman dropped Eliza suddenly. I didn't understand what had happened and then I saw a small paring knife in Eliza's hand. She held it by her side, almost hidden in her skirts, still. The other girl gaped, but did not move. They stared at each other, the space between them pulsing. The bell rang and was ignored.

Finally, Mr Simpson came out of the door and Eliza slid the knife into her pocket.

'What the hell are you all doing?' he shouted. 'Get back to work, you lazy cows!'

'Oh, Eliza,' Mary muttered as we moved towards the door.

'She'll get the chuck this time,' Lou said.

'She won't. You'll see,' Mags said. 'She gets away with it, Eliza.'

I stayed quiet as we walked towards the door. There were dark splashes on the cobbles, and the white glint of a tooth.

2

Frances

1984

The party started at midday, in Belgravia, and I spent most of the morning wishing I didn't have to go. We expected to be invited to the family parties – the drinks at Christmas or Mrs Maxwell's fiftieth – but this invitation, just for me, was a privilege I hadn't asked for and wasn't sure I wanted. It had arrived only five days before my father died, and when I heard the news, standing in my pyjamas in the kitchen with the men from the ambulance, an uninvited, unedifying thought formed: *maybe now I won't have to go to Antonia's eighteenth birthday party.*

But I did have to go, because even though I wanted everything to stop, it didn't. I took my exams and I got a summer job, and everyone said how well I was coping and then everything went back to normal again – apart from me. We kept the invitation on the mantelpiece and occasionally my mother would say, 'Isn't that kind of Antonia,' picking the card up to press it between her finger and thumb, testing the thickness, running her fingertips over the raised cursive lettering, before casually dropping it back down, as if I wouldn't be able to tell how much it meant to her.

I'd set my alarm clock for eight, but I'd had a bath, put talcum powder on, blow-dried my hair upside down, and it was still only quarter to nine. I'd always been quick at getting ready – I'd be first out of the school locker rooms or the C&A changing rooms, the only one waiting in the swimming pool foyer, ponytail dripping down my neck, eating crisps from the vending machine on an orange plastic chair. I didn't know what the exact skill was – I never felt like I was rushing, it was more that I didn't understand what took everyone else so long. What were they *doing* in there? I used to be proud of it, but now, at eighteen, being able to put your tights on quickly began to feel slightly shameful. Unfeminine, like bolting food.

I put my dressing gown on and sat in bed, trying to think of things to do. I thought about going downstairs to see if we had any cucumber to put on my eyes. I wondered if my mother had a face mask. I read magazines, searching for something that might tell me what to say or wear or how to behave at a party.

Finally, I allowed myself to start getting dressed. I tried to make the process careful and ceremonial: I put my arms through my bra straps and groped behind my back to fasten it, rather than fixing the clasp first and twisting it round as I usually did. I stretched my fingers into the toes of my white tights before rolling them up my legs. When I had put on my dress, I sprayed scent in the air and walked into it. It still took less than ten minutes.

'Oh, look at you, Frances, don't you look lovely!' my mother said when I came downstairs, putting her arm around my shoulders, and I blushed and laughed and pushed my head into her chest. I put on my navy cardigan and black shoes with the small heel and she insisted on taking a photograph of me standing awkwardly in the hall.

'Oh, Franny, you look *sweet*,' Antonia said when she opened the door, and I flinched, irritated before I'd even got inside the house. Antonia and her friends were the only people who called me Franny and it felt entirely wrong to me – too effervescent, too jolly – but Antonia had a manic need for abbreviation. Her dress was a dark shimmering blue with long sleeves and dramatic shoulders; it crossed at the front like a ballet dancer's, separating a smooth triangle of skin, the point astonishingly low. Her earrings were large and gold, her dark hair soft and full. My party dress – blue silk with white spots, covered buttons and a high neck – probably did look sweet and I understood that was not a good thing.

I stepped into the black-and-white-tiled hall. Antonia's house was so large it was almost uncanny: everything was overblown, from the grimace of the large brass letterbox and the doorknob like a giant's fist to the swollen cream pillars framing the door. The hall, the size of a kitchen, had a dark wooden dresser underneath a vast gold-framed mirror, where white lilies stood in a silver bucket surrounded by presents and cards. I laid my card and small bunch of tulips on it.

'Here, Franny-kins, have some fizz,' Antonia said as she led me into the living room. Under the large window looking out over the square, there was a shining wooden table with rows of champagne flutes and photographs in thick silver ovals, mostly of family but with one black-and-white portrait of a winsome spaniel. The carpets were as thick and soft as clotted cream. I remembered the first time we'd visited their house and my mother had said to Mrs Maxwell, 'Golly, white carpets, that's bold!' She'd laughed nervously, and though Mrs Maxwell was charming, I could tell she was puzzled.

The doorbell rang and Antonia said, 'Sorry, Franny, must get that,' and I turned towards the room, grasping my champagne flute. And as I turned, I became consumed by a feeling of dislocation, a feeling that had become very familiar to me that summer. I stared at the party, unable to move. All of a sudden, it looked deranged – the ruffles and sequins and jackets, the chatter and glee, the smoked salmon pinwheels and the beetroot salad, and, worse, the expectation that I should be part of it all.

It had started when my father died, this feeling, arriving without warning, at any moment. I would be waiting for a bus or picking something up for my mother at the grocer's, and I would start to feel peculiar, and then everything would feel peculiar: the ordinary people going about their business, while I could only stand and stare. The gulf between us felt vast: they were busy and unconcerned, shopping or eating or talking, and I was standing there, confused, holding an apple. It was impossible to explain what it was, this feeling, this gulf – if they noticed me, they would think I was an ordinary person going about my business too and I had no idea how to explain that I wasn't.

I stood there, unable to join in or to leave, knowing that the longer I was by myself, the stranger I would look, until two girls I knew from the Christmas parties, Felicity and Angela, waved at me. The horror of being thought rude made me walk over and say hello.

'Franny, hi! You look utterly fab,' Felicity said, kissing me on both cheeks.

'Oh—' I said, looking down, but before I could reply, Angela, in a red satin dress with flounces, was squeezing my arm and saying, 'We were just talking about Violet de Lacey. Have you seen? Tone's being *lovely* about it, but I'd be fucking furious if I were her.'

Violet de Lacey was always at the Maxwell parties and she was always doing something outrageous; people called her a hoot or an absolute nutter. She kissed a girl at Antonia's Christmas party and stole a side of salmon from Felicity's eighteenth. I looked in the direction Felicity was vehemently gesturing towards with her head and that was when I saw Nick for the first time.

Violet was with two men – they were men, not boys, that was the first problem, and they weren't in suits. They both wore T-shirts and loose jeans, and they had long hair, one loose and shoulder-length and the other in a ponytail.

'They weren't invited?' I asked.

Felicity shook her head. 'No, they were *not*. Apparently, she asked Tone if she could bring someone two nights ago and Tone said no, I'm sorry, we've done the numbers—'

'Which must have been really difficult for her to say—'

'*So* difficult – you know what Tone's like, she's generous to a *fault*, but she doesn't know these people and it's her *eighteenth birthday party*! And then Violet just turns up anyway with not one but two!'

'She said that she thought it wouldn't matter because it wasn't a sit-down—'

'As if she didn't know Tone's been going *crazy* about the buffet—'

'Apparently one of them's her boyfriend,' Angela said, downing her champagne. 'She was kissing him earlier, in this really *foul* way.'

'Well, what's the other one doing here then? Honestly, I think Violet's going to ruin Tone's eighteenth. Oh, James, hi!' She turned her face upwards to greet Antonia's older brother, who'd joined us.

James Maxwell and I had had a brief, banal conversation at the Christmas party and I'd been inordinately pleased with myself for sustaining it, despite his age, his looks, his height. Like the family home, he was too much: over six foot and so blonde he looked clean. He was twenty-one and training to be a barrister.

'Hello, Franny,' he said amiably. 'Have you just arrived?'

'Yes,' I said, all the other words I knew suddenly evaporating under his attention.

'James, Tone said you aren't coming to Gloucestershire this year!' Felicity said.

'Well, I've got exams—'

'Oh, you've got to come to Glossie-Possie!' Angela said. 'It's our summer of freedom.'

'Are you off to Oxford, too?' James asked.

'No, not as lucky as Tone,' Felicity said. 'Going to Bristol instead.'

'I didn't even apply. Too thick,' said Angela. 'So Bristol for me too.'

'What about you, Franny?' He turned to look at me. 'Are you going to university in September?'

'No, not yet,' I said, and then, for something to say, 'I'm thinking about applying to art school.'

'Oh, really, Franny?' Angela said. 'But I thought you were super-brainy.'

I was used to people thinking that, because I was quiet and diligent, but really I couldn't imagine myself at university. My school took pride in its art department, though, and I was quite good at drawing. I wouldn't be an artist, but maybe I would work in a gallery, or just be an interesting sort of wife, the kind who wore scarves in her hair and knew facts about *The Arnolfini Marriage*.

'Are you going away this summer?' James asked.

'I don't think so,' I said. We'd booked a holiday in Devon before my father died, but my mother and I had agreed without saying anything that we wouldn't go. 'I've got a summer job.'

'Oh, really? Where?'

'In a pub called the Black Hart,' I said. 'Behind the bar.'

'Oh, how *funny*!' Felicity said. 'I can't imagine you as a barmaid. Where is it? We'll have to come and see you! Can you get us free drinks?'

'In Hackney.'

'Oh God! I'm not going *there*!'

'Where's Hackney?' Angela said, but Felicity was fiddling with the clasp of her clutch bag.

'Does anyone want a fag?' she said, holding up a box.

'OK, but my parents said not in the house,' James said.

'Let's brave Violet and those horrible men outside then. Do you want one, Franny?'

I would have said yes, but when Helen at school had asked me to hold her cigarette for a minute at her eighteenth, it had felt strange and heavy between my fingers. Everyone had laughed at the way I did it and I thought if I couldn't even hold a cigarette convincingly, I probably wasn't going to be able to smoke one.

I went back to the drinks table and picked up a bottle of champagne. I poured it carefully, tilting my glass, and sensed someone coming up behind me.

'I'll have that when you're finished,' he said, and I turned round. One of the men Violet had brought stood behind me.

I handed the bottle to him. He topped up his glass, spilling some on the table. He took a long gulp and filled it up again, and then turned back to face the party, leaning on the table.

'Greetings,' he said, looking at me and holding up a hand. He had brown hair parted in the centre and finishing bluntly just above his shoulders. His face was angular in a way that might have been attractive: a square chin, sunken cheeks over protruding bones. His T-shirt was loose and grubby; I saw that the hem at the neck was fraying. It made me think of a boy at primary school who used to chew the tops of his T-shirts until they were covered in tiny holes and a dark V of saliva.

'Nick,' he said, not offering to shake my hand.

'Franny,' I said, since that was who I was at Antonia's parties. 'How do you know Antonia?'

'I don't, really. I know Jake. Violet asked us if we wanted to come to this fancy party with her and I thought, why not? See how the other half live.'

He didn't ask how I knew Antonia, but he didn't move away either. I could see Angela and Felicity through the French windows. He seemed unfazed by the silence, but I was frantically trying to think of something to ask him. I couldn't ask him what school he went to, if he had applied to university, if he was going away this summer. And then I remembered another way of starting conversations.

'What do you do?' I asked.

He laughed. 'Now there's a question . . . You mean as a job?'

I nodded, uncertain.

'I don't have one,' he said.

'Are you . . . at university?'

He laughed again, harder, performing. He shook his head and took another gulp of champagne. 'I'm on the dole.'

I blushed. I had forgotten about unemployment, or rather, it had seemed like an abstract idea, not something that I would encounter at a party. 'Oh, I'm sorry,' I said.

'Don't be. I don't want to work.'

'Really?'

He smiled at me. 'Why would I want to?'

'To . . . earn money?'

He shrugged. 'I have fairly simple pleasures. The dole covers food, cigarettes, the odd drink, and then I can always do a bit of work if I want something more. I live in a squat. No rent.'

My parents talked about squatters when we went on holiday, joking but nervously. I thought of them as mysterious housing thieves, who would move in when you went away, change the locks and leave you homeless.

'What?' he said.

'Nothing.'

'No, come on, what are you thinking?'

I tried to think of a polite way to say it but nothing supportive or encouraging was coming to my mind. 'I just thought— I mean, what about the people who the houses belong to?'

'They don't belong to anyone. They're empties.' He'd turned round to fully face me now.

'But someone must own them—'

'The council. But they're not doing anything with them.'

35

'Isn't it against the law?'

'Squatting? Nope,' he said, and the glee with which he said it caused the first unexpected surge of anger. 'Perfectly legal. Breaking and entering is illegal. Squatting isn't. Huge blocks of empty flats owned by the council – that's what's criminal.'

I looked over his shoulder at the groups of suited men and girls in sheer or shiny fabric revealing bare flesh. The room was getting more crowded now; the laughing and exclaiming had reached a different pitch. But I couldn't see anyone else I knew.

'I've shocked you, haven't I,' he said in an unapologetic tone of voice. He meant *I've made a fool of you.* The anger again: a jet of rage. He poured some more champagne in his glass and held the bottle out to me. I shook my head. He tried to lean on the table again, but slipped and the glasses rattled.

'What about this place? You think this girl, what's her name—'

'—Antonia—'

'—Antonia, yep, you think she pays rent here, do you? You think her dad does?'

'Well, no, I think he owns it—'

'Why should it belong to him, though? Who says it does? Why should some land belong to some people and not others?'

I was confused and curious, and tried to ask him how else it would work, but he interrupted and I realised then that of course he didn't want me to speak at all. It was another of those conversations that I wasn't expected to be part of, except to give sympathetic murmurs of surprise or agreement. He was going to say the things that he felt like saying, without thinking about whether or not I wanted to hear them, and I was going to exhaust myself keeping things civil and elegant and fair.

'Who signed us up to it? That's what I want to know. Why do we all just accept it?'

I was sick of it now. I looked out into the garden to see if Felicity and Angela were still there. He must have noticed because he looked me up and down and said, 'God, imagine being lectured about paying your own way by Laura fucking Ashley. Your dad pays for everything, I suppose, school fees, rent-free housing—'

'Oh, fuck off,' I said.

We looked at each other, surprised. I noticed I was shaking, but with relief. Then euphoria rose, fast and strong, until I was dizzy, floating. I walked away from him. Even that felt extraordinarily, satisfyingly rude. Angela and Felicity had come in from the garden and, as I joined them, Felicity gripped my arm.

'Oh God, we saw one of them talking to you, Franny. Are you all right?'

The party continued and the euphoria faded and that, and the anger, began to feel shameful: excessive, uncontrolled emotions. I managed another conversation with James and although I didn't say anything particularly brilliant I was pleased with myself for not saying anything stupid either. We watched Violet, Nick and Jake through the French windows; she screamed with laughter or kissed Jake on the mouth or hit one of them on the arm, and we looked at each other. Antonia joined us briefly and said, 'It's fine, I'm fine, it's absolutely *fine.*'

Eventually Nick and Jake left, but Violet stayed. When they walked through the living room, and the front door shut behind them, there was change in mood, a collective buoyancy.

'Thank God,' Angela said. 'Another fag, Flicker?' And I was on my own again.

I thought about going to the buffet, even though I wasn't hungry, but I looked over at Violet, who was now also on her own, tipping ash into the hydrangeas and smiling to herself. She looked comfortable, not abandoned, as if she was enjoying this moment between encounters, simply waiting for the next fascinating interaction to begin. Then she caught my eye and waved, and I went out into the garden.

I was always surprised that Violet liked me. I supposed I was a good audience – she didn't have to try very hard to seem outrageous to me. She baffled me in so many ways: she was always wearing something too tight or loose or torn or lavish, or everything at once, like the huge T-shirt she wore that day, cut off under her breasts, over a corset and a billowing black silk skirt. She always painted her eyelids black, the whole lid, and not with powder or eyeliner but a kind of thick paint, and although I'd talked to her many times before, I still found it impossible not to get distracted by them.

'Hello, hello,' she said, kissing me on both cheeks.

'Are you having a good time?' I asked.

'Same old, same old. The boys have gone to get hash, though fuck knows where they'll find any. I saw you talking to Nick earlier. He's great, isn't he?'

'Yes, really great.'

'Tone's pissed off with me,' she said, swigging from the silver hip flask she took everywhere with her.

'Is she?'

'You can see it all over her face. So I can't bring my boyfriend to her party just because he didn't go to Paul's or Westminster. Fuck that.' Then she stretched out her hand. 'I need a wee, are you coming?'

I would never have said no to Violet. I took her hand and let her pull me inside; the intimacy, the unnatural feel of foreign skin on mine, made my entire body feel odd. I wondered when I would be allowed to let go. There were one or two people waiting outside the downstairs cloakroom, so I followed her upstairs. She didn't stop to take her shoes off and so I didn't either, though I winced at the marks her boots left on the carpets. We went up two flights of stairs before she flung open a door and we were in a bedroom at the front of the house, looking out on the square. The window was framed by heavy curtains with a giant print of red flowers tied back with wide sashes, the pelmet fringed with thick twists of gold cord. There was a large four-poster bed swathed in folds of fabric and I couldn't help hearing my grandmother's voice: *if you want to know what the good Lord thinks of money, look at the people he gives it to*. Violet took me through a door to a bathroom, almost as big as the bedroom.

She looked at me triumphantly. 'I *knew* Fiona Maxwell would have an en suite!'

I stood uselessly in the doorway, panicking about getting caught, and also taking in every detail: the two basins next to each other set in marble, the vast bath, the fat white cakes of soap on floral dishes, not the misshapen lumps sitting in pools of gluey water on saucers that we had at home. And Violet, as she pulled her knickers up, the hair between her legs, her pale and blotchy thighs.

'I'm just going to fix my eyes,' she said and leant towards

39

the mirror, and that was when I realised how drunk she was because she started smudging the black paint, until it smeared at the corners, and her fingertips were covered with it. She left an inky print on her cheek and I grimaced.

'Oh fuck,' she said. 'Fuck. Fuck.'

'Do you want me to help?' I asked.

'OK, thanks,' she said, turning to face me.

She pushed herself up onto the marble countertop and I went back into the bedroom. Mrs Maxwell's dressing table was underneath the window: a swing mirror, two photographs of Antonia and James, and a pile of white cotton wool balls in a cut-glass bowl. I took a handful back into the bathroom, rinsed them and, positioning myself between Violet's legs, I stretched up to touch her eyes. I saw that, below the fine reed-like hair on her thighs, there were little black spikes on her calves. Last Saturday had been one of the hottest days of the year and I'd sweated under tights because I'd forgotten to shave my legs. It hadn't occurred to me that there was any other choice, and it astounded me that Violet was walking around, at a party, with unshaven legs, and there had been no consequences at all.

I leant forward and placed the wet cotton wool on her eyelids. It was difficult knowing how much pressure to apply: the way her eyeball felt below my fingertips made me queasy. At first, I made it worse, but with two more trips back to the dressing table, doing my best to ignore my guilt at the diminishing heap, I'd got it all off. She looked uncannily different; young and blasted and strikingly ordinary. Her skin was freckled. It was mesmerising.

'There,' I said. 'All done.'

She opened her eyes and smiled. And then she kissed me.

I knew that Violet kissed a lot of people, sometimes girls, but usually in public because it was an amusing and shocking thing to do. I didn't understand why she was doing it now. I also didn't understand why it didn't feel strange. She was kissing me in the same way that she kissed Jake, sloppy and unformed, but it wasn't that different from the time I'd kissed Jonathan at Helen's Christmas party.

She pulled away and smiled at me: a huge, intense smile. Then she put her hand on my cheek and said, 'Ah,' like I was a favourite pet. I moved away, blinking, and started gathering up the blackened cotton wool.

'I don't think I can redo your eyes,' I said. 'You'll have to do that.'

'Yeah, I'm not going to bother,' she said.

She jumped down from the counter, took my face between her hands, and kissed me again. I stopped thinking about the party downstairs or whether Mrs Maxwell would burst in; I was thinking only about the sensation, the warmth of her mouth, the way her lips moved, her fingers on my cheek. I was aware of her body, how close her breasts were to mine, the gap between her cropped T-shirt and her corset. I thought about what it would be like to put my hand inside it and then she said, 'Come on, let's go back downstairs.'

I zipped up her make-up bag and handed it back to her. Then I looked at myself in the mirror. My lips looked redder, plumper, but otherwise I looked unchanged. We went downstairs.

It took a while for the shame to set in but when it did, it was hideous. It was like swallowing something cold and heavy: I felt it drop down my centre and then spread until it was in my blood, circulating, inextricable. Kissing girls was just the sort of thing Violet did, but I had no reason to do it, apart from . . . what could I say? Drunkenness? A mistake? I had another conversation with James, but I knew it was no good. I was not the sort of person he would ever want to be with and it was stupid of me to think that I ever had been. I made myself stay until 4 p.m. and then left without saying goodbye.

I didn't want my mother to know I'd left the party so early, so I walked slowly through the stillness of the garden squares, past the fumes and grunting machinery of Victoria bus station, into the finicky elegance of St James's Park, with its pelicans and deckchairs and ice creams, and frothy unreal views. I walked down the broad sandy avenue of Horse Guards Parade, until I found myself in the great grey bowl of Trafalgar Square. Pigeon feathers, seed and ice-cream wrappers gathered round my party shoes.

I remembered coming here with my father and climbing on the backs of the stone lions that lay at the bottom of Nelson's Column. I took off my shoes, pulled up the skirt of my dress and clambered up onto the plinth. I sat on the hard stone, next to a giant paw, white crusted droppings next to me, looking down at the grubby marks on my tights.

Watching the tourists cheerfully taking photographs and holding out paper cups for the ragged birds, cold concrete on the backs of my knees, I finally confronted the worst thing about the whole business with Violet: I hadn't wanted it to stop. I couldn't say exactly what it was I had wanted, just that I had wanted something more. It was this curiosity, this appetite, that made me feel cold and squeamish. The girls I knew who I felt were good at being girls, like Tone or Angela, didn't seem to want things. They liked things – cigarettes, boys or clothes – but they didn't crave them. Every desire I had, whether it was for second helpings or the feeling I had when I touched myself between my legs, felt like a kind of failure, another emblem of the gap between who I was and the way I ought to be.

On the bus home, I decided that I would simply cut out the things that I didn't want to think about. I had no more invitations to parties that summer. I would refuse any more that came. Violet could say what she liked about me, they could believe anything they wanted, and I would never know. If I never thought about it again, then it may as well not exist.

I never had to see anyone from that party again. It was such a comforting idea that I almost started laughing. But, of course, that was not how things turned out.

Five days after the party, James telephoned me to tell me that he was going to Gloucestershire for the summer after all, but he'd very much like to take me to dinner when he got back. I sat on the stairs, stunned, writing down words he said in pencil on the telephone pad: 'Gloucestershire', 'August', 'somewhere in Covent Garden perhaps'. It seemed so far away and anyway, it would have been impossible to refuse, so we agreed that he would telephone me again at the end of August. I took the piece of paper I'd written on, folded it and put it in my drawer upstairs.

And then, a week later, I saw Nick again. One of the other bar girls left and I was offered the lunchtime shifts as well as the evenings. I found it suited me much better – I preferred being out of the house in the day, even if it meant wandering around aimlessly when the pub was shut in the afternoon. Ever since the funeral, the house had been in a constant state of upheaval, as my mother got rid of first my father's things, then most of hers, and then things that I thought of as ours: ornaments or kitchen implements. My mother had stopped wearing her wedding ring and when I mentioned it, she said, 'Well, I'm not married any more, am I?'

I had got the job at the Black Hart through Jessica, one of a handful of girls from my school who took the same number bus as me. She lived even further towards the end of the route than I did, in a large corner house of a crescent near Victoria Park. When I told her we wouldn't be going away that summer, she suggested I take over the job from her when she went travelling; it was just after the funeral and I was grateful for the distraction.

To get there, I had to catch the same bus we took to school, but in the opposite direction. Our house was on the border of Hackney and Islington and whenever I went out I almost always turned towards the centre of the city. I very rarely went further out. Jessica had described the bus route to me so I'd know where to get off, and the further away we got from the square I lived on, with its leaded windows and pointed facades, the less familiar everything felt. I noticed hollowed-out cars, ragged curtains hanging in the windows, mattresses in the front yards, and I got off on the austere high street, a row of newsagents with grilles in the doorways and shops with boarded-up windows and the lettering picked off.

I had to turn off the high street to get to the Black Hart, past the old hospital building and a little row of shops: E. Gibbon's Newsagent's and General Stores, Caribbean

Food Supplies, Unisex Hair Salon. On Saturdays there'd be a market, selling rolls of fabric or shoes or vegetables I didn't recognise in boxes, cardboard signs saying things like 'Okra' or 'Plantain'. The Black Hart was a large, old-fashioned pub – the walls outside were lined with dark, oxblood square tiles and the windows had diamond stained glass. Only the sign was new: 'The Black Hart' in chunky lower-case letters, white on black. Inside, there was a large rectangular bar in the centre of the room, which still had ornate wooden screens from when it had once been divided, and a high moulded ceiling. Pickled eggs sat like eyeballs in jars behind the bar; I dreaded being asked for one.

The evening customers dressed a bit like Violet, in a way that seemed deliberately confusing: the men had too much hair or the women too little. Sometimes it was different colours, or a man or woman would have it shaved at the sides and peaked at the top. They wore denim and leather and pierced their skin, and they created an atmosphere of energy and violence that I enjoyed watching from behind the bar, before I got the bus back home.

The lunchtime customers were different: a handful of men, middle-aged or elderly, sitting at the bar, tapping cigarettes into the metal ashtrays. I was surprised when they introduced themselves straight away and asked my name, but once I realised that they came in almost every day, I understood why they wanted to be on familiar terms.

On my second day shift, at around 2 p.m., Nick came in. It took me a moment to recognise him, because he looked smarter: his hair was pulled back in a rough ponytail and he had a clean jumper on. When he saw me, he stopped halfway to the bar. His expression, as he scrutinised me, tried to place me, was unnerving: a mixture of alarm and what looked like anger. Then he walked to the far end of the bar and pulled out a barstool.

'The girl from the party,' he said, taking some cigarette papers out of his back pocket.

'That's right,' I said.

He pointed a finger at me. 'Frankie, right?'

I nodded. It was close enough.

'I've not seen you in here before.' He started smoothing out one of the papers, filling it with tobacco. 'I can't say I was expecting to see you somewhere like this either.'

'It's my first day shift,' I said.

He nodded. 'I work round the corner. I usually come in for a quick drink after lunch.'

'I thought you didn't work?'

He spilt some tobacco on the bar and didn't look at me as he gathered it up. 'I do the odd morning as a school caretaker. It's useful to have a bit of cash sometimes.'

'I see,' I said. 'What can I get you?'

He ordered a double vodka and Coke – 'in a tall glass, lots of ice, fill it right up to the top'. I served him and then was called over by a man on the other side of the room. I always found the horseshoe shape of the bar unsettling: when I had my back to the rows of men at one side of the bar, it was often taken as an opportunity to mutter about my face or my body, particularly if I had to reach up or down to get something. I didn't think Nick would do this, but still, I was aware of his presence as I worked, even though he was only ever tapping his ash or staring at his drink when I looked over at him. When I next came to his end of the bar, he asked me if I'd seen Violet recently. Hearing her name again made my face go hot.

'Not since the party,' I said. 'How about you?'

'Nah, she and Jake broke up. I don't think I'll be seeing her again.'

Nick ordered the same drink again – 'tall glass, ice, up to the top, that's right' – and I went to clear the tables. Just before three, he stood up to go and caught my eye. I walked over and he said, 'It was nice to see you again.'

'You too.'

'Listen,' he said. 'We might have got off on the wrong foot.'

I didn't say anything.

'Well, like I say, this is my local and we'll probably be seeing each other again . . . so I wanted to apologise.'

'What for?'

'For being a prick.'

'When?'

I meant it, but he laughed and it felt like the most genuine thing I'd seen him do. 'I meant at the party. But I suppose any time.'

'All right,' I said. He stayed standing in front of the bar, looking at me.

'I was drunk. I can't remember exactly what I said to you . . .' He looked around the bar. 'Maybe I got you wrong. I'm sorry.'

I didn't know if he'd got me wrong or not – it was true that I didn't fit in at Antonia's party but I didn't fit in at the Black Hart either. I didn't say anything. I was beginning to understand that Nick had done something to me. He had turned off my desire to be nice and it was exhilarating.

He shook his head. 'You're so fucking hard to read, you know that?'

'OK,' I said, and he shook his head and left. I turned

around and smiled, putting the glasses on the shelf under the pickled eggs. I was never that rude to anyone. It felt wonderful.

Almost every weekday I worked, Nick came in. There was a precision to it – he arrived between five past and ten past two, sat at the same seat at the end of the bar and ordered a double vodka and Coke. He ordered the second at half past two and was gone by the time the pub closed at three.

He was different from the other men. Although they arrived separately, they often sat together and there was a camaraderie between them, but Nick kept his distance. The other men talked to me, about their jobs and their marriages, and paid me casual compliments about my appearance. Towards the end of the shift, things would turn darker and cruder – both the intimacies that were shared and the comments about the way I looked and what they would like to do to me. The other girls – Elaine and Rosa – knew how to deal with it, coming up with something witty or barbed to say in return: 'Nice tits,' a man with a belly said to Elaine and she said, 'Same to you,' and everyone laughed. But I never got used to it: each time I was surprised by how small and shocked I felt when men spoke to me like that. It was only much later that I realised that was the point.

Nick never talked about how I looked and he didn't speak to Elaine or Rosa either, not even to order his drink – he caught their eye, nodded, put the exact change on the bar, and they started filling the tall glass with ice. But he talked to me.

He mainly talked about himself and his life in the squat,

which turned out to be in a flat in an estate just around the corner. I didn't always understand what he was talking about but certain words and phrases came up again and again – The Swan, Naomi and Jane, anarcho-punk – until I pieced it together: The Swan was a pub where a lot of squatters gathered, Naomi and Jane lived below him in the block of flats, Naomi could be annoying, but he liked Jane, a lot. They thought they were going to get evicted soon, but Naomi had found this old factory building round the corner that they were working up to crack. Cracking a squat meant moving in. I never really understood what anarcho-punk was, but he spoke about it so much, I felt that I did.

He didn't ask me any questions about myself but I got the sense that he was trying to impress me. He started to bring me things – a paperback copy of *The Dispossessed* by Ursula K. Le Guin. A cassette of an album by a band called The Slits. I didn't feel like he really saw me – he gave me the book because I told him I liked reading, and he implied that I would like The Slits because I was a girl, like them.

And yet, he was changing me. I noticed things about our house now – the grandfather clock, the anaglypta wallpaper, my mother's housecoat. What had once seemed ordinary now seemed stifling and absurd. Sometimes I got the piece of paper I'd written on during James's telephone call out of my drawer and read the words again. I imagined us falling in love and getting married, and life becoming very easy. I thought I could do it too: I could learn to make lemon mousse and coq au vin, and choose curtain fabrics, and look after housekeepers. There would be summers in Gloucestershire and balls of cotton wool in glass bowls.

I wrote 'Frances Maxwell' on the piece of paper and then crossed it out.

But as the summer went on, the fantasy wouldn't settle any more. I looked out of my bedroom window at my mother in her quilted slippers, cutting the rosemary bush in the garden, and when I imagined being married, I felt an intense loneliness. I went over to my bed and put the cassette Nick had given me in the Walkman I'd got for Christmas. I didn't understand the music – but I listened to it dutifully so that I could tell Nick I had. And then, halfway through one of the songs, the singer screamed and my whole body shuddered with a sudden blast of energy. I felt as if I'd screamed myself.

3

Amanda

2019

The day I saw Lucy for the first time was the day I gave birth, which still feels appropriate to me now. It was also my first day of maternity leave, the first day I had not gone to work, except for holidays, for at least three years. I didn't take sick days. It was the first time I had woken up in the flat and not had anywhere to go.

I'd woken up at six-thirty as usual. I tried to go back to sleep but by the time Oliver left at seven, I was ready to get up. Before I got out of bed, I had to prepare myself for what I was about to do: moving didn't come naturally to me now. I took the stairs down to the kitchen slowly, keeping one palm flat against the wall. All the things I'd admired about the flat – the mezzanine platform above the kitchen, the suspended slats of wood instead of a staircase, the breakfast bar with stools instead of a table and chairs – now seemed at best inadequate, potentially treacherous. I filled the kettle and wondered what to do.

My flat was on the top floor of the building, at the back, and if I stood at the window, I could see down into the back yard, a communal landscaped terrace, with oversized deckchairs and curving red plastic furniture. I had never seen anyone in the building use it. But I liked looking beyond it, to the backs of the terraced houses: rows of gardens filled with children's toys, bicycles and barbecues, roofs hollowed out with skylights, slate and glass boxes tacked on the back. Every so often, an orange-and-white train went by. I put my hand on my stomach and sipped my tea.

The baby was always quiet first thing in the mornings and the stillness unnerved me every time. The relief I felt when something hard and hidden pressed into my hand almost made me cry. The fear of oblivion was always there, but recently it had been making itself known. I watched in disbelief as the flesh of my stomach rolled, curved and dipped: in the last few days, the situation – having a baby inside me – had started to feel crazy, unsustainable. It was going to have to come out. I thought I had understood that, but I hadn't, not really. *It is going to have to come out.* I decided to go and get a takeaway coffee, because I thought that was the kind of thing you did when you didn't go to work.

The building felt different, quieter, on a weekday but not as quiet as I'd expected. I smiled at a woman in her sixties, in jeans and fresh trainers, who I recognised because she was the only person who lived there who was older than me, and a woman in her twenties wearing short, wide trousers and heavy shoes with large buckles. One of the flats on my corridor had its door open and I saw a man wearing huge headphones, hunched over a laptop at the breakfast bar with a look of intense concentration.

I wasn't particularly friendly with anyone else in the building, but I could never resist sneaking a look inside the other flats, which were almost all studios, like mine. 'It's like a row of rabbit hutches,' my mum said when she saw it, and although it annoyed me, she had a point. The flats were developed almost twenty years ago, when it was more likely that someone in their twenties could afford to live in Hackney on their own. Now the turquoise paint in the hallways was getting grubby, and the Perspex-and-chrome barriers of the mezzanine platforms were scratched, and the studios were mostly occupied by couples: couples with bicycles and guitars leaning against the wall, indoor plants and copies of the same cookbooks. There was a building WhatsApp group but I got increasingly irritated with all the abbreviations and emojis, and then someone used the phrase 'no wozzles' and I put it on permanent mute.

The building was on the main road – a jumble of beauty salons, kebab shops and traffic. But just off it was the kind of street that estate agents namecheck, where they had a farmers' market on Sundays and the chicken shops and newsagents were slowly getting choked out by cocktail bars and florists and places where you could buy ice cream for your dog.

I chose the coffee place closest to my end of the street, not because I liked it but because it was getting harder to walk very far these days. It was small and cold, with unlikely seating: a plywood shelf or a stool that looked like an upside-down geometric bucket. The baristas always seemed mildly surprised to be working there and took your order with a baffled, kindly manner, as if they were humouring you.

I noticed the woman in front of me in the queue straight away because she was also pregnant. She had chin-length blonde hair with a thick dark stripe across her roots; I couldn't tell if it was deliberate or if she was growing it out. She had a nose stud and I was instantly envious: something to distinguish you in pregnancy, a continuity with your old self. Every day I felt myself getting less recognisable, disappearing into the only clothes that fitted – clothes I would never have chosen, that were either bland and cheerful or trying too hard not to be – and a badge that declared 'Baby on board!' with a jauntiness I almost never felt. I hated that fucking exclamation mark.

The woman at the front of the queue was talking to the barista, a slender black man in dungarees, a red-and-orange stripy jumper and brogues. 'I'm vegan,' she was saying, 'and I'm honestly not saying this to convert you, right – but dairy just tastes wrong to me now. It's, like, sort of rancid, like it's coating your throat.' When it was the pregnant woman's turn, she asked for an oat flat white and he told her they didn't have oat milk.

'OK, I'll have almond then. No, no, it's fine, I don't mind. I just prefer oat.'

He made a face. 'Just tastes like porridge to me.'

'Ah, you see, I quite like that. The oatiness. Almond's a bit sweet.'

She was wearing a pink shirt over a vest and pale-blue baggy jeans rolled up. I noticed that her legs were unshaven; I was repulsed without wanting to be. The milk conversation was still going on.

'Oh, goat's the worst,' he said, leaning on the counter. 'You think it's fine and then you get this sort of cheesy aftertaste.'

'Oh, yuck, sounds horrible.'

She waved – 'Bye, Michael, bye, bye, see you soon!' – and I ordered a flat white.

'Dairy?' Michael asked, and I nodded, feeling like I ought to have something to say about it, but I just tapped my card. As I did, I felt my stomach tighten, and then tighten, and tighten, until the pressure was implausible, unsustainable. I managed not to react, just to pick up my coffee and put my card away without Michael noticing. And then it stopped.

I walked on a bit, so I could go back through the residential streets; I'd noticed an estate agent's board outside one of the houses. Oliver and I had agreed that we'd take the flat off the market until the baby was at least one, and anyway, we couldn't afford these houses – we were looking at their copies further east – but I still couldn't stop myself looking at people's front doors and through their windows, as if someone else's curtains might tell me something about how Oliver and I ought to live. I was practised at it now, taking in as much as I could – the glint of a glass-topped kitchen extension, an outlandish light fitting – before it started to get unseemly, and then I turned back onto the high street, slowly moving towards home.

I keyed in the code for the gate outside my building and walked unsteadily across the cobbled yard. As I went through the front door and pressed the button for the lift, I began to feel a familiar kind of discomfort, a distant cousin to claustrophobia or panic. In the lift, in the narrow carpeted corridor, in the stunted hallway entering my flat, I felt like the walls were closing in.

Oliver said my centre of gravity was shifting because of the pregnancy, and he was right: I had lost all understanding of how much space I took up, where I began and ended. I bumped into things, I dropped things, I fell over. I'd once read that goldfish secrete hormones in the water

55

to help them understand their environment, and that was what stopped them growing too big for their bowl. But if you changed the water too often, they couldn't read the hormones and they didn't stop growing and then . . . flapping fins, bulging scales, gasping mouths. It was too grotesque to think about properly.

As I shut the door behind me and put my bag on the counter, my stomach tightened again, the same thing: rigid breathless shock, and then over. I took the last of my coffee – Oliver always teased me about how I dragged it out – and I drank it standing opposite the back window.

I had once loved this flat. I'd turned up to the viewing three years ago, sleepless, thin and jumpy, knowing it wasn't really what I wanted. I wanted a new-build, not a conversion, and although I was looking in east London, I wasn't sure about this part of Hackney. I knew it too well.

In the lift on the way up, the estate agent went hard on the history – *early twentieth century, preserving the industrial aesthetic.* He was called Julius and I don't suppose he'd ever known anyone who'd worked in a factory, which is why he made it all sound so pleasant. I didn't really like the idea of it: eating granola at a breakfast bar in a room where other women had worked, suffering, for very little money. Everyone wanted history – sash windows, fireplaces, cornicing, stained glass – but I didn't. Some things you don't want to be reminded of.

But I liked the exposed brickwork, the 'grand industrial proportions' of the double-height ceiling and domed windows. I liked how small it was. It was tiny and impersonal, and that was what I wanted, then. The life I'd had with David in our house in Highbury was the kind of life I'd come to London for – Ottolenghi starters, muted paint colours and organic veg bags – but by the end it seemed oddly dull and stressful, lying in bed worrying about what to do with a celeriac. This flat suggested the kind of person who didn't have time for any of that. Life – real life, the full, rich, interesting kind – was going on somewhere else.

I moved in three months later and I loved turning away from the traffic, up through the warren of corridors, to this small, still space that belonged entirely to me. Just after David and I separated, I'd got promoted at the newspaper and finally I could work the way I had when I'd started out, uninterrupted, focused, purposeful. I stayed as late as I wanted at the office, and came home to an unchanged room. I'd have a takeaway or a ready meal (the organic, no-preservatives kind of ready meal; I still thought all that stuff mattered, I just didn't want to do anything about it myself). I sat alone on the small sofa watching a box set or messing about with my friends on WhatsApp until it was time to look for the 10.30 headlines. I didn't panic if there was a story that I'd missed because I could just write it up then; I didn't feel guilty about sleep or stress levels any more because I wasn't trying to get pregnant, and there was no one to get annoyed with me about it. Sometimes I'd get a message from a friend saying they were thinking of me, or just checking in and wondering how I was getting on, and it took a moment to remember that this freedom, this solitude, was supposed to be making me unhappy.

I was happy now, standing in the sunlight, watching a train go by, but the happiness came freighted with a kind of foreboding. Was this going to be the last time I felt this way? 'Would you like to know the date you were going to have the baby, if you could?' Oliver's sister asked us a few days ago. 'Yes, of course,' Oliver said, at the same time as

I said, 'No.' 'It would be like knowing the date you were going to die,' I explained before I could stop myself, and both of them looked at me oddly. Of course I wasn't going to die in childbirth, I knew that, but when I thought about the birth, death was always there somewhere, black shapes hovering at the edges. I couldn't believe that the person I was now, drinking coffee in front of her window, was going to survive what happened next, and really, wasn't that a kind of death?

The baby book called them 'negative feelings'. *You may experience negative feelings in pregnancy*, it said, as though it was just another symptom, like heartburn. The feelings didn't matter, they weren't part of me; nothing to worry or think too deeply about. It ought to have comforted me, but in fact it did the opposite. Because these fears didn't feel like temporary afflictions, like cramp or swollen ankles. They were inside me. They felt real.

I tipped my paper cup back, draining it. I got a giant head rush, my stomach tightened again, but this time much harder and for longer, and then water started falling out of me.

In the birthing classes we'd been to, they talked about labour as a progression or a journey – *first stage, second stage, third stage, early, active, pushing* – but by the time I'd got to the hospital, and Oliver arrived – *oh, isn't that lucky?* one of the midwives said when I told her he worked at the hospital – I was in another world, where time slowed and sped up at random, and sometimes whole hours were lost. There were certain data points – *your amniotic sac is insufficiently ruptured; only two centimetres, I'm afraid* – but otherwise I was at sea. I bounced on a ball, I walked up and down stairs,

I ate a hummus sandwich. I walked along the corridors, and round the car park, and at intervals I was devastated with an internal power I didn't recognise, something I would be incapable of summoning. I pressed my hands into the walls of the hospital; I moaned; I paced around the birthing pool; I threw myself on the floor. My waters broke again, and still had to be broken a third time by a doctor; *temperature's spiked*; a group of people ran into the room to put stickers on my chest and disappeared; *we need to get you into proper labour now, sweetheart*. It had got dark outside. I was in a hospital gown attached to machinery by a needle on my wrist, a wire coming out of my vagina; *she has failed to progress*.

I was given a dog-eared laminated sheet to read, but I could barely absorb the list of horrible things that might happen to me, much less consider the percentage of risk next to each item. I handed it over and signed the piece of paper. A needle in my back, hunched over a pillow; *if you move, there's a risk of paralysis*. Stillness, machinery, graphs. *Heart rate's getting high, maybe drop it down a bit; fully dilated, you can start pushing; heart rate's spiking; I think she's going to need some help; we've got to get this baby out now, sweetheart*. I was sweating and furious; Oliver got me a hairband and tied back my hair. 'You look like you did the day we met,' he said, because I used to tie my hair back for work, and I managed to smile at him before I was told to push again. Then the universe shifted, suddenly, permanently. She was on my chest and I was swamped in contentment.

Oliver was crying and saying, *she's amazing, is she all right, she's amazing*, over and over again. 'She's fine,' I said, because I felt that I knew her. Then I said, 'I'm sorry, I think I'm going to be sick.' They didn't get the cardboard bowl to me in time. I threw up and the doctor who'd been calling me sweetheart had vomit on her face. Oliver said she would have been OK with it, but I saw her expression and I don't think she was.

When we got back to the flat two days later, it felt like we were returning somewhere we'd lived twenty years ago. The cars, the houses, the shops and cafés had a sepia tinge, receding against the blazing newness of us. Of the baby, who we'd called Iris, nestled in a car seat, her tiny head flattened from the ventouse, and me, bleeding, held together by stitches, still unused to the empty space between the zip of my coat and my belly.

Oliver carried the car seat across the courtyard and all I could think about was the time I walked across there in high heels with two bottles of wine in a carrier bag. I turned on my ankle and dropped the bag – the bottles smashed and there was red liquid all over the cobbles. I had a vision of Oliver falling in the same way; I could see the car seat turning over; her soft head on stone; blood. I thought about insisting on carrying it, but I still felt weak and unsteady; I didn't know if I could be any more careful. The idea that there might be nothing I could do to prevent it happening produced a cold horror worse than the original vision.

Oliver made me a cup of tea while I sat on the sofa, picking through the leaflets they'd given me at the hospital. There was one about all the ways that she could die, the horrible potential of duvets, saucepans and blinds. The leaflet was written from the perspective of the baby: *I could suffocate if . . . I could drown if . . .* I picked up another one about safe sleeping and read the 'simple rules to follow', which sounded more like superstitions or riddles. *The baby should wear a hat but never indoors. Don't let the baby get too hot or too cold.* I put the leaflet down again.

Iris was sleeping in a Moses basket next to me, making extraordinary noises: yelps, squeaks, grunts, barks. I had already googled this and apparently it was normal. Then she stopped and lay there, so still, so very still that I reached out and put my hand on her stomach. There was a lull – enough time for everything to unravel – *is this it? is this it? this is it* – then her arms flailed and the breathing jumpstarted again. I got out my phone and it said that babies sometimes stop breathing for a few seconds (what the *fuck*?). I kept my hand on her stomach after that just in case.

Two weeks later, it was Oliver's first day back at the hospital. I had read somewhere that on maternity leave it was important to leave the house every day and have a shower every day, so, even though I was exhausted, I forced myself out of bed before Oliver left for work. In the shower, alone, I cried. When I went back into the bedroom, I wanted to just pick the clothes I was wearing yesterday off the floor, but I knew they were covered in stale milk, so I put my dressing gown on, carried Iris downstairs, holding her tight, conscious of each step, so I could take a pair of leggings and a new maternity top from the drying rack in the living room. I got dressed in the living room because I couldn't face the stairs again and I was pleased with myself: a small achievement. The only mirror was upstairs, but I imagined I looked quite nice.

When Iris and I said goodbye to Oliver, he was crying and I did stupid things like make Iris wave and do a high-pitched voice saying, 'Bye-bye, Daddy,' because I didn't want him to know how afraid I was. He shut the door and I was alone in the flat. Then Iris was sick on my clean clothes and I had to get changed again.

I had planned to go to Mum and Baby cinema, even though it seemed unimaginable, that I might look after a baby in the dark while being shown a documentary about race in America that I'd chosen specifically to prove that I hadn't lost my mind. It was as if someone had asked me to take a grenade to the cinema. But I was good at making myself do difficult things. I moved around the flat, crazed, panicked, gathering up all the things we needed: pads for my nipples, pads for my vagina, nappies, wet wipes, extra clothes. I picked Iris up to put her in the pram, but gurgling sounds came from inside her and everything collapsed into liquid again: glossy ochre stuff on my arms, streaked on her leg. Little damp spots appeared on my T-shirt over my nipples. As I bent over Iris on the changing mat, laid out on the floor because we didn't have room for a table, the need to piss that I had been ignoring suddenly intensified, and I changed her nappy kneeling in a pool of hot liquid. I mopped and changed and stoppered us up all over again, but by that time we'd missed the film and I was ashamed at how relieved I felt.

Leave the house and have a shower every day. It sounded ludicrously, deceptively simple. I could not fail at this, not on my first day. I didn't know where we were going, but I put her in the pram and inexpertly manoeuvred it through the heavy fire doors and into the lift, scuffing the walls and banging the door frames.

Even though we had survived the birth, and the first two weeks, the black shapes were still there, lurking. In the past when I crossed the road, I believed that the traffic would stop at the lights, but now it felt insane to wheel the pram, with her tiny body encased in it, into a road where an HGV was driving and trust that the driver, who I did not know, who could be drunk or high or mad, would stop. The system seemed entirely insufficient. I waited until the traffic had definitely stopped before crossing and tried to make eye contact with the drivers and I was too slow: I was still on the road when the lights changed and the cars beeped and revved their engines. I got the buggy stuck on the kerb and panicked. By the time I made it to the other side, I was on the verge of tears.

I turned the corner and started heading towards the closest café and I saw the woman I'd seen the day I gave birth, with the nose stud and rolled-up jeans, coming towards me. She was no longer pregnant; she had a baby strapped to her with what looked like a very wide scarf with an exquisite geometric pattern. She carried a reusable coffee cup and looked tired. I wondered about smiling at her but decided that would look weird.

The café was on the other side of the road. To get to the pedestrian crossing I would have to cross several side roads and navigate stretches of narrow, uneven pavement. I watched people go in and out: I hadn't noticed that the doorway had steps leading up to it or that the door was so stiff. I had no idea how I would keep it open and get the buggy up the steps, without someone helping me, and although it was part of my job to ask difficult questions, the thought of asking someone to do this for me felt impossible. I stayed where I was, people moving around me, watching the door. I had never wanted a coffee so much.

Untethered, ordinary people opened doors, crossed roads,

typed on their laptops. I tried to make myself move, so tempted by the possibility of something hot and comforting, something familiar. I knew how to try, how to persist. I knew how to be stubborn, how to get in the way. I had built everything out of these qualities: what I did for a living, where I lived, who I was. And yet I couldn't do this. I turned around and walked home.

At home, I googled slings and found photographs of models draped in beautiful fabric that cost £250 and for a moment I was tempted. Maybe motherhood didn't have to be messy and austere after all? But then I looked at the functional options with rings and clips and adjustable canvas straps. I found a 'sling library', a place where they let you try out different options for free in a local church, and bookmarked the link.

I made myself scrambled eggs and the yellow liquid in the pan made me think of Iris's nappies. I dropped some on my leg when I was trying to eat it while holding her. I thought about how ordinarily I would get changed if that happened, but now there didn't seem much point. At four o'clock, she started crying and I didn't know how to make it better. I hadn't thought much about babies crying before – it was just something they did – but when Iris cried, all I could think about was how I had to make it stop, immediately. It was an urge, like hunger, and it increased with every intolerable second. When nothing worked, when she tore away from my nipple, unresponsive to bouncing or rocking or singing, I became desperate, deranged.

After an hour or so, she fell asleep, but Oliver's key in the door at eight still felt like salvation. I handed Iris to him and revelled in the extraordinary lightness, the slight lift of responsibility. I reminded myself that he'd done a twelve-hour shift in A&E and would be exhausted, but I couldn't make it mean anything to me, I didn't care – all I wanted was for him to take her. He talked to me about work, about how strange it was to be back, how he missed me and Iris. I tried to tell him about my day but it was hard to remember anything concrete. I went for a walk. I ate scrambled eggs. I decided to go to a sling library. I didn't tell him about not getting a coffee.

The sling library was a drop-in from ten till two. I thought it was annoying that you couldn't make an appointment but when Iris and I started the maddeningly open-ended business of preparing to go out, I realised it made sense. It was in a church that I had barely noticed before – another of those buildings, like health centres and community halls, that had emerged into the foreground in the last few months. Inside, there were long trestle tables heaped with fabric, among laminated signs for the toilet and stacked grey plastic chairs. I wrote my name on the waiting list attached to a clipboard. I couldn't remember the last time I'd written my name in pencil and I thought briefly about my office: the security passes, touch screens and the sliding glass barriers.

After half an hour a woman with grey hair and a toddler in a sling called my name. I walked over and then realised that I'd left the nappy bag on the chair and went back to get it. 'Baby brain!' she said, and I laughed, practising being this new kind of person, the kind who didn't mind getting called stupid to her face.

She wrapped me in various kinds of fabrics, while telling

me that wearing Iris in a sling would cure everything from wind to insecure attachment: 'When it's time for school, she'll be the happy confident one, skipping into the playground!' I was sceptical but seduced – what if it was true? Imagine if this changed everything and suddenly it all became easy. She patiently, kindly talked me through the ties and loops several times. Then she said, 'Now! Two free hands! One for coffee, one for cake! No housework!'

I had been told not to do housework before and I felt, as I so often felt since Iris was born, as if I'd been mistaken for someone else. It conjured up a different kind of woman, a different sort of home, where everything was basically clean and ordered, and housework was a kind of feminine indulgence that I just couldn't stop myself doing, like dusting ornaments or putting out doilies. But the flat, I had come to realise, was not built for this new mess and clutter. Perhaps other spaces could absorb it more easily, but within minutes of us simply existing, it looked insane. I didn't clean shit off the sofa or wash Iris's clothes to treat myself, I did it because I couldn't see any way round it, and if Oliver was at work there was no one else to do it. But I smiled and laughed and said, 'OK then!' as if she was the first person who'd said that to me.

I went out in the street with Iris in the sling, pushing the empty buggy. She fell asleep almost instantly, but so deeply it was sinister. Her breathing was almost imperceptible. I remembered the story that Oliver had told me, about the parents who walked into the hospital, with the baby suffocated in the sling. I had to stop and stand completely still with my hand on her back before I felt the tiniest, subtlest swell of movement underneath my palm. I had to stop again and again. I fussed with the fabric, to stop it covering her face, tried to catch a glimpse of myself in shop windows to check she wasn't too low, too high. It took me half an hour to get home. I ended up returning it to the library. Those black shapes again.

Two weeks later, I was feeding Iris on the sofa while Oliver was making dinner. I had become more practised at maternity leave, and there were now three moments in the day I held out for, savoured. One was when I walked out of the building in the morning and the cool air on my face made me feel instantly better: I had found a café that I could get the buggy into, and I bought a coffee and a croissant and then sat in the park by the hospital, thinking, *fuck, fuck, fuck.* Another was Oliver's key in the door. And then, when he'd had a shower, he would cook while I had a glass of wine with Iris asleep on me on the sofa, and then when she woke up, we would put her in her bouncer and eat together, and she was mostly remarkably content. I waited and waited for that moment and yet, when it came round, I often felt aimless and somehow disagreeable.

He was making salmon, green beans and some kind of complicated dressing that involved toasting seeds. He was getting frustrated – banging pans and shutting cupboard doors a little too loudly. The kitchen was under our bedroom on the mezzanine platform, so the ceiling was low and, like everything in the flat, it was just a little smaller than it ought to be. I imagined it was a very frustrating space to cook in, though I didn't know for sure because it was still always Oliver who cooked. He'd always cared a lot more about food than I did and when I got pregnant, he got even more obsessed with things like omega-3. He'd probably chosen the ingredients for tonight's supper to combine a specific set of nutrients to support breastfeeding and I ought to have been grateful for it, but in fact it only made me feel guilty about all the croissants and crisps I ate during the day. I was supposed to be grateful for his help, but everything unnecessary that he did made me angry: *can't you see what's going on? haven't you noticed this is a crisis?* His time had become my time and now he was messing around with sunflower seeds when he could have been holding Iris. I hated feeling like I had a claim on something of his, but there was no other way of surviving: I had nothing of my own any more.

The wine was making me chatty and I told Oliver about my day, the baby group I'd been to. 'And I thought that was it, we could go home, but then she said, "We're just going to do a little sing-song," and my God, I wanted to die. One of the dads just walked out but I couldn't manage it. So we had to sing along to this terrible version of "The Wheels on the Bus" blaring out of an iPhone.'

I kept waiting for him to laugh but he didn't.

'I don't really understand why you hate those groups so much,' he said. 'Oh fuck.' He took the seeds off the heat and there was a smell of burning.

'It's— They're awful. You would hate them.'

'I don't think I would.' He took the salmon out of the oven and touched the tinfoil. 'Ow.' He waited and then cautiously started to unwrap it.

'You'd find it boring. Everyone has the same conversations. About hypnobirthing and nanny-shares and dungarees.'

'I really don't think I'd mind it. I think I might quite like it. Not one single person at work has asked me about my paternity leave.' He flipped the salmon onto the plates.

'I mean, apart from the person who asked me if I enjoyed my time off.'

He bent over the plates, concentrating on the precise placement of the seeds and the dressing. It was the kind of gesture that had made me fall in love with him. A trace of that feeling was still there, but it was very distant now.

He started to set the table and I got up off the sofa, holding Iris, who was starting to stir and murmur. 'I was the one that said we should have done the NCT classes,' he said. 'You were the one who said you didn't want to sit around in a circle in your socks talking about your feelings.'

'Well, I didn't. I don't. That hasn't changed now that I've given birth.'

'I still think we should have given it a go. Maybe you need mum friends, I don't know.'

I didn't want to do NCT or make mum friends because all my life I had wanted to make things change and for things to happen to me, and I just didn't believe that was possible surrounded by women singing nursery rhymes. So far, all of the exciting, dynamic places had been the places men were – my course at Oxford, the newsdesk, the pub after work. Even though, at Oxford, I had to avoid saying certain words that made my Essex accent obvious. Even though a boy on my course said, affectionately, 'Amanda's hilarious: she looks so sophisticated and glamorous and then she opens her mouth.' Even though the elderly professor at my first seminar said, 'Are you sure you're in the right place, blondie?' Despite all that, I still wanted to be *there*, not here. Everything good in my life had happened there. And there was another reason, one that was almost too painful to think about, but I said it anyway because I was annoyed about the seeds: 'I didn't choose to bring a baby up with a load of women I don't know. I chose to do it with you.'

He sighed. 'What do you want me to do, give up my job?'

'No, I know, of course, you can't do that. But it doesn't make it any easier for me to . . . get through the day.'

'Look, you don't have to go to these things,' he said. 'You should enjoy your maternity leave. Why don't you take her to the Tate Modern or something? Somewhere you'd like to go.'

Because I am afraid. Because I can't get on the Tube without worrying that there won't be room for me in the carriage, or that people will resent me for taking up too much space, or imagining her falling onto the tracks through the gap between the platform and the train. Because when I'm out of the house, it is exhausting trying to contain her and me, feeling constantly apologetic, with the tinnitus of questions about her age, her sleep, whether she's too hot, whether she's too cold, whether I'm looking after her properly, and however much I hate the groups, they're the only place I get a break from that. They're only just better than staying in this tiny flat or wandering around the park by myself all day, not speaking to anyone till the evening.

Oliver was trying to unfold Iris's bouncy seat. We couldn't keep it up because there was so little space in the flat. I watched him for a moment. I could tell he was irritated with it, and with me for not helping, and I could see he'd reached that point where he wasn't really trying any more. For a moment it looked like he might have done it, and I was almost disappointed because the thing that had been building inside me might not have anywhere to go.

But then he said, 'Sorry, could you—? I can't ever get this right for some reason.'

'How come I know how to do it and you don't?'

He didn't say anything.

'I taught myself how to do it, I don't have this innate knowledge of baby equipment—'

'I'm just a bit crap with stuff like that—'

'I'm a bit crap with stuff like that too! But I have to do it!'

'I'm not here during the day! If I was here, I would know how to do it!'

It turned out that there wasn't anywhere for it to go after all. I was heady, almost vibrating, with anger. I wanted to hit the walls, I wanted to get away from him, but the flat was too small, and besides, I was still holding Iris.

In the baby book, there was a chapter on fathers. A lot of it was about sex: what to do if he wants it and you don't, what to do if you want it and he thinks your pregnant body is grotesque. And then how to involve him: *don't undermine him, don't sweat the small stuff, let him make mistakes.* But every other chapter in the book made it painfully clear that I couldn't make mistakes, because the small stuff – where she slept, how she slept, what she wore, how I fed her, what I fed her – could be fatal or damaging. I tried and tried and tried all day, and then I was supposed to sit back and watch him fuck it up. I didn't understand how I could do that. And the injustice made me furious.

When I met Lucy, Iris was six weeks old and I had finally admitted to myself that I was unhappy. I hadn't said any-thing to anyone else. I didn't want what came next: the grave looks, the hospital appointments, the medication.

I didn't know if it was what I needed, and anyway I didn't want it, so I carried on: adding peppy caveats to anything less than positive, punctuating my misery with exclamation marks and emojis. I shouldn't have been surprised that that was what I got in return: my feelings, raw and huge, fed back to me diluted. Rage became *we all get a bit irritable sometimes*, anxiety was *you don't know worry until you're a mum*. I was supposed to find what was happening to me ordinary and funny, but that made me feel like I was losing my mind even more. *If it's so normal why can't I cope with it?* But it was words like 'not coping' that I wanted to avoid.

I had decided to get a bus to a baby group – just a short trip, because I thought the more I did it, the easier it would get. I managed to get the pram into the right space and the seat nearest to it was free, so I could sit down and still keep hold of the handle. I had seen women leave their buggies there and sit further away but I couldn't do it; if this seat wasn't free, I would stand.

'Oooh, can I have a peek?' the woman next to me said. She was vast, in her fifties, with brown straggly hair. I nodded. She stood up and peered into the buggy. 'Oh. Is she yours?'

'Yes,' I said.

'She don't look it. Where's her dad from then?'

Another time I might have said London, but I didn't want to prolong it so I said, 'His mother was born in Jamaica,' and she seemed satisfied. Then she started asking me about Iris's name, her age, whether she slept through the night, and I had never in my life wanted to tell someone to fuck off so much. It was a constant acute pressure, like being on the verge of vomiting. But I leant my head back wearily and answered her questions.

'Was you in labour long?'

'Thirty-six hours,' I said.

'Oh gosh. Poor you. Still, it's better to do it that way, isn't it? My friend's daughter had three planned caesareans.' She said it as if it was like having three slices of cake. 'She got to choose the dates and everything. It don't feel right. Not to me, anyway. And are you feeding her yourself?'

I nodded.

'My friend's daughter's not. Says she don't want to.'

I tried to turn the conversation away from me. 'Do you have children?' I asked, gripping on to the handlebar of the buggy as the bus swayed.

'No,' she said. 'I wish I did.'

Suddenly the intense irritation turned to dread. The depth of feeling in her voice terrified me. I felt a burst of relief when she pressed the button on the pole in front of me, and I moved to let her get out. As the bus slowed down, she put her hand in the pram to touch Iris's face; I recoiled as if I'd been groped. 'Oh, she's gorgeous!' She stumbled and grabbed the handle of the pram to steady herself. She didn't let it go.

I kept my eyes on her hand. She ran it up and down the handle, her fingers on the catch that controlled the brake. I put my foot on the wheel and clutched the arm of the handle and told myself, *I'm ready, I've got her, I will not let her go.* The bus pulled in, she stumbled again, I lunged clumsily, and she laughed as she steadied herself.

'Oooh, you nearly took her with you then!' a woman opposite us laughed.

'Don't think Mum would be too happy about that!' someone else said.

I reeled back in the seat. Iris started to grizzle and I got off at the next stop, and took her out of the pram and held her. She seemed so vulnerable in the street, the hard cold paving below us, the speed of the cars. She stopped crying, but when I put her down she started again.

We did this two or three more times, until there was only five minutes before the group started. I forced myself to walk while she cried in the pram, desperately whispering comforting words to her. I had rarely felt so conspicuous or so fragile. *It is only five minutes.* I passed a mother with her baby asleep in a pram and I was consumed with frustration and rage: *why isn't my baby doing that? why isn't she sleeping like all the other babies?*

Finally, she fell asleep, just as we reached the community hall. The relief was instant and total. I wondered if she might stay asleep through the first part, or even the whole thing. Perhaps I could relax and drink tea, perhaps have a conversation. But the room was empty and a note, hand-written in marker pen and taped to the door, told me the group had been cancelled.

I decided to walk home down the street with the coffee places and shops that sold expensive socks and candles. The shops were small, with narrow doorways and steps up to the front, and everything inside them was minimal and delicate: bottles of ointment and fine gold chains threaded with tiny, indistinct charms. Ceramic bowls with paper-thin rims. Things that would be so useless to me now they seemed almost exotic. I remembered Saturdays in my old life, strolling in and out, idly looking for a birthday present for someone or something for the flat, coming out having spent more than I meant to.

I was calm when she slept, but also aimless: I knew this

moment ought to be treasured, I just didn't know how. As I got towards the middle of the street, I saw the nose-stud woman sitting outside a corner café, looking at her phone. She had a coffee and a plate of food with stuff drizzled on it and seeds scattered about. She was still wearing the beautiful sling; the baby was asleep in it. It looked nice. It looked like something I could do.

I had only been to this café once before. I remembered when it was a fish and chip shop, and it still had the original green tiles and sign outside. Inside, they had the same dark wooden tables and benches, and mirrors on the white-tiled walls, and there was still lettering on the windows offering live eels. They didn't sell live eels there now, of course. They sold eggs and cakes and toasties, just with unexpected additions like kimchi or tahini, as if nothing was enough on its own.

I used to not mind it, this trend for keeping the old sign and altering what was inside. You saw a Chinese takeaway with a bright red-and-yellow sign, and then it turned out to be an organic wine shop. The launderette, red letter-ing on a grey background, was actually a pop-up Thai restaurant. But recently it had started to unnerve me, in this patch of the city with layers of memories folded into one another, where everything was in the wrong place. If I looked in the window of The Swan now, I saw duvets and kettles; there were yoga mats and house plants in the Victorian school building; inside the old children's hospital there were king-size beds and T-shirts drying on racks.

The last time I'd been to this café, I was with my mum, when I'd just moved in to the flat. When I told her I was moving back to Hackney, she said, 'Oh God, what went wrong?' and it annoyed me because, although quite a lot of things had gone wrong in my life, I was hoping that this move was something right. When she came to visit, I tried to show her how different things were here now and she kept looking at the wrong things, like the man in a sleeping bag on the bench by the park or the woman fishing in the electrical recycling bin, her heels sticking out the back of her too-small shoes, filling a worn-out buggy with old adapters and extension leads. She pointed to the balcony of a council flat with piles of clothes drying on top of one another and said, 'Aren't you glad you don't have to hang your washing out like that?' And then, 'I just don't understand what all the fuss is about, why all these people want to live here now.' I was seething.

We were trying to find somewhere for a cup of tea, but nothing was right: there were lots of places that sold coffee, but they only sold lavender brownies or miso cookies, or sometimes vintage clothes, alongside it. She wanted 'proper cake, you know, a piece of carrot cake or something'. This was the last place we'd tried before we'd given up and we'd both been in a bad mood when she'd gone to catch her train back that evening. I hadn't wanted to eat a miso cookie either, but I felt like I had to pretend that I did, out of loyalty to the life I was creating, and I wished now that I'd just said that and we'd got carrot cake from the supermarket and eaten it in the park.

At the time, I hadn't noticed that the entrance to the café had three steep, uneven stone steps, but now I hesitated, unsure what to do, and then a man sitting in the window leapt up to help me, hoisting his end of the pram so enthusiastically that Iris's sleeping body was almost vertical. My heart was still racing as I paid for my coffee and food, but remarkably, every time I peered behind the muslin I'd pegged over the hood of the buggy, Iris's eyes were closed.

The seats were all taken so I said I'd sit outside. I had to ask another person to help me down the steps but the tables outside were full too. I hovered, stranded, and decided that I would have to walk away, that I would rather lose whatever ridiculous sum of money I'd paid for a coffee and a bagel than have to go in and out of the café again. Then the woman with the baby saw me and said, 'Do you want to share my table?'

'Are you sure that's OK?' I said.

'Yeah, of course.' She started moving her plate and coffee to make more room. I sat down next to her. It felt like refuge.

'How old—?' she said.

'Six weeks.'

'Snap,' she said, patting the sling. She stretched her arm out, so as not to touch the sleeping baby on her chest, and spilt coffee in the saucer as she lifted her cup. I recognised the rapid, unsteady way she drank it, that inability to do anything slowly. I couldn't even read a news article from start to finish now, only frantically skim it, picking out the most significant bits, in case I was interrupted before I got to the end. Then she said, 'I feel like I recognise you. Did you go to hypnobirthing classes in the yoga studio?'

I shook my head.

'Oh, OK, maybe not then. Maybe I've just seen you around.'

'Possibly. Do you live near here?' I asked, even though I was fairly certain she did.

'Yup. Just a few streets away, actually. Do you know Digby Street?'

I did know it. Oliver and I had looked at a house there once before we accepted that we couldn't afford to stay in the area. I could only vaguely remember what it was like – we had seen so many second reception rooms and side returns that the details had got hazy. But I knew that they were proper houses, family homes, with gardens and hallways and huge potential for conversion. I wasn't jealous – I didn't know her well enough for that – but I felt out of step, as if I had done things wrong already.

'How about you?'

'I live in a development on the high street. A converted factory.'

'Oh, sounds cool.'

'It is. It's just not very suitable for a baby. We tried to move, but we couldn't get an offer on it. You know . . . Brexit.'

I knew I was being boring but I was afraid of being any other way. When I talked to other mothers, I felt out of my depth, as if there were customs I didn't yet know about it.

'And how are you finding it?' she said, nodding at the pram.

I was about to say what I always said – *hard work, but amazing!* – but before I could, she took another gulp of her coffee and said, 'Sorry, that's such a shit question, isn't it? People ask me all the time and I never know what to say.' She put her cup down. 'I really don't! I'm all over the fucking place.'

I studied her as she stabbed wildly at her plate, cramming whatever haul her fork dredged up into her mouth, twisting her lips to keep in the bits that were threatening to spill out, and it didn't seem like a pose: she really did look all over the place. The other mothers I had met had a veneer of control, even as they were anxiously telling me how chilled out they were. It was so convincing that whether it was real or not didn't seem to matter.

'I never know what to say when people say, "How was your night?"' I said. My coffee and bagel arrived and I had another look behind the muslin. Iris was still sleeping. 'Half the time I can't even remember.'

'Oh God! I'm the same,' she said. 'The details, anyway. Like last night, he finally fell asleep on the living room sofa at – what? – three in the morning, and I know, you're not supposed to let them or whatever, but I've been waiting for him to go to sleep for three hours, how can I possibly move him? So I just lay next to him watching him, but why were we on the sofa in the first place? Why were we even downstairs? No fucking idea.' She put her cup down. 'It's like having sex when you're drunk. I have these really vivid, intense memories but, you know, I couldn't tell you how we got from one moment to the other.'

'It's more of a sensation than a . . . chronology, isn't it?' It was the best conversation I'd had since Iris was born and I wanted to keep it going, but I was beginning to feel nervous, as if I might end up saying something I wasn't supposed to. The sensation I was talking about was a mix of despair, exhaustion, frenzied anxiety, crushing loneliness – it was overwhelming and it was still inside me.

'Yeah, chronology, that's the problem, isn't it?' she said. 'Like the birth. I mean, people ask me about it, all the time, like they're doing this really noble, modern thing – "Oh, I'm going to let her talk about *her birth*" – but I don't know what to say. I don't know how to make it into a story. I clearly just need to figure out the short answer, but

79

I haven't yet so I carry on talking, saying random things, and their eyes are glazing over and I still feel like I haven't even begun to explain what it was like.'

'The trouble with the short answer is that then you feel like you're lying,' I said. My heart was starting to beat faster.

'Yeah, I know. And I could lie. It's not like people really give a shit anyway. But somehow I don't want to do that, I *can't* do that. Like, maybe I don't want to just turn it into a funny story about an epidural, I don't know.' She gulped her coffee. 'It's like the nights thing: some of the really vital details are missing. Like why did I take my pants off or why did they put that thing inside me? And then some things you'll remember forever. "Now, sweetheart, I'm just going to give you a little cut."' She flinched and blinked.

'I think we might have had the same doctor,' I said, putting my coffee down. 'Mine kept calling me sweetheart too.'

'Blonde woman? I can't remember anything else about her, to be honest.'

'That's the one. She told me my vagina would heal but "it'll never look quite the same again".'

She hunched her shoulders and turned her face away. 'Oh God. Why would you say that to someone?'

'I don't know. Anyway, now I'm too scared to look.'

I was almost dizzy. Being good with people had been part of my job. I knew when to be charming or flirtatious or chummy. I knew what kind of man would want to tell a young woman what the world was like; I knew the kind of woman who would be more comfortable if we both acted as if we were incompetent. I knew when to let people know about my first and when to say 'uni' instead of 'Oxford'. I knew when to disguise my accent and when to accentuate it, when to wear my glasses or contact lenses, to keep my make-up natural or do something wild. It was fun and I was good at it, and now that I was talking about vaginal tearing with someone whose name I didn't know, I missed it with an ache that was agonising.

She finished her lunch and pushed her plate away. 'Do you know any good baby groups round here?'

'I don't know if I know any good ones . . .'

'Oh, OK, I don't mean good. Fine? Bearable? I'm just looking for something to do. I feel like I'm doing absolutely nothing all day and I still don't have time to wash my hair.' She looked down at her baby's head. 'I feel kind of . . . untethered and at the same time, I mean, I've really never been more fucking tethered.'

I had hoped that having a baby might feel relaxing, the way it did when I spent time with friends and their babies, that petty anxiety would recede in the face of delight and joyful dedication to the most important task of all. But while there was no time to have a shower, there was endless time to think. Anxiety, it turned out, could breed and flourish if you sat on a sofa under a sleeping baby for three hours in an empty apartment. I couldn't concentrate or focus, but there was plenty of room for frantic, splintered thoughts – *feed or rock, are her lips still pink, is she still breathing, is she too warm, what does she want, feed or rock, what does she need?*

I liked being the kind of person who knew things and I wanted to be able to recommend a baby group, the way I used to be able to recommend a new restaurant or a conveyancer, but I didn't know any. She got out her phone.

'Someone told me about this singing group on Thursdays. Have you ever been to that?'

'Maybe we could go together?' I said. 'This week?'

I felt gauche and eager, but she didn't seem to mind and we exchanged numbers and names. We talked some more, and then the babies woke up and we introduced them, even though they didn't even know they had hands yet so why on earth would they care about another baby? Her son was called Stanley. Then Iris started crying and I began to feel panicked again, so I said that I had to go. As I wheeled the pram back home, I realised something: for the last half-hour, I had not thought about Iris dying.

II

4

Ellen

1909

'When's the baby coming then?' Mary said to me on Saturday morning, as we stood in the yard eating breakfast. 'Your ma's enormous.'

The weather was getting warmer. It could be fairly pleasant in the yard some mornings, even at half past eight, and that day the sun was already out, lightening the brick walls of the factory. We heard a train go by. I used to look forward to summer but this year, when I noticed light in the sky in the evenings, or the sun coming in through the windows, I got anxious instead. I did not know what this new season would bring. A life? A death? Two deaths?

'This month,' I said, although we never spoke about Mother's condition at home. Five months after Dad died, she'd stood up one evening while we'd been mending and I'd seen the ghost of that familiar shape and known that it was happening again. An understanding had grown between us, as she had grown. I knew that the midwife was expecting to come at the end of May. I knew that her address was on a piece of paper in the cash box where we'd stashed the money for her fee.

'This month! It's the thirtieth already,' Mags said, getting an egg out of her pocket. 'And I saw your ma dragging the coal in.'

'Well, she don't have a bloke,' Mary said. 'Who's going to do it for her? Anyway, it's the twenty-ninth today.'

'Oh, fuck yourself, Mary,' Mags said, flicking a piece of eggshell at her face.

'How do you always get eggs?' Lou asked, unwrapping her bread.

'Bloke next door's got chickens,' Mags said, taking a bite and showing us the crumbly gold yellow of the yolk.

'You lucky bitch,' Lou said. 'I'd love fresh eggs.' She took a bite out of her bread and turned to me. 'How did your ma get in the family way then, if she don't have a bloke?'

'She got that way before he died,' Mary said.

'The poor cow,' Lou said. 'Imagine finding that out. And she must be getting on, if she's got you.'

'My auntie had a baby at forty-six,' Mags said. 'The baby came out all right, but they couldn't get the afterbirth. The doctor had his hand up her, trying to tear it out, and in the end they had to take her to hospital.'

'Oh, fuck off, Mags!' Lou said, putting her hands over her ears. Dread bloomed inside me. I didn't know what an afterbirth was, or where the doctor had his hand, but the horror was plain.

'She was in over two weeks,' Mags said. 'My uncle said he would have starved if she'd been in much longer.'

'Was she all right?' I asked.

'Well, she looks all right. But my mum says she's not been herself since. She don't walk in the same way and she's scared of her own shadow. Don't leave the house much, unless she has to.'

'Hasn't she always been a bag of nerves, though, that one?' Lou said, and yelled as Mags shoved her.

The dread was always there now. I felt it when I saw a woman sticking out her belly with a hand on her back, a little girl pushing her sister or brother in a pram. In the mornings, when I had to shut the parlour door behind me, knowing I wouldn't be back for hours, I was full of it. I kept dreaming about the last baby, the one after Davey, limp and pale, like a piece of fish. It was only there five weeks. A little phantom visitor, it came and sucked the life out of the family, then went, and the house was filled with misery and grey light again. Another girl that didn't stay.

'I don't like babies,' Mags said. 'They always *want* something.'

'I hate 'em,' Betty said, kicking the wall of the factory behind her. 'My ma had *ten* and she kept every single one. She says my dad only has to look at her for her to get in the family way. "Here, Betty, hold the baby", "Betty, take the baby out", "Betty, keep an eye on the fucking baby." My whole bloody life and I'm sick of it.' She kicked the wall again.

All I could think about was that Betty's mother had survived each time. Ten times. The bell rang and we went back inside.

Saturday was a half-day at the factory and I had agreed to go to Miss Morton's straight from work. Her street ran parallel to the market, between the high street and the park. The houses started off a mix of good and bad, but when you got to the top of the hill, where Miss Morton lived, you knew straight away they were all good – it was still and quiet, and all the front doors were closed. I saw a girl sitting in the window, bent over her embroidery, and I thought for a moment about our old life.

When Miss Morton answered, I wondered if she had been cleaning the house, though I couldn't understand why she would have been doing that if I was coming or why she wasn't wearing an apron. Her hair was clumsily pinned back and coming loose, her shirt and skirt were crumpled and she had her sleeves rolled up. She wore no shoes and her stockings were dirty. As she turned around to show me into the parlour, I saw a giant hole in one of the heels.

The parlour was the same shape as ours, with a bay window at the front, but it was enormous. It was hard to tell if it was actually larger, or if it just looked that way because there was very little in it. They only had two easy chairs and a coffee table, a small table and a writing desk. There were books everywhere – splayed out over the arm of a chair, in a case by the fireplace, even a little pile on the mantel itself – but no ornaments or flowers, no looking-glass, wallpaper or rugs.

Another lady was sitting in one of the easy chairs with her feet on the coffee table. She didn't get up to greet me, but she put her book down and turned round, curling her feet up behind her on the seat, so she could peer round the wing of the chair at me and wave. She was the same age as Miss Morton, but much prettier, red-gold hair pinned back so it hung attractively around her pale freckled face.

'Ellen, this is Miss Horner,' Miss Morton said. 'Another of the volunteers at the settlement. She runs a club for working girls on Tuesday evenings, which I very much hope you'll attend.'

'It's wonderful to meet you, Ellen,' Miss Horner said. 'Miss Morton's told me so much about you. She tells me you're one of her best tenants.'

I flushed and looked down.

'Miss Horner suggested you could clean our windows,' Miss Morton said cheerfully. 'They get so horribly filthy here. And there'll be an extra sixpence for you.' She gestured to the table, which had two plates with crumbs and a crust on them, and empty teacups. 'I'm so sorry about our dinner things,' she said, unapologetically. 'We didn't have time to join the others in the dining room today.'

She showed me to a scullery at the back, looking out onto a large, pleasant garden. They had a wooden work box, with proper cloths rather than the bits of old shirts and sheets that we used for cleaning, and a large cast-iron bucket. 'I'll leave you to get on, Ellen,' she said, and I started filling the bucket and preparing the whitening agent. As I walked back down the passageway, I heard them talking in the parlour. Miss Morton sounded much jollier and bolder than she had in front of Miss Povey. On my second trip back, I heard them giggling.

When I came back in to scrub the passageway, they were quiet, but I moved stealthily so as not to remind them I was there. Then, as I was on my hands and knees scrubbing the floor, I heard Miss Horner say, 'You are coming to help on Tuesday, aren't you?'

'Of course,' Miss Morton said.

'Well, will you . . . tidy up your appearance a bit?' she said. Even though I couldn't see her expression, I could tell she was teasing. 'I know you rather enjoy going round like a char-woman but the girls won't respect you.'

Miss Morton laughed. 'Well, I don't think they respect

you. You looked like you were going off to a matinee yesterday. In the East End!'

'They like it. They like to see a bit of finery. Lord knows they don't get enough of it round here.'

'I went out without a hat or gloves yesterday and no one seemed to mind a bit. I must say it felt rather lovely.'

'You're going to end up looking like one of the natives if you're not careful.'

'I don't care.'

'You really don't, do you, Clara?' Miss Horner said affectionately. 'Lord, I wish I felt the same. When I get back home, I'm going to lounge around in pale silk all day, drinking coffee on a chaise-longue.'

'Well, it might not be that much longer for me.' Miss Morton's tone changed abruptly; she sounded sad. 'I had a letter from Father the other day. He wants me to come home. I asked for another six months and he may let me have that but then . . .'

'You think he'll stop the funds?'

'Quite possibly.'

'One can't do charitable work forever. Well, you can, but only if you don't mind ending up like Miss Povey!'

'Oh, heavens!' Miss Morton said, and they both laughed.

'Anyway, I'm longing to be back at home,' Miss Horner said. 'Imagine not ending every day exhausted and absolutely filthy. Imagine having servants. Imagine having all the hot water you please, without the Ghost hogging it all.'

Miss Morton laughed. 'Oh shush! She might be upstairs. We wouldn't know after all.'

'She's not here. She was at breakfast, being her usual utterly morose self, and I managed to get out of her that she had visits in Penn Street this afternoon.'

'Oh, poor soul. Penn Street isn't what one would call . . . salubrious.'

'A lock-up-your-spoons sort of place?'

'Exactly. Anyway, Bea, have you chosen a name for the club yet?'

While they were considering names, I opened the door of the dining room, the same room that Mother and the boys slept in at our house, just to see. Another bare mantel-piece, a long table with a white cloth and six plain chairs. I shut the door as quietly as I could.

When it came time for me to clean the windows, Miss Morton had moved from the easy chair to the writing desk. The dinner remains still had not been cleared. When I was finished, she came out to inspect the step and the passageway and told me how wonderful they looked. 'How sparkling! How welcoming! Oh, Ellen, you must be bursting with pride!'

'Now,' she said, 'your shillings, Ellen. Would you like them now or would you like me and Miss Horner to save it for you? You could collect your cards at the club on Tuesday.'

I said that I would like to save it, although I knew Miss Morton would be disappointed if I tried to withdraw it in the next two or three weeks, and that was when we would need the money most, for Mother's confinement. I may as well not have earned it. But Miss Morton looked so happy.

'How wise!' She saw me to the door. 'I shall see you tomorrow for the rent,' she called after me, and I turned round to wave at her, standing on the bright white step in stockinged feet, watching me go.

Back in our rooms, seeing Mother kneeling at the fire-place, polishing the grate, sweating, I felt the familiar rush

91

of relief: she was still there, still alive. But as I got my overalls out and rummaged in the drawer for cloths, the dread slowly started to return. We had survived another day, but we had so much still to come.

After we'd cleaned the house, and had tea and bathed the boys, I got ready to go to the market. Going to the market on Saturday nights was my job and I loved it, the way the streets filled up with fruit and meat and boots, and coloured awnings, men on the stalls calling out to me as I walked by, everyone infected with giddiness. I never went to the public house or a music hall, but I liked being around the people who did. I absorbed it all, got the food for the week and then was home before the fights and drunkenness began.

My hair was still damp and my face red from the steam of the copper, but I put on my smartest jacket and my second-best hat, took a basket and went out onto the street. It was already livelier than it had ever been in our old neighbourhood. A group of girls about ten or eleven were dancing barefoot around a pile of their boots and a pram with a baby in it. Young men, who looked like the kind who worked below us in the factory, sauntered past with beer bottles, in checked trousers and brightly coloured ties.

As I turned into the market, I saw the factory girls, standing by the fever hospital wall, just as they did at dinnertime, only now they looked even more extraordinary: dresses in turquoise, scarlet and purple, frilled collars curling up the sides of their necks. They wore close-fitting jackets and heeled boots that buttoned up the side. Instead of the caps, they wore hats with masses of folds, bows, feathers and ribbon, floating on rolls of hair.

Lou saw me first. She screamed my name as if she was calling for the police. Everyone stared and I walked towards them. They clambered round me, like dogs round meat, and Betty stroked the arm of my jacket and said, 'Well, will you look at this?' Lou unbuttoned it to get a look at the lining. Mags, in a deep-green dress and matching hat, starting patting my shoulder so hard it hurt.

'What are you doing out?' Betty said. 'I thought you was needed at home.'

'I'm going to the market,' I said.

'Oh, stay for a bit. She can, can't she?'

She looked up at Mary, who was smoking a cigarette. She stubbed it out on the wall, put the other half back in her jacket pocket and nodded.

'I've got to get the meat for Sunday dinner,' I said.

'Sunday dinner!' Betty said. 'Well, I never!'

'Can't you go tomorrow?' Mags asked.

'It's church,' I said, and they howled.

'See you then, Ellen,' she said, and I set off towards the meat stall.

When Miss Morton came for the rent on Sunday, she made me promise, several times, that I would go to Miss Horner's club for working girls on Tuesday evening. I could tell that Mother didn't like the idea – I wasn't, in her eyes, a working girl – and as a new week started, and the baby had still not arrived, I was getting more and more anxious about leaving Mother alone. But I knew we had to please Miss Morton, and when I arrived at the school rooms where the club was held, and there was a fire that I hadn't lit from coal we hadn't bought and a steaming copper tea urn on the schoolteacher's desk, I was glad.

Miss Horner and Miss Morton had arranged the school desks round the side of the room, like tables in a café with two or three chairs around them, and left a space in the middle. Next to the tea urn there were stacks of blue-and-white cups and plates, and buns piled on a platter. One or two girls were doing needlework at the desks and there was already a queue for the tea. I saw Mary at the back and joined her.

'I didn't know you were coming here,' I said.

'The tea's cheap,' she said.

When we reached the front of the queue, I noticed that Miss Morton did look tidier than usual – she wore a clean apron, though she'd got the corner of it caught in the string. But it was Miss Horner's dress I couldn't stop staring at: delicate stripes, billowing sleeves, long narrow cuffs and lace detailing. Her clothes made me think of visiting the dressmaker's where Mother had worked when I was small: secretly running my fingers over the grain of the cotton, the velvets, the rabbit fur, the pale fronds of ostrich feathers and the smooth coils of ribbon. They both looked delighted to see us when I reached the front of the queue.

'Ellen!' Miss Horner said as she handed us each a bun on a chipped plate and a warm cup of tea. I caught Mary looking at me.

'Have you brought any needlework with you this week, girls?' Miss Morton asked. 'Miss Horner would be very happy to help you with any mending or embroidery.'

'No,' Mary said, and she took her plate and cup and walked over to the desks. I looked down, shook my head quickly, and followed her.

She took a large bite of her bun and then asked, 'How

does Miss Morton's mate know your name then?'

'I whiten their step for them. On Saturdays.'

'Do you?' she said, taking another bite out of her bun, still looking at me.

'Miss Morton asked me,' I said. 'She thought it would be good preparation for a job in service.'

'I see,' Mary said, licking her fingers, pressing them on the crumbs on her plate and sucking them. 'I reckon Miss Morton thinks I'm too rough for that sort of work.' She yawned. 'I'd rather be on my own hook anyway.'

'Are the other girls coming?'

'Mags went down The Eagle on her bike. She asked me, but I ain't getting a bus all that way on a Tuesday.'

'I didn't know she had a bicycle.'

'She shares one with her brothers. I'm so jealous I could spit. She can go anywhere she likes on that bike.' She leant back in her chair. 'You know Mags is only thirteen?'

I put down my teacup and shook my head. 'No. I thought she was older than me.'

'She just grew quick. She's got two older brothers, boxers, like their dad, and she gets treated just like a boy. She gets everything they get: meat, eggs, fish. It's just her ma that holds back.' She took another sip of tea. 'She told me she's already got her Bloody Marys.'

I was confused and then I went hot and looked away. This happened to me so often when I was with the girls that I had almost got used to it.

'What about Lou?' I finally took a small bite of my bun. I had meant to savour it, but the sweet, warm, fluffy dough was too delicious and in three or four mouthfuls it was gone.

'Walking out with her bloke,' she said. 'Betty's gone

with her. To hang about with his mates, I suppose.'

When we lived near the park, I saw it all the time: girls like Lou or Mary walking arm in arm with working boys, round the park at weekends or through the market in the evening. Sometimes they sat by the lake with their arms round each other. It wasn't that I didn't want to get married – I supposed I would, one day – but I didn't understand how anyone could do the first bit, the walking out, the cuddling on the grass, without being afraid of what might happen to you.

When I was ten, Mother sent me to the Roman Road market for tomatoes. They had the ones she liked there, the pink ones, and as I was holding them, day-dreaming, a man came up to me asking if I was cold. I said I was all right, but he kept saying that I must be cold, with no scarf, and I should go with him and he would give me his scarf. I wasn't cold. But I let him take hold of my hand.

I was confused, not frightened, even when his grip tightened. It got so tight that I thought I couldn't snatch my hand back. I could have, of course, and I ought to have, but I didn't know that then, so I let him lead me down a narrow court and I didn't realise what he was doing when he wrapped his scarf round my neck or even when he pulled at the ends. I thought he was just trying to keep me warm. But then he pulled it tighter and all at once I understood, understood everything I had done wrong. I coughed and then I gasped, and I can still feel the wool burning the skin on my neck, my fingers at my throat, uselessly scrabbling. I didn't scream. If it hadn't been for the footsteps at the end of the court I would have died there, quietly, politely, and I don't know how long it would have taken for them to find me.

But he ran when he heard the footsteps and I crouched where he left me, panting, my face wet. My breath was hoarse and my throat burnt with the effort. The man who had saved my life without knowing it looked at me, disgusted, as he walked past. I covered the bruises on my neck for weeks afterwards. Five years later, my eyes still got hot thinking about it.

Mrs Thompson, on the other side of the park, had been strangled by her husband. Mrs Burnett's lodger had been beaten so hard by one of her gentleman friends that she died in the street. Afterwards, my mother and her friends would talk about the reasons these things happened, how the women they happened to were not quite nice – Mrs Thompson had been unfaithful, Mrs Burnett's lodger had had a lot of gentleman friends. The man with the scarf had mistaken me for a woman like that and that was what made me most frightened when I thought about it, the power he'd had to turn me not quite nice. Because if I had died in the street there, no one would have known that I'd gone to church on Sundays or helped with the boys' bedtime every night. I would just be another rough girl, a foolish girl, a whore. And the worst thought of all was that he wasn't mistaken. That he'd seen something in me, something I didn't know was there.

At the club, after tea and buns had been served, nothing much seemed to happen – some of the girls did needlework and Miss Morton or Miss Horner walked around the rooms and said things like, 'That looks splendid, Charlotte.' As it started to get dark, there was a knocking on the window and a pale boy's face appeared, leering, and then another, and some of the girls rushed to the windows and started banging on them. Miss Morton said, 'That's quite enough!' and pulled the green velvet curtains to. A few girls got excited and stood on one of the desks, and then leapt from chair to desk to chair, to see if they could make their way around the room without touching the floor. Miss Morton pulled them down. I sat watching the fire, and the patterns the flickering gaslight made on the pink walls, while Mary told me stories. She told me about the time Mags punched a bloke in the pub, or some of the things she'd seen at the music hall, or the time they'd been round to Lou's and her auntie who was on the stage had sung for them while Lou played the piano. I tried to make my tea last as long as possible.

At about half past seven, Eliza, the girl we'd seen fighting outside the factory, walked in. She was hatless and grubby, in a scarlet dress. It had probably been nice once, but there was a great tear in her skirt where you could see her petticoats underneath and half the buttons were missing. Her hair was loose and fell in tangled clumps down her back.

She had two friends with her. Their shirts were so thin and creased, it looked as if the fabric would disintegrate at any moment. Their sleeves were rolled up and their arms and aprons were tainted red. 'Oh God, it's the abattoir girls,' Mary said. No one said anything. The needlework girls stopped what they were doing and looked at each other uncertainly. Miss Morton stiffened and asked Eliza if she'd like a cup of tea in a bright, wary tone. Eliza just shook her head.

I couldn't stop watching her. She commanded attention, changed the air in the room, but she didn't seem to know or care that she had done it. We waited for something to happen, but she simply took a chair and drew it up next to the fire, rubbing her hands. Her friends followed. Miss Morton had said one of the rules was that no one was to sit too close to the fire, to avoid drawing heat from the rest of the room, but she didn't say this to Eliza. She began packing the tea urn away and turned round to take it to the back of the room.

Slowly, girls started to talk again, in low voices. The needlework girls picked up their sewing. I couldn't help glancing over at Eliza, who had taken her boots off and stretched her feet out in front of the fire. The holes in her stockings were so bad her toes and heels poked through, and I wondered how she dared show them: her toenails were curved and yellowing. Her boots were the worst I'd ever seen, the leather creased and cracked, and grey with dust. On one of them, the sole was held on by a grimy piece of string wrapped round the toe.

She turned her head and caught my gaze. She looked at me contemptuously and I blushed. I had always been told off for staring when I was little. But then her expression changed to one of revulsion.

She got up and flew at me, knocking me off my chair and onto the wooden floor. I was on my back, and she knelt on top of me and grabbed my hair with both hands and pulled. The pain was black, obliterating. I tried to rear up but she held me fast.

She looked as though she wanted to destroy me. I reached out and gripped her wrists, wrestled and kicked, but she was too powerful. I panicked. *Don't let me lose my hair. Don't let me lose my teeth.* There was a commotion around us – gasps and screams, the abattoir girls yelling, *scratch her, hit her, smash her face in*, Miss Morton and Miss Horner shouting to stop – but it all felt very far away.

Then a great dark energy rose from the depths of me, and there was nothing inside me but rage. Rage at the baby that was coming to sink our family, Mother for allowing it to, the horrible little rooms in Digby Street, the piles of boxes at the factory like gaping mouths. I gripped her forearms, my fingers pressed into her flesh, and I used everything I had in me to try to prise them off. I wanted to rip her apart; I wanted to be ripped apart. My breath was loud and hoarse, and I could hear my heart pulsing in my ears. The pain in my head had gone. I was floating. It was wonderful.

I couldn't get her grip to loosen with my hands so I let go. I tried to use my forearms to push hers apart and the heel of my hand collided with her chin. I heard a dull thump and she leapt back. My head hit the ground and I lay still for a moment, panting, before I sat up and touched my head. My hairpins were gone, and my hair was rough and wild, but it was still there. Eliza was standing over me with blood dripping from her mouth. My scalp started to burn.

She tried to wipe the blood off her chin with her hand but there was too much and she smeared it over her cheek and neck. Miss Morton passed her a handkerchief. Mary helped me to stand, and held on to my arm.

Eliza looked down and saw blood on the collar of her dress. She looked at me again.

'You *bitch*,' she said.

'We will not have fighting here,' Miss Horner said, but her voice was limp and shaky. 'Or that language. You must leave at once.'

Eliza stayed still, gaping at me.

'Are you all right, Ellen?' Mary asked, handing me my

hat. Miss Morton was at my feet, collecting my hairpins.

'Yes,' I said, quietly, putting the hat on, still staring. I looked at Eliza. The blood was not stopping, spreading all over her dress, splashing the floor. The rage had gone and all I felt was shame. 'I didn't mean—'

'Please,' Miss Morton said to Eliza, standing up. 'Please leave at once.'

Eliza picked up a teacup from one of the tables and threw it sulkily on the floor. It bounced but did not smash. Then she turned round and walked out of the room. The abattoir girls followed.

'She can't have meant you,' Mary said, putting her hand on my shoulder. 'She must have thought you was someone else.'

Miss Morton picked up the cup, took a deep breath and blew the air out through pursed lips. She walked over to the teacher's desk to return the cup.

'You didn't behave like I thought you would,' Mary said. 'You seemed like a different person.'

I caught Miss Morton staring at me as she packed away the tea urn. I tucked my hair under my hat and looked away.

At breakfast the next day, it was all the girls could talk about as they clustered round me in the yard.

'I still want to know who she thought she was fighting,' Mary said. 'I know she hates Jessica Winn.'

'Jessica Winn don't look nothing like Ellen,' Betty said. 'She's huge and her hair's curly. Anyway, she works on the same floor as Eliza.'

'So who was it then?'

'Ellen Budge?'

'What's Ellen Budge ever done to Eliza?'

'What's *our* Ellen ever done to Eliza?'

It was the most attention they'd ever paid me. I was embarrassed but I savoured the words 'our Ellen'.

'I heard she bit the top of her tongue off,' Mags said. 'That's what the girls on my floor are saying.'

'Oh, don't be daft,' Mary said. 'She bit it, she didn't bite it off.'

'Weren't you scared?' Lou asked. 'I'd be terrified if Eliza went for me. What if she'd had that knife?'

'I was scared,' I said, looking down, hoping that they wouldn't know about the rest of it. I was scared and then I was so angry I couldn't feel anything else. I was already ashamed of the rage, wondering if it had showed on my face, in my gestures. 'I was trying to get away from her.'

'It was a clever trick, what you did, going for the chin like that,' Mags said. 'She wouldn't have seen that coming.'

'It was an accident,' I said. 'I was trying to get free.'

They looked at me as if they were trying to decide whether to believe me or not. I could tell they didn't want to. I didn't know if I wanted them to.

'You held your own, though,' Mags said. 'That's more than most would have done. Here.' She scrabbled in her pocket and handed me an egg, round and smooth. I held it for a moment, heavy in my palm. 'You can eat it now. My ma boiled it this morning.'

'Oh, you cheeky cow! You said I could have that one,' Lou said.

'Well, I changed my mind, didn't I,' Mags said, and then they forgot about me again. The bell rang for the end of breakfast-time and I saw Eliza on the stairs. She was just ahead of me and I was sure I saw her jaw moving, as if she was still taking care of her tongue.

When I got home, Mother was standing by the fireplace gripping the mantel. She was breathing out through her mouth, her face turned up to the ceiling, eyes closed. Every part of her seemed to be working: her knuckles white, her eyes squeezed shut, her mouth gurning. Then she stopped and turned round and saw me. She walked over to the kitchen table and put the cloth on it.

'What's going on?' I said.

'Just a few pains.'

'Is the baby coming?'

'Not yet,' she said crossly.

I didn't ask again. I cut the bread and worked to scrape the very last bits of jam out of the jar, while Mother lit the fire and filled the kettle. There was only just enough jam for the boys – and they still complained about how thinly it was spread – so we had ours with margarine. We washed up, got rid of the dirty water, put the boys to bed, as if everything was normal, apart from these horrible interruptions when Mother would stop, clutch her belly, go to the corner of the room and press her hands against the wall and pant. Each one made me feel ill. The boys looked at me and I told them everything was fine and to stop staring.

At ten, we went to bed, and I was woken not much later by Davey, patting my arm insistently. I was still muddled with sleep, lifting my head slowly.

'Get in then,' I said, lifting the blanket, closing my eyes. He didn't move. I opened my eyes again. I saw that George was there too.

'She sent us out of the room,' George whispered. 'She's making too much noise anyway.'

I heard a groan from the other room and the clock struck midnight. 'Stay there,' I muttered, and went out into the passageway, knocking gently on the bedroom door. Mother opened it a little. She was red-faced and out of breath, but she looked ordinary, like herself. For a moment, I felt relieved.

'Ellen?' she said.

'Shall we get the midwife?'

She shook her head.

'Are you sure?'

'I've had six babies, Ellen. I know what I'm doing. Just look after the boys.' She shut the door.

'Now,' I said, going back into the parlour. 'Now then.' I tucked the boys under my blanket on the sofa. I heard a wild, unearthly sound from next door. 'It's all right,' I said. 'It's all right. Just the baby coming. Try and get some sleep.'

George turned on his side and curled up, but his eyes stayed open, giant and glassy. Davey curled up behind him and wrapped an arm around his waist and I sat at the end of the sofa with my knees up. Every time I heard a cry from the bedroom, I had to curl my fists and dig my fingernails into my palm.

George started to put his hands over his ears when the noises came. Finally, I told him to put his jacket on over his pyjamas and he went to fetch his shoes. I got the paper with the midwife's address on it out of the tin.

'Quick, quick, quick as you can, there's a good boy,' I said. Davey sat up with me and I put my arm round his small, trembling body.

Whenever a noise came from the bedroom, I gripped Davey tightly, while he shuddered. Mrs Atkins knocked on the door, eager to help, telling me she'd delivered half the babies in the street and laid out half the dead. I ought to have known. She was just the sort of woman who would consider herself a midwife.

'We have a midwife coming,' I said. 'But thank you.'

'Well, have you got everything ready for her? Is the bed covered? Do you have worsted?' She was close to me, almost pulsing in her desperation to come inside.

'Yes, thank you,' I said, shutting the door, though I didn't know what she was talking about.

When George came back, he was bent over, wheezing. 'She was asleep.'

'What?'

'That's what her bloke said. And he said he wouldn't be able to wake her because she'd been on the piss.'

'Don't use that language!'

'That's what he said!'

'Go back and tell him he has to wake her! Go!'

I stayed on the bed holding Davey. Every so often, in between pains, I ran next door to see Mother. She asked for water and I brought her a cup. She was starting to alter, her face whiter. She looked older and more afraid. Mrs Atkins banged on the door again. 'We can hear every pain. Is your midwife here yet?' The man next door shouted, 'Stop making so much bloody noise!' Davey asked me if Mother was going to die. George came back and told me the midwife had said she wouldn't come.

'She said it was too early. She said Mother wouldn't come off for a while yet. She'll come in the morning.'

The next time I brought Mother water, she was kneeling

at the foot of the bed, with her face in the blanket. The groans were going on for longer now and there was barely any gap in between. I couldn't leave her. I sat on the bed and stroked her hair while the pain was going on and when it stopped I ran into the parlour to check on the boys and ran back as quickly as I could.

Then the next pain didn't come. We looked at each other, confused. She got on the bed and curled on her side and I waited, next to her. She started to breathe more heavily and her eyes closed. I lay beside her on the bed. The baby wasn't coming after all. I felt my body droop with relief and my eyes start to close. The baby wasn't coming. It wouldn't come till morning, when the midwife would be here.

I must have dozed off because I was woken by Mother sitting upright, wild-eyed and raving. She threw herself on the floor onto her knees and started crying. 'Get Mrs Atkins,' she said. 'Get Mrs Atkins.'

I ran upstairs. For a second, I froze on the landing, faced with three shut doors, not knowing which one to knock on, before I banged on the one at the front of the house. Mrs Atkins flew out of the next-door room and down the stairs in her nightdress before I could say anything. She threw open the door of the bedroom; Mother had taken her nightdress off and was kneeling on the bed.

It could only have lasted a second, that moment, but I would remember it forever. There was a head – squashed, glistening, eyes squeezed shut, matted black hair, a slick of scarlet blood on the cheek – hanging between her legs. It had a face, my sister's face. A person half here, half not. Mrs Atkins ran to the bed and the baby flopped into her hands, bluish pink, coated in white lard and streaks of blood.

'Is she all right?' I asked. 'Is she all right?'

'Get me a clean blanket. Cloth, towel, anything. Start boiling the kettle. Then send your brothers to Mrs Rose at number five, tell her it's me who sent them.'

I was still for a moment, and Mrs Atkins made a low guttural noise of frustration. Then I began to move. I pulled the best tablecloth out of the orange crate and handed it to Mrs Atkins and then I took the kettle to the scullery. Everything – the tap and the bucket, the tapers for the fire – looked strange and bright, as if I'd never seen them before. I filled the kettle from the tap, lit a hasty fire, and then shepherded the boys out into an eerily quiet street. Mrs Rose answered the door and nodded sleepily when I explained. I realised I had no idea what time it was.

When I came back in, Mother was holding the baby close, wrapped up as if it was something from the grocer's. A coiled pale-yellow rope trailed down her stomach and under the blanket covering her. The baby was crying. Mother was pale and limp, head lolling and her eyes almost closed. Blood was soaking the sheets.

'Is she going to die?' I said, and they became the only words I could say, again and again: 'Is she going to die?'

Mrs Atkins didn't answer. Her hands and arms were covered in blood. 'A baby girl,' she said. She looked askance at Mother and then at me. 'She's very dark.'

I stood staring at her tiny face, until Mrs Atkins said, 'Scissors in boiling water now, Ellen,' and I went into the parlour and poured the water from the kettle into the saucepan. I put in the scissors from Mother's sewing box, fished them out with a spoon, and then handed them over. 'Ain't very sharp,' Mrs Atkins said, and she struggled with the fleshy rope, and I went back into the parlour and sat on the sofa, holding my face. I could hear Mother and Mrs Atkins talking in low voices, and when the baby squalled I started shaking. I heard more cries from Mother and I started to panic because I thought it was over, but then Mrs Atkins called my name and when I came in she asked for a newspaper. There was a large lump of meat, streaked with purple, grey and the colour of bone. It, like the sheets, like the rug, like the walls even, was smeared in blood.

'Ellen,' Mother gasped, opening her eyes. 'Make Mrs Atkins some tea, will you?'

I filled the kettle again, and got a teapot and some cups from the crate. I thought of the boys in a fit of panic, and then remembered they were safe. Everyone was safe. Everything was where it ought to be. Everyone was alive.

My spirits rose disturbingly fast. Everyone was alive. I could feel my heart beating, I could feel every drop of blood inside me. Alive. I whispered the word to myself again and again, as I reached up to the shelf above the sink to get the tea. I caught sight of a little red tin, where I had stashed supplies for after the birth: oatmeal, tea, coins and sugar. My face collapsed, suddenly wet and burning. I held the table and sobbed.

I sat on the bed, and the baby, my sister, was passed between me, Mother and Mrs Atkins. I fetched things. Mrs Atkins snored in the easy chair. I gazed at my sister's strange little face. I had been hoping for a boy, because the boys lived, but now that she was here I could not imagine wanting her to be any other way. I stared at her face and I thought even if she only stayed for tonight, for one day, I was glad she was here.

I must have slept for an hour or so, because I woke up

when the clock struck five and I remembered time: hours, minutes and seconds, all those harsh little divisions that carved up the world, that had once seemed commonplace and now seemed unbearable. I felt pulled to the house with a force that astonished me, but I had no choice. I washed, drank a warm cup of tea, and went out into the street, the sky large and inky. Everything had turned remarkable overnight.

5

Frances

1984

After the lightness of June, July was heavy and sprawling. London emptied out and I settled into the haphazard routine of quiet bus rides and shifts at the pub. Nick was still the only person, other than my mother, that I had conversations with. I told myself that I was going to use the summer to put together a portfolio for art school, and I once went to the National Gallery and did some sketches, but in the end, having something I was supposed to be doing only made it easier for me to not do anything at all. I was waiting, really: waiting for my exam results, waiting for James to ring, waiting for something unspecified to turn up. I sometimes wonder if I could have carried on like that for months or even years, the weekly rota at the pub the only moving element in my life. But halfway though July, everything changed.

'I had an estate agent visit yesterday,' my mother said when I came into the kitchen in my dressing gown and slippers to make breakfast before I left for work. I'd slept late, which I knew irritated her because she thought I should make use of the hours before the pub opened and

I never did. She was doing out the kitchen drawers and holding a carving fork with a brittle yellowing handle in front of her face as she said it. I knew then that the quiet, comfortable tedium of the summer was coming to an end.

As I filled the kettle, I peered into the cardboard box on the countertop. Egg coddlers, an ice-cream scoop, a chicken brick. A spatula, its pale rubber head crumbling at the edges.

'Why?' I asked. I lifted the kettle from the hob, judged its weight and put it down again. I reached for the matches.

'For a valuation. He said we shouldn't have much trouble selling it.' She threw the fork in the box.

'Why would we want to sell it?'

She shut the drawer and turned round to face me. 'I'm sorry, Frances. I thought you understood. We're going to have to.'

'Why?' I rummaged about in the tea tin.

'Are you going to make a pot? I'd love a cup.'

I got the teapot down from the dresser on the other side of the kitchen and she took her rubber gloves off and laid them over the side of the sink. 'This is a family home,' she said. 'I'm a widow, you're eighteen. There isn't much point me rattling around in it. And we need the money.'

'Where are you going to move to?'

'Well.' She smiled and looked down. 'I've always fancied living by the sea.'

'The sea?'

'Oh, your father never understood it either. He thought those seaside towns were dreary. But I always thought, imagine, being able to see the sea every day. Waking up every morning and it being there, just outside your window.'

We didn't say anything until the kettle began its disgruntled murmur. It turned to a high-pitched shriek before my mother said, 'For God's sake, switch that off, will you, Frances?'

'Sorry,' I said, turning the dial on the cooker and warming the pot. 'Don't you think you should think about it a bit more?'

She laughed. 'Oh, I've thought about it, believe me. I've thought about it for years.' Then she took off her glasses and rubbed her face. She put them back on and said, 'I'm sorry, I know it's a wrench. But you'll always have a room with me.'

'By the sea?'

'If that's where I end up, yes. But look, you're young, you should be in the city. Who knows what will happen with your results? Maybe you'll go to university. Or art school. This could be an adventure.'

'Do you want milk?' I said, even though I knew she did and the exact amount, and she nodded and said, 'Get a jug, won't you, Frances?' And then she turned round and opened up the cutlery drawer.

When I got to work, it happened again: the abnormal feeling. I took my apron, hot and crumpled, out of the dryer in the cellar, served the regulars – *how do you do it, Frances? how do you look so beautiful on a Friday morning?* – the lunchtime pints, filled wooden bowls with crisps – *just a half then, and one for yourself, darling* – but all the time I felt as if I was underwater. I could see light and shapes above me, but I was separated from everything else. Every movement met resistance.

I started to feel better in the afternoon, but I was still waterlogged when Nick came in after two. Everything was an effort – reaching for the tall glass, filling it up with ice, pushing the glass up against the vodka optic, counting the coins.

'Looks like we need to be on the move again,' he said as I shut the till. 'Council are on the warpath.'

'That's a shame,' I said, mechanically.

'Yeah, well, it had to happen at some point. We're talking about where to go next. Naomi is still on about this factory.'

'Oh . . . Which one is that?'

'The old factory building . . . on the high street?'

'Oh, yes,' I said.

He launched into an explanation of when they might move and how, and what they might do with the building, but it was too much, that day: I couldn't follow what he was saying, and keep an eye on the other customers, and the empty glasses on the tables, and the dishwasher running, and the number of crisp packets in the cardboard box. I started to feel angry with him: it felt as if he was flashing a torch in my face or banging a drum in my ear. I had to remind myself that he was only talking.

When he pushed his glass towards me for his second drink, he looked at me and said, 'Everything OK with you?' I managed to say, 'Yes, fine. Why?' but my voice came out distant and weak. He was the first person that day who'd noticed, who'd asked.

'You seem a bit off.'

I felt like I had to say something because I didn't want him to think I was being rude, but I didn't have the resources to make anything up. I told him about the house. He asked why my mum was selling it, and I remembered why I didn't want to talk about myself.

'Well, my father died in May,' I said, hoping if I spoke quickly enough and looked down we could ignore it, do without the moment where the conversation imploded and he'd get embarrassed until I said something reassuring, and get to the point where we pretended I hadn't said anything at all.

But Nick did not seem embarrassed. He put his glass down. 'Oh, shit. That's not very long ago.'

'No . . .' I said, fiddling with the edge of the tea towel hanging inside the bar.

'What happened?'

'He had a heart attack. In the middle of the night. When he got up to get a drink of water . . . My mum heard something and came down, but by the time . . . by the time . . .' My breath was starting to get shorter and my eyelids felt spiky. I realised I had not spoken about that night to anyone.

'And what about you? Where were you?'

'I woke up when the ambulance got there. And I came downstairs. But by that point he was already . . .' It was half-true. In fact, I hadn't been woken by the ambulance. I had been having one of my dreams, the dreams I couldn't properly think about during the day, about flesh and touch and warm, slick fingers, where I woke up to rapid pulsing between my legs. The dreams left me ashamed anyway, but this time I heard the voices downstairs and went out of my bedroom to listen, still hot and wet between my legs. It still made me feel horribly uncomfortable to think that I'd been asleep when he'd been dying, as if I ought to have been woken by the energy of it, or the world shifting, and I had somehow ignored it. The fact that I'd been dreaming made it even worse.

'Christ,' he said.

'At least he didn't suffer. He wouldn't have known what was happening.'

I said that a lot, and I had heard my mum say it, but I still didn't know if it was true. Heart failure, they said, and I couldn't help thinking about what that felt like, the moment between your body suddenly, unexpectedly giving in, and death. The horror, the fear, the desperation, alone on the kitchen floor.

He shook his head. 'It's shit either way. Illness is grim, but you have time to process things. If it's abrupt, it's just shit in a different way.'

I smiled and blinked.

'Maybe it's a good thing she's selling up. New start and all that. You have to move on at some point. Believe me, it doesn't get any easier the longer you leave it.'

'I know, but it feels . . . It doesn't feel normal, what she's doing. I mean, she's getting rid of everything.'

'Well, she's grieving, isn't she? It's not very nice to look at or be around, but that's what it is.'

I started pressing my eyelids, quickly as if they were hot, and said, 'Tell me about the factory then,' and he did and we didn't talk about my dad any more.

When he left the pub, he was a little bit softer and blurrier, as he always was, and he leant across the bar and gave me a swift, clumsy hug. It was the first time he had touched me.

'Take care, Frankie,' he said, and I couldn't speak, only hold my thumbs up.

Estate agents brought people to view the house, people right at the beginning of things. Women with large wire-framed glasses, their swollen bellies hidden under vast cotton dresses; men in brown corduroy trousers with toddlers in pushchairs. They were nothing to do with us, these people – a woman in her denim jacket, holding hands with a child in bunches and dungarees, talking about 'stripping all this out' in the hallway, while my mother and I sat silently at the kitchen table.

Meanwhile, I circled advertisements for bedsits in the local paper. And I looked through windows – in the flats above the shops when I sat upstairs on the bus, the basement windows under the steps of the houses on the way to the bus stop, the back of the flats when I took the shortcut through the council estate. I saw a man with no shirt leaning out of the window above the newsagent's, smoking a cigarette; a parade of ornaments behind net curtains; the fuzzy sloped neck of a bottle of Toilet Duck against frosted glass. I caught glimpses of nude mattresses, towels on pegs, pots of paintbrushes, hoping they would somehow help me to understand what I should do next.

Every time Nick came in now, he talked about the factory, how they were going to get in, how they were going to get the electrics going, how much space he thought there was going to be. 'We could have ten, twenty, thirty people living there even.' I told myself that I was simply enjoying his energy, but I liked the idea of it: the new space, this new way of living. Elaine behind the bar told me about the man she was lodging with who volunteered in a charity shop and came home with dresses for her to try on. She made me laugh uncontrollably, mimicking his voice – '"Do you not want to try it, Elaine? Is it not your size, Elaine? What *is* your size?"' And then one day she came in sober and red-eyed, saying she hadn't slept because he'd been trying to get into her bedroom and she'd had to push the chest of drawers against the door, but she was terrified it wasn't heavy enough.

'I think I'm going to try squatting next,' she said. 'I can't go through all that again.' I decided that I would ask Nick if there was room in the factory for Elaine.

I might still have stayed, waited to see if the house would sell, or where my mother moved to, if it hadn't been for that Sunday, when I got home and found a note on the kitchen table: '6.15 p.m. Gone to the shops – no eggs! Love M.' I put it down and went upstairs to change out of my work clothes. The door to my parents' – my mother's – bedroom was open. There was a gaping black bag next to the open wardrobe, and a pile of my father's shirts on the bed. His shoes piled on top of one another in a cardboard box.

I went into the room in the same spirit that I peered in people's windows: I wanted to look, without knowing what I was looking for. I hadn't realised she hadn't cleared the wardrobe – I had thought he was gone, but there was the impression of his feet on the wrinkled soles of his shoes and the line of brown-grey on the collar of his shirt. I felt as confused and vulnerable as I had the days after he died, when every room contained a handful of painful objects: his toothbrush in the mug, the bristles splayed; his matted towel on the hook inside their bedroom door. His watch on the bedside table, the strap bent and cracked at the place he always buckled it. Things that had been on his face, in his mouth, on his feet. I'd been angry with him, so angry I couldn't speak: it seemed rude, *slovenly*, to leave bits of himself all over the house, for us to deal with. I had to remind myself that he hadn't known he was going to die.

There were two drawers inside the wardrobe and the top one was pulled out. It had two green shoeboxes inside. I took one out and opened it, and saw a stack of receipts clipped together. The top one was from fifteen years ago. We used to tease him about his hoarding – the tins in the cellar, the manila folders full of bank statements – and he would smile and put his arm around my mother's waist and say, 'But answer me this: have we ever – *ever* – run out of baked beans?' I thought how much this would make my mother laugh.

There was a cellophane sleeve of photographs and I took it out, feeling happy and fond, expecting to see pictures of me and my mother. Instead it was full of black-and-white photographs of a woman I'd never seen before, naked. They were meant, I think, to be artistic, and for a moment I believed that they could have been a risqué photography project. But then I saw the flower pattern on the curtains and realised they were taken in this room. I set them down and picked up another pack, with more than a film's worth, this time in colour.

These were of a different woman in more explicit poses – she was naked on all fours or lying on the bed in lacy knickers, and there was an uncomfortable look on her face. I could see a half-full coffee cup on the bedside table and a full ashtray. My father's reading glasses and a little pile of coins. They were hideously amateurish. Presumably the person who took them – my father – couldn't see the fingerprint over the lens, the background detritus, the dimpled thighs, veins on the back of her hand. He only saw her.

I put them back in the sleeve, breathless, and picked up the receipts. The first one was from a restaurant in

Covent Garden. As I flicked through them I noticed the extravagance decreased: from hotels to B&Bs on the Essex Road, from pheasant to jacket potatoes. He had filed them chronologically and I was watching their romance unfold. Formality become familiarity, and finally it stopped on 12 May 1975. And then some miscellanea held together with a paperclip: a letter addressed to Margaret Robinson, confirming an appointment for a Dilation and Curettage. 'I Love You!' scrawled in biro on a train ticket to Peterborough. An order of service for Margaret Robinson, dated five years ago.

He had kept a used red toothbrush and a packet of paracetamol, half the blisters empty and wrinkled. An open box of Tampax. A nearly empty tube of something called 'personal lubricant'.

I stayed there too long. When I heard the door and my mother's footsteps on the stairs, I tried to put the lid of the shoebox back on, but I was slow and clumsy. 'What on earth are you doing, Frances?' she said, still in her coat, standing over me. 'What have you got there?'

Of course, I regret this now, but I let her kneel down next to me and pick up the photographs. 'Oh,' she said as she took it in. 'Oh.' It is a noise I cannot unhear. Pity and disappointment, with an edge of distaste. I still find myself reaching for the right thing to have said and done but I only sat next to her while she flicked through them.

'Rubbish, I suppose,' she said, and she tipped the box into the black bag.

The next day, I went into work and when Nick came in he was different, jumpier, more excited than I'd seen him before.

'We did it!' he said. 'We cracked the factory.'

I hadn't been able to think about the shoebox direct-ly, to untangle, or even properly identify, the horrible mixture of feelings it had provoked in me. It was a relief to think about something else, to absorb some of Nick's excitement. I turned around to fill his glass. 'Oh, was that this weekend? How did it go?'

'Easy! So fucking easy. A pane of glass was smashed – Jane just stuck her hand in, opened the catch and that was it. The ground floor's fucked – it's flooded at the back – but everything else – it was like a dream. So much better than we ever expected.' He leant forward onto the bar. 'When you crack somewhere, you just don't know what you're going to get. Empty buildings, they're weird places, Frankie. Sometimes it only takes a few months for them to fall apart. They look all right from the outside, but you get inside and they're already caving in. It happens so much quicker than you think. It's like the buildings need people.' I handed him the glass and he pushed the coins towards me.

'But this place! Plumbing's still in order, some of the lights were even working. We've chosen a room to start with on the top floor, so we're just getting that ship-shape, but there's loads of them, all the same. Jane's already talking about using the opposite room as a meeting space. I reckon if she has the right place – you know, to do some really serious organising – then something can start happening. Something big. Naomi wants to set up some creative workshops.' He lifted his drink. 'New start for all of us.'

I told myself I was thinking of Elaine when I asked: 'Who's moving in with you?'

'It'll be me, Naomi, Jane, and some bloke Naomi knows

called Malcolm. To start with. But the room's probably big enough for twice that. And there's another one opposite it, and below it.' He looked at me. 'Is your mum still selling up?'

I nodded.

'Well, it's a more-the-merrier situation, I'd say.'

He talked some more about the room and what they were going to do with it and then when he got up to go he said, 'You can always try it. At the squat, I mean. Spend a couple of nights there, get to know the others, and if you don't like it you can leave. Nothing to lose.'

When the door swung shut behind him, the respite was over and I was back where I started. I looked up at the clock: soon, I would have to go home.

A week later, I sat on the bus, carrying a suitcase and one hundred pounds in notes that I had withdrawn from my Post Office savings account. Nick lived in a block of council flats a few minutes' walk from the pub: a horizontal brick building with dark concrete balconies hedging brown front doors. I pushed open the swing doors on the ground floor; the lift had a piece of cardboard taped to it with 'Out of Order' scrawled in black marker, so I took the stairs to the fifth floor. The stairwell had square pale-yellow tiles three-quarters of the way up the wall, and on Nick's floor they turned pink, like a Battenberg. There were empty window boxes on the balcony and, while I waited for Nick to open the door, I peered in the one opposite. It was a third full of dark water, cigarette ends and a floating can of Sainsbury's cola, bisected with a sharp crease.

He opened the door, wearing the same frayed T-shirt he had when I met him. His eyes were red and swollen and his skin was blotchy. He yawned and turned round; I saw that his hair was fluffy at the back. I followed him into the sitting room.

'Morning,' he said, sitting down on the sofa and spooning milky cereal from a bowl on the coffee table into his mouth. 'Just going to finish this and then we'll be off.'

When Nick had talked about squatting, I imagined he lived somewhere entirely different from anything I'd seen before, but in fact the room was depressingly familiar. The wallpaper was greyish cream, with a porridge-like texture; on the wall nearest the door someone had started to strip it and fragments of a print with birds on it and mottled plaster showed underneath. They had given up quickly. In the middle of the ceiling, a single bulb was shaded by a cone of dimpled brown glass. There was a brown velour sofa, a matching chair and a pine cabinet.

Nick looked up at me and then said, 'You can sit down, you know.'

It felt too intimate to sit next to him on the sofa, so I sat gingerly on the arm of the chair.

'Are you sad to leave?'

'Not really. It was a good place, but I got five or six months out of it, so: time to go.' He took a gulp from a mug of cola. 'I reckon some old bloke must have died here and he didn't have any family, because no one cut anything off. I even had a phone for a bit. There's a toilet in the bedroom and these plastic handles everywhere too.'

'Did that bother you? That someone died here?'

'Not really, no. Not if it meant I had hot water.' He held the bowl up to his mouth to drink the last of the milk and sediment. 'All right,' he said, banging the bowl down and standing up. 'We're off!'

He drained the mug and took an ashtray from the top of the cabinet, tipped the contents into the bowl and put it in his rucksack.

'Do you not need the bowl . . . ?'

'Naomi and Jane have got all that stuff. Leave it for the next person, if there is one. Are you ready?'

'Can I just use your . . . ?'

'Upstairs,' he said, picking up his backpack.

I climbed the narrow staircase, and found the bathroom. I sat on the loo, which had a blue circle of carpet covering the linoleum at its base. The bath had a browning plastic sheet inside. There was no soap or towel, only an empty bottle of Fairy Liquid and a metal ashtray by the side of the bath. I rinsed my hands and dried them on my jeans.

'Come on then,' Nick said when I got downstairs. 'Let's go.'

I followed him down one flight of stairs and along the corridor to a flat below his. The window box was full of herbs and through the small rectangular window next to the front door I saw a woman wiping the countertop. Her off-blonde hair was pinned back and she had a small ring through her nose. I noticed a little alcove just outside the door; someone had put a tea light in it in front of a post-card saying 'Greenham Common: A Peace of the Action'. Nick banged on the kitchen window so loudly it made me jump and pushed his face against the glass. The woman gave a thin yelp, Nick laughed, she disappeared and then the door opened.

'Jesus, you frightened me half to death.'

'Sorry about that,' Nick said, insincerely. 'Naomi, this is Frankie. Frankie, Naomi.'

She was smaller than me, almost submerged by her

yellow sundress, which had wide straps and smocking at the front. Her shoulders were lightly freckled. She hugged me and held me tight; even though it was overly intimate, it felt natural. 'So good to meet you. Go on through. I'm just cleaning up the kitchen.'

'You don't need to do that,' a woman's voice called from the living room. 'The council are going to smash everything up anyway.'

'You don't know that,' Naomi called back, turning into the kitchen.

I followed Nick into the sitting room. The woman was sitting on the sofa, smoking a rolled-up cigarette. She was probably in her mid-twenties, tall and imposing, with thick brown hair pulled back in a stubby ponytail, wearing canvas dungarees over a grey vest.

'Jane, Frankie. Frankie, Jane,' Nick said, collapsing on the chair and shuffling through some papers on the coffee table. 'What's all this then?

She ignored him and kept looking at me. 'Frankie,' she said. 'Nick's friend.'

She didn't say it like a question, so I didn't say anything.

'Frankie works in the Black Hart,' Nick said. 'Go on then, sit down,' he said, nodding at me, and I sat beside Jane on the sofa, keeping a slight distance.

'Oh yes,' she said. 'Your bar girl.' She turned to me. 'Do you work full-time at the pub then?'

'I do four or five shifts a week. I'm waiting for my A-level results.'

'You're at *school*?' She looked at Nick. He got up and started picking at the filler in the holes in the wall. There were grey lines, ghosts of where shelves had been, across the alcoves.

'No, I've left,' I said. 'This summer.'

'Right. So you must be . . . eighteen?'

'Yes.'

'Stop interrogating her, Jane,' Nick said, turning round and sitting back down on the chair. 'She's coming to stay with us for a few nights. She's not applying for a job.'

'I think it's reasonable to want to get to know each other,' she said. She looked at me for a bit longer, then stood up and turned to Nick. 'Right. I need your help with some of the stuff upstairs.'

'So you do need a bloke around,' he said, standing up.

'I need your brute strength. And your van. That's about it.'

'You'd fall apart without me.'

'Feminist peace group falling apart without a man . . . I don't think so.'

'Can I give you a hand?' I asked, standing up.

She looked me up and down. 'No, you're all right,' she said. 'Don't want you straining anything. We'll get the heavy stuff out the way and you can do the boxes.'

She and Nick started bringing things down from upstairs and then started taking them out to the van. I was impressed by, and slightly envious of, the ease with which Jane did it: I could see the muscles in her bare arms stiffen as she carried shelves, mattresses and cabinets down the stairs, but she didn't sweat or stagger or get out of breath as I would have done. Naomi came in and out of the kitchen, carrying boxes. I asked if I could help several more times; at one point, Jane allowed me to carry a lamp.

There was a growing buoyancy in the flat. Nick was different around Jane, more animated, less sullen. Naomi seemed to get giddier: she dropped things and bumped into people and said, 'Sorry, sorry, sorry, I'm just excited, that's all.' Even though Jane was rude, I liked watching her take charge, telling Nick where to put things and what to carry when, and not to be so bloody stupid whenever he made a suggestion.

Finally, there was only my suitcase, Nick's rucksack and three boxes left.

'That's it, isn't it?' Naomi said. 'We can do that in one trip.'

'Looks like it.' Jane smiled, a rare huge smile, and then laughed as Naomi suddenly hugged her. Her head only reached Jane's chest. 'What are you doing?' she said, stroking Naomi's hair.

'I just can't believe it's really happening.'

'I know,' Jane said. 'It's been a long time coming, hasn't it?'

I picked up my suitcase, Nick put his rucksack on and they each lifted up a box. When we got outside, Naomi put hers down and took a camera out from the top.

'Right,' she said, 'I want a photo.'

'I'll take it,' Nick said, holding out his hand.

'No, come on, Nick, you should be in it,' Naomi said.

'It's your flat. It should be just the girls.'

'Women,' said Jane.

'Women, OK then. Come on, give it here.'

'Surely I should take it?' I said hesitantly. 'Then you can all be in it.'

'Oh, thanks, Frankie,' Naomi said, and she hooked the camera strap over her head and handed it to me. 'This one here,' she said, pointing to the button on top. 'We won't need a flash, will we?' I moved back towards the balcony and Nick moved with me, but Jane beckoned him forward.

'I don't like being photographed,' he muttered, but he went and stood next to her.

'Worried about your appearance, are you?' Jane said.

'Something like that,' he said, and I pressed the button.

A woman in her fifties with neat white hair and large pale-blue square glasses came out of the flat next door. She held on to the door frame to slide her feet out of check slippers and into a pair of brown loafers, which were waiting between the front door and the open iron security gate outside it.

'Mrs Harris!' Naomi said. A younger blonde woman with a pushchair followed her out of the flat. 'And Julie, we've not seen you in a while!'

Julie gave a guarded smile.

Naomi bent down towards the pushchair, where a child, perhaps around two or three, with fine white-blonde hair and a red jumper, was clutching a book. 'My goodness, you've grown. Hello, Mandy.'

'Amanda,' Julie said.

'She's so sweet,' Naomi said, standing up.

'Thank you.' Julie gave another tight smile.

'What are you lot up to then?' Mrs Harris asked.

'This is it. We're moving out.'

'Oh! That's a shame. Well, I hope I get someone as nice as you next.'

'We're only going round the corner,' Naomi said. 'I'll come and visit. Drop round some food.'

'Oh, I keep telling you, you don't need to do that! I'm perfectly capable.'

'I always make too much,' Naomi said. She held up the camera. 'Will you be in a photo with us?'

She laughed. 'Oh, you don't want me in one of your

pictures! Not exactly a dolly bird, am I?' She winked at Naomi.

'Come on! You're part of the story.'

'I don't know.'

'Please.'

'Oh, go on then,' she said, touching hair.

'Mum . . .' Julie angled her head towards the stairs. 'I want to get going.'

'We'll be really quick,' Naomi said, and Mrs Harris stood next to her at the door, beaming and holding her handbag in front of her with both hands.

'Take two,' Naomi said. 'I'll drop you in a copy when we get them developed.'

'Oh, thank you, dear,' she said. 'I would like that, you know, very much. I've enjoyed having you around. Keeps me young!' Naomi squeezed her hand.

I took two photographs and Mrs Harris went back to her daughter. 'Do you want a hand with the pushchair on the stairs?' Jane said, putting down her box.

'Here, I'll do it,' said Nick.

'Not with a fag, you idiot,' Jane said. 'Come on.'

She took the front of the pushchair and Julie took the back, and they carried it downstairs while Mrs Harris followed.

'Mum, you've got to speak to someone about that lift,' Julie said. 'And about that next-door flat; you can't have just anyone moving in here.'

We put the last few things in the van. The factory was only a short way down the high street, so Naomi, Jane and I walked. It was an austere building, a grid of large domed windows, some with panes cracked, set in dark-brown brick. The front yard was filled with rubbish: split black bags and broken furniture.

We went through the gate and walked over the cobbles through a cleared path to the doorway. Jane unlocked a new padlock on the door and we went inside, up a gloomy stairwell. The banister and concrete stairs were coated in dust and grime.

When we reached the top floor, we faced a huge window, which I realised, as I got closer to it, was the height of a door. I could see over the backs of the terraced houses, a metal train track strung above them. Jane opened the door on the right and we were in a huge room, separated into different areas with curtains pegged to washing lines. The floorboards were splintered and unpainted. Even with the curtains blocking the windows at the side, it was still the lightest room I'd ever been in.

There was a sink in the corner and a kitchen of sorts had formed around it: a hostess trolley, veneer with gilt edges, with a kettle and toaster plugged in to a cord extension, a few mugs, a bag of sugar and two saucepans. There was a wooden table with a rectangular space underneath it where a drawer ought to have been, and it was piled with plates, two washing-up bowls and a handful of mismatched knives and forks in a terracotta plant pot. Three cast-iron saucepans sat below it.

'It looks *amazing*!' Naomi said, putting her box down.

We made two or three more trips to the van. Nick and Jane brought two sofas and a coffee table in, which formed a living area in the centre.

'I sorted you out a bed,' Nick said, when everything was finally in, and he pulled back the brown-and-white silk curtain nearest the corner of the room. I saw a mattress on top of a few pallet boxes, slightly skewed. 'You're next to Naomi and Jane.'

'What about you?' I asked.

He pointed to the other end of the room, where curtains had been rigged up in each corner.

'I'll take that space, Malcolm can have the other.'

'Boys on one side, girls on the other?' Jane said wryly as she carried a suitcase towards the curtain at the end.

'Blokes like their own space, don't they?' Nick said. 'Thought you girls might want to chat.'

'Oh, fuck off,' Jane said, dumping the suitcase behind her curtain. 'Right, who wants tea?'

While the kettle boiled, I put my suitcase down next to my bed. I heard a train go by and noticed that the curtain dividing my area from Naomi's was actually a quilt, cream with stripes from different bits of material, lilac and purple and blue. I sat down on the mattress – it felt cold, almost damp, and there were light-brown patches ringed with a darker brown. I realised then that I had nothing to put on it.

I pulled back the curtain and went to sit on the sofa next to Naomi. Jane handed me a cup of tea. Nick sat opposite me on the armchair.

'So what do you think?' he said.

'It's brilliant,' I said. 'Did it take a lot of work?'

'Well,' Nick said, 'not too much more than usual, I'd say.' He talked me through what they'd scavenged from skips, traded with other squatters, favours they'd called in. In his ostentatious pride, his inability to see that he was boring me, he reminded me of my dad.

'Where do you . . . wash?' I asked hesitantly, and Nick said, 'Oh yeah!' and stood up. He showed me a room next door, with two cubicles at the end. One of the doors had come off and I saw an avocado lavatory in it. There were sinks outside.

'Is there a bath?' I asked, following him back into the main room.

'What do you think this is, The Ritz? No, there's no bath. We can wash at the sink.'

'I know somewhere you can have a bath, Frankie, don't worry,' Naomi said as she pegged back the curtain in front of her mattress. She started arranging a small group of coloured crystals by her bed. I went behind my curtain, sat back on my mattress and tried to summon the courage to ask.

'Naomi?' I said hesitantly.

'Frankie?'

'Do you have a spare . . . blanket or anything?'

'Oh, sorry, love, do you not have anything? Yeah, we must do, let's think . . . We might have something from the camp, hold on.' She went and rooted through the boxes and came back with a thin grey sleeping bag with diagonal red stripes on it. 'Here you go.'

'Thanks,' I said.

Nick had suggested I try it out for a couple of nights, but I knew when I left home that I wouldn't go back. I'd packed my suitcase, insisting I would be fine, that I didn't need any help, that I was eighteen, for goodness' sake. My mother had cried, and I'd felt guilty and ended up insisting even more. It felt impossible, after that show of independence, to go home and ask for a duvet.

It was midday. My shift didn't start until five that day, but I told them I had to get going and put my A–Z in my pocket. I waited a long time for a bus and then took the Tube to Oxford Circus. I walked into the department store we used to go to on Saturdays, went straight to the bed linen department, and spent a chunk of the money

I'd brought with me on the cheapest double sheet, duvet, duvet cover, pillow and pillow case. I paid for it quickly, not wanting to think about what I was doing, and then looked at my watch. It was two o'clock and I hadn't had lunch. I counted my change and, laden with linen, I went to the café and asked for a cup of tea and a sticky bun.

Sitting at the Formica table, I felt the weight of my childhood pressing on me. The feeling of the green leather padded benches underneath me, waiting to have my feet measured for shoes, the precise pressure of the metal bar on my socked toes. The intense lustre of the glassware section, cut-crystal decanters glittering under spotlights, and the terror of moving through them ('Now, I want you to be very, *very* careful,' my mother would say). The women with bronzed faces wearing white offering to spray scent on me; the smooth, steady pace of the escalator and lifts. And yet this neat, bright world, full of new things and possibility, was already starting to look peculiar. I went down to the ground floor, bulging bags knocking my calves, and stood, suspended in light and comfort, taunted by the opulence, watching women casually write cheques or hand over their dark-green account cards. Leaving home had been difficult, but somehow walking out of the department store felt even worse.

Downstairs at the pub, when my shift had finished, I ripped the bedding out of its packaging. I unfolded the sheets and scrunched them between my hands to try to disguise the fresh lines. I shoved the bags in the bin and carried the sheets home in my arms.

'Oh, you got bedding!' Naomi said when I got in. 'That's great. I was worried about you tonight.'

'A friend had it going spare.' I had rehearsed this during

my shift, had even invented a story about something I had exchanged for it, but decided I would only elaborate if asked.

'Looks like nice stuff,' Naomi said.

She was being kind, but the scrutiny was unbearable. I blushed and said, 'Yeah, it's all right,' and went behind the curtain to dump it on my mattress.

It turned out I didn't need a duvet, not that first week. We had the windows open all the time, but there was still a constant airless heat. Not the kind that you'd notice straight away, but after half an hour you had prickles of sweat at your hairline. Naomi was almost constantly in her sundress, hanging out of the window, smoking. 'Enjoy it,' Jane said. 'It's going to be fucking freezing in winter.'

Malcolm joined us two days after we'd moved in. He was mostly silent, with brown, tangled hair that fell below his shoulders. He told us he worked in a record shop in Islington and left at seven-thirty every morning to walk the five miles it took to get there. He'd brought his own chair, a small dark-brown velour armchair, and he set it apart from the rest of the furniture, near the window by his sleeping area. He put a stack of books and a cloudy dimpled beer glass filled with coppers on the windowsill.

Every day in the first week, Naomi wandered round the room waving a stick of herbs around, smoke curling up from it. She planted seeds in empty egg boxes and plastic pots and kept them in the kitchen corner, with earthenware bowls holding water and grains. There was usually something in her enamel saucepan on the hob and a bowl full of glossy aubergines, fennel, something brown and knobbly and hairy. Malcolm sat in his chair, reading and smoking, or drinking black coffee.

When I got home from the pub, Jane and Nick would have opened the glass door at the top of the stairwell and would be sitting with their legs hanging over the edge. I could hear them laughing and bickering as I came up the stairs. It opened to nothing, no platform or balcony between them and the four-storey drop. I felt queasy looking at it. They waved when I came in, but they didn't break off their conversation.

I didn't know what to do with myself when I wasn't at work, so I asked Malcolm if he knew a good local bookshop. He became unusually verbose, telling me about political bookshops, second-hand bookshops, feminist bookshops. Then he mentioned one nearby, slightly sneeringly – 'You know, just the usual stuff, new stuff coming out. Bestsellers.' I went there and came back with a stack of fresh books, feeling almost as guilty as I had buying the sheets.

6

Amanda

2019

Two days after I met Lucy, I went back into the office. There was a meeting about the investigations the paper would be running over the next year and of course I could have missed it but I didn't want to. I knew that things were going to happen without me over the next six months, but I wanted to at least know what they were. I had said that I would go to it before I went on maternity leave and I'd found the concerned, knowing looks – the implication that I wouldn't be able to manage, that they knew more than I did about my capabilities – unbelievably patronising and irritating. It made me all the more determined to prove them wrong, to show them that I hadn't changed, I hadn't lost control. I hadn't lost myself. I spent an hour working out how to use the breast pump, and expressed milk the night before, which left me peculiarly weak, as if the milk had been an integral part of me. I talked Oliver through how to use the steriliser.

They had said that I could bring Iris, of course. They said they'd love to meet her, and someone could hold her for me, but it was unimaginable. How could I take this

137

uncontrollable being – whose proximity turned me into someone anxious and scared – to a place where I needed to be slick and contained? And I was looking forward to being without her: whenever Oliver left the flat in the morning, I was crazily, desperately envious of him. He could close the door and leave it all behind him: the mess and the *work*. I savoured the thought of a proper outfit – a lace bra that didn't open at the front, shirts, heels, tights, a dress even. I could feel my old self waiting for me, ready to be inhabited again.

But when I woke up that morning, I didn't feel the way I'd imagined I would. It suddenly seemed a lunatic thing to do: the thought of her having even the slightest need that couldn't be met by Oliver, and me not being there, was unbearable. But the thought of calling my boss, letting people down, admitting that I'd made a mistake, was worse.

I started trying things on and began to panic. I knew I was more or less the same size as I'd been before Iris was born, because people told me. 'You're looking skinny,' the woman who worked at the newsagent's opposite me said approvingly after she'd congratulated me. 'Oh, you've really slimmed down!' a woman on the bus said to me after I'd told her how old Iris was. 'It's just breastfeeding!' I told them, and they smiled and nodded and said how lucky I was. I didn't say that sometimes after feeding I was so exhausted I didn't think I could stand up, and the physical labour of the days – the rocking, the feeding, the pram-pushing, the constant meeting of needs – frightened me because I felt so entirely incapable. I didn't say that I could be overwhelmed by desperate hunger at any moment, and I was scared that it would happen when I wouldn't be able to get something – because Iris was asleep on me, or because I couldn't fit the pram in the door of a shop – so I ate pre-emptively, whenever there was an opportunity, cramming food I didn't want or like into my mouth.

But it was as if what was left of my body had been re-arranged and I still didn't quite understand how. My stomach had got smaller but it was still slack, pooling in front of me when I lay on my side. The brown vertical line was still there, but while it was once a thin, taut hoop, it had collapsed into a loose stripe, a wavy watery line. My belly button was wide and deep, like a quarry.

My clothes were either too tight or too loose, or they simply looked wrong. And even if I knew it was unrealistic to expect to be the same eight weeks after giving birth, I had to go to the meeting and I couldn't go in leggings. I could hear Iris grizzling and, even though Oliver was with her, I knew that I wouldn't be able to stand it much longer. Even her mild unhappiness – not proper cries, just squalls and complaints – provoked something physical in me: the need to respond was not yet all-consuming, but it was there, like thirst or a full bladder, fracturing my thoughts. I would have to go downstairs in a minute. I looked at my watch. I had an hour before I needed to leave. But I still didn't have anything to wear. I rifled through the clothes on my bed as if that would reveal some new, magic solution, and, when it didn't, the panic increased.

When Oliver came up the stairs, I was standing in front of the mirror in my nursing bra, stiff circles of dried milk around the nipples, and the only clean pair of pants I had left: sheer black ones.

'Nice pants,' he said.

'Where's Iris?'

'Asleep.'

'What? Where?'

'Downstairs. I was rocking her and then she fell asleep, and then I put her down in the basket and she didn't wake up.'

'What the fuck?'

'I know, right?'

Suddenly we were both dizzyingly jubilant, him with pride, me with unexpected freedom. Maybe I could leave her. Maybe it was going to be fine after all.

'I mean it, nice pants,' he said, pushing me up against the wall and kissing me, and I said, 'Oh, come on, I have to go in a minute,' and then the only thing I felt was sudden ferocious desire, his body crushed against mine, his hand between my legs. At night, when I wasn't dreaming about death, I was dreaming about sex.

'Is it OK to leave her downstairs?' I whispered, taking off my nursing bra.

'It's fine. We're basically in the same room.'

'Is that weird, though?'

'We had sex before you gave birth and she was sort of next to us then.'

'I suppose.'

I picked up the failed outfits from the bed and dumped them in Iris's cot.

'Have you come?' he asked. 'Since . . . ?'

'A couple of times. I just wanted to know if everything was still working.'

'And is it?'

'Yeah. I'm still scared of the stiches, so I touched myself through my knickers. And . . . . I pissed myself when I came.'

'That's OK.'

'Is it, though?'

He put his mouth between my legs. We were fast, stumbling, scrabbling for a condom. He was inside me and I wanted to cry because I was thinking about the fact that Iris's head had been where his penis was now and even though I understood how that had happened, even though I'd touched the top of her skull with my fingers before her head came out, it still seemed impossible, a crazy trick, and I didn't know why I couldn't stop thinking about it or why it was making me want to cry. Then we heard Iris muttering to herself downstairs and we laughed. He pulled out and went to fetch her. I fed her on the bed, surrounded by a weird eroticism. After about twenty minutes, Oliver called up, 'Is she done?'

'I think so,' I said. He took her and then took my hand and put it between my legs.

'See you in a bit,' he said, kissing me.

I managed to find a combination of clothes that looked OK but they no longer felt like mine: I felt as awkward and inhibited as if I were wearing a clown outfit on the Tube. I had expected to feel free but instead I felt drastically out of place. I saw a man pushing a buggy and was assaulted by longing and panic and the feeling that something was terribly wrong.

It had been only six weeks since I'd been in central London but I had lost any ability to cope with it, to tune out the noise, the traffic, the crowds. Now they were overwhelming. I used to think about the people asking for money only fleetingly, as a distraction, an annoyance, but now the tiny temporary dwellings of cardboard flooring, blankets, sleeping bags, books and suitcases were almost unbearable. A young blonde woman sat on a cardboard box, with her knees against her chest, crying, and I wondered how I had ever managed to see this and not think about it. I offered to buy her something, and when I handed her the hot chocolate she'd asked for she didn't say anything or stop crying and I wondered what I had been expecting.

At the office, I tried to act normally. I'd had enough visitors and conversations at baby groups that it came naturally now: my life was a giant act of pretence. I made all the right jokes about sleep deprivation and epidurals, and I said that everything was fine and I was looking forward to coming back to work. But I hadn't kept up with the news, not really, sometimes scrolling on my phone during night feeds, trying to figure out how my replacement was getting on, what stories they were running. I was scared of getting found out.

The worst part was that I was so keen to pretend, to keep up, that I didn't look at the time. I thought the meeting would be quick, that everyone would want to get back to work, that I would be the one trying to prolong it. But people seemed astonishingly leisurely, making small talk or inane jokes, and as the meeting was coming to a drawn-out end I felt an intense pressure in my breasts. There was no clock; I didn't know how to subtly look at my watch. It was only coming out, looking at my phone, that I realised that it had taken over an hour. I had a text from Oliver: *sorry, I think she's hungry and she's refusing the bottle, any ideas?* And another one: *I'm really sorry, I can't get her to take it. what time do you think you'll be back?* My breasts were taut and painful to touch. I said goodbye to everyone, smiling, wanting to attack the people who asked me a question or said, 'Just wait a sec, I'll go down with you.' As soon as I was a safe distance from the office, I started running.

I was good in stressful situations. I knew that about myself. I didn't panic, I stayed calm, I just did what needed to be done. On the journey home I spoke to Oliver, who said she was totally fine, not to worry, just get there when I could, although I could hear the anxiety in his voice and her crying in the background. I told myself that it was all right – that she was being looked after, that she wasn't in any danger – and yet my whole body was vibrating. I had heard mothers say, 'Oh, it's so hard leaving her, I couldn't put her down even for a second' and I didn't believe them: it seemed irritating, cutesy, a pose. I didn't want to be that kind of mother and anyway I wasn't: I had been as desperate to be away from her as I now was to be with her.

I felt like pregnancy had come with a dizzying series of choices: home birth or hospital, breast or bottle, how long will your maternity leave be, will you go back to work, will you go part-time? And that with them came a choice about what sort of person I was going to be: was I going to be credulous or sceptical, new-age or modern, sentimental or rational? I assumed that when the time came I would make the correct choices, that I would pick a side and fight for it. I never thought that I would be hopelessly caught in the middle, that I wouldn't know what sort of person I was.

She'd calmed down by the time I got home. She wasn't even crying. But I still ripped off my shirt and the stupid bra that didn't open at the front and held her close, feeding her, feeling relieved and monstrous. I felt guilty, but that wasn't the worst part. The worst part was thinking that I might never be able to do something normal again. My old self had not been waiting for me after all.

★

By the evening, I was still feeling disorientated, but when it came time to put Iris in her bouncy chair, and Oliver was making roasted cauliflower with almonds and brown rice, I felt calmer. As I was pouring myself a glass of wine, my phone buzzed; it was Lucy, asking if I wanted to try the singing group we'd talked about.

'Hey, guess what?' I said to Oliver. 'There's a baby group at the Black Hart.'

'Seriously?'

'Yes. Isn't that weird?'

'Are you going to go?'

'I don't see why not.'

'Just don't pick up any men while you're there, OK?'

'OK, well, for a start, there won't be any men there.'

I told people that I'd met Oliver online, but that wasn't entirely true. We'd met five years ago, when I was covering social affairs and had to interview someone in A&E. We met in a side room at the hospital and, as we spoke, there were a few things I noticed straight away. I noticed that he was courteous, and that he paid attention, even when I was supposed to be the one paying attention to him. I noticed that he was mixed-race, although I don't know if I really thought anything about it. I noticed that he had fancy glasses. I noticed how he looked, of course, but although Oliver is nice-looking, he's not devastating. But that just made what happened next even better.

As I was putting my tape recorder away, he mentioned something about having been born in the hospital.

'Oh, really? I almost was.'

'Almost?'

'My mum was brought up round the corner, on the

Penn Estate? My parents were living there when she was pregnant with me, and then they managed to get a house in Essex just before I was born.'

'So you got out. Fancy.'

'Yeah, well, we all thought so. And then I went to Oxford and got into journalism and people let me know very quickly that, in fact, it wasn't.' I picked up my bag. 'My nana wasn't going anywhere, though, so I spent a lot of time here as a kid. I used to stay over at hers on a Saturday night and she'd take me to the library or swimming.'

'The leisure centre? Or the swimming baths?'

'The leisure centre. Of course. It had a wave machine!'

'Wasn't that incredible? I liked that boiling-hot children's pool at the baths, though. All those floats.'

I picked up my handbag. 'Listen, thanks for this. Are you going back to work now?'

He shook his head. 'I'm not working today. I came in to speak to you.'

'Oh,' I said. 'Well, I'm even more grateful now.'

'It's all right. I only live round the corner.' We walked towards the door together and he said, without looking at me, 'Listen, do you fancy a quick drink? It would be fun to talk more about, you know, all that sort of stuff, what it was like before. You don't often meet people who grew up here, now.'

I stopped at the door and looked at him. I wanted, so badly, to say yes. It was five-thirty; I hadn't planned to go back to the office. I could forget everything, for a couple of hours, and catch up later. But I had started my first round of IVF that week.

'I'm not really drinking at the moment,' I said.

'Oh, OK,' he said. He sounded disappointed but he didn't

give up and I liked that about him too: his persistence, his confidence. 'A coffee?'

'We could go to the pub and I'd have a soft drink?'

'Sure,' he said.

When I was little, the Black Hart had had a reputation for being rough, for being a squatters' pub. Now it served sourdough pizza, with the option of gluten-free bases and vegan toppings. They'd changed the sign back from the modern chunky lettering to something faux-Edwardian. The rust-coloured tiles outside and stained glass in the windows, and the ornate screens on the bar, had taken on a new significance: features rather than remains.

I went in the side door. The chairs and tables had been pushed back on one side of the bar and there was a rug on the floor, with children's toys on it, and some cushions round the edge. I saw Lucy straight away and simply recognising someone was astonishingly comforting, particularly when she waved and smiled.

There were babies everywhere and everyone was drinking tea, but at least I was somewhere familiar. I noticed that there were a surprising number of men there, and I was going to text Oliver to tell him, though when I counted it turned out to be only three. A woman with a guitar started playing and I sat down next to Lucy, on a soft buttoned cushion, and laid Iris on her back on the rug in front of me.

The woman started singing children's songs, but not ones I knew, which made it slightly more demanding and more interesting. She encouraged us to sing along when we'd picked them up, which I did, quietly, not wanting to draw attention to myself. We sang songs about breakfast and bears, and although I found it dissonant looking round at these women – presumably chefs, scientists, painters, marketing managers – all sitting together singing a song about bananas, I realised that I wasn't unhappy.

The next song was about an elevator going up up up up up and down down down down down and we were supposed to lift our babies up and down along with the chorus. I turned Iris to face me and, as I lifted her, she smiled down at me. My body jumpstarted with happiness, a demented, overwhelming gulp of joy. I couldn't stop myself returning her smile, even though I knew I was giving her a crazed, eager grin. For a second she stopped smiling and looked alarmed. But then she smiled again, and the room receded and I started laughing. I didn't care if everyone was looking at me. I didn't care what they were doing. This moment between the two of us was gigantic, total, the only thing that could possibly matter.

The song ended and the rest of the room became visible to me again. I was reeling from the fact that something so overpowering, so intimate, the kind of moment that happened in bedrooms, cathedrals and hospitals, had just happened here, on this dingy pub carpet surrounded by oblivious strangers and plastic bottles filled with beads.

We sang a goodbye song and then Lucy asked if I wanted to stay for a coffee. I said yes and went to get the pram, pushing it next to one of the tables at the side.

'Shall I get the coffee and you stay with the babies?' she asked, and I nodded, astounded at her confidence, in her baby, to be left, and in me, to take care of him. I needed to feed Iris so she put Stanley down in Iris's pram and I watched him wriggle in front of me and thought about messaging Oliver to tell him I'd actually enjoyed myself.

★

I wasn't drinking the night I met Oliver but I got drunk on the music and my short skirt, and his mood after three pints. We weren't on a date, because I was drinking lime and sodas and I had made sure to mention I was married; we just wanted to reminisce about the swimming pool and the library. But our conversation felt studded with connections, each moment where we thought or remembered or felt the same thing was like a little point of light, and two drinks in we were blazing, giddy with them. I asked where he went to school, hoping that he might say the local school, the one my mum and nana had gone to.

'Ah, no. I went to a school in north London, actually. A private school.'

I felt both sad and embarrassed that I'd got him wrong. He started to explain it; he told me later he always felt he had to.

'My dad left my mum when me and my sister were really small. He wasn't what you'd call . . . supportive, either financially or, you know, emotionally. His mum and dad, my grandparents, paid the fees for mine and my sister's schooling. I guess they thought that it was a way of compensating. I don't know.'

'I'm really sorry. How old were you when he left?'

'I was four. So I don't remember much about him being there. I've got some vague memories of the house we all lived in together but that's it. He's a photographer and he travelled a lot when we were younger, but even when he was in the country we didn't see that much of him. He went to some extraordinary places – and you know, some of his pictures are incredible. He really did have this amazing life, and people say all the time how brave he was, how dedicated, how lucky I am to have such a brilliant person as a father. I just didn't see that side of him. None of those qualities were any use to me, as a child.' He spoke easily enough, but I could hear the edge in his voice.

We were sitting at the bar; someone jostled me trying to get served and apologised. It was getting more and more crowded, with people coming in after work. I hadn't checked the time since we arrived, but we'd clearly been there longer than the couple of hours I'd told myself I would stay. I thought about suggesting that we try to move to a table, but I told myself that I would have to go soon. And I didn't want him to stop talking.

'I have some nice memories,' he said. 'Visiting him in the studio when we were kids, him showing me how to develop photos. Sometimes he'd ask me which print I liked best. And I guess I got an education out of him, like I say.'

'What was your school like?' I asked.

'It was fine. I mean, the teaching was good, I can't complain, and it's probably true what they say about private school and confidence. And, you know, there was a certain cachet to being from Hackney or Brixton or somewhere like that; all the boys in my year thought it was cool to be black and I probably milked it a bit, but I always knew I was faking it. Like everyone wanted to know about my cousins from the estate but they wouldn't have wanted to know about, you know, my mum's PhD or Sunday dinner at my gran's or anything like that. And then you're back home, seeing the kids you used to play out with, scared you're going to get hassle for not going to the local school.' He looked at me. 'I don't know why I'm telling you all this. Actually, I do know. You're still asking me questions.'

Normally, I would have apologised here, but the way he

was looking at me, and smiling, I decided not to. 'It's my job,' I said. 'And I'm curious.'

'You strike me as someone who's curious about a lot of things. Which is a good thing, by the way.'

'I'm more interested in some things than others.'

The best way to flirt is if the other person doesn't realise it's happening. I could never do that. I was ham-fisted when I liked someone: I talked about sex, I teased them, I fished for compliments. It just came out that way. I wasn't subtle or elegant or clever. Part of it, I think, was that I couldn't see the point in messing around; I'd rather just let someone know how I felt about them. But another part of it was trust: I believed that Oliver liked me.

It was one of those conversations where everything seemed to work, where you could never say the wrong thing because there was so much good energy there, and I knew that if something came out wrong he would probably know what I meant anyway. And I was enjoying being this other person so much, not the person I'd been for so long now, infused with failure: *some complications, I'm afraid. I'm sorry, I know this isn't what you want to hear.* I wasn't someone for whom sex was simply a way to make something happen, like an operation. I wasn't someone whose body routinely failed, who needed sedation and injections to make it work properly, and even then it still didn't happen.

That night, I was someone sitting on a barstool in a short skirt opposite an attractive man, and without noticing it we'd moved closer to each other and my thigh was edging into the gap between his. The joy of intimacy and attraction was dizzying and I knew he felt it too. Turned out my body worked fine after all.

When he was finishing his third drink, I finally looked at my watch. It was just after nine, that liminal time when, if it was a date, what happened next would have been decisive: more alcohol, getting some food, going home. But we weren't on a date, and I remembered something that I had to do.

I didn't always know how long I'd be out for at work, so I carried a needle with me, just in case. I was an hour late. I was suddenly infused with panic, scanning the evening for something I might have done wrong: what if the alcohol had entered my bloodstream by osmosis, what if there was second-hand cigarette smoke lingering on the people coming inside, what if I had ruined my chances to be a mother, just for these stupid few hours, pretending to be someone I wasn't with a person I'd never see again.

I went to the loo and in the cubicle I got the needle out of my handbag. My hands were shaking and I felt even worse. I jabbed it into my stomach, gasped, and went back out.

We sat opposite each other for a moment. We both knew something had changed.

'Another drink?' he said, but he knew the answer.

'I'd better be getting back.'

'Sure, me too.'

'It was really nice to meet you, Oliver.'

'And you.' He looked me straight in the eye. 'It would be nice to see you again.'

'I'll be in touch,' I said, in a way that meant I wouldn't, and he looked crestfallen. But I was married and I'd just injected myself in the stomach in a pub toilet.

When I got back, I was buzzing, and slightly dreamy, as if we had actually kissed. David was watching something on Netflix and I asked, casually, how long there was left of the episode. I had about twenty minutes. I told him I was going to bed early and then I went upstairs and made myself come thinking about what would have happened if I hadn't gone home.

When Lucy went to wipe Stanley's face, I noticed that instead of wet wipes she had a complicated set of little bags, taking a wet flannel out of one and putting it into another when it was used. We drank coffee and talked about sleep and breastfeeding and I said something about Oliver and then I asked when her partner had gone back to work.

'I don't have a partner,' she said.

'Oh, I'm sorry,' I said. 'I mean – I'm sorry I assumed, not I'm sorry that . . .'

She shook her head. 'Don't be. I know it's not the norm.'

I had all sorts of questions – why? how? – but I told myself not to ask them. I was still annoyed at how cack-handedly I'd approached it.

'I'm not really on my own,' she said. 'I had a baby on my own, but I live with a friend who's got a baby the same age. Also by herself. We're kind of a . . . very exclusive single-mum commune, I guess.'

A part of my brain was working furiously, a part that had felt dormant or underused for such a long time. There was a story there and I wanted to hear it. I always wanted to get to the meat of things, the kinds of things other people skate over or don't want to mention, and I had learnt through work that if you ask direct questions, people usually answer them. You don't often hear, 'I don't want to talk about that' or 'I'd rather not say.' Usually they tell you. But I also knew that too much intensity could be off-putting. If you want to get the story, you have to get people to like you.

I took a sip of my coffee and tried to sound casual. 'How did you meet her?'

'It was just coincidence, really. I'd met her a few times through a friend, but I more knew her from online. She's an influencer and I was trying to launch this clothing brand and we messaged each other a bit about that. But then she announced she was pregnant, same time as me, and I knew she was by herself. I had somewhere to live and a spare room. So it felt obvious. I feel really lucky.'

'She's an influencer?'

'Yeah, I mean, not like huge. Thirty thousand followers, something like that? She does interiors mainly, but she featured some of my clothes in some shots, which was pretty cool. I got some traffic through that.'

'Are you in PR then?'

'Oh no, the company's mine. I make the clothes.'

'What sort of clothes?'

She looked as if she was trying to remember how to speak a different language, the way I did on the rare occasions that someone at a baby group asked me what I did. 'So, it's women's wear, but kind of functional. I think it's actually really, like, a feminist idea, that women should wear stuff that's practical and you can move in. But hopefully not ugly. All sustainable fabrics, ethical manufacturing. I want to make pieces that people will wear for years, not just three or four times.' She suddenly looked embarrassed, as if she wasn't sure she'd got the wording right. 'That's the idea anyway.' Stanley grizzled and she unbuttoned her shirt and unclipped her bra. He turned away from her exposed nipple. 'No? OK then.' She started bouncing him up and down on her lap. 'I just feel like I spent way too much time in clothes that you couldn't actually wear, like backless, strapless, tight. Pulling up a neckline, trying to walk in heels. I feel like I wasted my life fighting my clothes.'

I knew what she meant but, when she was speaking, all I wanted to do was be a teenager in a backless dress and high heels, not in a milk-stained pair of leggings and a top that opened at the front. Iris was muttering in the pram so I picked her up and tried to feed her.

Talking to Lucy wasn't like talking to any of my other friends. She told me about being a flexitarian, and how she'd found someone to encapsulate her placenta, and said things like, 'Crystals are actually pretty mainstream now.' But she wasn't boring.

I had been told so many times that I would need a 'mum friend' to 'be boring with'. Someone you could talk to about feeding and sleeping, and all the things no one else gives a shit about. The thought had horrified me. It was that, as much as the socks or the nursery rhymes or being with other women, that had stopped me joining groups at the start. One of the things I'd immediately liked about my job was that it made me interesting. I liked having the inside track – I liked telling people what the Chancellor of the Exchequer was really like or what was really going on in the House of Commons – and I felt like I had temporarily forgotten how to do this, how to be this. I still couldn't concentrate on the news. On good days, which this one was turning into, I believed that I would get it back. In the meantime, I could talk to Lucy.

After I met Oliver, I thought about him a lot, despite being married, despite trying to have a baby with the man I was married to. Not all the time because I went back to being that other person, crying in a clinical waiting room, crying in the bathroom over a solitary blue line, crying in a café toilet when I saw blood in my knickers, crying when I saw a baby, crying just from the bleakness and the unfairness of it all. But I thought of him when I went past the hospital, and sometimes when I got a coffee from the place opposite, or when I queued for a takeaway wrap among people with NHS lanyards. I imagined bumping into him and what I'd say. I went over and over my favourite bits of our conversation in my head. The night David moved out, one of the first things I did was write a message to Oliver that I never sent.

But two years after the separation, idly browsing a dating app, one of the photos made me stop. I scrolled through the profile, my fingers trembling as I jabbed the screen ineptly. I thought, *wait, think this through, what exactly are you going to say?* but there was a bigger part of me that couldn't wait any longer, and I sent a message that began, *OK, this is going to sound weird . . .* He messaged back immediately. We went to the Black Hart for our first real date, and this time I drank whisky.

'When I met you before, you said you were going to leave A&E,' I said. 'Do something nine to five.'

'I know. And that was what, four years ago? And I'm still here.'

'Are you still thinking about it?'

'I think about it all the time. It's exactly the same as when I spoke to you – worse, probably, in terms of the stress, the shortages. And yeah, doing nights is just . . . It kills you. But it's still the best job I've ever done.'

'I don't think I understand that. I mean, it just sounds incredibly stressful and hard and . . . .'

'It's weird. I often think I'm weird. I like the feeling of crisis. It feels like someone's drowning, or falling, all the time, and you're all working together to stop it and then most of the time you do. Honestly, I sometimes don't know if there's a better feeling than that. People come in and they're really sick and you can make them better. I mean, you have a kind of power, you can make people better, and I know that sounds sort of fucked up and sadistic . . .'

'No, I get it,' I said. 'You like making things happen.'

'Yeah,' he said. 'I like making things happen.'

'I do too,' I said. 'I don't think that's weird at all.'

We went back to my flat. I don't even remember where we first kissed because it felt so inevitable. I remember talking and laughing as we were fucking, and a kind of urgent desire I'd never felt before. I remember how he made me feel in the weeks afterwards, after I'd come, lying next to him, flattened and emptied. Earthed. I'd spent my whole life grasping, reaching, pulling up, trying to be somewhere else. That was the only time I felt grounded. That was the only time I felt home.

I didn't want to treat Lucy like a feature, but I wanted to know more about how it worked in the single-mum commune, so as soon as she mentioned her housemate again I said, 'It must be nice having the support.'

'Yeah . . .' she said. 'I can't imagine doing it without Chloe. It's much less lonely. But then, you know, I can't ask her to get up in the night if Stanley's crying. That's when it feels isolating. That's when I wish I had a partner. Someone to share the nights with.' She laughed. 'It's insane, but the other night I was walking up and down the hallway at three in morning, I'd put him in the sling over my pyjamas, I was that desperate, and it was freezing and he was just in this little Babygro, so I put my coat on and wrapped it round him. I was in the hallway in my pyjamas and coat, with him in the sling, and Chloe and her baby were asleep upstairs and God, I really fucking hated her.'

'I don't think that's insane. And anyway, a lot of men sleep in the spare room.'

'Oh, you're just saying that to make me feel better. Does your partner sleep in the spare room?'

'No,' I said. 'But it's a studio flat and open-plan. So it's sort of impossible for us. And anyway, he quite often works nights or he has to get up for a shift, so either I'm on my own or I feel like I am.'

'Oh, OK. Well, I don't know, I've heard people say it's better to have one functioning human in the house any-way. So even if your partner's sleeping in the spare room, at least he's well rested and capable. Sometimes, with me and Chloe, it's like we're in separate worlds. Separate worlds of pain.'

'But then,' I said, 'your functioning human being isn't there. He goes to work for twelve hours a day and it doesn't really matter if he's a good dad or a great guy or whatever, because he's not there. He leaves the house and you're completely on your own.'

It's true that I wouldn't have cried if I hadn't been on maternity leave. Before then, I'd been a serious person: I visited prisons, visited cancer wards, visited a morgue, and kept my face set. I wrote about war and weapons, and terrorist attacks, and beheadings. Even as I was crying, I was narrating it in my head: a funny story about how I was so hormonal when I had a baby that I cried in front of women I barely knew at a baby group. And yet the anger and the abandonment were vivid and visceral and it would take a long time for them to fade.

Lucy didn't laugh or even acknowledge my joke about being a hormonal mess, which I couldn't stop myself making. She didn't say anything when I said how stupid I felt for complaining when she was on her own. She just handed me the napkin from under her saucer.

'It's colossally hard, isn't it?' she said, and I couldn't even nod.

One of the things I liked about Oliver was that he said he didn't mind not having children, and I believed him. The first person I'd slept with after the separation was a musician with long hair who was intensely serious and lived in a squat. We didn't have much in common, but that was the fun of it: when we found something in common, it was like finding gold in the earth. We went camping together even though I hate camping and he told me stories about the children he taught guitar to and I had a horrible feeling the conversation was going to go somewhere I didn't want it to. And it did: he told me how amazing he thought children were, and that he was so excited about having kids one day.

He thought he was being winning, because women like children, especially women in their late thirties, and imagine this man – this *very serious* man! – liking *children*, how unbelievably charming. But it made me angry, how blithe he was, and I said, 'You're thirty-nine, you're essentially single, you live in a squat. So when do you think you're going to have kids?'

He looked at me, uncertain. 'Well, it's different for men,

isn't it? I mean, you can father a child in your nineties.'

'You *can* father a child in your nineties. But have you noticed how the men in their nineties who find women a third of their age to have kids with tend to be billionaires?'

'Woah, OK, why are you—'

'Sorry,' I said. 'Sorry, I just—' I didn't even want to tell him, but I felt like I ought to explain why I was ruining things, so I told him that I didn't think I could have children. And he said, 'Don't they say if you give up trying, it just happens,' and I didn't tell him to fuck off, although I wanted to. I regretted it as soon as I'd started talking about it and something cooled between us. When we got home I cried, and I was angry with myself for being miserable because I knew we would never have had kids together even if I didn't have 'fertility challenges'. But the terrible thing was that I could tell he meant it – he did want kids someday. And now we'd had to acknowledge that we were never going to have a future together, that was enough to stop it being fun.

So when I started seeing Oliver, I brought it up after we'd only been together a few weeks.

'Well, I did always think I'd have kids,' he said. 'But then I never met anyone who . . . you know, it would have been the right thing with. And the older I get, the more I think I could imagine having a really nice life without them.' He looked down. 'There's also my dad. I mean, I'd be terrified to be a dad. I wouldn't have any idea how to do it.'

'What if you change your mind?'

'Well, there are things you can do, aren't there? IVF? Adoption? If we decided it was something we really wanted. But I mean, from everything you've said, it sounds like you're OK with it.'

That was the first point in my life that I realised I was. 'I suppose so,' I said.

'Well, I am too,' he said. 'So let's just cross that bridge when we come to it.'

Even though I had tried IVF and I knew about the complications and difficulties of adoption, and anyway I was already thirty-seven, I still felt a sense of comfort that I hadn't felt for a long time. There were things we could do, if we wanted to, but right now, we didn't.

'I know we don't need to think about this now. I just wanted to, you know, get the conversation out the way,' I said.

'I understand,' he said. 'It's out the way.'

But the most annoying thing about the musician was that he was right. Sometimes it does happen when you give up trying.

Lucy and I sat for a moment, while I gasped and stuttered in an attempt to get myself back under control.

'So your partner's out at work a lot?' she said.

'Yeah. He's a nurse at the hospital. A&E. It's incredibly stressful and he does long shifts and he's knackered all the time and he's a great dad and he says he'll do shared parental leave so I can go back to work after six months, and if he's not on at night he'll get up with her, even if he has a twelve-hour shift the next day, but actually there's not much he can do because she wants me, and the flat's so small she always knows I'm there, and he takes her out for walks in the pram at five a.m. . . . . but even, even all that, feels like a drop in the ocean, it feels like he has no idea what it's like to . . . to be on your own for that long. To not do anything else. I feel so bad saying all this, by the way, you know, when you don't have a partner—'

'Well, to be honest, it actually makes me feel better knowing it's hard for other people too. I mean, not that I'm not sorry for you. But a lot of the time I feel like I've done something incredibly stupid.'

After I'd cried, it felt easier to ask the question. 'What made you decide to do it by yourself?'

'I don't know if I'm a romantic, but I'm an idealist. The idea of going out there, you know, trying to find some-one just to have kids with made me want to kill myself. I was thirty-nine and it actually didn't seem that weird to me – I had this group of friends in our late thirties, none of us had partners, none of us had kids, and we were all talking about it all the time, you know: are we going to do something about it? Are we going to do it? And I suddenly thought: yes, I am.'

'I think that's really brave.'

'Well, that's only half the story. Because I decided to try to do something about it, but part of me thought it wasn't going to work. I thought, maybe I'll just do this so I can say I gave it a go, and then I can get on with life. And the IVF was so brutal, I didn't know how many times I could go through with it. But by then it had happened. It worked first time.'

'I had IVF too,' I said. 'Three rounds.'

'Oh God. But you got Iris.'

'Well, actually none of them worked. It's a long story,' I said.

Lucy had been bouncing Stanley on her knee and his eyes were slowly starting to close. She stopped bouncing and pulled him gently towards her but then he gave a strangled cry. She tipped her head back and closed her eyes. 'Oh, for fuck's sake, Stanley. What do you want?' She reached for her sling. 'I think I might have to go. Sorry.'

Iris had been remarkably happy on my knee while we were talking – from time to time I fed her or put her back down in the pram or picked her up again or squeaked a toy in her face. It amazed me how easy it seemed to look after her when I had something sufficiently distracting, and how hard it was to recreate these moments alone in the flat.

'Do you want to walk together for a bit?' she said as she stood up. 'Try to get them off to sleep? I still want to hear the story. About how you got Iris.'

'Yeah, why not?' I said, and I started putting Iris into her pram suit.

'I don't know if it's a great story after all that,' I said as we walked out of the pub and towards the park. I leant over Iris to tuck in her blanket, praying she would fall asleep or at least not cry. 'I tried for two years with my ex-husband, and nothing happened. And they did all these tests but there was no reason why it wasn't working . . . so we tried IVF. But the whole process just broke us and finally . . . well, it was quite exposing. We couldn't see a way of being together if it didn't work, so then it didn't seem like such a great idea to have kids together. So we split up. And then I was on my own for a while and I just thought I wouldn't have children. I'd been coasting at work, because I was exhausted by the IVF, and anyway, I thought I was going to have children so there was no point trying for a big job. Then the home affairs editor got poached by another paper and I took over. It felt so lucky, that something like that would happen just at that moment. I knew it was the kind of job you have to really go all in on, so I thought that's great, I'll just do this instead of having kids. And then I met Oliver, and three months in I got pregnant by accident.'

'Oh wow.'

'I was so shocked . . . I mean, what did I expect? I'd had sex education classes, I know what happens if you have unprotected sex. But I'd just been so used to failure, to protecting myself from it . . .'

I had never told anyone what actually happened. What had actually happened was that I had put off taking the pregnancy test because I didn't think I could go through it again, that reckoning with the immutable single line. The mockery of hope, the intolerable stasis, the confirmation that I was not the sort of person things happen to. I'd just wait till I got my period: the instant extinction of possibility.

But when it didn't come, and my body felt strange and full, I got out an old test. And this time, when I saw the single line, I was hit by relief, strong and unexpected, like a violent rainstorm. It was four o'clock on a Saturday but I had a large glass of wine at the breakfast bar, the sun coming in through the huge domed window, and every familiar thing gave me a surge of pleasure: the brickwork, my shelving unit, the wine glass that was a wedding present I'd kept without asking David. I had got used to it, I realised, the solitude, the joy of my work, the tentative happy hope of the early days with Oliver. I wanted things to stay the way they were.

The next day, I felt peculiar and it occurred to me that this bloated, full feeling, the feeling of things not being quite right, the feeling that made me think I must be getting my period, had been going on for some time now. I took a second test and this time I saw the whisper of a blue vein, a faint sign of life, and I started to cry, kneeling on the bathroom floor. I was still crying an hour later, for something else as well: I had spent years picturing this scene – the joy, the tearful phone calls to David, everything that was wrong between us suddenly evaporating. And this was not it. This was not what I had expected at all.

After the first scan, Oliver and I went and sat on a bench in the park near the hospital, him still in his scrubs and lanyard. I was still feeling sick and as though I had spent the last six weeks underwater. I had expected the twelve-week scan to be the moment it felt real – listening to the heartbeat, seeing the baby on screen. But as I lay on my back, flesh sticky, watching the silver-and-black image form on the screen, it still seemed abstract and surreal. They told me what they were showing me was inside me, but I still couldn't believe it.

A woman with pale skin, brown hair in a tangled greasy bob, was sitting on the bench next to us. She wore a dressing gown and socks and slippers.

'Oliver!' she said. 'You all right?'

'Yes,' he said, cautiously, steadily. I couldn't tell if he knew who she was or not. 'How's things?'

'You looked after me last week, do you remember? In A&E?'

He nodded. 'I do remember. And you're back?'

'Police brought me in this time. I'm on the open ward. I was out in my street threatening this guy with a knife.'

'Yeah, you probably shouldn't have done that,' he said, neutrally, but seriously.

'I was really unwell, really unwell. Besides, this guy, he's trafficking. He has this beautiful Somali girl trapped in his flat opposite me; it's not right. I lost it.'

'You could have called the police,' Oliver said.

'Yeah . . . You must know about snitches, though.' She emphasised 'you'. 'You call the police, the police let slip it's you, and then you become a target, don't you?'

'I can see what you mean,' he said.

She leant back on the bench and closed her eyes. 'It's shit in there. No routine. I preferred the closed ward, if I'm honest.' She opened her eyes. 'Is this your wife?'

'Partner,' he said, and it was the first time we'd used that word. 'I'm actually just on a short break right now so I can't really talk. But look, take care of yourself.'

'Yeah, you too, man. I appreciate what you did for me.'

'You're welcome. Take care.' He turned his body away from her, decisively but not unkindly. 'If it's a boy, what do you think of the name Joseph?' he said.

In that moment, I wasn't sure if I could be a parent, but I felt sure that Oliver could.

After that Thursday, Lucy and I started going to the music group every week. We did baby yoga on Tuesdays and had coffee together afterwards, filleting the class for things that annoyed us and crying with laughter. It was never really that funny, I was just hysterical with relief at being understood.

Then Lucy found another group on Mondays and asked if I wanted to try that out with her. Other days, we'd go for a coffee or walk together. We didn't see each other every day – there were family visits or weighing clinics or errands – but when we weren't together, we were messaging. Now there was a place that my circling thoughts could form – *what do I do? should I wake her? she's been sick!*

Lucy responded in the same way. A couple of weeks into our friendship, she messaged me asking if I thought she ought to give Stanley Calpol and I was astonished. All I could think was: *why are you asking me? how the fuck should I know?* It dawned on me then that she didn't understand that I was incapable, that she couldn't see it. I slowly got used to the idea, that she thought of me as someone who knew what they were doing.

Our friendship accelerated like no other friendship I'd had. In the space of a few weeks, we became each other's worlds – or rather each other's present worlds. She knew how many hours of sleep I'd had, how my milk blisters were, what kind of coffee I liked, Iris's nap pattern. We rarely spoke about work, or relationships, or anything that wasn't connected to our babies. But for the first time since I'd had Iris, I was surviving.

By the end of the year, Iris was three months old and things were getting slightly easier, as everyone had said they would, though I suspected that wasn't because Iris or I had changed, but because of meeting Lucy. Still, I couldn't say I was happy. I was still hungry for maternity leave to end. I didn't want Lucy to be my world; I wanted the real world back. At the end of March, Iris would be six months. I was going back to work, the winter would be over, the days would get longer and lighter. As 2019 drew to a close, I was counting the weeks till spring, when things would be normal again.

III

7

Ellen

1909

We named the baby when she was three weeks old. We still didn't know if she would stay, but she was different from the others, you could see that already. There was life in her. She was always wrestling, reaching and kicking, and she fed from Mother all the time, her wide-open mouth clasped to her. If it was quiet, you could hear her gulping and slurping as she fed. She stared intently at the light coming in through the windows. We called her Iris.

'She's a funny little thing, ain't she?' Mags said as we walked down the high street to get our dinner. 'I saw her the other day when Mrs Atkins was watching her on your front step. Lying in a box, farting, all red in the face with her mouth open. Like an old bloke.'

'The tiny ones give me the creeps,' Lou said. 'The way they look at you. Like they know something you don't.'

'What's she like, Ellen?' Betty said. 'Does she cry all the time?'

She didn't cry, much: if she did, she stopped when Mother fed her. Some nights, she wouldn't stop and I'd stumble into the bedroom and see Mother barely able to keep awake, and Iris squalling and fighting on the bed next to her. Mrs Atkins had said we were making a rod for our own backs if we spoilt her but the urge to pick her up was too great, so I took her in my arms, put my jacket on over my nightdress and walked up and down the passageway, where it was dark. She didn't cry but she didn't sleep either. She stayed in my arms, her eyes giant and bright, her body firm, arms and legs grasping and stretching. I sang or spoke to her in a whisper so as not to wake the neighbours.

Then, all at once, she'd change, like butter turning liquid in the pan. She went heavy, dropped into my arms, and her tiny, dimpled hand settled on my chest, fingers crooked and open like a spider's legs. Her eyes narrowed and then they disappeared altogether, only a tiny tuft of eyelashes sticking out of a heap of creased skin. The whole time I'd been walking the passageway, I'd been desperate to get back to bed, but as soon as it was possible I found I didn't want to put her down. The sky was usually lightening at that point and I sat on the sofa with her, her warm cheek melting on the skin of my chest, and I couldn't tell where I ended and she began. When I stroked the nape of her neck with my finger, I thought about my visits to Mother in the dressmaker's, and no material they had there could even come close to this: the exquisite softness of her fine dark hair on warm skin.

It was impossible to say what this was like. But I didn't need to. By the time we'd turned into the market street, they'd lost interest in Iris and were talking about Saturday night.

'Is there anything good on at The Castle, Lou?' Betty said. 'We've not seen a show for ages.'

'I've seen 'em all already, my auntie took me to the

matinee last weekend,' Lou said. 'Can't we just walk along the high street?'

'You just want everyone to see you walking out with Jim,' Mary said.

'Oh, shut up, I don't!'

'Why don't we go to The Eagle?' Mags said.

'It's too far, I keep telling you.'

'All right then, the Black Hart.'

'What do you think then?' Mary asked Lou and Betty, and they nodded and shrugged.

'Ellen?' Mary asked.

'I'm needed at home,' I said, as I always did, and they started talking about something else.

When I got home that day, there was a lady sitting on the sofa. The fire was lit and she was drinking from one of the good cups. Her gloves were pale green, with four buttons on each wrist. On the sofa beside her she'd laid a red notebook, a pen and various pamphlets, and a large card box, lidded and unlabelled. I couldn't stop thinking about how it had been made.

I guessed she was an inspector of some kind and they always made me nervous, even though I didn't think we were doing anything wrong. With the last babies, we'd been left alone, but now we had visits and pamphlets through the door. Every so often, since Iris had been born, I found papers with information about bottles or beds and I stashed them with the rest of the waste paper. I barely noticed the drawings of cots or babies as I wrapped bread in them or rolled them to light fires.

I watched her tentatively rearrange the cushions that I'd had my head on last night. I thought about sweat, flakes of skin and hair on her pale-grey skirts. I looked around the room nervously.

The rooms needed constant attention. Mrs Atkins had come in to help while Mother lay in – she refused money but after two weeks she had started asking if we could afford to get a girl in. We couldn't, so Mother said she was feeling much better and got up. She wasn't feeling much better. She still did her jobs, but she was moving and speaking more slowly, as if she wasn't ever properly awake. We struggled to tend to the rooms and Iris, and they were unforgiving. It was relentless, managing the mass of things we built up, just by being alive: tables laid and cleared, water carried in and out, fires lit and grates swept, blankets got out and put away. As soon as we'd done anything, eaten or slept or washed, we had to start work to remove all signs of it.

I took Mother's work basket off the table and tugged the tablecloth towards me to hide a stain. Mother introduced the woman as Miss Clavell, who ran a Mother and Baby Centre nearby. I sat down at the table as she asked the usual questions – wages, live births, stillbirths. I knew what we were supposed to say to these ones, but when she came to the questions about Iris – was she fed by the breast, by the clock, where did she sleep? – I didn't know what answers we were supposed to give. When Mother told her that Iris slept in bed with her, Miss Clavell explained that we could make a cot out of a banana crate.

'If you drape the material correctly, it will look just like a real cot, I promise you,' she said.

I was just starting to get fed up with her, wishing she would go so we could get the boys in and start laying the table for tea, when she leant forward and said to Mother, 'Now what have you eaten today?'

Mother looked startled. 'A bit of bread. I can't remember.'

She rested her elbows on her knees and clasped her hands. '"Feminine lunches", I call them. What woman hasn't been guilty? A woman needs a man to drive her to the saucepan and in your circumstances, my dear . . .' She picked up the box next to her, stood up and put it on the table. 'One of the ways our centres help babies is by keeping the mothers well fed. We organise community lunches on Mondays but in some cases we are able to provide parcels of food directly to the home.' She looked at Mother. 'Provided Mother is feeding by the breast, of course. The food is intended to nourish Baby.'

I came over to the table and opened the box. It was full of food, good food, bright, firm and fresh. I glimpsed the pink sheen of meat; white bone; smooth brown eggs; yellow potatoes. A frilly cabbage.

Mother stared at it warily. 'It's kind of you. But we don't need charity.'

I would not let the box out of the house. I wanted the food, and I wanted the time – the time I spent cutting and contriving the week's wages to turn them into meals, charming the grocer to put things aside for us, the Saturday nights at the market. I wanted the orange yolks, the brown gravy, the sour cabbage leaves.

Miss Clavell looked at Mother fondly, as if she was a dog that had done something clever. 'I do understand. I know many a deserving woman who feels that way.'

'I don't—' Mother began.

'Thank you ever so much,' I said. 'This will help no end.'

Iris woke and started making small moaning sounds. Mother quickly put her on the breast. Miss Clavell glanced at the clock on the mantel, picked her notebook up from the sofa and wrote something down.

'I assume Baby was due a feed?'

Mother nodded.

She gave us ideas about what to do with the food and spoke for a long time about porridge, and then she finally put her notebook away. 'I will visit you again in two weeks,' she said. She took a final look at the room. 'One last word of advice. It is marvellously tidy in here, the passageway is quite sparkling, and as for your front step, I applaud you.' I smiled. 'I'm sure you are awfully proud of your little home, but it's Baby who needs you now. Baby is more important than your front step.'

It was like being hit in the face. I felt the same rage I'd felt fighting with Eliza, quickening until it was all over my body. I wanted the food, but we would have to keep the house tidy for Miss Povey, and untidy for Miss Clavell, to find a banana crate to make a cot, make room for it in the bedroom, make porridge that no one would eat, feed Iris the way she wanted. It wasn't worth it. I thought about Mary's looks of disdain or Mags and her filthy mouth and I wanted to tell her to take her fucking food. *We don't need it, we don't need you!*

But it wasn't true. We did need it, and in the end, it would be worth it.

'We'll remember that,' I said. 'It's ever so kind of you to visit.'

On Saturday night, as I was carrying in the water for the bath, Mother saw my best jacket hanging on the door.

'You don't need to go to the market, Ellen,' she said. 'We'll have the chop from Miss Clavell for Sunday dinner.'

I poured the water into the bath. 'I'm going out with the girls from work,' I said, and then, because I knew she would find out from Mrs Atkins if I didn't say, 'They're going to the Black Hart.'

She looked at me but said nothing. I went out to get the last bucket of water and when I came back in my eye kept catching on something that needed doing – the knives, the bath, the grate. I felt sick. Iris started to complain and I lifted her out of her cot. I remembered when my dad would come home, after two or three nights away, red-eyed, foul-smelling. The piss stains on the sofa. My mother always said, 'It's worse in a woman.'

'I won't drink,' I said.

She got the towels out of the crate and put them by the fire to warm. 'Why are you going then?' she said.

'To be with the other girls,' I said. Iris cried louder and I turned around and began to walk up and down the parlour with her.

'The girls from work? The factory girls?'

'Yes, but they're not— They're decent girls.'

'I don't see too much point making friends,' she said. 'You'll be back at school once we're back on our feet.'

She was still moving slowly, much too slowly. It was as if the air around her had thickened, and it cost her to move through it. It frightened me, this change in her, but I couldn't allow myself to think about it for too long. We had survived the confinement, Iris was alive, Mother was alive. She had to be well. I had no more room in my body for dread.

I waited for Mother to stop me or say I could go, before I realised she wouldn't do either of those things.

'Ellen,' she said, putting her hands on her back and

arching upwards, turning her face to the ceiling. 'Ellen, just think, won't you, think . . .' She didn't say anything for a moment. 'We can't afford . . .' she said. 'Oh, hell! We can't afford to lose—' She sighed. 'Get the boys in, will you?'

I knew that she meant it was a stupid thing to do, a risk, and she was right. We tried all the time, we'd tried all our lives, to hide, to mend, to repair, to look presentable, to be respectable, and it wasn't just for show any more. It was for survival. The shame made me hot and uncomfortable and then it made me angry.

I went out to the street to get the boys. I was going to go anyway.

Mary knocked for me at eight o'clock, after I had bathed the boys. She looked extraordinary. Her dress was a deep purple, almost dark grey, and her hat was enormous, weighed down with ruffles and ribbons.

'Oh, look at you, Mary Cunningham!' Mrs Atkins said as we went past her on the front step. 'A man won't want to marry a vain girl, you know.'

'I won't get married then,' Mary said. 'Don't look much fun, if you ask me.'

Mrs Atkins shook her head. 'The way you've behaved since you started at that place . . . Twelve shillings a week and you think you can talk how you want.'

'Come on, Ellen,' Mary said, and we walked out of Digby Street towards the high street.

'Don't you have a dress?' she asked.

'Yes,' I said. 'But it's for Sundays.'

'I can get you one, you know,' she said. 'If you want. I run a dress club for the girls, we all order together, same pattern, and get it cheap. The bloke makes 'em out of what he can get so you don't get to choose the colour, but they usually turn out all right. We're doing it for the bank holiday.'

'Would you mind?' I asked.

We turned off the high street, down the street with the market stalls, by the fever hospital. 'The more girls we have in, the cheaper it is,' she said.

The walls of the pub were tiled in a deep red-brown, the colour running orange at the edges and almost black in the centre. Mary took us through a swing door at the side: the room was smaller than I'd been expecting, and I felt the warmth of the fire immediately. Everything shone: the beaten brass on the fireplace and the green tiles surrounding it, the tiny diamonds of stained glass at the tops of the windows, in pink, yellow, green and blue. The coloured stones in the combs in the barmaid's hair.

The room was empty apart from two men at the bar. The door swung open and Mags, Lou and Betty came in. 'All right, Kathleen,' Mags said to the barmaid.

'Turning into a bloody cowshed in here,' one of the men at the bar muttered.

'Go to the men's bar if you don't like it,' Mags said.

'If it was up to me, they wouldn't let you in at all.'

'But it's not, is it?' Mags said. 'So fuck yourself.'

One of the men stood up. I watched Mags, astonished. I knew she was strong but she was also small. She was a child. She stared steadily at him. She did not look afraid at all. Mary and Lou moved closer to her.

'You little whore,' the man said.

'All right then,' Kathleen said. 'I don't want fighting.'

Mags didn't move. I kept watching her face, looking for

a trace of fear, but it was as if she did not know what fear was. The silence went on a long time.

Kathleen said to the man sitting down, 'No trouble, please, or you'll be out on your ear.' Her voice was surprisingly harsh. He stood up and put his hands on his friend's shoulder. He was still looking at Mags. The hatred on his face made me shiver, but she held his gaze. He looked away first. Then he lifted up his jacket. 'Come on, let's go next door. I don't want to drink with a bunch of cunts anyway.'

'What did you do that for, Kathleen?' Mags asked as the door banged. 'I can look after myself.'

'I've no doubt you can but I've got enough to do without wiping you off the carpets. What are you having?'

'Come on, Mags, I'll treat you,' Mary said. 'What'll you have? And you, Ellen?'

'Quart of gin, please, Mary,' Mags said. Mary looked at me. 'Same for you, Ellen?' I nodded quickly. She leant over the bar casually and said, 'Five cups of gin, please, Kathleen,' and I watched as Kathleen took down five blue glasses and filled them with a small amount of clear liquid. Mary handed a cup to me and I took it with both hands.

As Mary handed over her coins, I noticed that the bar was shaped like a horseshoe and the room had been divided into three by ornate wooden screens. Opposite us, on the other side of the bar, there was another room, plainer and shabbier than this one. If I peered round the screen on the bar, I saw a room at the front of the bar, crowded, with only men.

I thought about pretending to drink the gin, but I couldn't do it to Mary, not when I knew how hard she'd worked for the money. I took a tiny sip and shuddered. My tongue slapped the roof of my mouth, and my throat burnt.

'What do you think?' Mary was watching me.

'Nice,' I said.

'You've got to get used to it,' she said, and I followed her to a table and chairs in the corner of the bar. The girls started talking about the bank holiday, getting louder and interrupting each other as they got more and more excited. I took another sip of gin. It was repulsive, though I began to see how the burning might feel warming, comforting.

'When's the bank holiday?' I asked, and they hooted.

'"When's the bank holiday?" Oh, Ellen!' Lou said.

'Four weeks,' Mary said, taking a cigarette out of her jacket pocket.

'How do you not know?' Mags said, looking at me as if I was the most curious person she'd ever seen.

'I don't like bank holidays,' I said, and they all looked at me as if I was crazy. 'I didn't use to work,' I said, trying to explain. 'It was just like a Saturday. We cleaned the house, went to the park perhaps.'

Dad was often on leave on bank holidays. We waited for him to come home from the pub, stewing in the heat, the agitation thickening, until we heard him at the door and Mother and I crowded round him, huddling him in before the neighbours saw, trying to persuade him, ever so nicely, to wash his face, brush his teeth and go to bed, without causing a fuss or making a scene.

'You'll have to come with us to Hampstead then,' Betty said. 'She can, can't she, Mary?'

Mary stubbed her cigarette out on the ashtray. She still had half of it left and she put it back in her jacket pocket with the matches. She nodded briefly. 'I know someone who can sort you out with money for the train.'

I didn't say anything. Mother hated debt; we were never even allowed to take an onion on tick. I was the one who'd had to take our things to the pawn shop when we moved and she still pretended she didn't know. Besides, to go out for an entire day, like my dad would have done, to abandon the house, leave Mother with the boys and Iris when I didn't have to, was unthinkable.

I sipped the gin again and as the fiery liquid made its way from my throat to my stomach it mellowed into something almost pleasant. I noticed that it was making me feel different: looser, more vigorous, lively. I wouldn't go to Hampstead but, as I listened to the girls savouring each detail of what they would wear and eat and drink, what time they would get the train, how much money they would borrow for treats, I began to feel happy.

Everything was so lovely that night – the way the firelight bounced off the coloured glass and the mirrors behind the bar, the high patterned ceiling, Kathleen's pink satin dress. The way the girls talked, the way they laughed. More people came in – mostly men, but also a woman and her young daughter. But the best thing was the way time stopped mattering. I didn't care what the clock above the bar said. I was free from the great store of hours and minutes and seconds that hung about my life.

'Fancy another one, Ellen?' Mary asked, and I said I'd treat her this time. I couldn't quite believe that I was walking to the bar. There were two young men sitting there now. I had to concentrate as I asked for the gins and handed over my coins, but nothing went awry, and Kathleen handed me five more blue glasses. I didn't even think about the money. Tomorrow, I would start counting the minutes and the coins again.

I was so pleased with myself, gathering up the glasses. I was changing into someone else: I was bold, I was bright, I was joyful. But before I turned to go back to the table, I felt something behind me. It was so quick, it was a moment before I understood what had happened, and by the time I turned round, the men were walking out of the pub. I thought it must have been a mistake. But it couldn't have been. It was so sure, so definite: one of the men had pushed his hand under my jacket and squeezed me, briefly, but hard, through my skirts. I could still feel it on my skin, as if he'd left an imprint.

All the boldness, the giddiness, went. I was not a different person after all, I was the same as I'd always been, but smaller, weaker, wet-eyed. I thought about Iris, plump legs, spine like a string of pearls, and I felt pulled towards home with a force that astonished me. I wondered when I would be able to leave.

'Ta, Ellen,' Mary said as I put the cups down in front of her. She took the second half of her cigarette out. As she struck the match, she said, 'Has Alice got the chuck then?'

'Well, she can't come into work, can she?' said Mags. 'Did you see what she looked like?'

'Oh, I couldn't look,' Lou said, grabbing her glass.

'It was horrible,' Mags said. 'Red and peeling and oozing . . .'

'Oh God!' Lou put her hands over her face.

On Friday morning, we had heard a crash and screaming, horrible cries, and the girls had rushed to the door but Mr Clifford had threatened to fine us and then give us the sack. We'd worked in a different way – agitated, nervy – all morning but I had never asked what had happened. I had not wanted to know.

'Who's Alice?' I said.

Mary took a puff of her cigarette. 'Girl on the second floor. She fell on the stairs bringing the hot water up and tipped the whole lot over her. It weren't so bad where she was wearing clothes. But her hands . . . and where it got her face.'

The water was heated in the cellar in a giant copper and we took it in turns to bring it up to make glue for the boxes. I hated that room. The steps leading down to it were steep and the wood was flimsy – it was barely more than a ladder. Two steps were missing at the bottom and Lou had told me that it was haunted by the ghost of an old foreman who'd broken his neck falling on them. She told me that, before I'd started, a girl on the third floor had set her hair on fire lighting the copper.

There were no lights in there; only a candle in a holder outside the room, which you had to light and carry in. You had to stand on a broken chair to put the bucket in the hot water, the steam burning your face. Every time I leant over the copper, I thought about falling in.

'Daft of her to drop it, though,' Mags said.

'I heard she was in the family way,' Betty said. 'And that was why.'

'Did she lose the baby?' Mags said, taking a packet of cigarettes out of her pocket. I still could not look at those boxes without remembering the hours I used to spend at home every day, folding and sticking the card.

'Course she did,' Lou said. 'My cousin lost a baby when a cow frightened her on her holidays.'

'Lucky for her, if she ain't got a job,' Mary said, stubbing the cigarette out in the ashtray.

'What will she do then?' I asked.

'Don't know,' Mary said. 'Turn tricks?'

'Not with a burnt face,' Mags said. 'And come to think of it, you might need your hands for that.'

They laughed and I took another gulp of gin. It had stopped making me feel happy. I felt lost and confused, and as if there was a great distance between me and everything I could see: the girls, the table, the firelight. I wanted my old life again. I wanted our old house. I wished I was still learning grammar and needlework, and that factories and pubs and fish shops had remained places that other people went to. I wished that I could still hear Dad coming in when I was in bed, even if he'd been drinking, even if he was being difficult, even if there was shouting and crying. At least I was used to it. I could still feel the man's touch on my skin.

'Did you see that story in the papers about the lodger who got murdered by her bloke?' Lou said. 'He told her he was a doctor and was giving her medicine – but all the time he was poisoning her.'

'I know her!' Mags said. 'Well, a woman who lives on my street knows the maid. She had to sit up with her, all night, while she was vomiting her guts up. She died early morning.' She smoked her cigarette. 'She said she had a lot of blokes calling for her, though. It was only a matter of time before one of 'em got her into trouble.'

'I don't know, Mags,' Lou said. 'There's getting into trouble and there's being done in. You don't expect your bloke to slip you poison.'

'Well, maybe she should have,' said Mary, and she stood up. 'Let's go.'

The walk home revived me and I started to feel a little

better: I was still myself, even after two cups of gin. When I came in the front door, I saw Mother walking up and down the passageway. She was pale and frantic, bouncing Iris vigorously.

'I don't know what to do, Ellen. I don't know what to do! I'm exhausted! Exhausted! If I put her down or sit down or even stand still, she'll scream and then she'll wake the boys.'

'Give her here,' I said, and the second part of my night began.

Three weeks later, we stood outside the fever hospital, drinking ginger beers from bottles.

'What if it's raining on the Monday?' Lou asked. 'Would we still go?'

It was a week until the bank holiday now and all the girls could talk about was if the weather would pick up. It was a cold, damp evening – it wasn't drizzling, but it had been on and off, all day. The pavements had darkened and droplets clung to the lamp posts.

I still hadn't told the girls I couldn't go. Their excitement had grown and grown, carrying me along with it, and I was becoming reluctant to break the pretence. I had to remind myself that getting into debt to go out on a bank holiday was the kind of thing that working girls did and we were still trying to behave as if I was not a working girl.

And Mother was still not herself, even though it had been almost two months since the confinement. Iris was getting healthier every day, and though it was joyful to watch, it was beginning to look eerie, like she was growing fat on something she'd taken from Mother. It was impossible to say what was missing – Mother still took in mending and made meals and did the cleaning, but some essence, some force had gone. It was like living with a ghost. I tried not to think about it but whenever I left the house in the mornings, the dread returned. I still went – to work, to the girls' club, even to the pub again – but the feeling of heady release as I shut the parlour door was mixed in with guilt and fear.

'Of *course* we'll go,' Mary said. 'We're not missing it because of the rain!'

'Wouldn't be much fun on the Heath, day like today,' Mags said. She was teaching Betty how to make a fist. 'No, like this, protect your thumb, that's it.'

'I don't want to be walking round all day in an overcoat,' Lou said. 'No one'll see our dresses.'

I tapped my feet, and opened and closed my hands in the folds of my skirt, because I was so tired I was scared I'd fall over if I didn't move. I was going in to Iris in the night more and more now; sometimes Mother didn't even wake up when she cried. I was often so tired I could barely stand, and I was afraid of dropping her as I stumbled up and down the passageway. Once, I thought one of Mr Atkins's rabbits had got in and swore I saw it lumbering across the floor. I tried to chase it away from Iris and then the dark shape dissolved and there was no rabbit after all. One night, I thought I saw leaves grow out of the ceiling. But then, after the horror of pulling myself off the sofa in the morning, the light and air revived me, until the next wave of desperate exhaustion or injection of restless, jumpy energy.

'My auntie says the sun always comes out on the bank holiday, however miserable it's been,' Lou said.

'Well, that's a load of fucking rubbish, isn't it?' said Mags. 'What about Easter last year? That's it, Betty, come on!'

'Oh, you bunch of . . . useless cows!' Mary said, turning round and kicking the wall. 'We are *not* missing it. I'm visiting Miss Reed tomorrow for the money and I'll tell her two shillings each.' She looked at me. 'You are coming, aren't you, Ellen?'

I hesitated. I couldn't have Mary borrowing money for me when I wasn't going. But a thought came into my head suddenly and unexpectedly: we hadn't needed to pay the midwife. I couldn't help thinking about the fee, still in the cash box, along with the money that I didn't spend at the market now we had the food. Mother didn't know anything about it. I was the one who managed our money now.

'Remember, they're still collecting for Alice,' Mags said. 'So we won't get our full wage on Saturday.'

Every Saturday, two girls from the second floor held out a tin for the girl who had fallen on the stairs and we each put a penny in it. I didn't like to think of her, but some days she got stuck in my mind and I couldn't shake her. I felt as if I could see her on the stairs, the pail tipping, her balance going, knowing she would lose everything at once: her hands, her job, her baby. And if that happened to me, wouldn't it be unbearable to know that I'd missed out on all that pleasure, all that colour, when I'd had the chance?

'All right then,' I said.

They flew at me and I stumbled backwards, letting them press me up against the wall. Lou screamed my name in my ear, Mags bit my cheek. I knew they were wild because of the holiday, but still, to be wanted, even briefly, even as a game. They let me go as suddenly as they'd come at me, and started talking about train timetables.

Mary brought the dresses to work on Saturday. She stashed the box under the workbench and I got excited every time my foot kicked it by accident. I followed the others to the back yard after work to look at them, knowing I'd be late for Miss Morton but unable to wait. When Mary opened the box, just glimpsing the fabric made my heart beat faster, and then she took them out, a mad unfurling of colour, high collars, lace, pin-tucked sleeves, billowing bodices and full skirts. One was turquoise, another purple, crimson, green stripes, red stripes. They were all sensational, but it was the red–and–white stripes that pulled me to them, a desire so strong I couldn't trust it. I couldn't take my eyes off it: so bold, so bright, so festive.

Mary chose first because she'd organised it and she wanted the purple. We pulled sticks out of Mary's hat to decide who would choose next and when we held them next to each other to compare, mine was the tallest.

At first, I didn't dare pick the red and white. I worried I'd look foolish or the other girls would hate me for picking the best one. I considered the green stripes, because it was halfway towards the thing I really wanted. But in the end, my hand reached for the red.

'Oh, I didn't think you'd pick that one, Ellen,' Lou said as Mary handed it to me and I held it close, tracing the stripes with my fingers. The others made their choices and held them up to the sky and against themselves, while I fingered the lace, the folds, the small red buttons down the front. I saw that the others all had the same white buttons, but the tailor must have found some red ones, just for my dress. Then Lou said, 'Ellen . . . do you always wear your hair like that?'

'Like what?' I asked.

'Pulled straight back. Don't you want a bit of a curl in it? For the bank holiday?'

I hesitated and she took a comb out of her pocket, pulled my hat off and loosened my hair. She stood in front of me, hairpins in her mouth, pulling my hair over my face so it tickled my skin and I couldn't see properly. I felt the teeth of the comb on my scalp and the pins dig in as she pulled it back from my face bit by bit, and then fixed it with the comb. Then she put her hat on my head.

'Oh, look!' she said, standing back. She gripped my arms and pushed me forward so the others could see. 'Look! With her hair done and a proper hat, Ellen looks quite nice.'

'Now,' Mags said, fishing in her pockets, 'look what *I've* got.'

She pulled out five feathers, white with tiny black spots.

'Mags! Where the hell did you get these?' Mary asked.

'Bloke next door, with the chickens, brought a funny bird back, like a giant chicken with spots all over it. He's ever so proud of it; you should hear the way he talks to it, like a lover. "Oh, my pet, my darling" – makes you sick. Anyway, I saw one of these in his yard, climbed over the fence and pocketed it. I kept looking out for more, but I weren't going to wait, not with the bank holiday coming up, so when he was out, I jumped over the fence, grabbed hold of the bird and plucked it.'

'You didn't!' Mary said.

'I did. It made such a noise. He'll never know, though. Don't you think they look smart?'

'They're beautiful,' Betty said, stroking hers.

'It's going to be *marvellous*!' Lou said, gripping Mags's head and knocking her forehead against hers.

On Sunday, it rained all day. I had to wear my best boots and jacket for church and dodged the puddles, huddling under one of our umbrellas with the boys. After dinner, I hung my jacket on the mantel to dry, then in the yard when there was a break in the rain, and put crumpled paper in the toes of my good boots and the top of my hat, lining them up by the fire, brushing smuts off whenever I went past.

On Monday, Iris woke me, just before five. Mother was in one of her deep sleeps, only twisting and moaning a little as I picked Iris up and took her into the parlour with me, while I dressed in my work clothes. I fed her some pap on my fingers, even though Miss Clavell had said she should only have milk till she was six months. We had no bottles and she was hungry. I put her in a crate and did some mending on the front step, watching her fold and curl. It was not raining but I kept looking anxiously up at the sky. It was covered over with dense, pale-grey cloud.

It had just gone six when I heard Mother shouting in the bedroom. I went down the passageway and opened the bedroom door. 'Iris!' she kept saying, wildly patting the bedsheets. 'Iris! Where's she gone? Who's taken her?'

'She's here,' I said. 'I got up with her.'

'Oh,' Mother said, sitting up in bed. 'Give her here.' She fed her, leaning back on the bedstead, closing her eyes. Her shoulder sagged and her arm drooped underneath Iris and I thought she might fall asleep again. I had a brief vision of her hold loosening, Iris falling on the bedroom floor, her tiny skull smashing. I pushed it away. I didn't have much time.

Back in the parlour, I went to the orange crate and carefully lifted up the tablecloths. I had hidden my dress underneath the good linen and every night after Mother had gone to bed, I'd gone over to peek at it. Even in the gloom of the parlour, the red–and–white stripes could still excite me.

I pulled my blanket round me and got dressed on the sofa. I had never put it on before and I was anxious that it might not look so miraculous as it had first appeared. The waist was too wide, which meant the fabric didn't hang as it should; the skirts were just a little too long. I grabbed some pins from Mother's sewing box and made a few tiny tucks to make it fit better. I pinned the hem crudely, thinking of Miss Morton and the way she held her skirts together with clothes pegs to stop them getting caught on her bicycle. I realised that I had missed a button at the neck and it came off in my hands as I was doing it up.

If anything was stained or torn or missing a button, we always had to take it off immediately. When things were harder, before Mother's job at the dressmaker's, she'd say to us, 'The only thing worse than being poor is looking poor.' Miss Jones at school had once praised me for my clothes in front of the whole class. 'Ellen's mother may not have much money,' she said, 'but her clothes are always clean and mended. She has made an effort.'

I looked at the clock on the mantel. I didn't have time to sew it back on but the thought of taking the dress off and putting on my Sunday best was unbearable. I wondered briefly if I would ever wear the dress again and a wave of sadness overcame me, but I had no time to be sad. Mother had a button box, but I didn't want to put it in with the ordinary buttons. I took my tea chest out from under the sofa and the key from behind the stuffed birds and unlocked it.

The tea chest had been my grandfather's and when I was about ten I was taken with it, the polished pale-brown wood, the red interior of the lid, the gilt borders. It was divided into two lidded compartments and I'd spent hours lifting the lids on and off, locking and unlocking it with its little brass key. After he died, I'd decided it was mine and held on to it, and Mother didn't say anything. I kept the little treasures that mattered to me there: a scrap of fabric I'd filched from the dressmaker's. An unusually nice stone. A London train map I'd found on the ground in the market, untorn and still readable. I had never been on a train, but I used to love tracing the railway lines, the wavy spine of the Thames, the splats of green for the parks. I loved saying the names of the stations to myself: Swiss Cottage, Brondesbury, Waterloo. Battersea Park, South Lambeth, Chelsea.

I put the button in the tea chest, locked it again and put on my jacket. It was dark grey and when I held it against the vivid red, the colours seemed to dull, as if they were sulking. My Sunday hat was not especially elegant, but Lou had given me some green ribbon for trimming and when I stuck the spotted feather in the band it looked decent. I took the comb Lou had given me and tried to curl my hair at the front the way she'd shown me and then I stood on a chair so I could see myself in the dress in the looking-glass above the mantelpiece. However much I shifted the chair, I couldn't see my whole body at the same time, so I crouched and straightened and tried to piece the different bits of myself together. I knew it was vain, but I couldn't take my eyes off her, that girl in the red-and-white dress with the spotted feather in her hat. I was visible. I was alight.

I took the hat off before I went to say goodbye to Mother. She and Iris had both fallen asleep. For a moment, I thought I wouldn't wake her, but then she stirred and looked at me, confused.

'What time is it? Are you off to work?'

'It's the bank holiday. I'm going to catch my train now.'

'What? A train? Where to?'

'To Hampstead Heath,' I said. 'I told you.' I had, but only once, when she was tired and distracted.

'Oh, yes. I remember,' she said. I didn't believe her.

'You don't mind me going?' I said, though I couldn't have stayed, even if she'd said yes.

She sat up in bed. 'What on earth are you wearing?'

'A new dress.'

'You didn't spend your wages on that!'

'I didn't buy it. One of the other girls lent it to me.'

'You look like an awning!'

She leant forward to look closer, and Iris moaned.

'It doesn't fit you properly. It's as clear as day it's not made for you. The pattern cutter's made a pig's ear of the stripes. And look, a button's already gone.'

I couldn't say anything.

'You look common, Ellen,' she said. 'I know you think you look stylish but you don't. Those girls think they're acting like ladies, I know, but I've made clothes for ladies for years, and believe me, a real one wouldn't be seen dead in something as gaudy as that.'

I was ready to run at her, hurl something, hit the walls.

Then her face turned pale and trembling, as if it had been jellied. 'You don't look like yourself,' she said, turning her face away. 'I don't recognise you. I don't know you.'

I walked out of the bedroom and slammed the door. George and Davey had put the tablecloth over two chairs and were eating their bread and treacle underneath it, giggling. I snatched it away from them.

'Don't leave that out to get filthy! Go and play if you're not going to help!' I hastily cut slices of bread and cheese and put them in a tin on the table. 'This is your dinner,' I said. 'Just come in and get it when you're hungry and don't disturb Mother and Iris.'

I stood in the parlour doorway, looking at the room, suddenly afraid to leave. Could I really go, when I was needed here? Then I heard Mrs Atkins say, 'Oh, Mary! A new hat? Your poor mother can't see any of that wage packet,' and I ran out onto the front step before I could think about it any more. I saw Mary in the deep-purple dress, the spotted feather in the gigantic hat with new trimmings. She looked wonderful.

'Ellen!' Mary said. 'Look at *you*!' I had been right after all. I did look nice. She took my hands in hers and squeezed them, and we ran out of Digby Street, hand in hand, along the high street, away from the factory, towards the station.

I had seen the track through the windows at work, heard the shudder and shriek of the train, but I had never imagined that I would go inside one, go into that dark brick building I saw on the way to church and up the stairs, clutching the small paper ticket that Mary had given me.

The platform hung high above the city, humming with people. Lou screamed our names when we arrived and Mags hugged me as tight as she could, lifting me off the ground. Lou looked us all over – 'You've made a bloody awful job of that hem, Mags,' she said – and then she asked if I wanted her to do my hair. I nodded and, while we waited for the train, she fiddled with the comb and my pins. I loved the feeling of her fingers in my hair, the little tug on my scalp as she pulled, and when she started to sing I joined in, even though I barely knew the tune and only a few words. The others started singing too, and by the time we saw the train at the end of the track, our voices were so loud it sounded demented. 'There!' Lou said, turning me round to face her as the train slowed in front of us. 'You look marvellous!' I caught my reflection in the train window before I boarded and I did. I looked marvellous. I saw a woman with a baby wrapped in a shawl and for a moment I thought of Iris, and then I didn't any longer.

The engine of the train was black, shining, magnificent. We clambered inside the golden-brown carriages, crushing each other in the doorway. The narrow wooden benches down the side of the train got taken quickly, but Lou found a gap, knelt on the seat and loosened the leather strap to open the window. She put her head out, clutching her hat, strands of loose hair whipping her face, and stayed there the whole journey. Mags snatched Betty's packet of cigarettes and ran off, dodging the crowds of people when Betty went after her, the men with their beer bottles shouting at them.

Someone touched my hand, and I turned round to see that Mary had found a space on the bench. I knelt on the seat like Lou, to see out of the window, while the train wheezed, honked and hissed. I felt like I was inside a beast. We cut through the backs of terraced houses, the roof tiles and chimneys closer than I'd ever seen them, and then suddenly we were above them, strings of miniature front doors stretching out like paperchains. I saw the names I recognised from my map: Mildmay Park. Maiden Lane. Kentish Town. Great clouds of steam curled past, light and white and clean, so unlike the grey, damp steam from the copper. And then we saw the green: leaves and branches and great flat plains of grass.

Coming out of Hampstead Heath station, I understood at once how different north was to east, with its rows of genteel little shops and red-brick cottages. We followed the crowds down a path lined with trees, the branches meeting at the top, a dome covered in leaves, and then came out onto a wide-open space.

We saw donkeys, food and beer stalls, games, rides, and as people started to wander off towards them, Mary led us even further through the Heath, past glassy plains of water. There were none of the fussy interruptions of Victoria Park – the neat little paths, lakes, bandstands, fountains – just grass and sky, the ground dipping and swelling, water pooling in puddles, rivers and ponds. Trees bursting into fountains of delicate grey-green or shocks of deep purple. And even on a dull day, it was bright, so bright. Without walls, buildings, roofs, without smoke, there was only light, more light than the factory floor on a sunny day, more light than I'd ever thought possible. The sky was colossal, everywhere, startlingly white.

We bought beers from one of the stalls and Mary laid an old sheet she'd brought with her on the damp grass. It was still not warm and the five of us huddled together on it. I didn't like the taste of the beer, but I liked the sharpness of it. Mags and Betty leapt up, running down the hill screaming, waving their arms, collapsing on top of each other and rolling down together.

Mary took off her boots and stockings, and pressed her bare feet into the grass. I copied her, shyly, my feet looking peculiar in the fresh light: the cracked white skin on the heels like smashed glass, a brown mole on the bridge of my foot, with two dark strands of hair growing out of it, the nail of my big toe mottled at the corners. I remembered my mother's story about her sister Catherine, who had taken her boots off to dance with some girls in the street and had them stolen, but the feel of the wet grass on my skin, soft and cool, was seductive. I lay back on the sheet, the earth soft beneath me, smelling the soil, and then, finally, the sun broke through the sky. My cheek felt warm as I fell asleep on the ground.

When I woke up, it was just Mary next to me. I sat up, my mouth sticky, my mind still cloudy, cold again.

'Where are the others?' I asked, wrapping my arms around my shoulders and rubbing.

Mary nodded at a group of boys at the bottom of the hill. One of them was sitting next to Lou, with his arms around her, while the others jostled and wrestled around them. Mags and Betty were with them, giddy as kittens.

'Who are they?' I asked.

'Jim's mates,' Mary said. Then she nudged me. 'Oh, don't look now.'

I turned where she was angling her head and I saw a group of girls with beer bottles. They were walking with purpose, marching, a little further down the hill to us; the girls at the back were almost running to keep up. Eliza was in the lead.

She had made an effort for the day, I could tell. She was in the same red dress she'd worn at the club, though it was in an even worse state than before. She was still hatless, though her long hair was piled up on her head. I recognised two of the girls in her gang from the club.

It had been some time since the fight and the fear I felt catching sight of her on the stairs at work or in the yard was fading. She hadn't come at me again, though I'd heard she'd been in several fights since: at the market, on the high street, by the canal. Still, I couldn't stop my heart quickening as she got closer to us. 'She don't care about the job, she don't care about anything,' Mary had said, and that freedom, that wildness, frightened and fascinated me. I didn't know what she was capable of.

When one of the abattoir girls nudged her, she looked up at me, still some distance away, with dislike and a certain haughtiness. I felt Mary tense beside me. I held Eliza's gaze, sensing that Mary was too. In the end, Eliza only spat on the ground and carried on walking.

'I don't think she's going to fight you again,' Mary said. 'She'd have gone for you by now if she wanted to.'

I knew Mary was right. I was relieved and disappointed.

'What do you want to do then?' Mary asked. 'Join the others?' She stretched out her legs. 'Or do you want to swim?'

I had seen men, and even one or two women, splashing about in the lake in Victoria Park. I had never once imagined I could join them. It seemed impossibly mad, to undress and get wet in a public park. But then I was here, on Hampstead Heath, on a bank holiday, and that had once seemed impossible too.

'I know somewhere good we can go,' she said, standing

up, holding out her hand. I reached for it and let her pull me up.

I followed her, and we walked higher and higher up the Heath. The crowds got thinner still, until we were alone for much of the walk. The stones and thistles on the uneven, unfinished paths began to hurt my bare feet. The pins were coming out of the hem of my dress and it was trailing on the ground, mud-stained. I thought again that this might be the last time I wore the dress, but now it didn't feel sad because I couldn't imagine a world outside this one any more.

I followed Mary into dark, quiet clearings between trees, where the ground was instantly damper and colder and pale light fell in stripes across the ground. We went up bright, open hills, looking down over roofs and spires. Then she led me down a track beside some woodland, separated by a wooden fence. She stopped and started to climb.

'Come on,' she said, landing on the other side and holding out her hand.

'Are we allowed?' I asked.

'I've done it before,' she said. I gripped the fence and, with Mary's help, climbed over. The trees were tall and the air was dank and cold. Ahead of us, I saw a huge pool of water, flat and brown, with patches of silver where the light fell.

Mary pulled off her hat, then her dress, then her corset and stockings, until she was entirely naked. I was unable to stop staring: another body, nipples huge like boiled sweets, curved bones under her neck and at the tops of her legs. Her thighs were dotted with red freckles, the hair between her legs was straight and red-gold. She ran towards the water, pushing back the reeds and screaming as she folded into it. I watched her head bob as she swam.

I had wanted things before but never in the way I wanted this. I was swollen with longing, craving the feeling of the water. My skin felt itchy. My hands shook as I fiddled with the unfamiliar buttons on my new dress. I edged my way towards the water in my stays and knickers and it was only thinking how brown the water looked and how I couldn't afford new stays that made me take them off too. I took out the comb Lou had given me and got closer to the water. It was only at this moment that I thought about the fact that I didn't know how to swim.

I walked right up to the reeds at the edge of the pond and stepped in. The cold water was shocking and the mud beneath my feet was deep, sucking at my skin. I took a few effortful, unsteady steps, letting the water rise up to my calves, and then suddenly the mud gave way and I was up to my chest in it. I started panting, panicking, consumed by the cold, my feet slipping beneath me. I managed to stand upright again and my breath and pulse steadied. It had started to rain: silver glints struck the surface and disappeared into the dark.

My arms looked golden under the water, unearthly, not my own. My stomach and legs were invisible, swallowed in murk. I began to want more of the cold and I dipped my chin under the surface, seeking out that pleasing sharpness, like licking a cut lemon. Black birds with red beaks sailed by and a giant bluish-grey bird perched in the borders.

I watched Mary cut through the water, wondering where she'd learnt how to do that, where all that grace and strength had come from. I thought about Lou's fingers in my hair, the way Mags's body moved when she was showing us how to fight. I was childish and foolish compared to them, but it made me so happy because there were so many things in the world to learn, there was so much to do.

Then the cold began to overwhelm me. I clawed my way out, gripping the reeds, and began to pull off my underwear, desperate to get the wet, cold cloth away from me. My flesh was red and rubbery, and my hair was wet at the nape of my neck. I stood in the sun for a moment, thinking how odd it was to be free from seams and buttons, wrinkled stockings, tough boots. A leaf had stuck to my neck, my feet and calves were almost entirely brown, and finer mud clung to my chest, like miniature tiger stripes. I saw a mole like a gravy stain at the base of my belly, just above the hair between my legs. I didn't know if I had ever seen it before.

Mary swam back to me and climbed out, and even though she was naked too, I reached for my clothes and got dressed again. I tried not to think about the fact that I wasn't wearing knickers. Mary didn't seem to feel the cold, pulling her clothes on her wet skin. Her hair was wild and tangled. I had never seen it loose before.

'Did you like it then?' she asked.

I nodded, and when she smiled again it was wide and kind, as if she took real pleasure in my pleasure. I felt like I'd never seen her smile before, not truly. As we walked back down the hill together, we didn't speak. I had no idea where we were, but I didn't care. I would have followed Mary anywhere.

We saw Lou and Mags first, on the sheet. 'Where've you been?' Mags shouted. 'What happened to you?'

I didn't say anything. I started putting on my stockings, trying not to think about how filthy they would get.

'Oh, Ellen, your hair!' Lou said. 'It's all falling down! And the pins have come out of your dress!'

'Oh, be quiet,' Mary said, sitting back down on the sheet.

I was tired, but in a different way from the way I normally felt. My arms and legs were heavy, but there was a flare inside me, a little stick of power burning. I had never been so hungry. We bought pies from a stall, crumbly and salty, but they didn't fill me up. I could have eaten and drunk all day, and I did: sharp sugary ices, crisp fried herrings, cold beers. I ran with the others. I laughed so much I felt dizzy. I watched the crowds milling and jostling, the children screaming on the rides, the men in the ponds, and it didn't seem so odd to me now, to swim in public. When we got home, I decided, I would ask Mary to teach me how to swim.

But then the clouds closed over for the last time, and the sun didn't come out again. There were spots of rain, and I felt the cold now, in my dress and jacket, the roots of my hair still damp at the back of my neck. I thought about the holiday being over, and the long stretch of days at work with nothing to talk about or plan, and a quiet horror crept over me, until it suffocated all pleasure. I started to remember home.

Eventually Mary shoved the sheet in her bag. It was streaked with mud and grass and I thought for the first time what a waste it was: it could have been saved and used for lining. We staggered back to the station and the mood on the train back was darker, more frantic. Mary and Mags argued about nothing in particular. Lou bumped into a man and he threatened to snap her neck if she came near him again. No one sang. When we piled out of the station, the East End was dirtier and smaller and more desolate than I remembered.

Mary said she'd stand us a gin in the Black Hart but I wanted to be at home. It was already much later than when I normally got back from work. The girls hugged me violently and I started to sob, strange sounds falling out of my mouth. I thought they would laugh at me, but then I saw they were crying too. Lou stroked the tears off my cheeks and kissed me. I stumbled back down the high street alone, thinking about how much I wanted to hold Iris. I felt as if I had been away for years.

I had never seen Digby Street so empty. Even Mrs Atkins was not on our step. As I turned into the street, I heard a baby crying; it struck me even though I knew it wasn't Iris's cry. The closer I got to number twelve, the louder it got, and when I went in our door I realised it was coming from the parlour. For a minute, I wondered if Mother had taken in someone else's baby, and then as I opened the parlour door and saw Iris alone, thrashing in the orange crate, I understood that the reason it did not sound like her was because it was not her usual cry. It was a howl, steeped in distress.

The noise was dementing. I picked Iris up, but she did not calm down, screaming and gasping in my arms. I went into the bedroom, struggling to keep hold of her, and I saw Mother sprawled on the bed, her eyes closed. I patted her shoulder; her eyes flickered but she didn't wake. I gripped her, yelled and screamed, and she stirred and opened and closed her eyes. Finally, she sat up, confused. She reached for Iris and I handed her over. Iris kept crying but eventually she found her breast and fed, her little mouth working furiously.

'What were you doing?' I said. 'Iris was screaming the place down.'

She looked bewildered. 'I was so tired . . .' she said. Her voice was weak and unfamiliar.

'How long were you asleep? Where are George and Davey?'

'I don't know . . . I was just tired, so tired. I couldn't keep awake, Ellen, I couldn't, so I put Iris in her box just for an hour. I just wanted an hour and then I'd see to her, and the house . . .' She looked at me, frightened. 'What're you doing back here then? What time is it now?' She looked around. 'Oh hell—' She began to cry.

'When did you put her in the box? How long has she been left?'

She started to cry. 'It was after you left, I just wanted an hour! I had to sleep for an hour! I don't know . . .'

'She's not been fed all day!'

'I don't know! I heard her crying and I tried to wake up, I tried, but I couldn't. I couldn't do it. It was like I was being held down—'

I looked down at Iris, gulping and slurping. My breath started coming more slowly again.

'Look, she's all right now,' I said. 'I'll light the fire.'

Mother was still crying helplessly.

'Oh, it doesn't matter! Stop making a fuss,' I said.

But she didn't stop. 'You don't understand, Ellen. It's my fault, it's my fault she's like she is.'

'Who?'

'Iris!'

'Like what?'

'All that's wrong with her, it's my fault.'

'There's nothing wrong with her. Or there wouldn't be if you hadn't been asleep all day!'

'I took drugs, Ellen! When I found out I was expecting . . .'

'What drugs?'

'Drugs! To bring about a slip.'

'A what?'

'To stop her coming! I tried to stop her coming. But it didn't work and that's why she is how she is.'

'She's not like anything!'

'She is.' She was crying again. 'Look at her!'

I did look at her, tiny lips sucking and squelching. Her eyes began to close and her mouth slipped off. I held out my arms for Iris, and she settled to sleep on my shoulder. The heat of her body seeped into mine like a medicine.

Mother pulled the bed covers off. 'I'll make tea. Did you eat?'

'I'll do it.'

'You've got Iris. Oh—' She stumbled as she got to her feet.

'Here.' I handed Iris back to her. 'You sit in the parlour.'

I didn't even lay the table. I cut two thick slices of bread, smeared them with treacle and handed them to Mother on a sheet of waste paper.

Her face changed as she ate; she became recognisable again. It was as if I was watching her grow another skin. I knew that we would never speak again about today, so I said, 'She's all right, you know. Iris. She's a healthy baby.'

She closed her eyes. 'Sometimes I hold her . . . and I can't look at her, I feel so guilty.'

'She's the healthiest baby we've had,' I said.

She opened her eyes and turned her face towards me.

'Do you think so?'

'Yes!' I said. 'She's fat, she's lively, she smiles. Look, she stuck up for herself today, didn't she? She was screaming the place down. She didn't give up. Not like the others. She's all right.'

She rested her head on the back of the chair and closed her eyes again.

'You won't understand, Ellen. Not now. You will one day.'

She took Iris to bed and I swept the crumbs from the chair and straightened the paper to reuse. I was too tired to get the sofa ready and I fell asleep on it still in my dress.

I woke up at two o'clock, needing to use the water closet. It was the first time for weeks I had been awake in the night without Iris and it felt so peaceful, making my way through the scullery in the dark. Then I remembered that I hadn't heard George and Davey come in. On my way back down the passageway, I gently opened the door of the bedroom and the four of them were there, asleep. Iris and Mother in the bed, both with their arms above their heads. The boys were sprawled on the mattresses as if they'd been thrown there, still dressed. I went over to the bed and crawled carefully under the covers, next to Iris. She stirred and I worried that I'd woken her, but I put my hand on her stomach to comfort her. Her eyes stayed closed as she wriggled, and then finally she was still again. Her breath slowed and deepened, and her stomach rose and fell against my hand in tiny, regular motions. I slept like that, my hand on her, feeling her breathe, till morning.

8

Frances

1984

Every day in the factory felt like a battle against the unfamil-iar. The things I had taken for granted – washing, eating, sleeping, brushing my teeth – now became little feats to be overcome. I washed with a flannel and soap, bare feet on peeled linoleum, one hand pushing on the swing door to stop anyone coming in. I lay on my mattress at night, listen-ing to the trains go by, looking at the little strips of different fabrics stitched onto the quilted wall beside my mattress, and I wondered how sleep had ever come easily to me.

We only had two hotplates, and besides I didn't real-ly know how to cook. After my father died, my mother stopped frying chops or mashing potatoes, or cooking a joint on Sundays. We ate eggs or mushrooms on toast or spaghetti with sauce from a jar, but now that it was just me, even that felt like an unseemly amount of effort. I made sandwiches mostly but I couldn't even manage my paltry little bag of ingredients: the milk quickly turned, little green spores sprung up on my sliced loaf, and I thought again how absurd the fantasy of me marrying Antonia's brother had been.

We had no telephone, but I didn't want to see my friends from school anyway. I still had my A-level results to come and I hoped that they would make me see things differently, delineate the map to the next part of my life. But the closer the date got, the less likely it seemed. I went to work, and then back at the factory I put all my energy into the constant challenges of physical existence, and I hoped that something would change.

My second Friday in the factory, I got in from work and saw Naomi kneeling on a cushion by the coffee table, chopping an onion. I went to put my bag down in my sleeping area and lay on my back on the mattress. I let myself relax for a moment, before I felt self-conscious and came back out again.

'Are you home tonight?' Naomi asked as I filled the kettle. I nodded. 'I think it's just you and me then.' She pointed her knife at the board. 'Do you fancy some of this?'

Naomi was always cooking and she always offered to share it with whoever was there. Jane sometimes ate with her; Nick and Malcolm always said no. Malcolm ate the same thing every day: toast and margarine and black tea for breakfast, ham sandwiches for lunch, and spaghetti with a garlicky tuna and tomato sauce at 6 p.m., after which he'd smoke and drink black coffee and read all evening. Nick ate whatever was on offer at the supermarket, bringing back piles of chocolate bars or cereal.

When you were squatting, I was learning, ordinary things became precious. Things I wouldn't have thought twice about at home – a cup, an onion, hot water – took on a new value, and people were always making exchanges, like an old bicycle for fixing the plumbing. I didn't feel

I had anything to offer Naomi in return for her cooking, and the idea of being in a kind of social debt horrified me, so I always said no too. That evening, though, I was tired and hungry, and I had run out of bread. The thought of eating something warm, which someone else had cooked, was terribly tempting.

'Are you sure that's all right? Can I give you money for the ingredients?'

'Don't be silly. It's nice to have someone to share it with – saves me eating the same thing twice a day.'

'Can I give you a hand then?'

'Don't worry. It's basically done. Should be ready about half seven.'

'OK. Thank you.' I made tea for both of us, took a book from my pile and sat on the sofa, while she chopped and stirred in the corner.

I wondered if I'd made a mistake when she handed me a bowl of brown mixture – glossy beans and greying aubergine poking out of the top, a few dark seeds, glinting pink, scattered over them. They looked beautiful, though not like food. But the bowl was warm in my hands and when I tentatively put a spoonful in my mouth it was unusually good. I had another one, and another, and I realised it was not just my low expectations and my hunger that made it taste so good.

'This is delicious.'

She blushed. 'Oh, thanks. It's all right, isn't it?'

'Where's everyone else?' I was scooping it in hurriedly now, unable to stop.

'Jane's at a meeting, and I reckon they'll go to the pub afterwards. Malcolm's at the cinema, I think. A film festival at the Barbican? He did tell me. And Nick's at his mum's.'

'Wasn't he there the other day?'

'Yeah, he goes back every weekend.' She looked at me. 'Did he not tell you . . . about . . . ?'

I shook my head.

'Well, I don't think he'd mind me saying . . . She's lost her mind, you know, she's not all there any more. They've put her in some kind of home. Nick visits every week, sorts the house and her paperwork out, but I don't think she even knows who he is.'

'Oh. I had no idea.' I had finished the stew and I put my spoon in my empty bowl.

'He doesn't like talking about it. It sounds like a real mess, if I'm honest. His dad died a few years ago and he's just got the one brother, who's not being much help, so it's all down to Nick.'

'That's awful.'

'Yes.' She sighed. 'Poor guy. What are you doing tonight then? Just hanging out?'

'Yeah,' I said. 'How about you?'

'I'm going to make some banners,' she said, nodding at a heap of fabric in the corner. 'Would you like some more?'

'Please.'

'Help yourself,' she said. 'There's lots.' I told myself I would just take a small amount, but I couldn't stop piling it into my bowl, until it was almost full. It was such a long time since I'd eaten hot food.

'What are the banners for?' I asked, returning to the sofa.

'I've got some friends still at Greenham,' she said, and I nodded even though I had no idea what she was talking about. 'I went there after I graduated, and I just loved it. Really loved it – that was where I met Jane and so many other amazing women. I said I'd take a break, so a group of us came to London and—' She gave a small, embarrassed smile and looked towards the window. 'A year later, I'm still here.'

She lifted a spoonful of stew out of her bowl and put it down again. 'I feel a bit stupid, you know, because I wasn't even doing the difficult stuff, the protesting, I was just in the support camp. And honestly, it was the most wonderful place I'd ever been. But then . . . It's just hard not having a home. I couldn't do it for too long. Anyway, I make banners for them and drop them there, with supplies, when I can.'

'Can I give you a hand?' I said. 'With the banners?'

'Can you sew?'

'A little bit. I can do running stich. I've never used a machine, though.'

She looked over at the pile. 'Yeah, OK. Let me just think . . . Are you good at drawing?'

'Yes!' I said, too eagerly, because that was one thing I knew I was good at.

She stood up, picking up her bowl, and I took it from her. 'Here, I can do that.'

'Oh, well, that would be nice.' She walked over to the fabric pile. 'Thanks.'

I washed up in the sink in the corner of the room while she arranged the fabric on the factory floor. 'OK then,' she said. 'Do you want to have a go at the lettering? Draw some big block capitals and then cut them out. It's not quite as easy as it sounds, but if you can draw, you should be fine.'

She had spread a rough rectangle of velvet, deep gold, on an old sheet.

'It's beautiful,' I said, putting my hand on it gently.

'Isn't it? I found some old curtains in a skip in a posh part of Islington. I used it for all sorts of things, and I've just got this bit left now.'

She handed me a pair of scissors, a triangle of white chalk and a tape measure. 'I reckon six inches high, for the letters. Give or take; they don't have to be perfect.' She got a scrap of paper out and scrawled on it 'WOMEN FOR PEACE ON EARTH'. 'You're probably not going to get all of those out of there, but I've got some other offcuts. Maybe do every other letter, so the different materials are spread out?'

'No problem.'

'I'll get the machine going. Do you want some music?'

I nodded. 'Anything.'

I smoothed the fabric out, tentatively made a chalk mark on it and rubbed it out, plastic clacking on the other side of the room as Naomi chose a cassette and put it in the deck. I began drawing, and music I'd never heard before, a female voice, began.

Naomi was right: it was harder than it seemed. The letters were rebellious: their arms sprawling, apertures bulging, the gaps between them spreading and shrinking. I felt like a child learning to do joined-up handwriting – what came out in chalk bore little resemblance to what I intended. But the work – brushing the chalk dust away, considering the line, standing back to see how they sat together – pulled me in, and then I was swallowed whole. My letters became stouter, my lines defiant. I found that a certain unevenness could actually be quite pleasing, and I worked to find the perfect measure of idiosyncrasy, half-listening to the swooping tones of the woman's voice from the cassette player and the rattle of the sewing machine.

When I had finished drawing, Naomi brought a canvas bag of scrap material to choose the fabric for the rest of the letters. She held bits out against the velvet and I could see immediately, without even being able to explain it, which ones sat best together, how the colours could change the gold from brilliant to dull.

'What about that one?' I said, picking an earthy floral pattern out of the bag.

'That one?' she said.

'Yes, look,' I said, holding it against the material. 'The gold picks out the purple.'

'Hey, yeah, you're right. Doesn't that look fantastic?' She went to turn over the tape. I spread out the floral fabric, my face burning with pleasure.

Naomi made coffee. I looked at my watch sometimes but these little interruptions meant nothing. I couldn't have stopped even if I'd wanted to; I was enclosed in the sensation of the scissors' blades slicing into velvets and silk. It was only when Jane came in that I noticed it was after eleven. Malcolm came in at midnight and we put away the material.

When I went to brush my teeth, I noticed the chalk dust on my jeans. Lying on the mattress, in my pyjamas, the music echoed in my head, and letters danced in front of me when I closed my eyes. Every emotion amplified until it felt like my body could barely contain it, joy and excitement pressing into my skin, ready to burst.

The next day, I saw letters everywhere: the cardboard signs scrawled in felt tip in the windows of pubs, the cigarette billboards, the cards outside market stalls or the newsagent's window, graffiti. 'No Travellers', '3 for £1', 'Thatcher Out!' I got back from my shift at the same time, hoping that Naomi would be there and she was. She offered to split the rest of the aubergine stew with me, and I drew and cut out more letters. She showed me some postcards and photographs she had of other banners and we talked about what sorts of images would work best: I drew doves on a fabric with a beautiful grain, so white it was almost blue, and trees on green silk. Malcolm was at home that evening, and he complained about the music until they compromised on something similar with a man singing, and he sat in his armchair, reading and smoking and getting up to make coffee.

On Sunday, we pinned the letters onto the giant white quilt that Naomi had been making on the machine, stood up and walked away to see if they were straight, got on our knees to adjust them, pinned them, and then we sat on the sofa opposite each other, the blanket over our knees, sewing.

'How are you getting on here?' Naomi said, biting a thread. 'I mean, without a bath and things. It feels like luxury after the camp, but I know it's not for everyone.'

'It's fine,' I said.

'My friend Clare lives in a squatted house round the corner – do you know Digby Street?' I shook my head. 'It's five minutes away, if that – anyway, they have a bath. I know she wouldn't mind us using it from time to time. Or there must be a Turkish bath somewhere.'

'There was one near my house,' I said. 'But I never went.' I remembered that my mother had said it was 'full of lesbians'. It only occurred to me then that that might not be true or it might not be a reason you couldn't go.

'Do your mum and dad live nearby then?'

I hesitated. I had told them I'd met Nick at the pub; I had not mentioned Antonia's party and, as far as I knew, he hadn't either. She must have known I didn't belong, not really; I couldn't hide the way I spoke, the way I behaved. But what I was beginning to like about the factory was the way it made the rest of my life – the anaglypta and housecoats and my dad's box of ghoulish hoardings – seem very far away and as if it mattered much less. And the next thing I would have to say to Naomi was, 'It's just my mum, actually,' and I found I couldn't do it, couldn't go through with another uncomfortable exchange about heart failure and how he didn't suffer, not when I felt I was starting again.

'Sorry,' Naomi said. 'I shouldn't have asked. Forget it.'

'It's not that—'

'No, it's OK, I understand,' she said. 'A lot of people you meet have a reason for squatting. Like Nick. Something to get away from. It's cool.'

I was looking down at my sewing, so it felt easier to ask, 'Is that why you're here?'

She laughed. 'Actually, no. I get on really well with my mum and dad. It was a whim, going to Greenham; a girl in my halls said she could get me a coach ticket and I thought, well, why not . . .? And when I was there, I felt different. I wasn't shy any more. I got through three years at university barely saying a word to anyone, but then there, being around all these women, they all had something to say and I felt like I could actually *do* something, change things, build a community. I still want to do that. But then you also meet a lot of people who are just into the drugs scene, or people like Malcolm who don't want to spend all their wages on rent, and I get that too.'

At nine o'clock, the door banged and Nick walked in with his suitcase. He looked at me and I immediately felt guilty, though I wasn't sure why. He strode over to his sleeping area and then came back out, going straight to the shelf by the sink.

'Got yourself a little apprentice, Naomi?' he said, opening a can of cola.

'Yeah. Frankie's been helping me out.'

'Nice for you.' He turned round and swigged from it, still watching us. Then he said, 'I'm going to take a piss.'

Naomi shook her head. 'He's always in a mood when he comes back from Surrey.'

When he came back, he took the can and a tall glass, and went straight into his sleeping area, pulling the curtains around his bed. Naomi and I continued to work, self-conscious at first, and then we started talking again in low voices.

Nick shouted, 'Girls, can you keep it down a bit?'

Naomi closed her eyes and bared her teeth, but called out, 'All right, sorry.' She whispered to me, 'Let's drop in on Clare soon.'

I had a day off on Wednesday, and Naomi said we should see if Clare or her friend Susie were at home. Their house was on a short street of terraced houses, joining two longer ones, in a little warren of residential streets. Some of the windows were boarded up or layered with newspaper, but in the middle of the row there was a house with a red front door and faded terracotta and cream diamond tiles leading up to the step. The path was buckling and there were one or two tiles missing.

A tall black woman with large wire-framed glasses

answered the door. I guessed she was about Naomi's age; she wore an orange jumper, narrow faded jeans and canvas trainers. Her curls were held with a pink band at the front, fanning out behind.

'Hello, you,' she said. 'Have you come for the bath?'

'Is that OK?' Naomi said, hugging her as she came in.

'Course. Come on in.'

'This is Frankie,' Naomi said, and Clare hugged me properly too, the way Naomi had when I'd first met her.

We squeezed past the bicycles lined up by the radiator in the narrow hallway, and Clare led us into a room on the right.

'Welcome,' she said.

'Can I go and get the bath going?' Naomi said. 'Sorry, I'm just desperate for a proper wash.'

'Go on up,' Clare said, walking out of the sitting room towards the kitchen at the back. 'I'll stick the kettle on.'

Their sitting room, a small room with a bay window looking out on the houses opposite, was a strange mix of the familiar and the new. There was a dark-grey mantelpiece, purple-and-yellow flowered tiles surrounding the fireplace. The hearthstone was cracked in two places. There was a sofa opposite the window, with the kind of pattern I might have seen at Antonia's house – pink roses surrounded by green leaves on a cream background – but there were patches on the arms where the fabric had been worn away and on one side the yellow-grey of the seat was almost completely exposed. There was no wallpaper or carpet or even curtains: the walls and floorboards had been painted bright white. Compared to my family home, with its rugs and pelmets and antimacassars, it looked nude.

On the wall next to the door, someone had made a

neat grid of nails – a tool hung on each one, with the name of the tool written in capitals in pencil below it. I walked over to the fireplace, which had roughly constructed shelves on each side, filled with books and magazines. Above it, there was a dark-brown oval mirror, with flyers and tickets tucked in the frame, the bottom half-obscured by a collection of things propped up on the mantelpiece – a record of the Slits album that Nick had taped for me, three naked women covered in mud on the front. A poster protesting a hospital closure, and various prints of different sizes: one advertising a peace march that had taken place three months ago, white block prints of doves against dark blue. The largest one, in the centre, showed an intricate line drawing of a tree, white on dark-green card, with the words 'There are so many roots to the tree of anger'. I was looking at the way the letters had been drawn, the way they sat together, the pleasingly uneven quality of the printing, when someone came in behind me.

I turned round and saw a small woman with wavy blonde hair cut in a jaw-length bob, a nose stud, and several hoops in her ears. Her jumper was huge and looked hand-knitted and her leggings were wrinkled at the knees. She had bare feet. I felt embarrassed to have been caught looking at their things, even if they were on display, so I said quickly, 'I'm Naomi's friend. I'm here for the bath.'

'Hi,' she said. 'I'm Susie.'

'Frankie.' I realised she looked familiar but I couldn't place her. 'Do you live here too?'

'Yes,' she said. She stood against the wall by the door and put her hands behind her back, as if she was folding herself away. 'Clare and I have been here about a year now.'

'It's nice,' I said, and then, to explain why I was standing near the fireplace, 'I like these prints.'

'Clare did them,' she said. 'She's really talented.'

I kept looking at her face and then it came to me. 'Do you work in the bookshop?'

'Yeah, that's right. Are you a customer?'

'I've been in a few times,' I said, looking down.

'Ah. Yes. You do look a bit familiar,' she said, but it was unconvincing. I blushed.

Then I heard Naomi on the stairs, calling, 'Come on, Frankie!'

I went up the stairs, allowing myself the briefest glance through the open doors on the landing. The back room was set up as some kind of studio, with a screen-printing table, bottles of ink and prints pinned on a washing line. The other two rooms had mattresses on the same pallet boxes that we had, white floorboards, rails of clothes and posters on the walls.

Naomi was at the top of another flight of stairs. The bath was in an attic room, under a sloping ceiling with sky-lights. There was a wooden shelf, warped and black with mould, between the bath and the wall, holding a couple of wrinkled magazines and a collection of spider plants in terracotta pots, papery tendrils diminishing into crisp brown points. Water came from the taps in arrhythmic spurts, and steam was rising off the water. Naomi tipped a bit of oil from a glass bottle under the taps.

'Take as long as you like,' she said. 'Just leave the water in for me, won't you? Do you want me to bring you up a coffee?'

'Yes, please,' I said, staring at the water.

I got in the bath and sat with my arms wrapped under

my bent knees. I tentatively picked up one of the magazines and it opened on the advertisements page, which offered rainbow jerseys, mohair sweaters, and dungarees 'with a comfy drawstring waist and slightly tapered legs'. There was an advert for something called 'a menstrual cup', which made me blush, and when I read the words 'What every woman should know about vibrators' I shut the magazine.

I sank beneath the water and looked up at the rectangles of sky above me. Naomi knocked on the door with a cup of coffee. She offered to leave it outside the door, but I was already so altered by happiness that I let her put the cup on the side of the bath, not caring that I was naked.

When I came down, the living room was full. Clare was sitting on the sofa and a black woman with short dreadlocks and a nose ring lay with her head in Clare's lap, her knees bent up. Jane had arrived and was sitting in an armchair, while Susie was curled up on a beanbag. Clare introduced me to the woman on her lap, Nya.

'Jane was just telling us about how they got into the factory,' Clare said. 'Were you there, Frankie?'

I shook my head and settled on a beanbag by the fireplace.

'So, yeah, once we found the smashed window, we were away. Though I did always say, we could have just smashed one ourselves ages ago and no one would have known—'

'I just think it's better if it's above board,' Naomi said.

'I know you do,' Jane said. 'Anyway, once we'd got the window open, Nick climbed in and let me in round the front. They hadn't even padlocked it.'

'What were you doing, Naomi?' Clare said.

'I was keeping watch out the back. And I tell you, I

wasn't even the one going in and I was still fucking terri-fied. I kept trying to smoke and I couldn't even do that, because my hands were shaking.' Naomi stood up and put a hand on Jane's shoulder. 'I really don't know what I'd do without people like you and Nick. I wouldn't have the courage to do any of this stuff.' Jane touched her hand. 'I'll go up to the bath then,' Naomi said. 'Unless anyone else wants . . . ?'

They shook their heads.

'So how did you two meet?' Jane said, nodding towards Clare and Nya.

Nya tipped her head back to look at Clare and smiled. 'The protest at the police station,' she said. 'It was my first time protesting with the group and, honestly, Clare was astonishing. Standing right in front of the horse. I thought you were going to get trampled or kicked.' She turned her face to Jane. 'But she didn't move. She didn't move at all.'

'Were you scared?' Susie asked.

'You know what, when it was happening, I wasn't,' Clare said. 'I started singing in my head – a woman at Greenham told me she'd done that, she said just to concentrate on the song and I did. I felt fine; I felt powerful. It was only when I got dragged away that I realised what was happening.'

'I was with this group in the pub the next day, having a debrief,' Nya said, 'and Clare turned up. She'd just been let go, and I was just—' She put her hand over her heart and tipped her face back again. 'I thought you were so brave and clever.'

'I just thought you were beautiful,' Clare said, stroking Nya's cheek.

'Oh God, stop it,' Jane said.

'Well, you did ask,' Clare said, and she leant forward, so that Nya had to sit up. 'Who wants to stay for lunch?'

We had lunch – red lentil soup in mismatched bowls – in a dining room behind the living room, with a round table in it, looking out into the small garden with overgrown grass at the back. Clare opened a bottle of wine. They all talked a lot, about books they'd read that I'd never heard of, the things policemen had said to them at protests, whether the different factions at the camp were a good thing or whether there should be more effort for unity. I listened, only partially understanding what they were talking about. I sometimes watched Susie, who did not say much either, though I sensed she was not shy, just observant.

Then Naomi asked Clare, 'Can you show Frankie the box?'

'That bloody box!' Clare said. 'Naomi, you're obsessed.'

'What's the box?' Nya said. 'I want to see it now.'

'Oh God, not you too. OK, fine,' Clare said. 'But this is the last time I'm getting it out.' She went into the kitchen and came back with a rectangular wooden box. 'We found this in the cellar when we moved in,' she said.

'There was so much in the cellar,' Susie said. 'I don't think anyone touched it for years. It was crammed with stuff no one wanted.'

'We're still going through it,' said Clare. 'Some of it was useful, but there was a load of old crap too. And yes, we also found this, which is going to keep Naomi happy for years.'

It had once had a lock, but the bolt had been forced out now. I opened it: the inside of the lid was red and it was divided into two lidded compartments with gilt handles.

I lifted one off and saw a small collection of things: a small red button. A pebble. What looked like a map, folded into a square. I took the lid off the other compartment and saw two pieces of pale-blue paper, folded into quarters. I unfolded them both, already feeling a sense of trespass, and saw that they were letters, on good-quality paper, written in blue fountain pen. It had the name Ellen Chase at the top, and the address of the house. Then there was the address of someone called Mrs Jonathan Maxwell in Gloucestershire, and the date: 15 December 1909. It said: 'Dear Ellen, I am writing to congratulate you . . .' I picked up the other one. It was from the same woman, dated 13 November 1911. 'Dear Ellen, I don't know why I should write now . . .' I put them down. It felt too intimate to read them.

'I wrote to the local archives in Gloucester and Hackney,' Naomi said, 'to see what I could find out about these two.'

'Naomi, you didn't!' Clare said.

'I was curious! Anyway, I haven't heard anything about Ellen yet, but there was all sorts about the Maxwell woman. She was part of a "notable Gloucestershire family", the man said.'

I folded the letters and put them back, replacing the lid. It was starting to make me feel uneasy.

'So what did you find out?' Susie asked.

'Well, she married into this family and then her husband died in the war and left her a rich widow so she became some kind of philanthropist. Apparently, they've got all sorts of stuff about her there – letters, photographs, she even wrote a memoir. I'm thinking of making a day trip, just to take a look.'

'You don't have a job, do you, Naomi?' Clare said.

'Shut up.'

'So if she's from this notable family, what was she doing writing to someone who lived here?' Susie said.

'Well, that's what I mean! That's what I want to know.'

Jane started shaking her head. 'Naomi, you have far too much time on your hands. Why does it matter?'

'I find it interesting, that's all.'

'What *difference* does it make?' Jane said, scraping the table with her unused knife.

'Well, what difference does anything make?'

'Now there's a question,' Nya said.

'Who wants coffee?' Susie said, getting up. I started clearing away the bowls and took them into the kitchen.

Two weeks later, Naomi travelled to Greenham to deliver her banners. When I got back from my shift on Thursday, the room was empty, Naomi's fabric folded in neat piles by the sewing machine. I realised I felt lost without her; she was almost always there, cooking or sewing or knitting something, and I'd come to rely on the companionship. I tried to read, but I kept picking up the book and putting it down again, wandering over to the windows to look at the rooftops and washing lines, filling the kettle and forgetting to put the hotplate on, picking up the small scissors on Naomi's sewing table and slicing the air with them, jumping when a train went by.

When Nick came in, I was embarrassed, but he didn't seem to notice that I was aimlessly wandering about. He was carrying a Sainsbury's bag; he put it down on the kitchen table and got out a packet of Quavers and a can of cola. He opened the bag, walked over to the sofa and held it out to me. I wasn't hungry, but I took one, to be polite.

He went to the cupboard to get a glass and a bottle of vodka. Since I'd moved in, he had stopped coming to the pub, though he was still out for most of the day. I didn't know if he'd changed his hours or just went somewhere else to drink. Perhaps he thought it was too much, to see me every day when we lived together.

'Where's Jane?' I asked.

He poured the vodka into the glass, a bigger measure than a double. 'Some meeting: feminism, anti-racism, something like that.'

'Are you not going with her?'

'Not really my thing. I don't mind planning stuff, doing stuff, but it's a sitting-around-talking one. All that "Have you read that book, isn't everything terrible, wouldn't it be lovely if everything changed?" Not for me.' He poured the cola into his glass and then squashed the can between his hands. 'I'm a man of action, you could say.' He held up the glass. 'Want one of these?'

I shook my head and he came and sat opposite me. All at once, it felt unbearably formal to be alone together, without the constant interruptions of customers or dirty glasses.

'I feel bad that I've not really seen you since you moved in,' he said. 'Are you getting on OK? I mean, it looks like you like it, since you're still here.'

'It's great,' I said. 'I love it here.'

'You and Naomi are getting very pally.'

'I really like her.'

He didn't say anything for a moment. He took a gulp from his glass and then said, 'I suppose she filled you in on where I go at weekends.'

'Yes,' I said. 'I was sorry to hear about your mum.'

'It is what it is.'

'Is she very ill?'

'Her mind's gone. I mean, she's completely doolally, has been for ages now. Sometimes she knows who I am, I think, but most of the time it's just gibberish. But she's happier now, she's just accepted it. She doesn't panic so much any more. I still go and see her because . . . well, what else do you do?'

'How long has she got . . . to live?'

He laughed. 'How long have any of us got? She could outlive me for all I know. I mean, she's not going to get better but she's not getting worse, not at the moment. She's just stuck. And I'll be going back and forth between here and there for as long she stays that way.'

Another train went by. He looked towards the window. 'It sounds horrible – and I wouldn't say this to too many people – but it's almost the worst part, having to be in two places at once. When I'm here, I want to be . . . in it, you know, and every time I feel like I'm getting close to something, it's back off home again. Sleeping in my childhood bedroom. Back to being the person I was.' I guessed he must have had something to drink before he came in; I recognised the loose, maudlin way of talking from the pub, after he'd had two drinks. He started tapping his hands on his knees. 'I feel like I can't settle anywhere.'

'I know what you mean,' I said, and I did.

He looked at me. 'I sometimes think we're quite alike in that way.'

'Really?'

'When I first met you, at that stupid party, I thought you were just one of Violet's Sloaney mates. And you're not like that, are you? You've got more depth. But you don't really strike me as one of Naomi's gang either.' He looked at me and smiled. 'I mean, apologies if I've got you wrong there too, but I don't really see you as an activist.'

I smiled weakly. 'Maybe I just don't fit in anywhere.'

'Well, join the club,' he said, leaning back in the chair. 'Join the fucking club.'

We were still for a moment. I felt sad and deflated. He was probably right. I loved being around Naomi, Clare and Susie, even Jane, but I didn't understand half of what they talked about and I rarely spoke about myself. Nick was the only one who really knew anything about me.

He got up suddenly. 'Have you ever taken a look round the rest of the place?'

I shook my head. I never liked thinking of all the empty space below me. I knew the others found it exciting – they talked about meeting spaces, workshops, community lunches – but when I passed the closed doors on each floor, I had to stop myself thinking about the cavernous unknown rooms behind them, and took the stairs two at a time.

'You want to go exploring?'

'Why not?' I put my book down. The idea was gently frightening, but I had nothing else to do. Perhaps if I saw what was behind the doors, with Nick there to protect me, I would feel happier, knowing what was underneath.

'Come on then.' He grabbed the torch we kept above the sink. 'I've got something to show you. I think you'll like it.'

On the other side of the window where Jane and Nick smoked, there was another room the size of ours: the same eight giant windows, brick walls, rafters. It was half past eight and the sky was losing light now; the streetlamps and the windows of the houses were beginning to glow against the navy sky. It was uncanny seeing a room the same as ours, but without us. It was empty, only a few abandoned sheets of newspaper on the floor. One of them showed a faded picture of a blonde girl with no top on, the stripes of a shoeprint across her torso.

'This one's ready to go,' Nick said. 'We could do anything here. We could even have another bunch of people living here if we wanted. But there's three other floors underneath us. We've barely got started. Come on.' I followed him down the stairs.

I lost my bearings quickly after that. Occasionally we found a room with strip lighting, but often the only light came from the moon, casting oblique shapes through the giant windows, or Nick's torch. The walls and ceiling liquefied into shadow. We walked in and out of rooms, through a haze of corridors and stairwells. Sometimes, it was so dark that I lost all sense of space; I missed steps, crashed into walls.

So much remained. Long metal lockers with overalls hanging in them, a sink with splatters of rust, like bloodstains. In the corner, a bloated pile of white fabric, perhaps someone's shirt, and a pair of black loafers. Empty metal shelves, hooks hanging from the ceilings, scattered paperwork, a filing cabinet. Cardboard boxes, litter. Shelving lay drunkenly on one side, coils of rope spilling onto the floor, a chair without a seat. There was an open cupboard with old sheets of paper cascading out, light and creased and yellowing like old skin.

In one of the rooms, there was a mattress and a blanket, and a cassette player.

'Someone obviously got here before us,' Nick said. 'But they haven't been back, so . . .'

When we got to the ground floor, we opened the door to the room at the back that had flooded. The water was completely still, glinting in the moonlight, a liquid floor. We went outside. There was light rain on my face. Nick showed me the yard in the back, filled with rubble. Something dark flew past my face and I jumped.

'Bats,' Nick said. 'Look.' I looked up and I saw dark shapes in the sky, darting and flitting.

'I've never seen bats in London,' I said.

'They like the rubble,' Nick said. 'They like destruction. Come on, this is what I wanted to show you.'

Back inside, Nick led me to a door at the bottom of the staircase. He opened it and there were seven or eight concrete steps, leading to a cellar. I could only just stand up in it, and Nick had to crouch. He turned on a switch on the wall and strip lights just above our heads began to flicker. Only a few of them were working; odd bands of harsh white light and the rest in darkness. It was full of junk. Desks and filing cabinets, notebooks and telephones. An old-fashioned cabinet with lots of drawers.

There was a doorway at the side which led into a clearer space, covered in dank carpet. Nick could stand up in it.

'What I was trying to say upstairs, Frankie,' he said, and I knew he was drunk now, 'is that I'm sorry if I get moody, you know, after the weekend . . .'

'It's fine, honestly,' I said. 'I understand.'

'It does my head in, being around all her stuff. I should get rid of it but she's not dead, is she? I sort through a bit at a time but it never really makes a difference. I don't know what to do with half of it.' His voice cracked. 'There's stews she made in the freezer.'

'At least you've still got her things,' I said. 'And you've

got the time to decide what to do with everything.'

He shook his head. 'You don't want time. Seriously, Frankie. We cleared my dad's stuff right after he died, in those first few weeks when you're too crazy to think about what you're doing. We should have done that when she went into the home, just got rid of everything. But the moment's gone now.'

We were still for a moment. It was cold and I wanted to go back upstairs, but he made no signs of wanting to leave.

'Has your mum sold the house yet?' he asked.

'We had an offer,' I said. 'It seems to be going ahead.' I rang my mum every week, from the phone box near the station. There was one closer to our house but I chose not to use it. I told her that I was fine and said a few things about my week, but there was so much she couldn't know about my life now.

'It sounds like your mum's moving on. That's good. Jesus, I'd love to move on. But I understand it's not great for you, seeing the house go, if it's where you grew up.' He turned to me. 'Do you miss your dad? Sorry, stupid question: of course you bloody do.'

It was a stupid question, but in another way it wasn't: I still had to think about my answer. Fond memories of him came into my head all the time – often unexpectedly, like an assault – and I felt a desperate, sad kind of longing, but also anger, vivid burning anger, because the lies he'd told us, the other life he'd had, made the memories seem cheap and fake.

Nick looked at me, and there were only a few seconds when I realised what was about to happen, how close his face was to mine, how intimate the conversation had become. He kissed me. His mouth felt strange but not unpleasant.

I had only kissed two men – and Violet, though I tried not to think about that – and as I moved my mouth against his, I worried that I would betray my lack of experience. Then he began clawing at my clothes in clumsy but definite movements, and I realised how stupid I had been.

The kissing didn't mean anything. He was an adult, I was an adult now, and adults didn't kiss: they had sex. At some point – moving in to the factory, going to the cellar with him, talking to him about his mum, kissing him – I had agreed to this.

I swung between pleasure and disgust. There was some sensation there, but the reality of what was happening kept intruding: his saliva cold on my nipples. His skin on mine felt intense and alarming. I was cold. I didn't want to undress. Sometimes he did something that felt good and I felt a kind of relief, but then he stopped doing it and I wouldn't have known how to ask him to do it again. He pushed against me and there was a moment of collision; I panicked that my body was letting me down, that he would think I was frigid. But finally he was inside me on the damp floor.

Kissing Nick, it turned out, was just like all the other times I'd found myself unable to refuse things. It was every invitation to a party I dreaded, every drink I didn't feel like, every conversation that bored me, every time I'd laughed at a weak joke. It was no surprise, really, that I let him kiss me, no surprise that once he was inside me I just waited, hoping that he would move and make it more comfortable. Sex with Nick was a culmination of everything I'd ever been taught. It was the way I'd been built. When it was finished, I wiped his semen off my thighs, suppressing a gag, so that he wouldn't think I was rude.

9

Amanda

2020

Oliver was aware of it first. He started bringing hand sani-tiser home from work and insisting we wash our hands after collecting the post or taking in online shopping. He bought dried beans and yeast and flour – 'just in case'. I was barely skimming the headlines now – stuff about cruise ships, quarantines and cancelling events. It felt like reports from a distant world: something there, not here.

At the end of February, I was holding Iris outside the bathroom while Oliver brushed his teeth before work. He wasn't talking much and I asked if he was OK.

'Just didn't get much sleep last night,' he said, rinsing the toothbrush.

'Oh. Right.'

'I know you had less sleep than me. And I have tried giving her a bottle—'

'I know! I know you have. And it doesn't work and it just makes things worse, because she knows I'm in the room because we only have one room and I know that's the situation, and I know there's nothing either of us can do about it, but it doesn't make it any easier to get by on three hours' sleep. It doesn't.'

'I was awake last night, you know. When you were with Iris. I know I'm not feeding her, but I'm lying awake, worrying about you, what's going to happen when this thing hits, what's going to happen at work, how we're going to protect Iris . . .'

'Well, I'm sorry for you, but also, when you say that, all I can think is, I would just fucking love to be able to lie in bed while someone else dealt with Iris. Even if I wasn't asleep. Just lying in bed not doing anything, while someone else took responsibility for her, that would be fucking amazing. And you know, after a night like last night, I would give anything – anything! – to walk out of here at six-thirty in the morning and go somewhere else for twelve hours, I would just fucking *crave* that—'

'You wouldn't last five minutes in my job. Especially not at the moment.'

'The difference is, people respect you! You get paid! You're doing something people consider worthwhile—'

'You think people respect me? Everyone hates me. Everyone in triage hates me because they've been waiting for hours to get seen, everyone in the corridor on a trolley hates me, and I don't blame them, of course I don't, because I would be angry too, but it's exhausting being the target of that every single day—'

'You said yourself you feel like a hero at work sometimes. I mean, Jesus, a hero, that is just so far from . . . To go from feeling like you matter, like people see you, to . . . to walking down the street with a buggy, and at best I'm irrelevant, invisible, but then I try to do something like get on a bus or feed Iris and all of a sudden you're in the way or you're doing it wrong or you're taking up too much space . . . I feel like I'm disappearing! You don't understand – even I don't understand why it feels like this—'

'No, no, you're right. I can't possibly imagine what it would be like to walk down the street and people make a snap judgement about you, based on a single thing about you. I have absolutely no idea what that feels like.'

'OK, fine, but—'

'Look, we've done this before. It doesn't get us anywhere.' He came out of the bathroom and put his coat on. 'I'm going to be late for work. What are you doing today?'

'Visiting my nana.'

'Is that a good idea?'

'Yes. Why wouldn't it be?'

'Why do you think?'

'So, what, she's never going to see her great-granddaughter again because of this . . . virus?'

'I'm just saying, be careful. Maybe don't hug her. Maybe she shouldn't hold Iris.'

'Oh, for God's sake, Oliver!'

'Look at the modelling. Look at the modelling. It's terrifying, and it's one thing lying awake at night thinking about intensive care units in the car park and food supplies, but I cannot cope with your *denial*—'

'Well, I can't cope with your . . . panic room stuff!' I said. 'Can't we just deal with it when it comes? Oliver, I'm barely getting through each day. I can't start prepping for the apocalypse as well, I just can't.'

'I'm going to be late for work.' He picked up his keys and left the flat.

I was shaking with anger when I got Iris dressed but, stepping out into the high street, I felt better, the way I always did when I felt the air on my face, even if it was cold, even if the sky was grey and seemed to hang over us like a tent. I sat in the park by the hospital and had my coffee and croissant, looking down at Iris, the sugar slowing my adrenaline while the caffeine dredged me awake.

My nana was still in the same flat she'd lived in all my life and if I looked at the pale-yellow and pink tiles in the hallway in the right way, they could still make me feel excited, as if something incredible was going to happen. It usually did – sweets, bacon sandwiches, and when I got older, cash, slipped into my hand for 'a couple of ice creams'. My mum always drummed it into me that Hackney was dangerous, the estate even more so – *don't use the lift, be careful in the hallways, don't go on the main road, don't play in the back gardens* – but nothing could shake the feeling of safety and happiness when I was inside her flat. It was only later that I noticed things like the dirt on the wall above the tiles, the cobwebs hanging on the hexagonal lamps.

Most of the block was privately owned now. There were one or two middle-class couples, with a taste for bicycles and mid-century furniture, but mostly the flats were tenanted. On one side of my nana, there was a family with four children; on the other side, different people came and went all the time. When the door was open, I'd seen mattresses in the living room.

The iron gate that had been in front of the door for years, the gate my mum begged her to remember to keep locked, had been removed after Grenfell, but her outdoor shoes were still just outside the front door. Each door had a little niche in the frame just outside it – sometimes people put tealights in them or postcards; there was a couple who were artists, who had some weird agonised little paintings in there. My nana always had a china figurine of a girl in a pale-green dress striding out, with 'Thursday's Child Has Far to Go' written on the base – she'd bought it when I was born on a Thursday, like her.

She answered the door, beaming, in pale-grey slacks with a sharp crease down the front, and I thought how much smaller she looked, hunched under a pale-blue jersey. She started crying as soon as she saw me with Iris – my mum said she had been crying a lot recently. I pushed the pram into her living room and followed her into the kitchen, where she was filling the kettle and I saw plates with sandwiches and sausage rolls, enough for a party, all covered in clingfilm on the table. It was ten o'clock and I guessed they had been ready for hours.

'Nana, I don't think I can stay for lunch. Iris'll need a sleep, so I'll have to take her out.'

'Oh, it don't matter, I just didn't know if you'd be hungry.'

'To be honest, I'm hungry all the time now.'

'There you go then,' she said, and she took the plate of sandwiches into the living room and unwrapped them on the coffee table. She took the chair and held out her arms and said, 'Give her here then.' I hated waking Iris when she was sleeping but I couldn't think what else I could do except pick her up and hand her over. I sat on the sofa and reached for a ham sandwich, cut into a triangle. For a moment, I saw the bread, the ham slices and the processed cheese through Oliver's eyes – *you don't know what is in that stuff*, he'd say – and then I ate it, and another.

She lifted Iris up and down and made faces at her. 'Oh, this takes me back. Your mum was still living here when she was pregnant with you, you know. You were here when you were in her tummy.'

Sometimes I tried to imagine it: how she'd brought up three children here, with the tiny kitchen and no garden, and then lived here with my mum and dad, three adults in this flat. I thought about me and Oliver greedily hunting down extended kitchens and I felt ashamed.

'How's her daddy? How's Oliver?'

'He's fine. Working hard. It's a tough winter at the hospital.'

'He's a hero, you know.'

I ate another sandwich.

I settled back into the sofa. I was so used to being tense now that in the rare moments when I relaxed I was keenly aware of the physical change, the way everything loosened. Everything I could see in the room brought a rush of fondness and pleasurable nostalgia – the 1950s sideboard, the cocktail cabinet that was never opened, the oatmeal carpets – each thing layered with overlapping, connecting memories. Oliver said that my voice changed when I talked to my nana, that I sounded more East End, though she still teased me about my 'posh telephone voice'. I wondered why I hadn't brought Iris here before and realised that it was only since meeting Lucy that I'd felt strong enough to cope with it – the thought of managing the stairs and the often-broken lift and the narrow walkways with the pram.

Iris started to wriggle and kick her legs. 'Oh, you're a strong one, aren't you? You're a fighter, aren't you? Just like your namesake.'

I'd known we had a relative called Iris, who my mum and nana talked about fondly, though I couldn't quite remember what was so interesting about her. It had been in the back of my mind when we'd chosen the name.

'Was Iris your aunt? Or great-aunt?'

'A cousin. My dad's cousin. Iris Chase. She was a doctor, and in those days it was rare to have a lady doctor, never mind one coming from round here. You'd have to fight to get yourself that kind of education. My dad said they was the posh relatives, you know, her mum had the haberdasher's, but they still wouldn't have had much. And she worked through the war, you know. I can't remember all the stories now, but I remember the way my dad used to talk about her, ever so proud.'

'That's right, I remember now.'

'I'll have some pictures of her somewhere.' She handed Iris back to me and went over to the sideboard. 'I've still got all the boxes, you know, from my dad's, and there'll be something in there. She was in the newspapers a few times and a family like ours, getting in the papers, you wouldn't throw something like that away. He'll have kept it.' She started opening and closing drawers and taking out boxes; I could tell she was getting distressed. 'I just wish I could remember where . . .'

'Nana, don't worry about it, honestly.'

'Next time you come, I'll have them for you.'

She brought the sausage rolls through and sat Iris on her lap, and it almost made me cry, seeing them together. We talked about Iris and what my mum was like as a baby, and what I was like, and a bit about coronavirus – 'It'll take more than a virus to finish me off, don't you worry.' But then Iris started to fuss and my nana said, 'Oh dear, you want your mum back, do you?' and we tried passing her back and forth, but I knew she really needed to sleep.

As I was packing up the nappy bag, my nana came back with a little plastic envelope that the bank used for coins, filled with notes.

'Here you are, love, you and Oliver get yourself a cup of coffee.'

One of the things I liked doing best with my nana was teasing her about how decadent my life was – she pretended to be appalled when I told her David and I had bought a dishwasher or spent thirty pounds on cinema tickets. Whenever I got fish and chips delivered, I tried to remember exactly how much it cost so I could shock her with it. But she knew that you didn't need a wad of notes to buy two coffees, not even at the sort of places that I went to.

'Nana, come on. This is way too much.'

'I don't need it, I don't spend anything.'

'Well, save it then.'

'Buy Iris something nice with it.'

'She's five months old, she doesn't need anything. Save it for a rainy day.'

'I have savings, thank you. I'm going to be absolutely fine.'

I had once tried to talk to her about the cost of care, how it would obliterate her savings, but it hadn't gone well, unsurprisingly. I took the notes and put them in my handbag, feeling guilty and ridiculous and loved. 'Thank you.'

She nodded towards the sideboard. 'You know everything's in the top drawer, don't you, for when I die? Everything you need is in there.'

'I know that, Nana. But you're not going to die for ages. You're a strong woman. Like Cousin Iris.'

'Well, just in case.'

'You'll outlive me. You'll outlive my Iris.'

'Oh, I hope not!' She came to the door and blew me kisses as I pushed the buggy into the lift.

When I came out of the block, I saw the fish and chip shop opposite. I could never believe it was still there. My grandad used to go across on Friday nights when I stayed over and we'd eat it out of the paper on our laps, as a treat. I'd sleep in the spare room next to my nana's sewing machine and then have as many bacon sandwiches as I could eat in the morning. In the early days with Oliver, we were walking down the high street together, talking about what it used to be like in Hackney when we were growing up, what we missed and what was still there, and he told me he still had a soft spot for the little 'fish and chip shop opposite the estate. We used to go there a lot. I think it's still there, really blue eighties lettering.'

'You mean the Frying Machine?' I said.

He stopped walking and turned to face me. 'You've been to the Frying Machine?'

'Something of a regular.'

He started laughing and kissed me. 'You're perfect! You're actually perfect!'

A week later, I found out I was pregnant.

The next morning, I was up with Iris at 4 a.m. I saw I had a message from Lucy, sent a couple of hours before. *Hello from the night feed. Weather looks terrible tomorrow. Do you want to come for tea and cake at mine?*

'I'm going to Lucy's house today,' I said when Oliver got in from the night shift.

'Oh, right.'

'I've never been before. I want to see what it's like.'

'Didn't you say she lived on Digby Street? It'll just be one of those Victorian terraces we've seen hundreds of already.' He went into the bathroom to brush his teeth. I turned back to the living room and started texting Lucy on the sofa.

'I'm sorry, I'm just so shattered,' he said, coming in from the bathroom. 'It was a horrible shift. I need to go straight to bed.' I didn't look up. 'If you do go to see Lucy, make sure you sanitise, won't you?' he called down from the stairs.

I had sometimes walked down Digby Street, trying to guess which house was hers. It was an unexceptional street, the kind of terraced houses with bay windows that you saw all over Hackney, but I still found it impossible not to process the details, taking a mean satisfaction in expensive things I didn't like.

Lucy's house was number twelve and I expected it to be one of the glossier ones – anthracite paint and wooden shutters. In fact, it was slightly unkempt. I struggled with the buggy over the path up to the front door; the ground was uneven, buckling and erupting under the faded red and cream tiles, and there were several diamond-shaped cavities of dirt where a tile was missing. The front yard was almost entirely filled by a wonkily constructed metal bike shed.

Lucy came to the door and let me in to a narrow hall-way, which curved around a steep staircase ahead. Iris and I squeezed past two buggies, various hats and coats hanging on pegs along the wall and rows of shoes under the radiator. I followed Lucy into a room on the right.

I realised I'd had a clear image of her living room: big

open spaces, the kind of minimalist Scandinavian aesthetic that I'd coveted online. But, in fact, it was oddly old-fashioned: a small front room, with a sofa (one I recognised from being aggressively advertised in the supplements of the weekend paper) opposite a bay window. There was one other chair, a standard lamp with its paper shade slightly askew, and the curtains were a splashy seventies print of browns and oranges. There was a dark wooden oval mirror above the fireplace.

We hadn't said who would bring the cake, which I knew meant we both would. I'd left the house especially early so I could go to the café near baby yoga because I knew she liked their Portuguese custard tarts, and then I remembered that she'd said something about trying to cut out gluten, and that her flexitarianism sometimes encompassed veganism, so I went to another café, and got two different cakes, just to be safe.

'Oh, very nice!' she said when I got them out: little miniature creations with peaks of fondant and petals on top. She pulled out a Percy Ingle carrier bag and put some iced buns on the table. I'd tried too hard. Of course, the cruder thing would turn out to be posher.

'I'll put the kettle on,' she said. 'Is it OK if I leave Stanley here?'

'Of course,' I said, thinking, *as long as he doesn't do anything*, and she put him on his back on the playmat.

I sat on her softened sofa, looking at the houses opposite, and listened to the kettle boil at the other end of the hallway. Iris fed for what felt like less than a minute before she pulled away crying and a fine white jet of milk sprayed on the sofa. I tried to get her to latch back on, but Lucy came back while I was struggling with her.

'Sorry,' I said. 'I don't know why she keeps doing this.'

'Oh, Stanley's doing that too,' she said.

'Don't you find it really—' She finished my sentence for me, only she said 'annoying' at the same time as I said 'distressing'.

'Annoying, distressing, yeah,' she said. 'Do you want to pass her here?'

I did, and Iris went quiet.

'Magic touch,' I said weakly.

'Different touch,' she said.

'This is a lovely house.'

'Thanks,' she said, and she sounded slightly awkward.

'How long have you lived here?'

'I actually only moved a few months after Stanley was born,' she said, and she still sounded evasive. Finally she said, 'It used to be my aunt's. She died a few years ago, which was really sad, obviously, but she left the house to my mum and she gave it to me.'

She seemed ashamed of owning the house, trying to pass it off as a random bit of good fortune, as if having family members who could hand down London houses like cutlery was just a quirk of fate. I was suddenly jealous – all Oliver and I wanted was a house like this and she'd just been given one. It was the way I felt when someone's relative or godson walked straight into an internship on a national paper, which then turned into a job, after I'd spent years on local papers, writing about escaped cats who'd been found after three months or local schoolboys who'd won a competition. I didn't know if it was justified any more, this feeling: I had my flat, after all, and although, unlike her, I was proud of owning my home (I liked to think it was my work ethic, my persistence), it really had been good fortune that David and I were able to buy a flat in Highbury before prices got out of control and he'd been fairer than he needed to be in the divorce. I sometimes caught myself in the local deli, wearing the same jeans as the woman in front of me, discussing orzo recipes with the woman behind the counter, exactly as if I belonged in this life, not really knowing how I'd ended up here or whether I was play-acting any more. Iris started grizzling again and Lucy handed her back to me.

'It was squatted for years before she bought it, but she got lucky – the squatters had made quite a nice job of it. Everyone thought she was totally crazy moving here in the eighties.'

I didn't say that my grandmother had lived here her whole life, that in fact the story about how she made tea for the squatters when they moved in next door in the eighties was one that we told again and again. I didn't say that I was almost born here, because I knew when not to make things uncomfortable.

I had been standing, absent-mindedly rocking Iris while we spoke, and I realised that she had closed her eyes in my arms. I very gently moved to the sofa and turned Iris round so she was resting on my front. She wriggled but stayed asleep. I exhaled.

'Here,' Lucy said, passing me my tea. She sat down next to Stanley, who was still on his back on the mat, and handed him a toy.

I had thought that all of maternity leave would be like this – doing something you wanted to do, only with a baby beside you – but in fact these moments were rare, exquisite. Mostly, when she fell asleep it hamstrung me: keeping me pinned to the sofa or walking in the rain, flicking back the muslin to put a hand on her chest. If there was something I wanted to do – have a conversation, eat or drink – she was awake, needing something immediately.

'Where's Chloe?' I asked.

'Oh, she's staying at her mum's.' Lucy looked down at Stanley on the mat and started playing with his fingers. 'She does that quite a lot now.'

'Is her mum helping out then?'

'Seems to be. Chloe didn't know if she'd really be into it, her mum. The grandparenting thing. She had Chloe super young, she's only mid-fifties and she looks, like, younger than me. She's certainly cooler than me. But anyway she loves it apparently. Chloe goes to stay with her, well, every couple of weeks now, so it must work. I said I wouldn't mind if her mum stayed here, but I guess she likes it there.'

'Has your mum come round?'

'Yeah, when Stanley was born. They're a bit further away, my parents. And she and my dad have always been pretty clear, since I told them I was going to do this. They said they'll come and visit, but they've done it once, raising children, they're not doing it again. They're not going to be, you know, full-time grandparents, which is totally fair enough. I mean, I'm a feminist, I can't complain about unpaid domestic labour and then go round extracting it from my own mother.' Her voice changed; she sounded on the edge of some darker emotion. 'Everyone says to you, "Oh, could a relative not come and help you? Can someone not help you out in the night?" – like there's this army of old women who are totally happy just to go round changing people's babies and doing their washing-up. Not everyone has someone like that and anyway, why should they? The women, I mean? Maybe they want to have their own lives now.'

She looked down at Stanley. 'You know that really annoying thing, when you're pregnant, and everyone looks at you with a face full of doom and a knowing glance and says, "Ooh, enjoy it while you can"?'

'Very much so.'

'OK, well, imagine how much worse it is when you're going to be a single mum. I was *infuriated* after a while, like, come on, it can't possibly be as hard as all that. It doesn't *look* very hard . . .' She laughed. 'And now— And now, I mean, I can't say I wasn't warned, can I? I can't say I didn't know it would be hard or I didn't know I'd be doing it entirely on my own. My mum said she wasn't going to be a proper granny and yet there was just this tiny part of me that thought . . . maybe when he was here . . .'

She smiled wryly and stood up and took her cup of tea from the mantelpiece. 'I'm too optimistic. That's my trouble.'

'That's nice. That's a good thing.'

'Optimistic, naive. Same sort of thing, isn't it?' She sipped her tea and looked down at Stanley. 'She has been to stay a couple of times, Chloe's mum, and she's not really here for me, but she's fun to have around and it's good having an extra pair of hands. She's this really famous fabric designer . . . You might have seen her on Instagram.' She got out her phone. 'Let me see if I can remember her name, it's different to Chloe's. Ah-ha! Here we are.'

She passed me her phone and there were squares of dark, intense fabrics: octopuses, leopards, ships, on dense colours, with the name Violet de Lacey written above it.

'Very cool,' I said, handing back her phone.

'This is one of hers,' she said, walking over to the sofa and picking up a cushion. 'Apparently she was this real wild child before she had Chloe – she's got all these amazing stories about how she saw Bowie live, that sort of thing. And now it turns out she's number-one granny.' She looked at the coffee table. 'God, sorry, you haven't even had any cake. Here, I'll do you a plate.'

She started cutting the cakes and buns and putting them on the plate for me. I thought about how Oliver would react, knowing that she hadn't washed her hands, that I hadn't washed mine. I had reluctantly put some hand sanitiser in my bag, but there was no way I was going to ask Lucy to use it or wake Iris by getting up.

'Are you disappointed?' I said as she passed me the cake. 'With how things turned out?'

'Disappointed . . .' she said. 'I mean, yes. I'm also angry a lot of the time.'

'With Chloe? Or your mum?'

'Well, I can't be angry with Chloe, can I? She doesn't owe me anything and I'd probably do the same if I were her. And my mum and dad – like I said, they're just doing what they always said they'd do. I'm angry with . . . society? With myself? Like, how did I fuck it up so badly? I feel like I've done something stupid and selfish, and I'm letting him down already.' She gave her head a tiny shake. 'It's not that I wish I hadn't had him, or that he wasn't here, it's not that, it's just sometimes what's needed from me feels so huge and I don't feel up to the job. Not remotely. And that just scares me so much . . .' She looked up. 'Sorry. I'm not usually so depressing. It's just there isn't anyone— Isn't—'

'I know,' I said. 'I know.'

Soon, it wasn't just Oliver: everyone was talking about the coming apocalypse or quarantining, though usually as a nervous joke. I still thought they were being melodramatic. It wasn't until the second week in March that I started to accept that something really was happening.

We went to a singing group on Friday and the woman running it said, 'Well, I would say see you next week, but of course we don't know if we'll be here next week.' Some of the women at the group joked about setting up a forest school for when the nurseries shut. I thought, *thank God Oliver's taking parental leave*, and wondered idly whether this thing would mean I couldn't go back to work, but the thought of endless maternity leave just seemed too improbable, too nightmarish, to be real. When I went into one of the local shops, they were talking about whether they ought to install a Perspex screen.

On Saturday, Oliver had a day off. I'd said I would get up with Iris because he'd had so many night shifts the week before, but he was awake at six. He kept saying, 'We have to make a plan, we have to make a plan,' so I suggested that we take Iris out for her nap in the morning. He stayed with the pram when I went into the coffee shop and I was already starting to feel different, aware of the space between the people in the queue, the ghosts of other people's fingerprints on the cups, the door handle.

'You can still see people outside, though, can't you?' I said as we walked towards the marshes. 'I thought it couldn't spread outside.'

He looked at me like I was mad. 'No. No, Amanda, that's not true.'

'Oh.'

'They've already locked down Italy. And now France. They're saying you're going to need passes to leave the house.'

'That's ridiculous!'

'It's not ridiculous. It's true.'

'But that's not going to happen here.'

'It is going to happen here. And I'm going to be exposed to the worst of it. I have no idea how dangerous it's going to be, and Iris . . . she's still so young. I don't know if I can stay in the flat with you.'

'What? Where would you go?'

'My sister's? Her spare room's in the basement. I could isolate there.'

'Oliver, this is crazy.'

He shook his head. 'I've been thinking about how to do it, all week, and there's no way we can live in that flat together and not . . . be contaminated. People at work are talking about getting tents and sleeping in the garden and we don't even have a fucking garden!' His voice broke. 'Also, I don't know if I can bear it. To be around her and not— hold her.'

I gripped his hand on the handle of the buggy. 'Oliver, we'll work something out. Besides, I'm going back to work in a couple of weeks. You're going on parental leave.'

I saw him looking at my hand. I took it away. 'Amanda,' he said gently. 'I don't think that's going to happen.'

My mind was working furiously, trying to make sense of things he would never understand. I had pieced together a bearable existence, a mechanism made out of baby groups, coffee, fresh air, sleep in the buggy, and Lucy. I knew these things sounded meaningless to anyone else, but they meant survival to me. I didn't have the resources to start again. I thought of the early weeks of Iris's life, standing in the rain, wishing I could call Oliver, knowing his phone was in a locker in a hospital corridor somewhere, thinking about what it would be like to walk with the buggy out into the traffic. I was not going back there again. I couldn't.

On Monday, I went through my usual routines, but life was already beginning to feel different. Everything had taken on an unstable, temporary air. I noticed a tent had been erected in the hospital car park for coronavirus patients. I walked around the streets, not quite able to understand what I was going to lose, only knowing that I would lose something. I angled the pram into the lift – back to the flat for the home straight: tea, bath, bed – and as I was feeding Iris on the sofa, looking out at the window, I re-membered the last time I had felt this way: the final days of pregnancy.

By Thursday, there was no bread left in the supermarket and a queue outside the artisan bakery. Lucy and I talked about whether we ought to stockpile Calpol. The singing group was cancelled, so we walked on the marshes instead and every person we passed was talking about it – *they're going to close the schools tomorrow – so they'll lock us down next week, I reckon – the little place on the corner has loads of para-cetamol left.* We sat on a bench, looking at the acres of green and the city ahead, and we talked about whether we could see each other any more, if we could go for walks 'but just keep really far apart and not face each other'.

On Friday, when the schools closed, and Oliver left for work at six-thirty, I let Iris chat to herself in the cot while I went downstairs, took out a notebook, got out my phone and looked up suggestions for things to do at home with a baby. Someone on Instagram talked about filling a plas-tic crate with beans and letting the baby play in there: a 'sensory bin'. I wrote: *free play? make a sensory bin?* I didn't even have a plastic crate. Oliver would go crazy if I used our dried beans. I shut the notebook.

Lucy and I hadn't answered the question of whether we could still see each other — we were still talking about a hypothetical scenario, even though it was almost upon us. But there must have been some understanding between us not to suggest meeting up because neither of us did. I wanted to, so much — I kept reaching for my phone — but I told myself I needed to practise being by myself indoors. I needed to know if it was possible.

I took Iris for a walk in the morning so she could sleep. The café was now takeaway only and I did not go in. It felt strange walking with no purpose — I realised how often I tried to tack an activity or errand on to taking Iris out, to make it feel as if I was achieving something — but this time I simply took her down to the park and round and back home to the flat when she woke up.

Manoeuvring the buggy in the lift, down the corridor, through the door, past the breakfast bar, folding it up, putting it under the stairs, had not got much easier in the past six months. It was 10 a.m. and my day's activity was over. I put Iris on a playmat while I read the book that Oliver had bought about baby-led weaning. I boiled beetroot and carrots and put them on her tray. She sucked two of the carrot sticks and one piece of beetroot. The book had said that this counted as success because she had tasted and engaged with them, but it didn't feel like it; it felt like a crushing waste of time and energy. She threw one of the carrot sticks on the floor and I trod on it. I went to get a cloth.

It wasn't so bad, clearing carrot off the floor, or it wouldn't have been if I just had to do it once, if daily life now wasn't a relentless cycle of things erupting and me restoring them – milk on the sofa, carrot on the floor, shit on the hat, piss on my leggings. I thought about what Oliver would say if I tried to tell him just how depressed and angry the carrot on the floor made me, and how he wouldn't understand – that somehow, taken together, these constant tiny frustrations amounted to something larger and darker.

Everything I saw depressed me. The cot sheet and sleep bag and Babygro that I'd put in the machine this morning because her nappy had leaked in the night; the tiny leggings and vests and giant socks on the drying rack that I needed to take off before I could hang them out; the pan full of livid pink water on the hob; the bib that needed sponging. Iris was starting to get fussy because she was tired.

I tried to get her to nap in the cot because if next week we weren't allowed to go out, we needed to practise. I could get her to sleep in my arms but, unlike at night, she woke up when I put her down. I tried a few times – getting her to sleep in my arms, putting her down, her crying, picking her up, getting her to sleep again, putting her down – and in the end I had to put her down in the cot awake, not because I really thought she would go to sleep, but because the frustration, the desire to be anywhere else but here, was turning into anger, pure rage, and I was afraid of it. But it was a mistake because although my desire to leave the cot, to be by myself for just a minute or two, was overpowering, as soon as I got downstairs she started crying and the desire to go back up was equally strong. I tried not to give in to it, because she might fall asleep by herself and the books said that this was part of nap training and anyway I needed to wash up, but I couldn't wash up, it turned out; I could only sit on the sofa with my knees up and my hands over my ears. I went up after five minutes.

Getting her out of the cot, putting her in her pram suit, getting her in the buggy, felt like defeat. I was tired, so tired, and hungry because I hadn't eaten since breakfast. It felt like a point of pride not to leave the house a second time so I planned to wheel her up and down the corridors, but she was crying a lot now and I didn't want to annoy the neighbours, so I took her down the lift to the car park below the flats.

We rarely used the car, but the bin room was at the back of the car park. It was almost always empty, and desolate: if I saw anyone else – a figure in the shadows, coming out from behind a concrete pillar – I felt a sharp injection of fear before I recognised one of the tenants, holding a plastic bag full of cardboard. This time, I rolled the buggy up and down under the electric lights, the sound of her crying magnified by the echoes, tears falling down my face. When she finally fell asleep, I was shaking. I didn't want to risk waking her by taking her upstairs, and besides, I didn't want to be in the flat. I sat in the corner of the car park with the buggy and got out my phone and messaged Lucy.

She replied instantly: *I miss you too!! Yeah, it's going OK so far. Chloe and I keeping each other sane. But now she's saying if there's a lockdown next week, she doesn't want to be in London and she doesn't want her mum to be on her own so she might go and stay there for a few weeks. Makes sense I guess but I'm freaking out.*

I messaged her back and told her about walking in the underground car park and it felt a little bit better, having told someone about it. When Iris woke up, I went back up to the flat and I folded the clothes on the rack and put the others out and washed up and boiled some more vegetables that she could hold in her hands and then threw them in the food waste bin when she didn't eat them. I messaged Oliver with a photo, saying, *not a fan of broccoli!*, even though I knew he wouldn't pick it up. I bathed her and fed her, waiting for her to fall asleep in my arms, judging the exact moment to put her in her cot, getting it wrong, picking her up again, trying again, getting it right. I went and sat on the sofa and cried, silently, so as not to wake her, feeling like the walls of the flat were getting closer.

When Oliver came home, at seven-thirty, he wouldn't touch me until he'd taken his clothes off and put them in the washing machine. He started crying on the sofa because he said he was so afraid and I didn't go to him because I didn't know whether I ought to touch him and also I was annoyed that he was crying so loudly when I had had to do it silently because I didn't want to wake Iris. My phone buzzed and I looked at it while he had his face in his hands. I saw Lucy's name and the words: *this might sound like a really weird idea but if there is a lockdown and Chloe does move out . . .* I felt a surge of excitement and then I was floored with utter relief.

Lockdown was announced on Monday and I emailed work asking if I could extend my maternity leave. On Tuesday morning, I packed a bag and Oliver and Iris and I went down to the car park. We had made the plan – for me to go and stay at Lucy's and for him to isolate in the flat – in only an hour. After all the prevaricating the week before, it had all happened almost instantaneously.

We had spoken very little all morning, beyond practicalities. It was only when I was buckling Iris into the car seat, not looking at him, that he said, 'I think you're being selfish.'

'What?'

'You don't seem to care that you're moving out. It's like you're looking forward to it.'

'You were the one who said we needed to live apart! It was your idea! This is the most practical way of doing it. You don't have to put your sister at risk, I don't have to be stuck in a tiny flat by myself.'

'But we're not going to see each other. For weeks.'

'What do you want me to say? I don't know what the other options are! I will go mad if I have to stay there by myself, Oliver, and it's dangerous for you and Iris to be near each other . . .'

'I know, I know. You just seem excited about living with Lucy.'

This was the moment, the moment that had undone me and David, when someone knows you so well that you can't hide anything from them. I did care about living apart from Oliver, but not enough. I wanted me and Iris to survive more. And he was right: I was excited about living with Lucy.

'You seem to be pretty happy about taking her away from me . . .'

'I'm not taking her away from you! This is the whole fucking problem, isn't it? I *have* to be with her, so if we can't be together then . . . what do I do? Believe me, I wish every day I had your . . . freedom, but I don't, and I don't have the capacity to mediate your relationship with her as well. You have to do that. And I know it's hard at the moment—'

He laughed. 'You have no idea, no idea *at all*, what my

job has been like these past few weeks. You have no idea anyway – you think work is . . . lunch with some Westminster aides or whatever – but this has been the worst winter I've ever had to deal with and then I come home, and time with Iris is just taking her out so you get a break and I'm on the marshes at five a.m. with a pram and I can't even see her because she's covered in a cloth like a fucking . . . *parrot*, and I think, is this what fatherhood is? Not interacting with her, not even seeing her face? I want it to be more than that, to be so much more than that, and I have no idea how to get there. But you don't know anything about this because I don't think you care about me. I honestly don't. I think you care about Iris and that's it now. And this fucking *Lucy* woman—'

'Lucy's there! She's there every day, when you fuck off to work!'

'Well, you just seem to be enjoying your time with her an awful lot, for someone who's claiming to have this existential crisis about motherhood.'

'Well, you know what? I think you enjoy it too. Your job. Oh, I know you complain all the time about the shortages and the cuts, but I think you love it. Saving lives. Being a hero. Sometimes I think you're more like your dad than you know.'

'You bore me,' he said. 'When you go on about Lucy and her stupid clothes and her fucking placenta or whatever, I'm bored. You bore me.'

I had been here before as well. The moment you know exactly the right thing to say to hurt someone. I suppose I knew Oliver and I would get there eventually. I just hadn't expected it to come so soon.

★

We didn't speak on the car journey. It was only when the car slowed on Digby Street that my anger began to dissolve, though it didn't turn into anything remorseful or generous: it turned to fear. I had known Lucy for five months and now I was going to live in her house, with instructions not to leave it, indefinitely. I had only visited once; I hadn't even been upstairs. I tried to take Iris's car seat out of the car without waking her, but of course it didn't work and I resigned myself to the fact that the day would now be a little worse. When Oliver lifted her out and said goodbye to her, I had to turn away. We mumbled goodbye to each other and he kissed me on the cheek. I lifted Lucy's door knocker.

In the last few days, I had thought about nothing else apart from how to orchestrate this precise situation. But it was only now I had got what I wanted that I realised how little I knew Lucy. I didn't know if she had brothers or sisters. I didn't know if she'd ever been in a long-term relationship. I didn't know what she used to do for work before she'd started her business, or what she liked to eat in the evenings, or what she would wear to a party. When she opened the door and said hello, she was slightly too loud and slightly too jolly, and I knew she was thinking the same thing.

'Here, come on in,' she said, and I put my bag and the car seat in the living room. 'I'll *show you to your room*,' she said in a stagey voice, and I carried Iris up the stairs, which were carpeted. Compared to the stairs in the flat, it seemed like a soft-play area, and I realised the weight of anxiety I held every time I took Iris up to bed or downstairs in the morning, fingers gripping, feet placed deliberately, catastrophe stuck in my head like a jingle.

'So me and Stanley are in here,' Lucy said, gesturing to

an open door at the front of the house. I saw an oval cot and the corner of an unmade bed, a dummy and a bendy giraffe on it. 'And you guys can go in Chloe's room – old room – next door, if that's OK.' Chloe's room overlooked the garden, with a double bed and a travel cot next to it, a small dark-grey fireplace with earth-red hearthstone tiles. It was tidy and plain, but clearly someone else's room – there were pictures above the bed, clothes on a rail, a few bottles still on the bedside table.

'This is great. I really can't thank you enough for this,' I said. I could not imagine living here.

'Oh God, honestly don't thank me – I would go crazy on my own.'

We walked back out into the landing and she pointed out her studio at the back of the house. 'Not that I've been in there for – God, nearly six months now. It might just end up being Stanley's room.' She gestured to another flight of stairs. 'Bathroom's in the attic, I'm afraid. Dodgy seventies conversion.' We turned to go downstairs. 'I'm sorry it's still a bit ramshackle. I had all these plans when I moved in here – get rid of everything, knock through, extend the loft – but I didn't know how long it would take to get pregnant – or crucially how much it would *cost* to get pregnant – so I ended up not really doing anything with it. But in some ways I quite like it. Loads of the stuff was here when I arrived. I quite like the history.'

For the rest of the day, we did what we normally did, the carousel of milk, purées and naps, everything feeling slightly more forced and difficult in unfamiliar circumstances. I felt anxious all day about whether Iris would sleep in the travel cot, but after an agonisingly tense bedtime, she did. I felt exhausted from the strangeness and when Lucy suggested I have a bath while she made supper, I said yes, if only because a bath was a novelty after three years in a flat without one.

The bath was positioned under the roof, with a wooden shelf between it and the sloping ceiling. Lucy had put scented candles in glass jars on the shelf, along with succulents in geometric concrete clumps. I moved the fancy silicone bath toys out of the way and I put down a glass of wine and a book I had been pretending to read for six months. I watched the sky darkening through the skylight, and I wondered if I had ruined it all with Oliver, for no reason at all.

'What do you miss most?' Lucy asked me, two weeks later, as we walked towards the river, Stanley in the sling and Iris in the pram. We did this walk every morning now and I still disliked this part of it, seeing the grilles, darkened windows and closed doors of the shops and cafés.

'I miss swimming,' Lucy said. 'I mean, not that I've been since Stanley was born, but now I really want to.'

'I miss cafés,' I said.

Lucy liked this kind of conversation – every day we made lists of things we would do when we could. But there was an understanding that we had to say things that were small or trivial. We weren't allowed to say 'family' or 'work'. I never said 'Oliver'.

Oliver and I had stayed angry at each other for a couple of days, sending brusque text messages about logistics, and it quickly became exhausting. I knew that we needed to keep in touch so that he could see Iris on screen. We cried on the phone to each other and apologised and said I love you again and again, but there was a limpness to it all. We knew that we hadn't resolved anything. When it worked with his shift patterns, I video-called him with Iris before she went to bed, and it left me with a dull kind of misery that I had to shake away.

It was usually easier when Lucy and I reached the park – the empty roads felt peaceful, if slightly eerie. It was more crowded than the streets, though, and we had to keep contorting ourselves to keep space between us and the dog walkers and other parents, jumping nervously at a jogger's heavy breathing.

'Playgrounds,' Lucy said, as we passed the roundabout and the slide with tape wrapped round them. 'Stanley's only been on the swings once.'

When we came back from the walk, Lucy set up a play-mat in the living room – they were both sitting up now but not crawling, and there was a window of time, after they'd slept and before they got too hungry, when they were happy sitting together, only needing a small amount of intervention. I went to the kitchen to boil vegetables for their lunch.

The day before I'd moved in to Lucy's, I'd tried to buy bread and I couldn't find it anywhere, so I'd brought some of Oliver's flour and yeast with me. The bread I made was serviceable and the salt-free breadsticks I made for the babies, using a recipe from Oliver's weaning book, were nothing like breadsticks, actually pretty disgusting, with a wet, almost cake-like texture and a pale, limp crust. But Stanley and Iris ate them anyway. 'This is great, Amanda,' Lucy said about the bread, and even though it wasn't, that was enough to make me feel pride in it.

When I made food for the babies, I was usually making

something else as well. I made the food of my childhood: cottage pie and macaroni cheese, Black Forest gateau and trifle. Lucy had a piping bag and one afternoon I made misshapen éclairs, with obvious holes where I'd filled them, while Iris sat in her highchair watching me.

Lucy was exactly the same, only she made things that she thought would save us, and the planet: things with pre-soaked beans and no animal products. She had an organic veg bag delivered and we agreed that one of us would go to the shops once a week, which I performed like a raid, jumpy, every movement loaded with potential disaster. We talked incessantly about what ingredients were available and which weren't. My old life of swaggering in and out of shops, throwing avocados in a basket, tapping my card, fifteen pounds here and there, now seemed very far in the past, a distant era of insane extravagance.

That day, while the broccoli was steaming, I decided I wanted to make the chocolate cake that I used to make at my nana's house. I rang her and asked for the recipe and she told me she couldn't remember where it was written down but that she'd find it for me. She sounded anxious and I wished I hadn't asked.

'Don't worry about it, it was just an idea. I can find a chocolate cake recipe anywhere.'

'I'll find it. Drop it round when I go to the shops.'

'What? I thought your neighbours were getting your shopping.'

'Well, it's ridiculous, her doing that for me, when she's got all those little ones to look after. I told her, they'd have had to put me in the loony bin if I'd been stuck in that flat all day with the three of mine, never mind four. So I just ask for a few things, you know, because I don't want to trouble her, and the rest I can just get myself.'

'But you're not supposed to leave the house. I'll go for you, if you don't want to bother this woman!'

'I'm not having you doing that. I should be helping *you*, you've got a baby, Oliver's at the hospital all hours, you're living with a stranger . . .'

'Nana, it's dangerous for you—'

'Oh, don't be silly. They used to call this place Murder Mile, you know. When the squatters moved in next door, I made them a cup of tea and helped them carry their boxes. I said I'd rather have you lot than those junkies in the stairwell. And when your mum went on about their hair and the way they dressed, I said, "Julie, what does it *matter* if a fella's got long hair? Or if a girl's got a ring in her nose?"'

'Nana—'

'When the council wouldn't do nothing for us, I mopped the floors myself. Me and the little girl with the ring in her nose next door, we cleaned the urine and what-have-you from outside the door every morning. And your mum moaned about it but do you know where I was brought up—'

'I know, Nana, the bottom two rooms—'

'The bottom two rooms of a house by London Fields. No bathroom. No kitchen. We had to have slipper baths. This was before the war, but it weren't that long ago, not really. My dad went to school barefoot because he couldn't afford shoes. That's where you come from, you know. And then your mum complains about this place, but I said, "It's a damn sight better than some of the places you could have been brought up, let me tell you—"'

'I know, I know, but this is a different situation.' Iris starting fussing and I looked at the broccoli on the stove. 'Look, I've got to go, but please, please just be careful.'

Mostly, I tried to ignore any feelings of discomfort about the virus. When I saw masked figures walk past the bay window or heard the words *you must not leave your house*, I was stoical, defensive, the way I always was when I got bad news. I told myself that we would be protected – by our age, by our good fortune. It was distasteful to worry when there was real tragedy going on.

But there were things that were difficult to think about. The numbers. The thirty-eight-year-old mother who died within forty-eight hours of contracting coronavirus. The six-week-old baby; the thirteen-year-old dying alone in a room. The healthcare workers who had died, whose faces had started appearing in the paper or on posters in people's windows, most of them non-white. The ease and speed with which everything I knew and relied on could be taken away. The undetermined chunk of Iris's childhood that she would never get back.

I didn't want to think about any of this. I started making a banana cake instead.

Iris wouldn't sleep in the cot for her lunchtime nap, so I went on another walk with nowhere to go. I noticed that another café had opened up for takeaway, the one run by the two Turkish sisters, and I went in to get a coffee, excited by the novelty. They had started selling groceries and I picked up some oat milk for Lucy. I thanked the woman who served me slightly too profusely and talked to them for slightly too long. 'Me and my sister, we're not lazy, you know?' she said, and there were tears in her eyes. 'We've worked hard for this. I don't want to lose it.'

Eventually, I found myself at the bookshop on the main road, where my nana used to take me when I was little. The sign on the door said 'Closed' but there was a woman in there, in her fifties, her long brown hair streaked with grey and pulled back in a messy chignon, wearing jeans and a cashmere jumper over a Liberty-print blouse. She came to the door when she saw me peering in. I stepped back, to give her some space, and asked if they were open, even though they clearly weren't.

'We're not, but if you email us with an order, you can come and pick it up. Or we'll deliver it if you're local.'

'Does Digby Street count as local?'

'Digby Street . . .' She smiled. 'Yes, that counts. Here—' She wrote down her name – Frances – and email address on a piece of paper and handed it to me. I noticed holes in the elbow of her cashmere sweater and the wrinkled leather of her brown brogues. 'I suppose there's a better way of doing that now, but old habits.'

Peering behind her into the bookshop, I felt like I was going back in time. It was smarter than it had been twenty years ago, of course, but I could still see the slightly dingy carpet, the plastic carousels of children's books, the rubber-lined step at the back where I used to sit reading by myself, Nana waiting patiently for me.

I heard Iris cry in the buggy and my mood changed immediately. I think Frances saw it on my face.

'Oh dear,' she said. 'I would say to come in and feed her but I don't suppose we can—'

'No,' I said. 'No. I'll just walk back with her, it doesn't matter.'

She bent over the pram and made faces at Iris, rattling

her toys, which stopped her crying long enough for me to gather my resources and rethink my entire afternoon.

'Do you have children?' I asked Frances, hoping for a point of connection.

She shook her head. 'It wasn't for me,' she said with a touch of sadness, and I felt incredibly stupid.

When I got back to the house, I saw our next-door neighbour, a woman in her sixties with a blue silk headscarf, coming out of her house. She asked me to wait and went back inside, coming back with a plastic bag full of fruit, saying, 'For the little ones.' I nearly cried as I thanked her. When I got in the house, I saw that a folded piece of paper with my name on it had been put through the door. I unfolded it and saw the chocolate cake recipe, in pounds and ounces, in my nana's curling handwriting, as familiar to me as the lines on her face.

Lucy was in the kitchen chopping garlic. Stanley was still napping and I had to suppress a surge of jealousy. 'I left some clothes out for you on your bed,' she said.

The weather had changed suddenly – we'd gone from stuffing Stanley and Iris into pram suits to thinking about sun cream and hats – and I realised that I hadn't packed anything appropriate to wear. Lucy had offered to lend me some things. I took Iris upstairs and she sat on Chloe's bed while I tried Lucy's clothes on. I didn't feel especially hopeful – it had been months since I'd liked anything I'd worn. My maternity clothes – the little heap of soft, stained and durable fabric in the two empty drawers that Chloe had left – were starting to feel more and more dispiriting. It wasn't only the weather: I was changing too. Some of my favourite outfits that I'd worn in Iris's early days, and which I'd thought looked quite nice, now made me feel depressed.

Lots of Lucy's clothes weren't right but there were one or two things that would do – a sleeveless blue shirt dress, a stripy T-shirt. I picked up a dark-green printed shirt and could see from the label that it was one Lucy had made herself. It didn't look like the kind of thing I normally wore – too smock-like, too unstructured – and I thought, *I don't know about this, Lucy*, as I did up the buttons and pulled the cuffs down. But when I saw myself in the mirror, I felt a glint of excitement.

After months of stretchy jersey, the light fabric felt cool on my skin. I liked the wildflower print. I liked the colour. I liked the pin-tucks at the shoulders. I liked thinking about Lucy making it. I sized up how it would work with Iris – it was dark enough that it wouldn't show up stains and the print would disguise it anyway; it buttoned at the front so I could feed her.

I looked at myself in the mirror for probably a bit too long. I could recognise my own reflection again – not entirely, but it was certainly getting more familiar, connected, at least, to the person I was before pregnancy, before Oliver, before David even. There was a continuous line running through us all. But as much as anything, I was simply enjoying having something new to wear. I hadn't felt that kind of ordinary, uncomplicated pleasure for months, and I gasped with relief because I'd thought it had gone forever.

After we'd given Stanley and Iris tea, and bathed them upstairs, I sat on the end of Chloe's bed, holding Iris in my arms as she fed, feeling her body grow heavy and watching her eyelids droop. Soon, I knew from the precise angle of her eyelashes that her eyes were closed, not closing, and I knew from the weight of her body that it was safe to slip my finger between her lip and my nipple. She started as she came off the breast but I held her close and she grew heavy again. And then, from the way her arms fell, the sound of her breath, the movement of her chest, I knew it was time to try to put her down. And though I'd been waiting for this moment all day, I stayed on the bed, as I did every night, just staring at her face, fixated on the beauty of her slightly parted lips, the swell of her cheeks, the swoop of her dark eyelashes. It was an astonishing privilege to watch her sleep.

It was only the fact that she might wake up – and then contentment would switch immediately to untenable frustration – that made me stand up and gently place her in the cot. I held my breath but she stayed asleep, even as I switched the light off and closed the door gently behind me. Lately, I had been getting it right more often than not.

It was a strange kind of expertise, which sometimes worked and sometimes felt like no use at all. An arrangement of skills that I had learnt, painfully, all by myself, unknown and useless to anyone apart from me, and they would remain that way forever. The hardest thing about the past six months was that everything that was important to me in that time, everything I had worked at – it was all destined to go unseen and unacknowledged. I would go back to work and pretend it had never happened, go back to talking about other things, the things that mattered. The feeding, the sleeping, the love, the attention – no one would ever know or care about any of it, apart from me and Iris. The best part of living with Lucy wasn't being able to walk out of a room to go and get something, or going to the loo by myself, or having someone to talk to when I was pushing the buggy. It was having a witness.

After we'd eaten together and Lucy had gone to bed, I rang Oliver in the attic bathroom, to say goodnight, whispering so as not to wake the babies. I got into my pyjamas and rubbed in the sticky paste-like hand cream I'd bought online, but it seemed to have no effect on the red raw patches on my wrists and fingers that had appeared after only a few days of constant handwashing. I crept downstairs and into Chloe's room. Iris stirred, making a strange keening wail that I was starting to understand meant she was barely awake. I got under the covers and lay there for a moment, sick with adrenaline, waiting to see if it would turn into a full cry of distress, but she stopped, and then, as the silence continued, my heart gradually slowed and I could breathe more easily.

I turned onto my side, wondering how long I would have in bed alone tonight, before Iris would wake up and I would put her in next to me, despairing at committing to the half-sleep I got when she was with me, and at the same time delighting in the feel of her tucked in next to my stomach, the place she'd slept when she was newborn, the place she'd slept when she was inside me. Just before I went to sleep, I congratulated myself on getting through another day, another marker in this strange endurance event. And then I thought about getting up in the morning and doing it all over again and I felt so happy.

IV

10

Ellen

1909

By the time September arrived, the bank holiday felt like a dream. Mother still looked hollow and limp, but when I got home from work Iris was happy, and there was always a full crate of shirts and trousers for George to take to the tailor's on Saturdays. He'd come back with more, and no messages. We kept the house in order. Iris grew and grew – she could grow in a day. I would come home and find a different baby to the one I'd left: eyes burning, cheeks round, folds in the fat of her legs. It was difficult to believe that anything was wrong.

Miss Clavell came every two weeks with a box of food, and I went out with the girls on Saturday nights and to the club on Tuesdays. I still went to clean for the ladies on Saturday mornings, and I began to enjoy it – not the work, which I resented after a week at the factory and keeping our own house together, but the little glimmers of life. The mess of papers on the writing table, the creased pair of gloves dropped on the arm of a chair, the hatpins on the windowsill. Once, I saw an open bottle of sherry on the table, four small glasses engraved with curlicues at the mouth, sticky red collecting in a triangle at the bottom, a packet of cigarettes lying next to them. When I scrubbed the passageway, I listened to them complain about the Ghost and a Miss Dawson who I took to be in charge of them and how hard the work was, and sometimes very dull things like the number of water taps in a tenement block. Miss Morton had been to a matinee last weekend. Miss Horner went home for a lunch party for her father's birthday. Her sister was expecting twins. 'She's absolutely enormous. She said, "Frankly, Bea, have you ever seen anyone so huge?" I said, "Frankly, Lettie, no."'

The first Saturday in October, Miss Horner answered the door, yawning, and showed me into the scullery. When I was out on the step, Miss Morton came home on her bicycle, red-faced and hatless, clothes pegs still in her skirts. She greeted me warmly and carried her bicycle out to the yard.

When I went in to scrub the passageway, I heard Miss Morton say, 'What did Miss Dawson want yesterday then?'

'Oh, Miss Povey had had a word with her about my tenants in North Street. I'm afraid I let them rack up a bit of debt.'

'Oh, Bea, you didn't!' Miss Morton sounded genuinely shocked. I lifted my bucket as quietly as I could and started scrubbing closer to the door.

'Yes, stupid of me, wasn't it, but when it came to it I couldn't bear to do it, to chuck them out. Every Sunday she said she'd have the money next week and she seemed so desperate, I kept hoping she'd come up with something. Anyway, Miss Povey found out she was a . . . working woman, shall we say.'

'Oh, Bea!'

'Yes, and she was working in the house! And a drinker. Miss Povey threw her out quick as she could but she found out about the bad debts and, well . . . you can imagine. I showed her the case notes, said how could I possibly have known? But I'd been sloppy with the references . . . Oh, she went on at me!'

'What did she say?'

'The usual business. Helping the right sort of person. "We are not here to help sluts or drunks! This is not the Salvation Army, Beatrice!" You can imagine.'

'I can,' Miss Morton said.

'I thought that was the end of it, but she'd evidently spoken to Miss Dawson about me and I had to go through it all again this morning. And she got on to the girls' club. She heard about the fighting we had at the start.'

My face turned hot. I had stopped scrubbing to listen and I began again, furiously.

'How on earth did she hear about that?'

'Oh, it'll be one of the old gossips who sit on their steps all day. Anyway, she was saving it all up to throw the book at me. She doesn't think the club's up to much. It's not enough to give the girls a good time, apparently, though Lord knows they could do with it. I need to improve their *character* as well.'

'There's the needlework, Bea.'

'The needlework! The girls who wanted that have all stopped coming. It's perfectly clear I don't know the first thing about it. No, they all want ghost stories round the fire and buns and dancing, and frankly I don't blame them. But Miss D wants Bible studies and hymns.'

'What did you say to her?'

'Oh, I told her what a rough set of girls they were, how

difficult it was to do anything with them, and at least if they're at the club they're not getting blotto on gin. She agreed with all that. And then I said I'd organise some talks or lectures. I've asked Gwen to speak to them – you know Gwen, my old Girton friend.'

'Gwen? Isn't she a raving socialist?'

'Well, who else will I get? The Earl of Asquith?'

'But Miss D won't want you to turn them all into Fabians, will she?'

'I won't put it that way. An interest in politics, I'll say. In their futures.' She sighed. 'And then it all got rather personal. She'd found out about our little sherry party. "We are here to influence the working classes with our good character, Beatrice. It is not for them to influence us!"'

'Oh, good heavens!'

'Well, look, I'll be home soon. I don't know if it matters what Miss Dawson or Miss Povey think of me.'

There was a silence and I took the moment to knock on the parlour door and began work on the windows. I saw a coffee pot still out on the table and mismatched crockery with crumbs. They were quiet the whole time I worked and I thought about the Black Hart that evening, about the blue glasses and firelight and what Kathleen would be wearing. When I'd finished, Miss Morton raved about my work and said she'd add the money to the savings account.

She turned to Miss Horner. 'If only all our tenants were like Ellen, Miss Horner!'

I smiled shyly and then, as soon as I had said goodbye and heard the door go behind me, I started to run.

When I got home, Mrs Atkins wasn't on our step, and Mother and Iris weren't there. None of the cleaning tasks had been done – the grate was still dirty, the knives sat in a basket. I wondered if they had gone to drop the mending off instead of sending George, but a fresh crate of unfinished trousers stood by the sewing machine. I put my head out of the door but I couldn't see Davey or George among the children playing out. I didn't want to ask one of the women in their doorways. I didn't want them to think anything was wrong.

I told myself to get on with the tasks and wait till Mother got back, but I couldn't settle and I ended up wandering about like a cat, picking up a task and then abandoning it before I'd finished. It was half past three before Mother came back, shining with sweat, carrying Iris on her hip.

'Where've you been?' I asked.

'Oh, never mind about that, Ellen, you could at least have made a start in here! What on earth have you been doing since you got back?'

'I've—' I looked around the room at the half-completed tasks.

'Come on, you get Iris off to sleep while I do the grate. No sign of George, I suppose? Well, you'll have to do the knives again.'

I took Iris in my arms and watched Mother curiously. She was out of breath, but there was an energy, a liveliness to her, that I hadn't seen for a long time. She was moving more quickly now. I watched her take off her jacket and hat and hang them on the back of the door. It occurred to me that I hadn't seen her wear them since Iris was born. She hadn't left the house, apart from to go to church. And yet she was still in her old cleaning clothes – her patched woollen skirt and the shirt that was thin and creased like an elderly woman's skin. I couldn't believe she had worn them out of the house. I took Iris to walk up and down the passageway, and heard Mother singing hymns as she took the grate apart.

On Tuesday, when we got to the club, the chairs were arranged in rows and another lady stood by the desk at the front with Miss Horner and Miss Morton. As I queued for tea with Mary, I could see that they were behaving differently around her. Miss Horner made jokes about the neighbourhood and the slums, as if she expected the visitor to find her shocking, and Miss Morton was eager and breathless and said things like, 'Oh, that must have been *extraordinary*!' The lady looked ordinary enough to me, sipping her tea gravely, and watching us intently as we took our buns and tea. We ate them in our laps in the second row, and after more girls had arrived, Miss Horner clapped her hands and used her very loud voice to call for quiet and introduce us to Gwendoline Hartley, who had studied at Cambridge and was now a journalist.

Miss Hartley spoke fiercely about labour strikes and wages. She spoke about women's work and maternity benefits. Although I lost the thread early on, I felt that she was describing something I understood, even if I hadn't known how to explain it. I knew that it was unfair – the pay, the rules, the fines at the factory, the way Mother worked to keep the house together and also took in mending – but I hadn't expected someone like Miss Hartley to care, beyond food parcels or help with the rent. I hadn't begun to think that anything could be any different. She talked about justice, hope and victory, and I began to feel excited. Miss Morton gazed at her, enthralled, and Miss Horner was smiling with pride. But the whole way through, Mary shifted and sighed tetchily next to me.

When the talk was over, and Miss Horner was saying goodbye to Miss Hartley at the door, Mary pushed her chair back and stood up. 'Let's go. I want to go to the Black Hart.'

We never went to the Black Hart on Tuesday. 'But . . . it's not even gone seven. Miss Horner said she was going to tell us *her* ghost story this week, the time two ladies walked through her bedroom in Shropshire.'

'They're all made-up anyway.'

I followed her out and I saw Miss Morton watch us go. Mary walked quickly and didn't say anything to me on the way there. The mixed bar was empty apart from two old women sitting at the bar. Mary treated me to the first round, while I took a table in the corner. I tried to get her out of her black mood, making jokes about Miss Hartley's hat, telling her a story I'd seen in the papers about another poisoning, trying to get her going on factory gossip, but she remained sullen and I began to worry that I'd upset her. Finally, I asked her what she thought of the talk.

'It was all right.'

She took out one of her half-cigarettes and lit it. She was looking away from me now, staring into the distance, tapping some ash on the table, then stubbing it out and pocketing the last quarter. Finally she said, 'Did you like it?'

'Yes,' I said. 'She seemed so . . . full of energy, so vigorous. It rubbed off on me, I suppose.'

'She talks like we're stupid. Like we don't know it's unfair. What are we supposed to *do* about it? Don't help hearing about it from someone like her.'

'Well, those things she said – the strikes and the laws and all that.'

'What difference does it make? That strike she talked about was twenty years ago. Before we was even born. And we're still here. Working ten-hour days for twelve fucking shillings a week.'

'Well . . .' I was trying to hold on to the feeling that Miss Hartley had given me, to turn it into words. 'She said that progress was . . . slow . . . and . . .'

'Aren't you scared?' Mary said. She didn't sound scared. She sounded angry.

'Of what?'

'Of what it's going to be like. After we leave the factory. Marry some bloke, endless babies, wash day every week, gossiping on the step, never enough of anything. I don't want it.'

'You might marry someone well-off,' I said, and she laughed bitterly.

'Where would I meet this well-off bloke then? Round here?'

'You don't have to get married,' I said, although there was no woman I knew in the neighbourhood who wasn't.

'Stop at home forever? Handing over your wage to your ma every week? It wouldn't be much better.'

'You could be a spinster. Like Miss Povey.'

We didn't say anything for a moment.

'That's the difference between you and me,' Mary said, a strange half-smile on her face. 'You look at ladies like that one today and think you could be like that.'

I blushed. 'I don't think I could be like that,' I said quickly. 'I just thought—' I couldn't find the words. That I could take something of hers, some of the fierceness and bravery, and borrow it, wear it occasionally. Make something else with it. 'I thought things would get better,' I said finally.

'Why?' she said.

'Because they did. For a time. We didn't have much when I was little, and my dad was working away, and the babies died, but then Mother got a job at the dressmaker's and finally in the haberdasher's and we were all right. We had the house near the park and her wage, the boys were at school and I was going to stay on too. They said I could have been a schoolteacher. And then things got worse again and we moved here, but I always thought— I thought . . . we'd get back to how things were.'

'How?' She gulped the rest of her gin.

'I'll treat you this time,' I said.

I walked up to the bar. Kathleen had her back to me, pouring jugs of beer for two children I half-recognised, collecting them for their mum and dad. While I waited, I tried out different ways of resting my hands on the bar, moved my feet further apart and then closer together again. I looked at the two women next to me, sitting on stools.

I recognised one of them, though I wasn't sure where from – they were in their fifties, most likely too old to work at the factory. Neither of them wore a hat and the woman closest to me seemed drunk; she had her elbow on the bar and she was resting her face in her hand, and she was talking too loudly.

'"Can you get off my step?" she says. "I want to whiten it." Bitch. You're no better than the rest of us even if you did work in a shop.'

'Ah, she's all right, Ruth,' her friend said. She was facing forwards, sipping her beer.

'She acts like she's too good for us. Like butter wouldn't melt in her mouth.' She sat up and took a gulp of beer. 'But listen to this, Annie,' she said, holding her finger up. 'I was talking to Jane Rose last week and we both said we'd noticed something funny. She's a widow, she says, and her husband died just as she's got in the family way.'

I went hot. My fingers started dancing on the bar.

'Yes, we all know that,' Annie said.

'That's right, we all know the story, the poor woman, made a widow just as she's expecting. But Jane says to me, she says, the baby was born in June. The beginning of June! She remembers it because she took the two boys in. And if the husband died in July, which is what they say, then that's a long time between him dying and that baby being born. It's a long time to be carrying a baby, if her husband got her in the family way before he died.'

Annie started counting on her fingers and then stopped. 'Oh! Well, some women do carry their babies late, don't they? Matilda carried our Bill nearly a year. He was enormous when he finally came.'

'All right then, Annie, but listen to this. Jane says that he died of an illness. It weren't an accident. Seems funny he'd be asking for that from her, right at the end.'

'I don't know, Ruth, perhaps that was his dying wish!' They collapsed in laughter. I clutched the gold rail on the bar.

'Jane says she's seen her taking the baby out at odd times, while the little ones are at school and the daughter's at work. She ain't got nothing with her when she comes back, no shopping.'

'She's allowed to leave her house. And if it *was* her

husband . . . the poor woman. She must know what everyone's saying about her.'

'But if it was another bloke, Annie, what a little whore!
Her husband couldn't have been long in his grave while
she was . . .'

'Well, we all need something to cheer ourselves up after
a burial, Ruthie!'

They were laughing again. I realised that Kathleen had
been standing in front of me for some time and Mary
was now standing beside me. I asked for two cups of gin,
though my voice sounded distant. Kathleen got the cups
from behind the bar.

'You all right?' Mary asked. I nodded.

'You're not listening to those two old cows, are you?'
she said. She raised her voice for the last words, and they
turned round. Annie saw me and looked horrified, nudg-
ing Ruth. She turned round and stared at me rudely, with
blank eyes. Mary picked up the cups and I hurriedly put
money on the bar, and we walked back to our table.

'Women like that will talk about anything,' she said,
taking a swig of gin. She sounded kind, but there was a
cautious edge to her voice too.

'It's not true!' I said. 'What they were saying.'

'Of course not,' Mary said. 'They're a pair of old gossips.'

Mother could have carried the baby for years and I still
wouldn't believe it. The woman they were talking about
was not my mother. She didn't think she was better than
anyone else. She was afraid, like Mary, like we all were, of
losing the little things we'd got, the things that Miss Morton or Miss Clavell smirked at or took for granted. The
white step, the stuffed birds, the Sunday best, the job in
the shop, it mattered. But I also knew that, whether it was

true or not, people would believe it. And I had to make sure it was not what Miss Povey or Miss Clavell believed.

I finished the gin and Mary stood me another. We walked home, exhausted and confused. The streets were blurred and shifting. Mary started singing and I sang along too, my voice weak at first, then getting stronger. As we stumbled down the high street, I saw Miss Morton on her bicycle leaving the club. She had noticed us, I knew it.

On Saturday, I went straight from the factory to Miss Morton's. I didn't stop to talk to the girls in the yard or walk some of the way home with them, as I used to. I was prompt at quarter past one. I tried harder this time, to do everything as well as I could, and when I got home Mother wasn't there again.

'Where've you *been*?' I asked. 'We always clean on Saturdays.'

'I took Iris out for a walk. It's good for her to get some fresh air. Stop asking so many questions.'

I didn't go to the Black Hart that evening; I stayed at home and helped Mother with her sewing. When Miss Morton came to get the rent on Sunday, I remarked how much Iris looked like our father. I took bread for breakfast and lunch every day. I mended every tear in our clothes, replaced every missing button, I cleaned our curtains twice a week, I cleaned the smuts from the window twice a day, and cleared the table and washed the crockery the moment we'd eaten. I remembered to tell Mother not to whiten the step when Miss Clavell was coming and I went round the parlour, leaving a few things out, before she arrived.

I began to put money back in our cash box and started

stashing bits of oatmeal and tea, the way I had before the confinement. It seemed easy, at first. All I had to do was try harder to do the things I knew I had to do anyway – save, not spend, clean the house, not drink – and no one could say that we were not of good character, no one would suspect that any of the rumours about us could be true. I had no idea about the depths of loneliness and sadness I would feel on Saturday evening, watching Mary out of the window, walking down Digby Street in her best hat, while I mended stockings, and then, as the evening wore on, how restless, how tethered, how angry I would feel. It was the same way I felt mid-afternoon at the factory and now that it was here, in our home, it was unbearable. And late at night, when I struggled to get to sleep, or if Mr Cunningham and Mr Rose woke me up coming home drunk and making noise in the street, the anger turned to fear. I was scared, in the same way Mary was: I was scared of how things were going to be.

A week later, when I went to Miss Morton's to clean, she looked pale and distracted when she answered the door. When I was working on the passageway, I heard her snap at Miss Horner about the mess.

They passed a few minutes in silence before Miss Morton said, 'I'm sorry. I'm in a foul temper this morning.'

'So I see,' Miss Horner said lightly.

'I've had a letter from Father. He's quite serious this time. He wants me to come home.'

'Ah. When?'

'In a month or two. There are all these parties he wants me to attend. He wants me to find a husband, you know.'

They both started laughing, gulping, choking.

'Oh Clara, I shouldn't, I'm sorry!' Miss Horner said. 'But I don't think I've ever seen you in a dress.'

'Well, precisely! But I suppose no father wants a spinster for a daughter so there we are.' Her voice was unsteady with sadness. 'I know – I know! – I've been so lucky. To have this year. Dear Daddy – a lot of fathers wouldn't have let their daughter go anywhere near the East End, much less paid for the privilege.' Her voice went quiet. 'But I don't *feel* very lucky.'

There was a silence before she said, hesitantly, 'Do you ever feel, Bea, that we've not done much good?'

'Oh, always,' Miss Horner said. 'The ideas I had when I came here! The wonderful things I was going to do! And then, well . . . either the natives don't care or you realise it won't make the blindest bit of difference.'

'I had such energy! When I arrived. I wanted to *improve* things, to help.'

'Oh, so did I! But . . . tea, a bit of dancing, cheap rent, clean windows, it's not *nothing*. Perhaps that's the best we can do.'

'That feeling. Of having *purpose*. Vigour. Oh, it was wonderful! I'm afraid that I won't ever feel that again.' Miss Morton's voice went quiet. 'When I think about a lifetime of embroidery and calling cards, and managing the house, well, I can't help but feel . . . rather low.'

'It could be a lot worse, Clara. Think of what some of the natives go through.'

'Oh yes, I know, I know. But if I could have done some-thing, something like your friend Gwendoline . . . I shan't get the chance now.' She spoke more firmly. 'I'm not brave enough anyway.'

'Aren't you getting tired of it? I am. The filth and the

noise and the *work*. I just want to go home now and get on with it. I'm fed up with waiting.'

'Get on with what?'

'Well, life, I suppose. I want my life to begin.'

'I don't think I feel like you, Bea,' Miss Morton said, and her voice had got even smaller and less steady. 'I thought my life had begun when I got here. Now it feels like it's closing in again.'

I thought I heard her crying and then Miss Horner said, 'Oh Lord . . .'

'I'm sorry,' Miss Morton said, and then they were quiet.

'I'll miss you, Clara,' Miss Horner said.

'And I'll miss you,' Miss Morton said.

When I got home, Mother was out again.

George was nowhere to be seen, so I started cleaning the knives and I tried to decide if Miss Morton leaving was a good thing. I told myself that most likely it was. There would be another Miss Morton and Miss Horner, and the new ladies wouldn't know that I had been to the Black Hart and perhaps they wouldn't hear the stories about Mother, and we could start again and they would see that we were the right sort of people after all. But it did not *feel* like a good thing. It made me feel unstable, as if everything in our lives was coming away.

I saw Mary go past our window and I felt a wild longing. I wondered where she was off to. Then I heard her greet Mrs Atkins and there was a knock at the parlour door. Mary had never been inside our rooms before.

'Where's your ma then?' she said, walking into the room and looking round. I had the same feeling I had when the health inspectors came: that we were about to be found out for something, although I couldn't have said for what.

'On an errand,' I said.

'Very nice,' she said, nodding at our mantel. 'Fancy. Fancy for Digby Street, anyway.' I didn't say anything.

'Lou says her auntie can get us tickets to a show at The Castle tonight.' She spoke abruptly, as if she was organising who was going to make the glue on our bench. 'Do you want one?'

I shook my head. 'I'm needed at home.'

'"Needed at home"!' She mimicked me. 'You're always needed at home these days. What're you needed for? And you don't walk out with us to get dinner no more.'

'I come to the club,' I said.

She looked the way she had after Miss Hartley's talk, sullenly furious. 'I don't understand you, Ellen. Do you think you're too good for us now?'

'No!' I said. 'I'm needed at home! Why does it matter to you anyway?'

'It don't matter,' she said, turning round. 'I don't care.'

She left the parlour and I had to hit the wall to stop myself crying. When Mother got in, in that curious state of energy and briskness, I wanted to run at her, the way Eliza had at me that day in the club. I made a start on the windows instead.

The next week, I hung around with the girls before work, but I could feel them slipping away from me. I felt invisible again as they talked about the show they'd seen and Lou imitated the main act, twirling and chucking herself about in the yard behind the factory. By the end of the week, they'd stopped asking me to walk down to get dinner with them and I unwrapped my bread on the factory floor with the other girls who worked there. At the club on Tuesday, Miss Horner looked disgruntled and sat on her chair behind the desk all evening. She said she was feeling too faint to tell a story this week. Miss Morton snapped at a girl for spilling her tea. When I went to their house on Saturday, she was morose and distant. Miss Horner had gone out and there was no conversation to listen to.

When I got back home, I found a girl sitting on our step. I immediately knew she was not from Digby Street. She was about eight years old and she looked like one of the slum children from school: bare feet and a face coated in grime. Someone had done her hair in plaits, but not well: her parting was crooked and one plait was fatter than the other. 'Are you Ellen?' she asked.

I nodded.

'Your mum says to come to twenty-two Penn Street.'

'I don't know where Penn Street is,' I said.

'Give us a penny and I'll show you,' she said. I felt in my pockets. I wasn't usually soft; I knew she would have got a penny for coming with the message, but I was too bewildered to argue with her.

Penn Street was on the other side of the high street, past the factory, a narrow, miserable court of cottages with flat, plain fronts. It smelt awful; the houses dumped their slops in the street. I avoided the rotting vegetables and bones outside number 22, and went in the open front door. There was a staircase in front with the banister ripped out, most likely stolen for firewood.

In the front room, I saw a woman sprawled on a straw mattress, asleep with her mouth open. She looked as if nothing would wake her. Iris was lying on her back in an old drawer, crying, and Mother was on the sofa with a baby in her arms. Her shirt was open and the baby was feeding from her.

She was calm when she spoke to me. 'Ellen, I need you to take Iris for the afternoon. She's being a right pain.'

'What are you doing?'

'I need to feed the baby.' She nodded towards the sleeping woman. 'She's got no milk.'

I picked Iris up and she struggled in my arms. 'All right, all right, Iris, calm down. How do you know these people?'

'Mrs Atkins did the delivery. She said I was the only mother she knew with milk.' She looked down at the baby. 'Poor thing would have died.'

'But what about *us*?'

'What about who?'

'Us, our family! How do you think it looks, you sneaking over here?'

'I'm not sneaking anywhere, thank you. Now, if you can take Iris out, I'll put this little one in the drawer and tidy up a bit in here.'

We both looked round the room. It was hard to know what could be done. The grate was broken and piled up with ash. One of the windowpanes had gone completely and was covered over with an old sheet. There were no curtains.

Then someone else wandered in: a girl wearing a ripped shirt and a skirt that was so worn it was almost ragged. Her black hair was roughly pulled back and she was carrying a saucepan. She looked at me and I recoiled in recognition.

'Hello, dear,' my mother said kindly. 'Are you a relative?'

'No, I live at number twenty, don't I.' Eliza gestured with her head to the left. 'I was told to bring this.'

'Thank you, dear,' Mother said. 'Put it on the table.'

She nodded and walked out.

'Come on then,' Mother said. 'Take Iris. She's driving me up the wall.'

'Are you going to stay here?' I said.

'Well, she's tired, poor little thing, she's so weak. She keeps falling asleep, so it's better I wait around till she wakes up and then I can give her some more milk.' She put her gently down in the drawer, which was lined with a blanket I recognised from home. She spoke with a voice so gentle, it made me ache for a time I couldn't quite remember. 'There you are, poppet. You get some sleep.'

'Don't you care what people think? You coming some-where like here?' I said.

'Poor little thing would have died,' she said again, and in that moment she felt completely mysterious to me. I carried Iris out of the house.

Eliza was waiting in the street and, although I pulled Iris tighter, I realised that I was not as afraid as I once had been.

'I didn't expect to see you somewhere like here,' she said. 'You keep turning up, don't you, like a bad penny.'

I didn't say anything.

'Is that your ma?' she said.

I nodded.

'It's a nice thing she's doing,' she said. She nodded at the window of number 22. 'No one thought that baby was going to live. Poor cow's got no one.'

Iris grizzled in my arms; I moved to go.

'I'm sorry about that night. At the club,' she said. 'I thought you was someone else.'

'I'm sorry too,' I said. 'About your tongue.'

'It weren't so bad. I weren't expecting it, you see. If I'd

seen it coming—' She looked at me intently and I had to look away. 'I wouldn't let you get away with something like that again.'

It seemed such a long time ago now and I realised how much had changed since the fight, how much I'd grown and how much I'd lost. I turned my face back and met her gaze.

'I wouldn't let *you* get away with something like that again.'

I turned around and walked out of Penn Street.

That night, I went to the market, even though we were still getting the food from Miss Clavell. Everything was making me tetchy that evening: bathwater splashing my shirt, the creeping itch of sweat on my face, Iris's stubborn shrieks. The need to leave the house was sharp and vicious, growing worse, until finally I announced I was going out on an errand. It was unkind of me, to leave Mother with the bathwater and the boys still up, and I felt guilty, but as soon as I left Digby Street I felt light and loose.

It hurt to see the girls standing by the fever hospital and I tried to get past without being seen, but then Mary called my name. I felt so happy, thinking that they still wanted to see me. I could just talk to them for a few minutes, on my way to get the shopping; surely no one would begrudge me that.

As I approached, I saw something was different. They weren't laughing or talking all at once, the way they used to. Lou was fiddling with a cigarette box. Betty was facing the wall, poking the toe of her boot where the wall met the paving, shifting bits of dirt around. Mags was not with them.

'You ain't seen Mags, have you, Ellen?' Mary asked.

I shook my head.

'She was at work this morning. She said she was coming tonight.'

'She'll have changed her mind,' Lou said, but she sounded cross, not consoling. She took a cigarette out of the box and put it back in again.

'And gone where?' Mary said.

'Somewhere else! With her brothers. She don't always come out with us.'

Mary shook her head. 'Her brothers ain't seen her. No one's seen her since this morning.'

Lou kicked the wall. Betty put a hand on her shoulder.

'She'll be at work on Monday, with a tale to tell. You'll see,' Betty said.

'I have to go to the market,' I said.

'All right then,' Mary said. They didn't ask me to stay.

I barely thought about Mags that night, or Sunday. I thought about myself, sulking about how I'd lost all the things that made life bearable. When she did come into my head, sometimes, fleetingly, I wondered where she'd gone or when she'd turn up. I thought that she would be at work the next day.

I remember everything about the next morning. By rights I should have forgotten it. I sometimes think of the other world, where I got up, washed and walked to work, and the memory of it folds into the memories of the hundreds of other mornings. But this one is set apart from all the others now, forever. I can remember thinking about Mags as I dressed, wondering what story she'd have to tell when I got into work. I can see my fingers on the buttons of my good shirt. I can smell the coffee from the coffee shop as I walked down the high street. I can remember the last few seconds of ordinary life, as I walked through the gates to the yard, moved through the milling workers, and saw the girls.

Mags was not with them. They were still fidgeting, expressions flickering like the light from a gas lamp. I started to feel something in my stomach.

'She'll have hooked it,' Lou said as we walked up the stairs.

'On her own?' Betty said.

'With a bloke.'

'What bloke?' Mary said.

'A secret bloke. She don't have to tell you everything!'

We walked into the factory room and had barely sat down at our workbenches before we heard the howl. It was uncanny, not quite human. We all looked up, startled, including Mr Clifford. We heard a loud yell, then boots on stairs. The other girls were coming out. I don't know who did it first, but someone must have thrown down their work, and then we all did, clattering down the stairs.

When we got to the ground floor, we could see girls pooled round the door to the cellar. They were not speaking. One or two of them were sobbing hysterically; others had red, bloated faces. The cutters and scorers began to appear. Mr Simpson stood by the door. He looked frail and elderly. One hand was shaking, the other was tugging at his grey hair.

'What happened?' Mary asked the girl next to her.

'A girl went in to get the copper going,' she said, 'and there was a body at the bottom of the steps.'

'Oh God,' Mary said, and she didn't sound like herself.

'They think she's been there all weekend.'

A vision came into my head of Mags on a train, holding hands with a man. Suitcases on the seats beside them, staring out of the window, the steam curling, the yellow-brick houses and chimney stacks folding into leaves and flowers, leaving Hackney and the factory and all of us behind. It was so strong, that vision, I felt like I could touch it. I wanted to lose myself in it. We were not told until much later, but I must have known, even then, that she was the girl at the bottom of the steps.

Mr Clifford pushed his way past us to the mouth of the cellar. 'Sir! What's going on?'

Mr Simpson stretched his arm through the door, to light it with the candle in his hand. Mr Clifford clapped his hand over his mouth. 'Oh,' he said. 'Oh.'

'The stupid cunt,' Mr Simpson said. 'What are we going to do now?'

I wanted to destroy him. I wanted to rip his hair from his head, smash his face against the brick wall, split him open. But I couldn't lose everything, so I didn't. Mary and I stared straight ahead. We didn't even touch.

I I

Frances

1984

When I think about the factory days now, I think about Sundays. I am almost certainly romanticising it – perhaps it only happened like that once or twice, for a few hours. But in my memory, it isn't an experience so much as a feeling, a certain quality: of industry, peace, intimacy. None of us were religious, and only Malcolm worked regular hours. We were supposed to be creating a new and different sort of life – and yet the rhythms of the traditional week were inside us. On Sundays, everyone was at home.

Naomi would start cooking in the morning; Jane and Nick argued and smoked, wrote in notebooks, counted leaflets. Malcolm read or listened to his Walkman. Sometimes we would go over to Clare and Susie's for lunch, or we would eat together at the factory. Sometimes Nick would join us, and even Malcolm would eat his ham sandwich near us, hunched protectively over it on one of the vinyl chairs. I would help Naomi sew or I would draw: odd pencil sketches of the building, the giant windows, the beams and corners, or the kettle on the hostess trolley. I was always pleased with how they turned out, though I couldn't think what I'd do with them when I'd finished. One or two of us would be doing our washing and we'd all scrabble in our pockets for coins for the launderette.

If I walk past the building now, on a Sunday, I am overcome. I would give anything for one more Sunday afternoon.

I had been at the factory six weeks and already I missed the dull, airless heat of the summer. When I'd packed my bag, in August, I hadn't imagined that I would still be there when the seasons changed and I had no warm clothes to wear. My winter coat was probably still hanging in the upstairs wardrobe at home, unless it was in a cardboard box – something else I didn't like to think about.

Clare lent me a denim jacket, still with her Greenham badges on, and Naomi lent me a jumper and a scarf she'd knitted. The scarf was long and thick, with an intricate pattern of green, yellow and cream; I wore it and the jumper every day, for as long as I could ignore the musty, sour smell. When it got too much, I soaked them in a tub, squeezing out grey-brown water, and wrapped myself in a blanket while I waited for them to dry.

The space was too big to heat properly, so we bought two small bar heaters and moved them around, depending on who was sitting where, and argued about the exact positioning of them. If I put a cup of tea down out of their range, it was cold by the time I picked it up again. I clutched a hot-water bottle on the sofa, and at night I slept in strange contortions, tucking my hands under my armpits or closing a knee round the opposite foot.

I rang my mother once a week, usually after a trip to the launderette. I didn't want the others to know I was doing it, so I squeezed into the phone box with my bag of clothes, still warm from the dryer, my paperback and purse resting on top. At the beginning of October, she told me that James Maxwell had rung.

'James. Fiona's son, you know? I explained that you didn't have a phone where you were, but I said I'd pass on the message when we spoke.'

'Oh, well . . . thanks,' I said.

'We had a rather nice chat, actually. He's a lovely boy. He said he was just back from driving Antonia to Oxford.'

'Right.'

She sighed. 'He left a number. Would you like it?'

'All right then.'

I felt around in my pockets. I decided that, if I couldn't find a pen, I would just pretend to take the number down, but there was a biro in the pocket of Clare's jacket and I scribbled it on the title page of my book.

'It did sound like he wanted to speak to you,' she said, and there it was again, that note of slightly desperate hope that was there whenever she talked about the Maxwells. I said that my money was running out, even though it wasn't.

I walked back, feeling the same unspecified discomfort that I always had after the phone calls to my mother. I disliked thinking about home, or life beyond the factory, at any time, but some pieces of news – my A-level results, the house sale, Oxford University, James Maxwell – made the unease particularly acute. They reminded me that I didn't know what to do next. That there was potential for a future for me but I didn't know what to do about it.

At the factory, that didn't seem like so much of a problem; just being there was absorbing. Daily life had become less of a struggle, but it was complicated enough that reaching the end of the day fed and washed, with reasonably clean clothes to wear, an envelope of cash from the pub in my pocket, felt like a satisfying achievement. Clare had helped Naomi set up a screen-printing table in the room next to ours and they started running workshops – I helped occasionally, setting out bottles and paper and card among enthusiastic young women in ink-stained overalls. When we went round to Clare and Susie's for a bath or lunch, I enjoyed the liveliness, the energy, of their conversations, even if I still felt I didn't have much to say. I went into the bookshop again, when Susie was working, and we talked for a long time about the writers we liked; the next time I visited Digby Street, she lent me a stack of books.

Once, when I'd been at a loose end one afternoon, I'd even gone to the Digby Street house alone. It had taken a lot of courage, to go by myself unannounced, even though neither place had a phone and I knew the others did it all the time. But when Susie answered the door, she didn't seem to think it was strange that I wasn't with Naomi. It turned out she was there by herself, and we had a cup of tea on the front step in the late-September sunshine. Walking away, I'd felt uncommonly happy at the thought that I was becoming a small part of their world. And yet I still had the feeling that I was in a fleeting dream. At some point, I would have to go home.

James had rung once before, at the end of August, and I had done nothing about it. I was amazed that he'd bothered to ring again. At first it seemed impossible that I would return his call, but I disliked the idea of being rude. I imagined ringing him and saying that I couldn't go out for dinner if he asked. But if he took me to dinner, we would probably go somewhere nice – tablecloths and napkins, hot food, heavy cutlery, candlelight, good manners. It would be warm and light; I might eat something that had been cooked in an oven, not on a hotplate. It all seemed very luxurious suddenly. I couldn't quite remember what James looked like now, but I imagined a faceless figure – older, cleaner, more responsible – sitting opposite me.

When I got home, Nick and Jane were sitting at the window at the top of the stairs, with their coats on and a blanket over their legs. It was getting dark earlier now, and we could see figures in the lit windows of the backs of the terraced houses. They waved when they saw me, and then turned towards each other again, passing a joint between them.

Our room in the factory was empty. I switched on the strip lights and one of the bar heaters, and went over to the kettle. I heard Nick say, 'See you then, mate,' and the door open. He came in, still in his coat, rubbing his hands, and I felt a mixture of excitement and dread.

I had had sex with Nick four times now, and it always started with moments like these, when we were unexpectedly alone together. It was always the same: we'd start talking, the way we used to at the pub; often it would turn more intimate – about his mother or my father – and then we would end up in the cellar together, me on my back on the damp floor.

When we were talking, I remembered why I used to like him coming into the pub. I liked his stories, and the fact that I didn't have to impress him. When I was at Clare and Susie's dinner table, listening to conversations about abortion or camp politics or whether motherhood was a pillar of patriarchy, I was out of my depth – often I liked that feeling but sometimes I didn't. And Nick was still the only person who I had talked to about my dad.

I disliked the sex – my face near the foul carpet in the cellar, sometimes uncomfortable, sometimes in pain, until he suddenly made a noise, and jerked away from me as if I were poisonous, standing up, then crouching next to me, lighting a cigarette in cupped hands. Just afterwards, doing up his jeans, he'd look at me with something like alarm and disgust and that was the worst feeling: that even he wasn't enjoying it. Men were supposed to like having sex with women; the idea that he didn't infused me with a sense of deep failure. The fact that nothing ever changed made each time a little bit more unpleasant – no intimacy or fondness was being fostered, only a kind of stagnating distaste.

I made myself a cup of tea while he took his coat off and took a packet of currant buns out of his Sainsbury's bag. He sat on the sofa, tearing open the packaging, and took a bite of one still in the packet. He looked up at me. 'Sorry, I'm starving. Do you want one?'

I shook my head.

'What?' he said, smiling sheepishly. 'They were on offer.'

'I don't think I've ever seen you eat a proper meal,' I said.

'No time. No time to eat meals when you've got to save the world.'

'Is that what you're doing?'

'Yes. Well, helping Jane save the world.' He stood up and went to the cupboard. 'How about a drink?'

I shook my head again. He made himself a drink and we sat on the sofa together. He ate another bun. He told me about a protest that Jane was planning at the town hall;

he seemed enlivened by the idea even though he said he'd be at home when it was going on. When he got up to make another drink, he asked if I wanted one too.

We'd talked for longer than we usually did and I started to wonder if we wouldn't have sex after all. I felt enormous relief, and then guilty about it, as if it was something I ought to want, and worried by the thought of not being desirable enough. I said yes to a drink.

'How's your mum?' he said, coming back to the sofa and handing me a mug with vodka and cola in it.

'I don't know, really,' I said. 'She seems OK, but . . . I've not been back home since . . .'

'Does she know where you are?'

I shook my head. 'She thinks I'm staying with friends.'

'That must be hard on her,' he said.

I took a gulp from my mug. 'She actually seems . . . happy when I speak to her. She's excited about the move.'

'That's good, though, isn't it? New start and all that.'

'I suppose . . . but it doesn't seem . . .'

'She's got to move on, Frankie.'

'I know, but what if . . .'

'What if what?'

My heart was beating faster. 'What if she's happier now than she was when he was alive?'

We were quiet for a moment. I drank more of the sickly mixture in my mug and a dreamy, unstable feeling grew.

'What was he like, your dad?' Nick asked.

When he was alive, he was my father: I never thought I'd have to describe him, turn him into good qualities and funny stories and amusing flaws, the way he had been in the eulogy or people's letters. I knew I could reach for the adjectives and anecdotes that he'd been boiled down to, but the truth was, I didn't really know what he was like. There was a whole side of his life I had known nothing about.

'He was having an affair,' I said. 'More than one, probably. I found out after he died.' I had never said the words out loud, and they sounded much simpler and more neutral than my feelings about my father were. It was a temporary relief to hear them.

'Did you?' he said slowly. 'How did you find out?'

'Going through his stuff . . . after he died.' I began to wish I hadn't said anything. I didn't want to talk about the shoebox with Nick.

'Does your mum know?'

I nodded.

'Did she know before he died?'

'I don't know,' I said. 'We never talked about it. She didn't seem that surprised. Perhaps.'

He finished his drink and looked up at me. 'People can live with all sorts of things.'

'But he lied!' I was suddenly finding this conversation unbearable. I got off the sofa and went to stand in the kitchen, so I wouldn't have to look at him or be close to him. 'He lied to us, for so long.'

He spoke more quietly. 'Are you angry with him?'

'Yes!'

He stood up and walked over to me. He put his hands on my shoulders. 'Look, I know it's difficult to understand. Adult lives are complicated. Maybe it was hard for him too.'

I didn't want him to see how angry I was and I turned my face away. He kept his hands on my shoulders, looking straight at me. Finally, I returned his gaze. The tension was horribly exquisite. The thrill of being desired, dread at the possibility of being rejected, the squeamishness about the sex – it all churned together until I had no idea what I wanted any more. He took my hand. Knowing what Nick wanted made it easier.

Back in the cellar, after it was finished and he was sitting up, I lay on the floor next to him, staring up at the underside of the floorboards above me. I thought, as I always did, that I must find a way to stop this, to not let it happen again. Then I sat up and crossed my legs. I wondered when we'd go back upstairs.

I noticed that he was making odd gasping noises. I turned to look at him. He was staring straight ahead, his mouth open, his jaw juddering. I didn't realise what was going on until I saw tears on his cheek. I touched his arm tentatively and he jerked away. Then he stubbed his cigarette out on the floor violently, and his face resolved itself again.

'Come on,' he said. 'Let's go.'

As we made our way up the stairs, I looked at my watch. It was only half past seven. I sat on my bed behind the curtain, feeling the familiar stickiness between my legs. I picked up the paperback with James's number in it. Then I went to the phone box.

It took me a few days to get through to James, since he couldn't call me back, and his landlady got more and more abrasive, until she told me firmly that James had said that Wednesday evening would be a good time to call. When I did get through to him, I found myself getting flustered, apologising for not ringing sooner, but he sounded delighted to hear from me. We made a date for dinner on Friday the following week.

I did not tell anyone about the date, but for the rest of the week I treasured the knowledge of it. I thought about it when I had to drag myself out of bed in the night to go to the toilet, shivering, bare feet on cold linoleum, light coming in through the uncurtained windows. I thought about it when I ate another disappointing sandwich, when Jane said something cutting, when I felt particularly young and ignorant in front of the others, and when Nick and I were alone together on Saturday night and ended up in the cellar again.

The week of the dinner date, I started to feel ill and panicked, wondering if I wouldn't be able to go. I couldn't tell what it was exactly. Sometimes I thought it was a mutation of the old feeling, the not-normal feeling; I often felt as if I was underwater. Sometimes I thought it was flu. I was exhausted; standing behind the bar towards the end of the shift, I felt that it was taking all my energy to keep upright and if I relaxed for even a second I would just collapse. Tiny actions – brushing my teeth, calculating someone's change, getting a new box of crisps from the cellar at the pub – took so much effort I started to dread them. But the idea of trying to get hold of James all over again, to tell him I couldn't go, leaving a message and then worrying about whether he'd got it – even thinking about it exhausted me. It would be easier to go.

When I'd left home, in a moment of optimism, I had packed a burgundy cord A-line skirt and a twisted knot of black tights. The ceremony of getting ready seemed even stranger than it had before Antonia's party: encasing my legs in stretchy woollen material felt almost as odd as dabbing my eyelashes with a sticky bristle or smearing coloured wax on my lips under the strip light in the bathroom.

I put Clare's jacket and Naomi's scarf on over my purple paisley shirt. I took the badges off Clare's jacket and I looked at myself in the bathroom mirror. The make-up had made me look worse somehow, jarring against my sallowness. My skin looked like it was slowly disappearing, like a worn piece of fabric: the shadows under my eyes, the blue veins above my cheekbone, starting to show through. But I was too tired to take it all off.

I could have gone straight out, but I didn't. I hesitated outside the door to our room. I wanted and didn't want them to notice me, wanted and didn't want them to know I had plans that didn't involve them. I opened the door and went in to say goodbye to everyone.

'Oh, wow, you look nice, Frankie,' Naomi said. 'Where are you off to?'

'To meet a friend,' I said, and regretted it. It just drew attention to the fact that I never met friends. Jane looked up from the sofa.

'Where are you meeting her?' she said.

'It's a him,' I said, and the attention was excruciating. I couldn't look at Nick. I had told myself that I wasn't doing anything wrong: having sex in a cellar did not require any kind of commitment. It still felt like a betrayal.

I took two buses into town because it was cheaper than the Tube fare, shivering on the top deck. When I got to the restaurant, confronted by James in a suit and a tie, I realised it would have been better if I hadn't made an effort. Compared to the other women there, with their amplified hair and shoulders, I looked old-fashioned and prim. I didn't know whether it was shyness or tiredness, but forming words became so difficult it was almost painful. I kept stopping mid-sentence until James finished for me, usually with something different to what I had been about to say, but I was only grateful to be helped.

I had been looking forward to the food, but, holding the menu, any appetite or desire was occluded by the anxiety that I might choose something messy or inappropriate – red meat seemed too masculine, fish too complicated, coq au vin too hearty. Was duck too extravagant? James made gentle recommendations and spoke to the waiter. We talked about the summer and the parties he'd been to, and I ate slowly and carefully as if I'd never used cutlery before, terrified of spilling or staining or looking greedy. I tried to avoid talking about where I lived, but he got it out of me.

'Gosh, Franny, you are *brave*,' he said. 'And there I am thinking that I'm roughing it in a bedsit.' He asked me more and more about it – 'No *bath*! Golly' – and it was nice to feel amusing, but then it started to irritate me. It was my life, after all, not an anecdote, and although it didn't quite match what I was inside, neither did the restaurant or the food or the women with their ballooning sleeves and gigantic belts. The food, with its sauces, creams and gravies, suddenly felt horribly rich.

He insisted on hailing a taxi to take me home, even though he had to stop three before we could find one that would agree to drive to Hackney. He gave me a ten-pound note for the fare and I fell asleep on the leather seat.

I felt sick when I woke up the next morning, as if the wine and the restaurant food hadn't been digested properly. I was disgusted with myself for eating and drinking too much, and when I had to be sick in the pub toilets I felt wretched and ashamed. It lifted after that, but I still felt wrung out and separate from the rest of the world. On the way home, the nausea rose again and I was sick outside the newsagent's. I thought I would feel better the next day, but I didn't.

It came and went, for days, then weeks. The smell of Naomi frying onions made my stomach lurch. Food was mostly inedible and I stood, dazed, in the corner shop next to the pub, holding different things in my hands, trying to decide what, if anything, I could stomach.

The waves of sickness brought a crushing sense of fore-boding and shame. And then the awful thought formed and I counted the dates, trying desperately to remember the last time I'd started bleeding, but not managing it. I kept trying to work it out, as if I might come upon some new information that would tell me something – *if it start-ed on Wednesday then that would mean ten days late* – but my memory was too patchy.

The sickness carried on, like erratic tides, until one morning, over a month after my dinner with James, I felt it lift, as I clung to the cup of herbal tea that Naomi made in a pot every morning. The change was instant, like someone had switched on a light. I stood up, radically better, only aware of how horrible it had been now it was no longer there. I was desperately hopeful.

A week later, I woke up in the night, wet between my legs, and held my hand up to my face to see the streaks of blood on my fingers, and I was filled with relief. I got up to get a pad, fixed it to my knickers, and lay back, light-headed, happy, imagining everything I had feared being gently washed away.

It was only when I woke up again, and there was more blood, and more, more than I could ever have expected, that I began to feel afraid. My stomach cramped violently. I went to get another pad, but there were none left in my shoebox – I was too embarrassed to wake Naomi or Jane. I folded up an old T-shirt and put it under my hips. I closed my eyes and tried to fall asleep, desperately hoping I would wake up and everything would have returned to normal, but my eyes opened every time my stomach seized. I don't know how long I lay there, tears running down my face, the pressure getting more intense, feeling the blood on my thighs, the sheets. Soon, I was too scared to move. I thought that if I stood up, everything would fall out of me, not just blood, but my entire insides, guts and bones.

Eventually, I rolled off the bed and took my knickers off. The T-shirt was soaked through. I didn't have a choice. I crawled through the curtain separating my area from Naomi's and knelt at the side of her mattress, looking at her face: she was on her side, mouth open, eyes closed. She shuddered and gave a small yell.

'I'm sorry, I'm sorry,' I whispered.

'What's going on? Are you OK?' She wasn't whispering and I was terrified of waking the others.

'I need . . . I'm bleeding . . . Could you . . .?'

'Shit, you look awful,' she said. She got up, picked up the torch by her bed and pulled back the curtain. I stood up and followed her, and saw the disaster of my bed for the first time, drenched in scarlet. Dark purple clots the size of blackberries. Then what I'd feared came true: everything did come out of me in a burst of pain and pressure.

'Naomi, Naomi, Naomi, Naomi,' I said, panicking, and she directed her torch at me and said, 'Oh shit.'

I looked down at the fleshy form on the floor between my feet. I was slow to read it at first, but in the glare of the torchlight I saw a curved shape and understood exactly what it was. I cried out.

'It's OK,' she whispered, coming towards me and taking me in her arms. 'It's OK. Come on.'

She helped me get to the bathroom and I sat on the toilet in one of the stalls, Naomi kneeling in front of me. I couldn't stop thinking about it lying on the floor by my bed and I knew that it would mark me forever. I leant against the tiles on the wall. She took deep breaths and I copied them. She held my hand, which wouldn't stop shaking, jabbering against her palm. Sometimes she sang to me and I remembered Clare saying that she'd sung in her head when she'd had to face the police horse and I did the same thing. Sometimes I said, 'It hurts,' or 'It's just so much,' and she would say, 'I know, I know,' and I believed that she did. When I think about the factory now, what I lost and what I regret, I think about Naomi.

Time lost all meaning. After a while, I felt like things were getting easier, and there was less blood, although why I felt that I can't remember. I was collapsing into Naomi's arms, then she helped me back to my bed and pulled my sheets off in a bundle. We looked at the thing on the floor and I whispered, 'I don't know what to do, I don't know what to do.'

'Here,' Naomi said, and she came back with a Tupperware box and a tea towel. She was careful with it, but it still felt wrong. I wanted, so badly, to say sorry to the baby, for not being better or stronger, for not being able to keep it inside. She got me a new pad and laid a blanket on the bed. I was suddenly terrified that, if I went to sleep, I would die. I could barely move, I was losing consciousness, but

I was afraid that if I closed my eyes, I wouldn't wake up.

I kept saying, 'Am I all right? Am I all right? I feel so weird,' to Naomi and she said, 'It's OK, I'll stay here,' and she held my hand.

When my alarm clock went off, I didn't know if I'd slept. There had been no boundary between being awake and asleep, no moment where I forgot what was happening, but Naomi was no longer there, so time must have passed. I lay on my back for a while, crying quietly, and then I heard Naomi whispering my name. I didn't reply, but she pulled the curtain aside anyway and came in, holding a cup of tea.

'Here you go,' she said. It wasn't the usual tea; it was a bright-yellow liquid with some green leaves in it. It tasted earthy and lemony and stained the china; it wasn't totally unpleasant. She put a new pack of sanitary towels on the mattress.

'Do you have work today?' Naomi said.

I nodded.

'Here,' she said. 'Get dressed and I'll come out to the phone with you.'

I pulled on my clothes. My flesh felt odd under my fingers. I patted my neck and my cheek experimentally. They didn't feel like they belonged to me any more. When I came out, Jane was sitting on the sofa with Naomi. She looked at me, concerned and anxious, and I was suddenly mortified.

'Here,' Naomi said, handing me a plate with some toast on it.

'I'm so sorry, Frankie,' Jane said.

I ate a bite or two of the toast, and realised I was desperately hungry. It had been such a long time since I'd wanted food.

'I'm fine,' I said. 'I can go to work.'

Naomi shook her head. 'Frankie, I think you should see a doctor.'

'I'm OK, though! I feel fine.'

'Jane knows someone who— It can get really compli-cated. We need to get it checked out.'

'Look, it's just round the corner,' Jane said. 'We'll come with you.'

I shook my head weakly.

'Come on,' Naomi said, holding out her hand. 'I'm going to show you something. Something you'll like.'

On the way to the hospital, we turned into Digby Street and into the front yard of a house at the end. I knew it was empty. I could spot empty houses instantly now; the way I could tell if someone on the bus was sleeping rough, no matter what they were wearing. It wasn't the newspaper plastered over a cracked pane of glass or the mattress in the front yard; it was a certain expression, an air of defeat. Naomi pushed open the door and we walked in. The hall reminded me of home: the wallpaper, the ceiling mould-ings, the telephone table. But the wallpaper had streaks of brown on it and there were boxes stuffed with old news-papers lined up by the walls.

She picked up the phone and handed it to me. There was a dial tone. I held it to my ear, looking at her stupidly, until I realised.

'They didn't cut the phone off!'

'Exactly. Clare told me about it. We can use it whenever we want.'

I left a message for Dave at the pub and told him I had food poisoning. Then Naomi, Jane and I went to the hospital and waited on fold-out chairs. A nurse in a blue uniform came out to see us, and looked at us suspiciously.

'What's this then?' she said. 'A mother's meeting? Which one of you is here to see the doctor?'

I put my hand up tentatively.

'Well, come on then. Doctor's ready.'

'Can I come in with her?' Naomi said.

The nurse looked suspicious. 'Does she want you to?'

'Yes!' Jane said. She looked at me. 'Sorry, Frankie. Do you?'

I nodded.

'Go on then.' She sighed and we followed her into the consulting room.

The doctor asked us to sit down and the nurse made a show of getting the extra chair. He must have been in his sixties, and he was kind and polite to me as he asked me to tell him why I was here. I found myself lulled by his thick silver hair, his upper-class accent, the way he said 'my dear'.

I tried to explain, but the words I knew were inadequate. A miscarriage sounded so simple; a mishap, a misstep. I had to make him understand that something had gone terribly wrong, that I had thought I was going to die, but I didn't know how. I was tired again, and I could feel the warm blood collecting at the top of my legs, and I knew that it couldn't have been normal because women lost babies all the time and I couldn't believe it would be like this. I noticed him glance down at my hands and it took me some time to realise why.

He spoke to the nurse first, calling it a spontaneous abortion, and I misunderstood, saying, 'No, no, I didn't—!' until he finally said to me, in a voice that was too loud and slow: 'It's all right, my dear. It's a miscarriage. You lost your baby.'

'No, no, it was worse than that— It was— I think there must be something wrong—' I said.

'Well, let's have a look then, shall we?' He spoke to me as though I were a nervous animal. 'No need to worry, just jump on that couch and get undressed, yes, that's right, everything off, please, Nurse will help you, that's right, there we are, no need to worry, my dear. I'll be very quick.'

Naomi held my hand through the examinations. I was wearing only my jumper and T-shirt, covered in a thin sheet. Head tipped back, the unnatural positioning of the stirrups, the cold metal inside me. He asked if we'd seen the products of conception, and Naomi let go of my hand and moved down the bed. I knew she was showing him the Tupperware box. I heard the slight pop of the plastic lid, and the doctor saying neutrally, 'Yes,' and then to the nurse: 'Clinical waste.' Naomi said, 'No, I think we'll have that back, thanks.' I was grateful although I wouldn't have dared say it myself.

It was only at the end when he said, 'Well, it all seems to have come away; I don't think you'll need a scrape,' that I started to cry.

The doctor stood up and walked round to be next to my head. When he spoke, his tone was kind, paternal. 'Now, what's wrong with you, young lady?' he said in a jolly tone of voice.

'I'm sorry,' I said, but I couldn't stop crying, my face and vocal cords beyond my control.

'Oh dear,' he said, putting a hand on top of my head. 'There's no need to get upset. You're very young. Plenty of time to have lots of babies. Though I would advise waiting until you have a ring on your finger.' He moved back down to the end of the table. 'All in all, I'd say you've been very lucky.'

'Almost finished now, my dear,' he went on, and then to Naomi: 'Would you mind waiting for your friend outside?' She looked anxious and kissed the top of my head, but she did leave and then he sent the nurse out of the room too. Then he said, 'I'm just going to do a quick internal exam.' Before I had time to think about what was happening, he thrust his fingers in my vagina, pressed hard, and left them there. I can still remember the expression on his face.

When we came out of hospital, Jane was still waiting for us. She and Naomi took me to a chip shop on the opposite corner to the pub, an old-fashioned kind with green tiles outside and 'Live Eels' still etched on the window. I sat on a wooden bench below a large mirror, opposite Naomi and Jane, and looked up at the menu on the chalkboard behind the counter. Everything sounded obscenely wonderful – mince on toast, pies, chips. I had barely spent any of my wages since I'd arrived at the factory; the idea of paying for something as ephemeral as a meal seemed crazy. Naomi said she was going to get a steak pie and chips, and I said I would have the same.

'I didn't know you ate meat,' I said when she came back from ordering at the counter.

'Sometimes,' she said, and I handed her a note from the envelope my wages came in.

'Was the exam OK?' Jane said.

I nodded.

'He said everything was fine?' she said.

I nodded again.

'Well, that's good,' she said. 'Keep an eye on it, though, won't you? If anything feels wrong, we can always come back with you.'

Naomi turned to Jane. 'You'll like this, Jane. He said she should wait till she had a ring on her finger.'

'Oh, for Christ's sake!' Jane said, and she and Naomi laughed, and then I did too, shaking, relieved. 'God, they're dinosaurs, the lot of them.'

The food came and it was the best thing I'd ever eaten – warm, thick pastry, dense gravy, salty potato slabs. I could almost feel my insides rebuilding as I ate. Then I thought of something I wished I hadn't.

'Jane,' I said, tentatively, 'how did you know what happened? Did you hear us in the night?'

'I heard you get up and then when you were talking . . . I put two and two together.'

'But you don't think . . . Would the others . . . have heard?'

'I don't think it matters,' Jane said. 'The blokes wouldn't come near this sort of thing, even if they did know what was going on.' She looked at me. 'But I don't think they did. I was next to you. They're right over the other side of the room, remember.'

Nothing had happened between me and Nick since the dinner with James; I guessed I'd somehow put him off, either by letting him know about James or by looking and feeling so awful. I hadn't had the energy to interrogate it, only been grateful, but now I was resolute: it would never happen again. I would not be connected to him any more than I already was.

'You won't tell anyone, will you?'

'Of course not,' Jane said.

317

'Is it . . . to do with that man you went for dinner with the other day?' Naomi said.

'James? No! No, it was nothing like that.'

They looked at each other, surprised. I realised that James was the only person I had seen outside the factory for weeks.

'Then, is it—?' Naomi said.

'Naomi!' Jane said.

'Sorry, sorry, you're right. You don't have to tell us anything. Of course.'

But they knew. Jane lit a cigarette and turned her face to the wall. 'Idiot,' she muttered, and I didn't know if she was talking about Nick or me.

When we got back to the factory, Jane took my sheets to the launderette and Naomi brought a blanket to the sofa and put the kettle on. I raised my knees and put the blanket around them.

'I'm sorry about bringing the . . . box,' Naomi said. 'I didn't know if you'd want me to, but Jane said it might be helpful at the hospital, and I thought I should . . . but I can get rid of it. Whatever you want.'

'I don't know,' I said. 'I don't know what to do with it.'

Naomi went over to the trolley to make the tea and I saw her backpack leaning up against the sofa. I opened it, captivated and scared, and took out the box. It was still wrapped in the tea towel inside. The box felt unnaturally light. I had no desire to look in it, but the thought of the bins, the toilet, was awful.

'Let's take it outside,' I said.

I put on my scarf and Naomi went into her sleeping area to get her coat. We went down the concrete stairs, Naomi holding the box. I was beginning to feel light and hollow again; I was still losing blood. The yard was full of junk, and I remembered the bats, so we ended up walking down the high street and through the green until we ended up in the marshes. I stopped in a clearing between the trees and shrubbery lining the path by the river. It was dark and cool and damp, and I knelt on the bare earth under the tree, scrabbling at it. Naomi handed the box back to me.

'Do you . . . What about the tea towel? And the Tupperware?'

'It's OK. I mean, I probably won't reuse it,' she said, and I laughed, a kind of dark, breathy, shaky laugh.

'Here you go,' she said, once I'd covered it over with earth. She took a little brown bag of seeds out of the pocket of her coat and scattered them over the top. 'Is this OK?' I nodded. 'I can't actually remember what these ones are. I hope it's something nice, not . . . fucking parsley or something.'

We laughed again, the same exhausted, shaking laugh. 'Parsley's all right,' I said, still crouching by the earth.

'It's something, isn't it?' she said, and she held out her hand to help me up.

I was surprised at how quickly my body recovered. I still had dreams about things coming out of me: something grey-brown and leathery, like a tough steak. Something yellow-white, like old bone. A large, boneless hand, soft and slippery with sausage-like fingers. 'It's a trial,' the doctor explained in my dream. 'Your body tried making a hand, but it didn't work.' But some days I was shot through with unexpected euphoria, grateful that I had survived.

In the last days of November, we had a few unexpected

days of winter sun. I was standing at the window, drinking tea, looking out over back gardens and rooftops, when Naomi told me she was going up to Hampstead Heath.

'I think this is going to be my last swim of the year,' she said. 'It was freezing last time. But I don't want to miss the sun.'

'I'll come with you,' I said, putting my mug down.

'Are you sure?' she said. 'I mean, seriously. It's going to be cold.'

'I'd like to go. I've never been,' I said. Hampstead Ladies' Pond was somewhere else that my mother had said was 'full of lesbians'. Stoke Newington was another. 'I don't want to wait till summer.'

We took the train that we saw go past the back of the factory. I had never taken an overground train in London before and although the platform was desolate and bare, and the train was delayed, I felt a tentative dizzying excitement at being above the rooftops. I could hardly concentrate on what Naomi was saying on the journey, taking in the great gas rings by King's Cross, the tiny slices of life from open windows.

We got off at Hampstead Heath station – Naomi said she preferred the walk from the west side. I admired how clean and neat everything seemed compared to Hackney as I followed Naomi onto the Heath, past the heads bobbing in the mixed ponds and the men's, then down a shaded path and through a gate with the sign 'Women Only'. As we walked towards the changing hut, a woman stood in front of us at the end of the path, wearing only grey knickers and a grey woollen hat. She had one breast, jellied flesh, areola the colour of rotten apples, and a scar next to it across flat, plain skin. I found it impossible not to look: the tiny starbursts of varicose veins on her dimpled thighs, striped with black hairs. Her stomach was ripe and creased, belly button disappeared in the folds. I had never seen a woman like that naked; the women who displayed their bodies were watertight, flawless. And yet, there she was, erupting all over the place, looking entirely at peace. In the field to our left there were naked women everywhere, rubbing floppy bodies with towels, drinking from Thermos cups.

I was relieved that Naomi wanted to change inside, and I undressed the way I'd learnt to at school: unclipping my bra without taking my T-shirt off, snaking my arms out of the sleeves and straps, and then pulling it out of the bottom. We came out, my feet freezing on the wet concrete, and stood in front of the unformed mass of water, messily circled with trees, randomly punctuated by red-and-white rings. The water was brown, and a sign warned us it was cold and deep.

I did not want to go in at all, repelled by the murk of the water and the fear of the cold, but in the end my desire not to look weak in front of Naomi was greater. The wet metal of the ladder was sharp on my feet and when I reached the water the cold was worse than I expected. I pressed my lips together and stepped further down the ladder. When I was in up to my waist, I allowed myself the slightest, imperceptible pause before letting go of the rails, turning round and folding into the water.

The shock was intense and I suppressed a yelp as I swam. I could think about nothing else but the cold: it obliterated everything. My breath became loud and hoarse and my heart was beating fast. I forced myself to keep moving through the water.

It was only when I reached the first life ring that I was

able to think of something other than the cold. Everything I could see was twice as bright: clear and delineated. A bird skimmed the water before rising up into the sky and the wind left ripples like fish bones on the surface. A cormorant sat on the life ring, spreading out its wings, the light filtered through its feathers. Bright turquoise beads for eyes, a dash of yellow on its beak.

By the time I reached the boundary rope, the water had become seductive. I dipped my face in it, I turned on my back, and the sensation on the back of my skull was delicious. Now everything had receded – not just home, but the pub, the factory, the high street – it had all faded, set against the brown water, the curling leaves next to my face. I wanted to stay in forever. And then suddenly I was freezing again, my body started to tremble violently, and I swam as fast as I could to the metal steps.

When I got out, I felt weak, as if I had none of the reserves left to stop me erupting into tears, which I did, sitting on a bench, dripping wet and sobbing. The lifeguard came over and asked if I was OK, but I couldn't speak. Naomi sat next to me and wrapped a towel around me, and I cried for the child that I could never have mothered.

'I'm sorry,' I said, when I could speak.

'Happens more than you think,' the lifeguard said, touching my shoulder. 'But you need to get warm, as soon as you can.'

Naomi took me into the changing rooms, where I was shaking so much and my fingers were so numb that I was scared I wouldn't be able to dress myself. My skin was covered in vivid red dots. I put on my clothes, wrapping my scarf tightly around my neck, but it felt as if it made no difference. The cold was inside me.

Naomi took out a Thermos and gave me a plastic cup of tea. We stamped our feet and she held me close and rubbed me vigorously. Then we stood in the meadows together, in front of the pool of water on the other side of the ponds, holding hands, watching the swans.

In December, Susie invited us to dinner to celebrate Clare's birthday. The house at Digby Street had become almost like a second home. It wasn't just the hot water and the company, but the form of it was comforting. Sometimes the effort it took to will the bare factory room into home got tiring. The hallways, walls and curtains were a re-assuring antidote.

Dave at the Black Hart offered me a bottle of sparkling wine at cost price and I paid for it out of my tips. I took it into the kitchen where Susie was bent over a chicken, in a large striped shirt tucked into high-waisted jeans, sleeves rolled up, tenderly rubbing buttery fingers into the crevices. She looked up when she saw me in the doorway.

'I brought you this,' I said, holding up the bottle.

She looked up. 'Oh, hi. That's nice of you.' She turned towards me and held up her hands, slick with grease. 'I can't . . . Can you put it in the fridge?'

She'd pulled her hair back, but it was so short, large chunks had fallen across her face. She tried to push them out of the way with her forearms without getting butter in her hair. It was only partially successful; I wanted to do it for her. It was the first time I'd seen her not in a jumper and it was almost shocking to see the shape of her body underneath the shirt, the fullness of her breasts, the way her waist tapered at the top of the jeans. 'Of course,' I said, and I had to move past her to get to the fridge at the back of the kitchen, aware of the narrow space between our bodies.

Susie had lit tea lights on the mantelpiece in the dining room and even put out a cloth. It was just the five of us; Nya was no longer on the scene. Once, when Clare and Naomi had been making prints in the factory, and I'd come in to bring them a cup of tea, I'd shyly asked Clare what had happened with her.

'Oh, it didn't work out,' Clare had said, taking the cup. 'Thanks, love. I'm actually seeing someone else now.'

'Clare! You didn't tell me that. You sly fox,' Naomi had said, and Clare rolled her eyes and I sat on a stool and watched them work.

After we'd had the chicken, and the sparkling wine, and a Viennetta with a candle in, Naomi said, 'I don't want to be a downer on your birthday, Clare, but I finally managed to look up Ellen – you know, the girl who lived here, with the letters and bits in the box.'

I knew that Naomi was still curious about the box. She'd come back to the factory a few weeks ago, thrilled that she'd come across the letter writer's, Mrs Maxwell's, memoir in a second-hand bookshop on the Charing Cross Road. Jane was performatively disinterested, but I listened to her and she gave me updates as she read it, about this woman's philanthropic work in the East End and her fundraising for the suffrage movement. She'd annoyed her late husband's family by selling a Rembrandt drawing for the cause. But I hadn't heard anything about Ellen.

Jane raised her eyebrows and pushed away her plate, but Clare said, 'Oh yes?'

'I found her records. She died in 1916. She was only twenty-two.'

'Ah,' Susie said. 'That makes me a bit sad, actually.'

'I did get teary looking at the dates,' Naomi said.

'Did it say how she died?' Susie asked.

'Sepsis. Probably childbirth.'

'So she missed Armistice. That's a bummer.'

'It probably wasn't that unusual,' Jane said. 'Particularly for women round here. Childbirth, poverty, miscarriage.' I thought I heard her hesitate, but I could have imagined it. I had to look down. 'Domestic abuse.'

'It's still sad,' Naomi said.

'It was a long time ago. You didn't know her.'

'Not that long,' Naomi said. 'She could have been your grandmother. Great-grandmother. Anyway, isn't that all the stuff we're supposed to be trying to change?'

'I thought so,' Jane said. 'But I don't see how you're going to change anything spending all day in the archives.'

'I don't spend all day in the archives.'

'That's true. Sometimes you spend all day sewing.'

'That's not fair! I made those leaflets for you, didn't I? And it's not just about what I make – we can teach other women how to use the presses and then who knows—'

'Yes, but at some point you've got to actually fucking do something! It doesn't matter how much . . . artwork you make if you're never going to take action! You haven't helped me at all with the plans for the protest. You said you were taking a break after Greenham and how long has it been? A year?'

'I'm just still figuring out what I want to do . . .'

'Naomi, you go on and on about the suffragettes and those bloody matchgirls, but you know you wouldn't have been able to do any of the things they did.' Jane was trying to speak lightly again, but her voice was getting louder and less controlled. 'They'd be setting fire to the letterboxes and you'd be worrying about everyone's post.'

'Well, I would, but so what? There were other ways of protesting, weren't there?'

'Like what? Chaining yourself to railings? Hunger strikes? It's all a disturbance, isn't it? Why should women have to damage themselves in the process? Why aren't we ever allowed to turn it outwards?' She pushed her plate away. 'You like all those stories because it was a long time ago and there was a happy ending. But you would have been useless if you were actually there.'

'No, she wouldn't,' I said. I surprised myself and clearly the others too, who were all looking at me.

'Really?' Jane said. 'Well, what do *you* think, Frankie? Come on, it's not like we've heard anything from you about all this. What's the best way to make change? Direct action? Breaking the law? Peaceful protest?'

I didn't say anything.

'Those are quite big questions, Jane,' Susie said. 'I think it's OK if she doesn't have an answer.'

'I just want to understand where she's coming from,' Jane said, looking at me intently.

'Look,' Susie said, more assertively than usual, 'I think we should talk about something else. Because it's Clare's birthday.'

'Yes!' Clare said. 'It *is* my birthday.' She had an odd expression on her face and she took a sip of her drink. 'It's my birthday and I've got some news.' I noticed that Susie was watching her, affectionate and anxious.

'OK then,' said Jane. 'What's this news?'

'I'm getting married.'

'You're fucking kidding,' Jane said.

'Yes. I mean no, I'm not kidding. Not straight away. But he asked me and I said yes.'

'But you've only been seeing him, what, a few weeks?'

'Three months. But we're in love. We're going to try to buy a place in south London.'

'You're going to be someone's *wife*? Are you going to take his name?'

'Why do you care?'

'Because— The whole point was that things were going to be different! That we weren't going to get enmeshed in this! If you love him, why don't you just be with him? Why do you have to get married?'

'Well . . .' Clare took a deep breath. 'I'm also pregnant.'

The words hurt, unexpectedly and sharply. I couldn't look at her.

Jane shook her head. 'Clare. Just because you're pregnant, you don't have to get married. You don't have to have the baby.'

I began tapping my fingers on the table. I felt like I was going to be sick.

'But what if I want to?' Clare said.

Jane didn't say anything.

'What if I want to have kids?' Clare said. 'What if it's all I've ever wanted? I want to be someone's mum. And I know you think that's a bad thing, but I can't help it being true.'

Jane started scraping the tablecloth with her knife.

'And I told you,' Clare said, her voice rising. 'I told you the stuff I felt conflicted about, that motherhood means something different to me, and you didn't listen, because it doesn't fit. How I feel, the stuff I care about, it doesn't fit in with your worldview, so you just block it out.'

'It just feels like you're giving in! Giving up. It was so bloody hard – to come here, fight for everything, go against everything that was expected of us. And now you're just going to take the easy route.'

'So now you think I've let you down.'

'Well, you have!'

'Why do you always make me feel like I have to choose?' Clare said. 'Do I want to have a baby or do I want to stop the bomb? Do I care more about the women's movement or a black man getting shot in the head by a policeman? Do I want to be an activist or a housewife? I'm sick of it! Why can't I have everything?'

'But it's all connected! That's the point! Racism, sexism, capitalism! We're trying to make a better world.'

'It doesn't feel connected! You don't make it feel connected! You're so fucking single-minded! You never think of how things might feel different for other people!'

'Maybe you have to be single-minded to get anything done!' Jane said. Then she said, limply: 'Anyway, you can't have a family in a nuclear war.'

'What are you going to do? Just not meet anyone? Keep living without any kind of intimacy?'

'I thought we had friendship,' Jane said. 'I thought that would be enough.'

No one said anything. Jane got up and went into the front room to get her jacket. Naomi started clearing the plates and apologising, and then we heard the door slam. Naomi and I took our belongings from the front room and hurried after her.

We caught up with her, but she still walked slightly ahead of us, all the way home. I tried to keep the space between us even and we walked in a kind of procession.

Someone shouted, 'Fucking dykes!' and I jumped. I rarely got attention on my own, but we often did when we were together. I'd put the badges back on Clare's jacket after my date with James, my hair had grown longer and wilder, Naomi's piercings, Jane's dungarees – as a group, we looked different, and if someone noticed, it felt threatening.

We turned into the factory gates and Jane undid the padlock to let us in. She went straight to her curtained area. Malcolm looked up and then went back to his book.

A week later, I went to visit my mother in Kent. When the house sale had gone through, over a month ago, we spoke on the phone and she asked me to pick up the rest of my things before she moved. I put it off and put it off and eventually she stopped asking. And then she invited me to her new house, near Whitstable.

I told everyone I was going to visit a friend in Brighton, which they must have thought was odd, since I hadn't mentioned a friend since my dinner with James, and then I took the train to Whitstable, and walked along the coast to her new house.

It was about forty-five minutes' walk from the station, towards Seasalter. The town felt desolate in December, with limp tinsel in the windows and only a few people out in the streets. And then the cafés, oyster bars and pubs disappeared altogether and I walked down long stretches of deserted beach, past dilapidated beach huts and misshapen groynes, the wood warped into deep crevices. The wind was fierce, and my feet felt beaten by the heavy stones of the beach.

Her house was a small bungalow on the seafront, with a huge glass window at the front. We had a cup of tea, watching the sea, and I revelled in how uncanny the living room felt, all the things from our old house rearranged. We talked about the town and what Christmas would be like, and I picked up as many of my things as I could manage, then walked back down the beach.

By the time I reached town, I still had an hour before my train. I passed a fish and chip shop and ducked in, through a sterile waiting area with a takeaway counter to a steamy room at the back with pinewood panels and painted yellow walls. I asked for haddock and chips and a cup of tea.

'That's going to play havoc with your diet,' the man at the table next to me said when it arrived on an oval plate, and I blushed. He looked me up and down. 'Oh, not to worry, you're slim enough!' he said, and turned back to his dinner.

At about two o'clock, the café started to clear. I watched the people that were still there idly: an old woman in a knitted bobble hat reading the paper and eating chips. I was dimly aware of a family behind me: a small boy asking 'Why?'; the mother sounding increasingly fraught.

When I'd finished my food I went to the ladies, and when I came out I caught a glimpse of them. The mother was saying, 'No! Sit properly!' to a child wriggling on his seat, putting his feet on the wall. The father was reading the newspaper. The child's face looked deeply familiar and for a moment I was confused, wondering why the face of this child reminded me so much of someone who was not here. 'That's not sitting properly!' the mother said, and then to the father: 'Can you give me a hand here, please, Nicholas?' The man put down his newspaper and looked straight at me.

He was wearing different clothes: cords and a shirt. He'd shaved and slicked his hair back. This must be something to do with his mother, I thought. The children must be his nephews. But when the youngest boy turned towards me, it was like looking directly into Nick's face. It wasn't just the likeness – the colouring, the shape of his mouth – there was something else as well. The resemblance that hit you on first glance that would have been there even if their features were different or their hair different colours: the ghost of Nick's expression crossed this boy's.

'Daddy, he got more chips than me,' the second boy said.

Nick touched the woman's arm and said something to her – she looked up at me, bemused – and then Nick got up and walked towards me. He stood opposite me, too close, so I had to lean back slightly to look at his face.

'Hello, Frankie,' he said, pleasantly. My heart was beating faster. 'Fancy seeing you here.'

'Yes,' I said. 'Who's that you're with?'

He looked at me with such concentration and scrutiny it scared me. 'You're something of a dark horse, aren't you?' he said. 'You told me you were going to Brighton this weekend.' He cocked his head to one side. 'Fancy going for a little walk?'

'I haven't paid,' I said.

'Here.' He thrust his hands into his pockets and took out a shiny leather wallet, one I'd never seen him carry before. He put a note on my table. 'Come on.' He took my wrist, with a subtle pressure, and turned his head to his wife. 'Back in a minute,' he said. She nodded unhappily.

We came out onto the little row of shops and he led me away from the station, keeping hold of my wrist.

'Is that your family?' I asked.

331

He didn't say anything. We came out onto the high street – it was now almost empty. I saw a few faces in the lit windows of the pub on the corner, impossible to reach. It was colder now, and the sky was greyer, and he pulled me down a narrow alley running between the shops. There was barely room for both of us between the brick walls and dried spattered bird shit at my feet. The other end of the alleyway, towards the seafront, was very far away.

'I don't have time for small talk, Frankie,' he said, still gripping my wrist. 'You don't tell anyone – *anyone* – about this encounter.'

'You lied to me! To all of us!'

'I mean it, Frankie. Do not breathe a fucking word.'

'Why shouldn't I?'

'Because I'm *telling* you not to.' In that instant, the way he said it, like a parent or a teacher, we both knew he was losing control. He was panicking. I had never exploited that moment in a classroom before, the moment the teacher's authority slipped. But now I did.

'Well, you're a fucking liar, so why would I do anything you tell me? Why would you do that, to her, your wife? Your . . . children? What are they going to think when they find out? Lying, and lying, just so you can have your other life, fuck girls you meet at parties—'

My voice was breaking and I was childishly hitting out at his chest with my free hand. All at once, he let me go.

'Is that what you think this is?' He laughed. 'You think I do this to get *sex*? This has *nothing* to do with you, Frankie! OK?'

'Does Jane know? Does your wife?'

'No! *No!*' He was sweating now and his voice was getting hoarse. 'No, and they aren't going to. This stays between us. I am this close – this close, Frankie! – to getting what I want, and I am not going to let your little . . . *day trip* fuck it up for me. I'm not. I'm just not.'

He let me go and crouched by the wall with his face in his hands. 'You're a kid, Frankie, I know you don't get it. You don't understand what it's like, you can't understand . . . The training, the paperwork, the arse-licking, making tea for Oxbridge cunts, all to get *here*, right where I am now. And then spending years with these . . . tossers, going to meetings, pissing about with leaflets, thinking please, please, for the love of God, just do something I can report back on, you useless, useless fuckers.' He took his hands away from his face and looked up at me. 'I haven't slept for nine months, Frankie. You can't, not properly. You're on edge all the time, can't just switch it off at night. I'm fucking terrified of going to sleep, thinking what if I go under, what if I shout something out in my sleep, what if they find something? What if they already know and they're waiting, so they can *do* something to me? And now – *now!* – it's paying off. Jane's finally fucking doing something, so I can close it up, get my round of applause at Scotland Yard, be done with the whole fucking lot of them. I am not going to let that go because of you.' He put his head between his knees. He was trembling and I could hear him panting loudly. Then he jumped up and hit the wall with his palm. He must have done it harder than he meant to because it startled him and he shouted, 'Ow! Fuck!' and rubbed his palm.

We were silent for a moment. Then he said, 'I mean it, Frankie. No one can ever find out about this.'

'Why should I lie for you?'

'Because—' He took my wrist again. I could tell he was

getting back control. He squeezed harder. 'Because if you don't, there will be consequences.'

I would never have imagined it could hurt so much, the pressure of his fingers on my wrist. I thought about my veins bursting. He pinned my arm back against the wall. I was horribly aware of his strength, his casual force, the brick wall near my head.

For my whole childhood, I had felt reassured by the police. I thought of them as people you turned to if you were lost or there was some sort of accident; they were the people who would help. It had never occurred to me to be afraid of them, until I came to the squat and started absorbing the stories – women getting dragged away on protests, Clare's brother getting stopped three times in a night, squatters nicked on trumped-up charges, or picked off the street, thrown in the back of a van and beaten up. I was no longer someone to be protected. I had crossed over without realising. He kept hold of my wrist.

'What's going to happen to Naomi and Jane?' I asked.

He let go of me suddenly. 'Naomi? Nothing's going to happen to Naomi. What would I nick her for? She doesn't *do* anything. I knew from the moment I met her she was going to be a waste of time. Jane's always been the one – the one I held out hope for.' He looked at me and laughed. 'But why would you care about what happens to her?'

I rubbed my wrist. 'Because . . . I don't want her to go to prison!'

'Jane doesn't like you, Frankie. She never has. She doesn't trust you.'

'I don't think that's true! Why wouldn't she trust me?'

'This stuff! Stuff like today, lying about where you're

334

going. Jesus, I would never have gone anywhere near you if I thought you knew Kent. Not having any friends. Not having any kind of life outside the factory, not that bothered about activism. It's completely fucking obvious you don't belong and they're trying to work out what you're doing.'

I started to tremble. 'I do belong—'

'They know your name's not Frankie.'

'It is my name!'

'Jane went into the pub, asked if you were there one time you were on your break. They said they'd never heard anyone call you that before.'

'It's a nickname.'

'A nickname no one calls you. It looks weird.'

'Why was Jane in the pub?'

'Checking up on you. She's getting paranoid at the moment, which is another reason that I want to finish up and move on.'

'Naomi likes me,' I said.

'Naomi! You think she decides what goes on in that place? Listen, if you tell Jane about today, believe me, you will really fuck things up for yourself, I will make sure of it. You'd be obstructing a police investigation, you know that? You know how serious that is? And I can just tell Jane that you're lying: chances are she'll side with me and then you'll be out. Or you can just wait until I'm finished, carry on enjoying your little holiday from real life or whatever it is you're doing, go back to your mum, and you never have to see me again.'

'OK,' I said, because I didn't know what else to say.

'Good.' I could hear his breath become slower and deeper. I wanted nothing more than to be out of this alley, up on the beach, to see the openness of the sea. He leant back on the wall in front of me and lit a cigarette.

'I thought they were your friends,' I said. 'I thought Jane was.'

He flicked the ash of his cigarette onto the ground. 'I don't give a fuck about any of them. I just want to go back to my normal life.'

'Why don't you then?'

'I've got to finish the job first. Then I will.'

'But you said you'd really worked for it. Why didn't you just have a normal life in the first place, if that's what you want?'

He took a drag on his cigarette and looked up at the sky. 'I don't know. Didn't want to be stuck behind a desk for thirty years or be some crappy local policeman. Wanted to do something more with my life than all the DIY, bike-rides-with-the-kids stuff. But I've done it now. I'll be able to get Jane for something. Conspiracy at least. Then I'll ask for a transfer and go back to my old life.' He tapped his cigarette. 'Can't bloody wait.'

'OK.'

He looked at me. 'What?'

'Nothing.'

'Oh, don't do this, Frankie, it's so fucking irritating. Just tell me what you're thinking.'

'It's just . . . you seem to like it. When you're there. You seem to like the life. You seem to like Jane.'

He turned towards me and for a moment I thought he was going to grab hold of me again. 'That's a load of crap. Haven't you ever heard of acting?'

'OK. You're a good actor.'

He stubbed out his cigarette. 'I'm not talking about this

with you any more, Frankie. This conversation didn't happen. I'm going back to my family.'

I got back to the factory on Saturday night. Nick's absence – that night and for the rest of the weekend – began to feel like a photographic negative staining the room. I spent the weekend dazed, dismantling the images I'd formed about his life in Surrey – the hospital visits, the stews in the freezer. I imagined him looking after his children, getting into bed with his wife. And then I had to dismantle everything he'd ever told me, even from the day we met. I combed over what I could remember of his family – the ages of his children, his wife's clothes, her face – the same way I had, unwillingly, combed over the memory of my father's photographs, because that was all I had that was true, real. The worst part of the betrayal was not the sex or even the baby, because with those things I had still kept some part of myself back. It was when I thought about what I had said to him about my father that I felt the most sick, stupid and ashamed, when I'd been honest and he'd been lying. And now I was lying too. Every time I looked at Jane, I felt guilty and afraid.

Nick came back on Sunday night, and the others were out. It is hard for me to remember everything about that night. I know that I said I didn't want to go down to the cellar, and I know that he said, 'Oh, come on,' and grabbed my wrist, but I can't remember the precise degree of force. I remember being afraid, but I don't know whether he made me afraid, whether the fear came from him or from me. How could I ever know? I remember taking off all my clothes at the sink afterwards, scrubbing between my legs with the flannel, and then scrubbing again, and again.

And then having to get rid of the cloth, balling it up, squeezing it out, burying it at the bottom of the rubbish bins outside and then still thinking about it there. I put the clothes I was wearing in a ball in the corner by my mattress, and three days later, I put them in the bin too.

12

Amanda

2020

In the middle of April, a celebrity I hadn't heard of did an Instagram post about one of Lucy's jumpers, and she spent our morning walk on her phone, talking to her business partner about stock and orders. She kept saying, 'Sorry, sorry, sorry about this,' to me, but she was clearly excited and I found I was too. Despite our arbitrary markers – a different walk for each day of the week, alternating cooking days, cocktails on Friday nights – I was still finding it hard to distinguish between days. Change was thrilling, even if it was happening to someone else.

When we got back, she breastfed Stanley on the sofa, trying to type on her phone at the same time, saying, 'Fuck,' whenever it slipped out of her fingers or Stanley detached. She seemed like a different person, filled with a new kind of energy. I told her that she should go and work upstairs while I looked after Stanley and Iris.

I sat on the sofa, watching them on the playmat together, surrounded with toys. Although I'd spent a lot of time with Stanley, Lucy had always been there, in the next room at least; I'd only been alone with the two of them for small amounts of time. I didn't know what I'd do if both of them needed me at the same time and I felt a brief pulse of panic at the thought.

As the sun came in through the bay window, I watched the babies pick things up, chew them and put them down again. A couple in face masks walked past the window. I remembered when I'd first gone to the singing group with Lucy and she had left me with both of them for just a few minutes, and how impossible it had seemed then. This was happening more often now: things that used to frighten or distress me, or take disproportionate effort, passed without me noticing.

After half an hour, I carried them both into the kitchen and strapped them in the Scandinavian highchairs that Lucy and Chloe had bought, while I went back to the living room to fetch the playmat and the toys. Unlike the houses on both sides, Lucy's kitchen had not been extended, but the narrow strip of concrete between the kitchen and the garden wall turned out to be a good place to put the playmat, outside the open door. I put sun cream on them – the thick, insoluble kind Lucy bought that advertised all the things it didn't have in it – and the new organic cotton sun hats Lucy had insisted we order from an independent retailer. They sat on the playmat while I made them an omelette, turning back to take things out of their mouths or exchange toys. I cut the omelette into strips, took it outside and sat on the back step, watching them eat. Stanley in particular was delighted; he was laughing so hard I thought he might fall over. Iris started laughing and then I did too. Lucy's studio looked over the garden and I could hear her voice through the open window, just catching phrases: 'So what are we saying: another run on pre-order? Should we do it in teal as well? Or just stick with the coral?'

It was a moment of rare alchemy, when everyone was doing something they wanted to do, and I felt as though everything might be OK. These moments used to feel like respite – seconds on the life raft before being sent back out to sea. Now, I could almost believe that I'd reached the shore.

My phone rang and it was Oliver.

'Hey, how are you?' I said.

'Fine. I'm at home today.'

'Oh yeah, you said.' I put another couple of toys in front of the babies and took the bamboo plates into the kitchen.

'It's pretty weird, actually. I live for these days and then I go for a run and it's like, what do I do now? I've got a stack of books but I can't seem to make the words go in.'

I felt a surge of irritation – imagine having *too much* time to yourself. I could tell myself that being alone in the flat would be difficult, if you were used to working hard, if you were lonely, if you missed your daughter, but it didn't stop me craving it. It was so wildly distant from these days I'd now got used to, a tinnitus of small activities, a constant meeting of needs.

'I think it's odd because I was in the Green Zone the last two shifts, you know, normal A&E, and no one's there. I've never seen it like that. No one's coming to hospital. Don't get me wrong, it's nice to get the break, but it's eerie, and you know on the other side of the partition, everyone's going through hell . . . I don't know if I need that much time to think right now.'

I put the phone under my ear, got out Lucy's chopping board and started cutting up grapes. 'Do you want to come round? We could sit on the doorstep and you could stay on the street. Or we could wave through the window.'

'I can't. I just can't. Not if I can't hold her. It kills me when you send me photos of her and FaceTime—'

'I know.' I took the grapes out and sat back down on the steps, watching the babies intently for signs of choking.

'Is this crazy? Should you move back in? I can't tell any more.'

It had been three and a half weeks since we'd seen each other. Lockdown had just been extended for another three weeks. We talked about the separation endlessly, but inconclusively.

'I don't know. But look, we've done it now. Let's not fuck it up by me moving back in too early.'

'I look at the figures every day, you know. Thinking about when we can get back to normal. Anyway. Tell me what you're up to.'

'I just made the babies an omelette.'

'The babies? You're looking after both of them?'

'Lucy's upstairs – everyone's going crazy about one of her sweaters and she's got loads of orders.'

'Everyone wants loungewear, right?'

'That's it.'

'I have to say, in all the time I've known you, I don't think you've ever made me anything. Not even an omelette.'

'It had spinach and potatoes in it. All the food groups.'

'I feel like I don't know you,' he said, and then there was a strange pause.

'Yeah, well, they loved it. Stanley loved it so much I thought he was going to choke.'

'I bet they did,' he said. Then his voice changed. 'I can't believe she's eating food. I read the book, you know the

one I got you with the pictures of cute kids eating straw-
berries, and this was when I was supposed to be on parental
leave and I was actually really looking forward . . . looking
forward . . .'

'I know,' I said. 'I would be in the office now.' It felt unbearable, just then, to be surrounded by the ghosts of the
lives we ought to have been leading. Then Stanley went
bright red in the face, and got redder and redder until it
looked like his skin would burst. I walked over and sniffed
him. 'I've got to go. I've got to change Stanley's nappy.'

Lucy came back downstairs to put Stanley down for his
nap, and this time, both he and Iris slept in the cot. I was
having to take Iris out less and less now, and I was getting
used to, even allowing myself to anticipate, the time apart
from her. Lucy and I usually ate lunch together in the
garden, but today she said she had to go back to work. I ate
a leftover strip of omelette and looked at my phone. After
about half an hour, I knocked on the door of her studio.

'Do you want lunch?' I said.

'Oh, thanks, yeah, I would, I just . . . want to make the
most of this nap.'

'Why don't I make something and you can have it afterwards, when he's woken up?'

'Would you mind?'

I shook my head. 'No, it's fine,' I said. I knew I ought to
go downstairs, but I was curious. 'I've never been in here
before.'

The studio looked out over the garden and the backs
of houses, as my room did. The house opposite had an
incomplete structure projecting out of the back, the open
mouth of it covered over with tarpaulin, piles of roof tiles

343

and planks of wood on the scaffolding. The project had obviously been abandoned some weeks ago. It made me feel anxious every time I looked at it.

'Have you seen that building site?' Lucy said. 'At least we don't have a bloody great hole in our house.'

'They're still living there, though,' I said. 'Do you always see that guy working on his laptop?'

'Oh yeah, I watch them all the time. I really want their kitchen. It's so nice it looks like . . . she's in a TV drama and something bad's going to happen to her.'

Lucy's desk was a huge sloping plane of wood underneath the window that took up most of the back wall. There was a sewing machine and a cracked mug with an artistic print on it, stuffed with pattern scissors, pens, triangular chalk and safety pins. The desk was covered with hundreds of drawings of clothes, as well as notebooks, order slips, packaging. There were two full clothes rails, and shirts and dresses hanging on a cupboard door. A pinboard leant against the wall to the left of the window, covered in pictures taken from magazines, fabric samples, wallpaper samples, a photograph of white blossom against green leaves.

'That's beautiful,' I said, pointing to a scrap of fabric.

'Oh, thanks,' she said. 'I like that one too.'

'Did you study fashion then?' I asked.

She shook her head. 'No. I studied English.'

'So how did you know how to do this?'

'I taught myself. I started making designs and drawings, and looking at clothes that I liked and trying to work out how they were made, and then I just talked to pattern cutters and manufacturers and . . . it went from there.'

'You *taught yourself*? What the fuck, Lucy?'

She looked embarrassed. 'Well, I didn't know if it was going to work when I started out. It was a risk. But people wanted to buy my stuff, and I just got better every time I did a collection, and it just grew . . .'

'I can't imagine doing something like that.'

Looking at her, I was struck by the longing I felt – for the peace, the space, the freedom. The possibility for focus and concentration so unlike the splintered days of the last seven months. I remembered looking at Oliver's mother's desk in the same way, when we went to visit when I was seven months pregnant – she'd caught me staring and laughed. 'You get it back, you know,' she'd said. She was probably right. But the possibility that I wouldn't still haunted me.

That evening, in the kitchen, listening to Stanley murmur to himself on the baby monitor, Lucy was still excitable from her day. It was her night for cooking, but I'd said I'd do it this time. She opened a beer and handed me a glass of wine.

'I just can't believe it. My phone's been going all day. We've completely sold out of pre-orders. We've got a waiting list!'

'It's great. I'm really pleased for you.' I had to look intently at the onion I was chopping, because I was pleased for her, but jealous too. There was something about her that I recognised and wanted for myself. I told myself that I was going back to work too, as soon as this was all over, as soon as the nurseries reopened.

'You know, these last few weeks, we've been busier than we've ever been. Even with everything else that's going on, people are buying stuff. I feel like people are *getting* it, you know: these ideas about comfort and functionality and beauty . . . Anyway, I spoke to Sophie, my business partner, today and she thinks I should start planning a new collection.' She looked at the baby monitor. 'Oh, just shut up, will you, Stanley? I got out my scrapbook again, where I keep these little images, sketches, bits and pieces. I couldn't help myself. I mean, it's ridiculous. I can't launch a new collection now.'

'Sounds like it's good timing,' I said. 'We're through the first six months of maternity leave.'

'Oh, well, I'm self-employed. So I'm not really on maternity leave.'

'I know, but if we were in the normal world, we'd be thinking of getting childcare, going back to work.'

She shook her head. 'I'm not going to get childcare for Stanley. I'd *like* to keep the business going, you know? I'll do what I can with naps. Or if Chloe comes back, we talked about doing a kind of collective childcare thing . . . But to be honest, I just thought I'd keep it ticking over as long as I can. Sophie said she'd take the reins while Stanley was small, but if it's not working with me, well, she can launch a collection by herself, start taking a larger share or something. Even buy me out, if she wants to.'

'But how will you . . . I mean, don't you need to go back to work?'

'I've got the house. And even though it was a headfuck, the good thing about getting pregnant quickly meant that I still have savings. But I was going to put something aside anyway, because I didn't want to get pregnant and then not be able to spend any time with him. I wanted to be in a position where I didn't need to work until he was at least two.' She took a sip from her beer. 'Why, what are you going to do?'

'The original plan was that we'd do shared parental leave. I'd take six months' maternity leave and then Oliver would do three months. But I mean, that isn't really realistic now . . .'

'Oh, wow. Six months. That's so early.'

'It's pretty normal in my industry.' I threw the onion into the pan and it spat. I knew that Lucy was a different kind of person to me. I'd known it from the start of our friendship. I shouldn't have expected her to feel the same way as me about things.

'Still. God. I couldn't do it, I don't think.'

'Well, lucky you don't have to,' I said. I hadn't meant to sound so acerbic, but it didn't look like she'd noticed. She was holding the baby monitor and staring at it.

'Oh, for fuck's sake, Stanley! Right, I think I'm going to have to go in. Have I got time?'

I nodded and she went upstairs. I told myself I was irritated by her insensitivity, her inability to see what it was like for me, her blithe certainty that there would always be money. But it wasn't just that: I felt betrayed. We'd become close talking about how hard we'd found motherhood, and now she was signing up for another two years of it? *This is temporary*, I told myself. *This isn't normal life. You'll move back in with Oliver. You don't have to stay friends with Lucy. You'll go back to work.*

But I didn't like thinking about going back to work. So while the sauce was cooking and Lucy was still upstairs, I looked up what was coming in Lucy's organic veg bag and worked out what I could make with it. Sophie dropped round some of the stock, because there were so many orders she couldn't complete them by herself, and after Lucy and I had eaten, we sat at the kitchen table packing soft pale-pink sweaters into compostable packaging and sticking address labels on them.

When I was seven months pregnant, Meera, the deputy editor, said that we should have lunch. 'You're terrified, right? About going on maternity leave? Don't worry, I'm going to tell you what you're going to do.' She had three children under ten, and once, when I'd been reading a high-end magazine in a café, I'd seen her quoted in an article about combining work and motherhood. She always wore beautiful clothes and seemed so calm, so authoritative in everything she did. I was hoping, I suppose, that she would lend me something of what she had – the apparent ease of moving through the world.

We met in a café near work. She wore a flame-coloured silk blouse, so sharp and clean that I wanted to touch it, dark-grey trousers and gold asymmetrical earrings. Her fingernails were painted olive green. We established the parameters – mid-September, a girl, six months, shared parental leave – and she smiled warmly in the right places. Then, when our food arrived, she said, 'So you want to know what you're going to do when you get back, right?'

I nodded.

'You're going to hire a nanny. You're going to get a cleaner. The nanny's going to cook or you're going to order food in. You're not going to give a shit about homemade birthday cakes. That's not important: the important thing is the time you spend with your children. Everything else: you outsource. And you don't feel guilty about it.'

I had already looked at my salary, and childcare costs, and I had struggled to see how I would make nursery fees work, let alone nannies or cleaners or ordering food in.

But to mention it, to bring up the fact that my partner was a nurse, while her husband was a hedge fund manager, felt deliberately disruptive.

'You'll have to pay the nanny to do bedtime, because you know as well as I do, if you need a legal sign-off or the briefing comes in late, you have to be there. But you'll make it back for bedtime some nights. You can ask to work four days a week and that's fine, they'll probably let you. You spend your fifth day *with your children*. It's the quality of the time that matters, not the quantity. But when you're in the office, for those four days, that's when you are going to *prove* to them that they haven't made a mistake. You're always going to go the extra mile, you're going to be the one who puts their hand in the air when they ask who's going to write that morning briefing. You're going to prove that you haven't disappeared. You're going to show them you're still in the room.'

I yawned by accident, then laughed at myself. 'Sorry – I didn't mean that, like . . . It does sound tiring, though.'

'Tiring? It's bloody knackering. Listen, I have a full-time nanny and believe me, I've heard the stories, I know how lucky I am with her. She does the kids' laundry, she makes food for the freezer, she knows when it's non-uniform day for Black History Month or Odd Socks for Autism or whatever the hell it is this week. She makes bloody rainbow cakes! She used to be a pastry chef, actually. And I still have an A3 whiteboard in my kitchen with everything on it because I have to keep everything in my head.'

I had ordered something I would have wanted to eat before I got pregnant, but I couldn't digest food in the same way and I didn't want to wake up in the middle of the night, as I had last night, crying because there was acid in my throat and I couldn't breathe. I couldn't believe how heavy and slow I felt and I didn't want to feel it because I saw women work up until the last two weeks of pregnancy all the time. I wanted to be the kind of woman who said, *oh no, I don't need a seat, thank you.*

'You'll have to have everything in your head because life happens. The nanny will take holiday or the cleaner's kid's sick, Mina's got chickenpox. There's a meeting at school about Leila's behaviour. Life happens! You can't keep it out, it gets in the way, and anyway, we're not robots. The trick is not to let it get in the way in the office. There'll be weeks when everything goes belly-up and I'm the one holding everything together, but they don't know that. I'm still proving, even now, that they haven't made a mistake.'

She sensed that maybe she'd gone too far. Perhaps I was looking anxious. She changed tack.

'But you'll do it. You'll have your baby and you'll take your six months or whatever and then you'll go back and you'll think, "I can't do it, I can't go on." But you must. And then you'll have another baby and you'll think, "I can't do it, I can't go on." But you must. Because we need women like you.'

I had expected a trick, a tip, but I felt worse than I had before – what she was saying sounded impossible, not just in terms of money but in terms of energy. She sensed me wavering. She was looking at me carefully.

'You've heard the one about "working twice as hard for half as much", right?'

'Yes, of course! It just doesn't seem very fair.'

'Fair! Of course it's not fair! Is it fair I nearly didn't get my first job in journalism because they thought I wouldn't "fit in with the drinking culture"? No. But I was the best candidate on the day, so maybe they had doubts but in the end: I got the job. And I worked my arse off as a junior reporter, as I'm sure you did, and I wasn't going to lose everything I had when I became a mother. I wasn't going to let that happen.' She leant back in her chair. 'Fair! God! You can wait till everything's fair, but you'll be waiting a long time. Or you can just get on with it.' I wondered if I'd ruined my chances already, marked myself out as weak, insufficient.

She made eye contact with the waiter. 'Could we have the bill when you're ready? Thanks so much. Look,' she said to me. 'It's your choice at the end of the day. No one's judging anyone. But when I'm at the school gates or a kid's birthday party, I don't see that many women like me and I don't see that many women who've given up their jobs completely. What I see is women who have shrunk their careers to fit – gone part-time, taken a less demanding job, not moved on somewhere else because they don't want to lose the maternity leave for baby number two.'

The waiter put the bill in the middle of the table – I did a fake reach for my bag; she waved a hand at me and got out her wallet.

'You take your foot off the pedal now, you never get back to where you were. I don't see that many women who don't work at all, to be honest. I see a lot of women living with faded dreams.'

She tapped her card on the machine. 'It's your choice at the end of the day.'

Two days after the Instagram post, Lucy and I sat in the garden after we'd eaten, at the wrought-iron table and chairs her aunt had left behind.

'If everything opened up tomorrow, what would be the first thing you'd do?' Lucy asked.

I looked back at the house. The sight of the blackout curtain on my bedroom window, and the thought of Iris sleeping there, and Stanley next door to her, made me so happy. The kitchen window starting to glow as the light faded.

'Do I have Iris with me or not?'

'Say both. One with Iris, one without.'

'OK . . . With Iris, I'd go to that singing group in the Black Hart.'

'Good one.'

'Without . . . a restaurant, maybe? How about you?'

'Maybe the same . . . Definitely the singing group. With-out . . . I don't know. Go out somewhere. Get a babysitter. Go on a date.'

We had been friends for months, had been living to-gether for nearly four weeks, and I was conscious that she had never mentioned romantic relationships to me. I had always been curious, but followed her lead – I never asked about it.

'I can't imagine going on a date now,' I said carefully.

'I actually interviewed a babysitter two weeks before all this happened. And yeah, when I was talking to her, I felt like it was all hypothetical. Like, OK, sure, you'll come to my house at seven-thirty and I'll go out? She was a teen-ager! Then she spilt her tea on the sofa and I just thought: *no*. I mean, she was mortified, but I didn't care about the sofa. I just thought, *what if you spill your tea on Stanley?*'

'Maybe you don't have to do it right away.'

'No, but . . . I have to make it happen. Otherwise, what, I never go out? I never meet anyone? And you know, companionship . . . sex . . . These things matter.'

I hesitated before asking but I didn't want to miss the opportunity. 'Was there anyone you thought about having children with? Before Stanley?'

'Well, yes,' she said. 'I mean, I was with someone for ten years. We were planning a family.'

'Really?'

She nodded.

'What happened?'

'He left me. For someone else.'

'Oh God, Lucy, that's awful.'

'Yes. It was.'

'Did you have any idea before . . . you know?'

She shook her head. 'I'd like to say all the stuff that you say about David . . . That it was dead for ages, that I knew all along it wasn't right, but there's no point lying about it. I can piece things together with hindsight. I can tell you now what was wrong with him, what was wrong with me, why it would never have worked, but that wasn't what I felt at the time. It was pretty humiliating, actually: begging him to stay, that sort of thing. I was just wrong. I got my whole life wrong.'

'Don't say that – it sounds like he was an idiot.'

'I don't know – he probably did the right thing, didn't he, if he didn't want to be with me? He's still with the other woman. They've got children now. I'm just part of their origin story.'

'I had no idea about any of this,' I said. 'I feel like I've been inattentive or self-involved . . .'

'It was actually such a relief to meet you and realise you didn't need to know. It made me feel like it was part of the past now. And I'm slightly allergic to pity.'

'Me too. That was actually the worst thing after the divorce – the way people treat you.'

'As if you're contaminated. And the way they try to reassure themselves that it won't happen to them *in front of you*: "Oh, that's so awful. But I think the reason Ben and I have such a strong relationship is . . ." I mean, could they not wait till they got home to make themselves feel better? Do it in private?'

'I had that too.'

'Anyway, at least you've got Oliver. I've bought myself a lifetime of being pitied, having a child on my own.'

'I don't know if I do have Oliver, any more.'

'Really? Oh, come on, surely not.'

'I said some horrible things to him before I left. We haven't even been together that long.'

'But you've been through the pregnancy together, and the birth. It must have been at least a year?'

'Eighteen months now. Long enough, I suppose. And you're right, actually, sometimes I think that's just an excuse. I think even if we had been doing it for ten years, like me and David, I don't think it would have been any kind of preparation . . . So what if we'd gone to a lot of restaurants together? Who cares if we liked going to the same museums as each other? It wouldn't have been any kind of preparation for what came next. Sometimes I think I could have picked anyone off the street and had a stab at it and would have had the same chance of success.'

'That can't be true.'

'I don't know. That's how I feel sometimes.'

'Look, don't judge it on now. This is just a strange time. We'll get through it, we'll come out the other side, and you and Oliver will work it out. I bet you will.'

I laughed bleakly. 'You said that to me about getting through the first six months of motherhood. Do you remember? You said things would have got back to normal by now.'

'Did I? Well, sorry, I'm not psychic. It would have been a bit weird if I'd predicted this, wouldn't it? When *this* is over, we'll go back to normal.'

'It's not going to happen like that, though, is it?' I said. 'You know, when we talk about all the fun things we're going to do when it's over – that's not going to happen. There's not going to be one day when it's all over and we don't have to worry any more. It's still going to be there. Even when the lockdown's over, we're going to be worrying about touching and breathing and hugging, for God knows how long.' I looked down. 'Sometimes I can't imagine what normal life looks like. I don't know what it is any more.'

We were still for a moment. I looked at the house again, the kitchen interior now a clear, bright image set against the dusk. Some days, walking Iris up and down the hallway to get her to have a quick nap before bed, bathing her under the skylight, kneading dough on the kitchen table, I couldn't believe that this house would only ever be a fragment of her childhood. The bay window, the oval mirror above the fireplace, the tea chest with the red interior and the gilt edging that Lucy sometimes put lavender or rosemary in – it all felt like part of me now. I couldn't believe that I would have to leave.

'Well, maybe some of that's true,' Lucy said. She looked away and then she got up. 'You'll be fine,' she said as she walked into the house. 'You and Oliver will be fine.'

★

The weekend after my lunch with Meera, I wrote down figures on pieces of paper and Oliver and I talked, the way we always did, but with more urgency: about our salaries, moving somewhere cheaper, only having one child, nanny-shares, nurseries, childminders, commuting from outside London. Nothing worked.

'I can always get her from nursery if I'm on nights,' Oliver said. 'Then you'd have till seven.'

'If you were on nights, you'd have to leave the house at six-thirty. Which would mean me leaving the office at five-thirty. Which I can't always guarantee I can do. And we can't afford to pay a nanny till eight every night just because I might not make it back.'

We kept on talking – 'How would we even get her to nursery? I'm usually working before six anyway', 'Maybe I should change my job', 'Maybe *I* should change mine' – before we came to the end, exhausted, no closer to a solution.

'We could move out of London,' Oliver said. 'I could get a job somewhere else. You could commute.'

'Where to?'

'Near your mum? She could help with childcare?'

'And our child will be the only mixed-race kid in her class?'

'I survived.'

'I tried *so fucking hard* to get here, it would feel like going backwards—'

'Fine, but don't pretend it's about her if it's about you.'

When I'd been doing IVF, covering social affairs, filing three stories a week instead of three stories a day, I watched Julianne, a senior reporter, trying to negotiate with the lawyers and the newsdesk to get her piece signed off before

6.30 p.m. and taking calls from her nanny at the same time. I watched her getting increasingly agitated – 'Have you given him Calpol? What did you say his temperature was? Shit, OK, OK. I can't, I can't right now, I'll be done soon. Look, have you tried putting him in the bath?' I wasn't scared then; I was just curious about how she'd let it happen to her, how she'd allowed herself to get into that situation. I didn't think it would be like that for me. I would find a way of handling it better.

When I finally got pregnant, I was scared. I began to study women like Julianne for evidence that they were doing things differently, that I would not make the same mistakes that they did. It was the same defensive fear with which I approached people's stories of early motherhood – *I would just sleep-train my baby, I would just give my baby a bottle, that's an extreme situation, she just had postnatal depression, that's just a horror story.*

'Look, at least we've got the flat,' Oliver said.

'That we can't live in with a child.'

'Yes, but you don't have a mortgage. Come on, we've been so lucky. If you were just a few years younger, you'd never have been able to buy in London . . . We couldn't afford childcare and rent.'

I stared at the pieces of paper. 'But it *still* doesn't work. I don't see how I can do my job when the baby's here. And if I can't do my job when I've had a child, then the people in the room making things happen or writing about the things that happen are going to be men with wives or women with rich husbands or women who don't have children. I don't want it to be like that.'

'Maybe that's how it is,' Oliver said.

'I'm not going to give up on this,' I said. 'I'll find a way to make it work.' I went into maternity leave without a plan. I thought I'd figure it out.

Four weeks into lockdown, Lucy asked me to cut her hair. She had stopped dyeing it when she was pregnant and now it was dark until her chin and blonde to her shoulders.

'Really? I actually think it looks quite good like that,' I said.

'I'm fed up with it. Please.'

She ordered some scissors online and I said I would do it at nap-time, if both of them went down OK. She went upstairs to have a shower and Oliver rang.

We had been talking more and more about when to move back in together, circling through dates and figures, with no clear answer. Whenever I tried to imagine it, being back in the flat, by myself for most of the day, I felt the same loneliness and helplessness I'd had in the first weeks of Iris's life – that I wouldn't know how to look after her or what to do with her. I told myself that she was older, that I did know what to do with her now. But still, the feeling was there.

'It wouldn't be like going back to how it was before, you know,' Oliver said. 'You've seemed so much stronger recently.'

'I know,' I said. 'Of course. I think we should just wait until the best time—'

'It will break me to miss much more of her childhood.'

'I know,' I said. Lucy walked into the room, with wet hair. 'I've got to go.' Lucy took a chair from the kitchen table and sat down in front of me, with a towel around her shoulders. 'Are you sure about this?' I asked.

'Yep. Definitely. Time for something new.' I cut across

the blonde stripe. Wet strands lay on the kitchen floor. It was strangely satisfying.

'How are things with work?'

'It's slowed down a bit now,' she said. 'Which is probably good. This week has been manic. I've never spent this much time apart from Stanley before.'

'Has it been weird?'

'A bit. It's more weird that it isn't weird. I really trust you with him.'

I felt happier than I'd expected. I bent down and put my face close to her head to check if the lines were straight.

'It's almost chilling, though, because sometimes . . . sometimes I forget. At my desk, speaking to the manufacturers, sending out parcels, I feel like the same person I was before I had him. Like he hadn't happened. It scares me, how easily I can not think about him.'

'Is that scary? It sounds quite nice. I'm always scared I *won't* get back to how I was before.'

'I have dreams about forgetting him. All the time. I dream I've left the house and I'm doing something else and then I remember, shit, no one's looking after him. And I'm trying to get back as quickly as possible, to work out . . . work out . . .' She took a deep breath. 'What will have happened to him when I get back? Will he have fallen down the stairs or pulled something on top of him? Or will he be OK? Like, how would he die? How long would it take him to die? If no one was looking after him.'

'Oh God, Lucy.' I crouched down next to her. 'That's not going to happen.'

'I thought . . . when I had him, I'd stop caring. About work, or my clothes, or anything else. I thought my business would just seem trivial and he'd be the biggest thing in my life, and it would be . . . fine. And now, when I think about letting it go, letting Sophie take over, losing it just when it's starting to take off – it's breaking my heart. But I don't want to feel like that.'

I stood up and started cutting again.

'You know, my mum said she never wanted kids,' she said. 'My dad persuaded her.'

'Oh . . . but she changed her mind when she had you, right?'

'No!' Lucy laughed, but I'd never heard her laugh like that before. 'She said she regretted it.'

'Really?'

'Yeah. She was dead against me having Stanley. I've had therapy and I've made my peace with it and I'm not the same person. I'm going to do things differently, but when I have those dreams . . . I just worry I wasn't cut out for it either.'

'Lucy, you're an amazing mum.'

'Oh, everyone says that. *Oh, you're an amazing mum, you're doing so great.* It doesn't mean anything. I always think, *how would you know?* You see me for half an hour with him when I'm holding it all together. It's just something you say to cheer people up. No one actually knows.'

'I've seen you with him for a lot more than half an hour,' I said. 'And fine, maybe you're not an amazing mum. I don't think I am either. But I think we're OK.'

'What, the "good enough mother" stuff?'

'Yes! And I hated that when I heard about it because I don't want to be good enough. I've never wanted to be good enough my whole life. I want to be fucking fantastic at everything I do, and when I had Iris, it felt like I'd been given the most important thing in the world to do and I *hated* the idea that that was going to be the first thing in my life that I cared about and didn't do well. I still hate that. But I don't think I can be amazing, I just can't, so maybe . . . maybe a good enough childhood . . . Well, I think that's a lot. I think what you're giving Stanley is a lot.'

I had stopped cutting and had my hand on her shoulder. She reached up and touched it.

'Look, I'm not going to cut any more,' I said. 'I don't know if it's completely straight, but if I keep trying to even it up, you're going to end up with no hair.'

She held up a mirror. 'It's perfect.' She put the mirror down and smiled sadly. 'I'm going to miss you.'

I went to get the brush to sweep up the hair. 'It'll be nice to have Chloe back, though,' I said.

'Oh, I don't know if Chloe's going to come back.'

'Really? Why?'

'Just a hunch. We've been messaging . . . She hasn't said anything as such but she seems happy, her mum's looking after them both. I thought she might do it before, actually, just go and live with her mum. And maybe, well, having you here made me think . . . This' – she gestured at me – 'was more what I had in mind when I pictured it. I don't know if it worked out the way I wanted with me and Chloe.'

'Why not?'

'I don't know. I've been trying to figure it out. Maybe because she's a bit younger than me, she's at a different place in her life. Maybe it's easier now the babies are older. Or chemistry.'

I was more pleased than I thought I would have been at the word 'chemistry'.

'Don't feel you have to rush back, anyway,' she said. 'I think I might have a spare room for a while.'

'The thing is, I have to go back, because, you know, Oliver's Iris's dad and I have to go back to work and . . .'

'Oh yeah,' she said. 'It's just up to you, that's all I'm saying.'

At the end of April, I had got off the phone with Oliver and was clearing the kitchen after Iris had gone to sleep. I was starting to think about something for me and Lucy for dinner. I heard her on the stairs and then she came in and reached for a beer.

'All good?' I asked.

'Yes,' she said. 'He's still chatting, but . . .' She held up crossed fingers. She took a wine glass out of the cupboard and poured me a glass of wine. Then she walked to the back of the kitchen and looked out over the garden.

'Did you see they've started work on that house again?' she said. 'The builders are back.'

'Is that legal?'

'I don't know. Anyway, I'm not sure I'd blame them if it wasn't.'

'I just spoke to Oliver,' I said, taking some potatoes out of the fridge.

'Oh yes?' She turned away from the window and came and stood next to me as I started peeling them into the sink. 'How's he doing?'

'OK. He says things are starting to get quieter at the hospital. It's pretty clear it's past the peak. And Iris isn't really at risk. So we think it's time for . . . you know.'

'What about you being alone in the flat?'

'I'll be back at work soon.'

'Really?'

'Yeah. I mean, depending on when nurseries open and whether I can get Iris a place, but if all that goes ahead, yes. I could extend my leave to a year, probably, but I've extended it once already.'

'Wow.' She shook her head.

'What?' I said.

'She just seems so young, that's all. I mean, they're babies. Do you want a hand with those potatoes?'

'No, it's fine, I don't mind. Well, like I say, I was supposed to be back now.'

'And you were OK with that?'

'Yes! It's not like what you do. I can't just choose not to launch a new collection or work in nap-times. The world doesn't go on pause when I'm not there – someone else is doing my job. Right now. I've handed over everything I've worked for – all my contacts – to someone else, and the longer I'm away, the more I feel like I'm . . . losing everything.'

'Do you have to go back five days? Like, is there a part-time version of your job you could do?'

'Oh, yes! *Yes*, there is – there actually is a version of my job which I can do part-time and get paid the same, and it's equally fulfilling, and I don't lose any status within the company. Thank God you pointed it out – I tell you what, I'll ring up on Monday and ask if I can just do that job instead.'

She looked sulky. 'Fine, sorry.'

'Look, I know you want to take two years off or whatever, but I think it's actually a bit insensitive of you—'

She groaned. 'Oh, for God's sake. I didn't think we had to do that here.'

'Do what?'

'All the looking-after-people stuff. Not ever saying what you really think. Can't upset anyone, got to keep everyone happy, so just pretend you don't have any opinions about anything. I get so tired of all that . . . remembering to be self-deprecating all the time so that no one feels offended. It's exhausting! I can't be bothered! I think it's important for babies to be around people who love them when they're small. Why can't I just say that?'

'You can say what you like. But Oliver's a nurse, Lucy. I don't own a house I could raise a child in, I don't have two years' worth of savings, I can't just . . . dick around with buttons during nap-times and see what happens. It's not a choice for me—'

'Well, if it's not a choice, why are we even talking about it?'

'All right then. It's not a choice, but also I don't want to. I don't want to keep doing this! I don't want to sing nursery rhymes and make mushed-up apple! I went into journalism because I wanted to make a difference, I want-ed to change things. I wanted to do something important. Something that matters.'

'Well, I think what I do matters.' She held up her beer bottle. 'I might go and sit in the other room while you do this then.'

'I don't . . . Of course I think it matters, I just . . .'

'You just don't want to do it yourself.'

'No . . .'

'I'm glad you had a good time with me,' she said, turning round in the doorway. 'I'm glad you enjoyed your little holiday, but you can go back to real life now.'

'Oliver's my partner, Lucy,' I said. 'He's Iris's dad.'

'Sure,' she said. 'This was only a temporary thing anyway.'

'Right,' I said.

We ate together, mostly in silence. After I'd cleared up, Lucy went back to her studio. I went out into the garden where it was warm and light and sat on one of the iron chairs, with another glass of wine.

It would be over soon, this strange emergency state and Iris's babyhood. I had known that it would – I had thought about it all the time for the last five weeks, counting down days, making lists, savouring memories and hopes for when it was all over. From the beginning, we had been preparing for it to end.

Three days after Iris was born, I had curled up on the sofa, clinging to her, crying. I knew I'd made a terrible mistake and all I could think about was how easily she could stop breathing, and how easily I could stop her breathing, and I was terrified of what might happen, of what I might do. (My milk crashed in the next day: my breasts were hard, huge, unrecognisable. *Baby blues*, the midwife said.) I knew then that I would not find it 'surprisingly easy' as I'd hoped. I could not just 'carry on as normal, but with a baby'.

After that, all I wanted was my old life back. I wanted not to be leaking milk and blood. I wanted to wake up in the morning and my first thought not be, *when can I go back to sleep?* I wanted to be able to choose when to go to bed, to choose when to wake up, to choose what to wear, instead of picking one of three or four outfits off the floor. I tried to live in the present as everyone said I should, to treasure every moment, but really I was waiting: waiting for spring, waiting for Iris to grow up, waiting to go back to work.

And now, there was bright sunshine, and Iris's fluffy pram suit and her woollen hat felt like artefacts from an ancient era. And I was still waiting: to move back home, to get back to work, to get a vaccine. But it was different now, because a horrible little thought that I tried to bury was surfacing: what if normal life didn't exist any more? I could not imagine a world after this. I didn't want to go home. I didn't know how to look after my child without Lucy. I could not afford to do my job. I couldn't manage the long days alone. I was attached to a man I didn't properly know. Over the past six weeks, my vision of normal life had been getting thinner and thinner and now it was ghost-like.

My real fear was this: that my life was here now, in this liminal space, waiting for something indefinable that never came. I would move into the next phase of endurance and wait for it to end, and there would be another phase and another and another, and then it would all be over, Iris's childhood, my life. It would be over, and I'd wished the whole thing away.

Lucy came out holding my phone. 'Someone's really keen to get hold of you,' she said.

I looked down and saw it was my mum calling. I think I already had a bad feeling as I answered, but I can't be sure. I spoke to her briefly and then I went back in. I stood in the hallway, watching the little crescent of ink-blue sky above the front door.

Lucy came out of the front room and stood in the doorway with her arms folded. 'Everything all right?' she asked sullenly.

'My nana's died,' I said.

V

13

Ellen

1909

They found Mags at the foot of the broken staircase, her head on the hard floor. One of the steps had finally given out. The candle she'd been holding had set her dress alight; we didn't know if she'd died from the fall or the burns. The last time we'd seen her was at Saturday breakfast – a girl on her floor said she'd been looking for something she'd lost from her pocket just before we went home. She must have gone down to the cellar to look for it before the factory shut. We didn't know if she'd died instantly or over hours or a day.

I thought about what would have happened if one of us had waited for her on Saturday. If I hadn't run straight to Miss Morton's but had lingered with the girls, would I have suggested we go looking for her? If Mr Simpson had checked the cellar before he locked the place up. I thought about what a corpse lying somewhere for a day and a half would do to a place: what it would send out into the air, what would settle in between the bricks or gather in the corners.

I had never liked the smell of the glue, but now the

rotting, animal smell was unbearable. A girl turned over a pitcher of it and I wanted to vomit at the sight of the steaming rubbery stuff pooling on our bench. The girl lost time clearing it up and had to work an extra half an hour. I retched for days afterwards.

I couldn't work the way I used to. My fingers were slow and I kept making stupid mistakes, but I wasn't the only one. The piles of failed boxes grew bigger. Lou spilt boiling water on a girl's hand and the girl threatened to cut her face with a fish knife. A girl on Mags's floor, Sarah, nicked her finger on the card, and they said it was just a paper cut, the kind we all got from time to time: a clean slice, spilling scarlet. But hers wouldn't heal. It turned into a glistening crater instead. She wore a bandage on her finger and the yellowing stains on it grew bigger during the day. She got slower and clumsier until she couldn't work any more. I didn't see her again.

I hated going down to the cellar, but we all did, so we took it in turns the way we used to. I tried to think only about my feet on the stairs and my hand on the candlestick, to be careful and deliberate and not make a mistake. I had to concentrate, very hard, on the job I had and not think about Mags, but when I came back out, my body was shaking and I wanted to cry.

An article had appeared in the local paper about the accident, criticising the factory and working conditions for women and girls in the local area – the low pay, the long hours, the fines system, the fetching and carrying of card and hot water, the cellar steps. They were all things I'd known were unfair, but like with Miss Hartley's talk, hearing another person say it made it feel new. In the paper, Mr Simpson was quoted as saying that the factory was perfectly safe and the girls were well treated. A girl told us that she had overheard him in private calling Mags 'a clumsy little fool'.

'Any one of us could've broken our neck on that drop,' Lou said one breakfast-time as we stood in the yard at the back of the factory. 'There was girls going up and down all day.' It was cold now, and we had to stamp our feet and clutch ourselves to stay warm. We still preferred to be outside.

'And he ain't even replacing the steps,' Betty said.

'My auntie says we should organise a walkout,' Lou said. 'She said they walked out of the biscuit factory when she was younger and they got a shilling more for their wage.'

'He'd find some other girls to work for him instead,' Mary said. 'We're cheap, he knows that.'

'Not if everyone walks out, he couldn't,' Lou said.

'And how are you going to get everyone to walk out then? There'll always be girls who'll stay because they need the money, and I don't blame them. And how do you suppose any of us would get by without our wage, come to that?'

'Maybe we could speak to Miss Horner's mate,' I said. 'Gwendoline Hartley. Maybe she could help us.'

'How? Pay all our wages?'

Lou hit the wall with her fists. 'We've got to do *something*! He – that . . . *cunt* – can't get away with it.'

'But I don't care about the pay!' Mary said. 'I don't want an extra fucking shilling a week! I want to burn the building down with Mr Simpson inside it. I want Mags to come back. That's what I want. But we can't do that, and she isn't coming back, so what's the point in talking about walkouts.'

There was a current running through the whole building – it surged and faltered throughout the day, but it was there all the time, agitation and discontent murmuring under everything we did. Mr Clifford and Mr Simpson were rattled. They shouted, issued fines, punched girls in the back. Mr Clifford even hit a girl round the face one time. But there was nothing for them to worry about. We didn't know how to turn it outwards. We were the ones who got hurt.

Miss Morton and Miss Horner were not themselves when I came to clean. 'I'm so sorry about your friend, Ellen,' Miss Morton said, in a weak, shocked voice, clutching my hand, and I had to look away because I didn't want to cry. When I visited the next week and the next, they were subdued and preoccupied, and their front room was quiet as I scrubbed the passageway.

Miss Hartley picked up the stories in the local paper and wrote something in one of the nationals about the scandalous working conditions in the East End, but it was like reading about someone else: Margaret Card, fourteen years old. They made her sound frail, pitiful, like a bird with a broken wing, like the other poor women we'd got used to reading about, the poisoned lodger or the Ripper girls. Women you expected to get hurt. When I thought about what Mags was really like, and how little anyone understood that, I wanted to scream.

Three weeks after Mags had died, on a Sunday night, I found myself awake at four o'clock. When I heard Iris cry, I got up, scooping her out of Mother's bed. She was getting easier to settle now and I only walked her up and down the passageway for half an hour or so before she fell asleep in my arms. This time I did not put her back in the bed or try to sleep next to her. I sat on the sofa and held her close to me, and I started to cry.

I tried to do it quietly so I wouldn't wake her. I tried to stop my chest from juddering as my breath quickened and I shook my head to try to stop my tears falling on Iris's head. I was not crying for Mags or myself. I was crying for Iris.

She was five and a half months now, far older than the babies who had gone. She was on the side of the living now, she had been for months. But that didn't matter because, even if she survived her first year, even if she lived to be my age, even if she was alive when I died, one day it would end. I tried to soothe myself, but I could not escape the thought, as certain as it was unbearable: her life would end. And I thought about what was waiting for us: the lost babies, the punch in the back, the endless struggle to make the wages last. Why bother? Why bother, if it was all going to end with you lying on a cellar floor, neck broken, body burnt, for an entire weekend? I had believed things would be different for Iris, that her life would be better. Now, I wondered why I'd believed that. I held her close and she slept, oblivious, in my arms.

In the end, it was Eliza who began. I went into work on Monday, drained from my wakeful night, and covered the boxes, slowly and dolefully, the only way I knew how to work since Mags had died, until the breakfast bell rang. In the yard, as I was eating my bread and dripping, we heard that Sarah, the girl with the infected finger, had been sacked. I did not think much about it. It was unfair, but it was only her finger. She hadn't been burnt like Alice or died like Mags. The bell rang and we went back upstairs to carry on our work.

It was eleven o'clock when we heard the sound of boots, dozens of them, on the stairs. We looked at each other, startled, and then ran to the door. We could hear them on the stairwells below us: girls running, faster and faster, out of the factory. We ignored Mr Clifford shouting at us, as we clamoured at the window at the front of the building. At first we saw nothing: just the empty cobbled yard. And then Eliza came out, and then more girls after her, and then more and more, until a whole crowd of them gathered there.

I looked at Mary, astonished, and then at the abandoned card and glue on our benches. It was as if we were seeing the room from very far away; everything was familiar but changed. The girls' faces – bright, alive – did not look the same. Then there was more noise on the stairs, footsteps echoing up the stairwell, louder than before. Then the commotion was just outside our door. The girls on our floor were coming out.

I wish I could say that I chose to go, but I didn't. I was pulled along by something else, some great dark energy that was bigger than any of us, as I ran down the stairs, letting myself be dissolved into the crowd. In the yard, I stood among the girls, bewildered by the feeling of fresh air on my face in the middle of the morning. I had not been outside at this time on a weekday for months. Mr Simpson came out and shouted at us to get back inside. None of us moved.

Eliza led us out of the yard and down into the high street. We were already getting looks, fifty girls walking down the road in a mass. No men or boys had come out.

I had no idea where we were going or why – I don't know if any of us did – but just to be out, to be moving, to no longer be contained by the factory walls: it was the most extraordinary feeling, uncanny and marvellous. We followed Eliza to the marshes and sat on the grass and the story was told again and again: Mr Simpson had asked the girls on Mags's floor to sign a piece of paper, saying that Mags and Sarah had not been mistreated. Eliza was the first to refuse. She was threatened with the sack if she didn't sign, but she spat on the floor in front of him. He threatened to smash her face in. She still refused to sign. She walked out, and the other girls followed.

There was a demented feeling of release. Girls took their boots off and danced. When a girl got up and ran back towards the factory, the crowd yelled at her. I sat on the grass, giddy with the unexpected freedom, but also lost and confused. Mary sat next to me, staring straight ahead, and I could see from her expression that her mind was working.

We sat out all day. Girls left to get food at dinnertime; a few didn't come back, but most did with pies and herrings and potatoes, and we shared out our shillings between us. By the time I got home that afternoon, I felt exhausted and permanently changed.

'Oh, good Lord, you weren't with them girls today, were you? Out on the marshes?' Mrs Atkins said as I came past her on the step. I didn't say anything. She shook her head. 'Oh, your poor ma.'

Mother was in the parlour, at the sewing machine. 'Oh, Ellen,' she said when she looked up.

I sat down in the easy chair. I felt weak and paper-thin, as if I could disintegrate any minute.

'Did you hear about it?'

'A group of girls that size walking down the high street? We all heard about it. I thought you'd have more sense.' She stopped the sewing machine. 'You can go back to-morrow. Tell him you've been silly. If the others stay out, he'll be grateful for the work.'

'We're not going back,' I said. 'We agreed.'

She hit the table with her hand. 'Ellen!' she said. 'You can't do this to us. I *need* you, I need your help.'

I didn't say anything.

'What will we do? What will we do without your wage? We can't survive on . . . this!' She stuck her hand into the work basket and held up a fistful of shirts and collars. 'And we'll lose the rooms, if it carries on! We've never been in debt in our lives. Not to mention what Miss Povey will think of you.'

'There's cash in the tin,' I said.

'And how long will that last? Oh, Ellen, I know what walkouts do. I've seen it. People starve. Iris! Iris, Ellen. Iris needs you.'

I couldn't speak. All I knew was that my old life, my life from a few hours ago, was unreachable. I did not want to keep going, but I knew that I couldn't go back.

'Ellen!' she said. 'What on earth will we do?'

'I don't know,' I said.

It was Eliza who began but Mary who organised us. She called for me in the evening and told me we would meet back in the yard the next morning to form a picket line. Only a handful of girls went in but the men, the cutters and scorers, pushed past us. We sent girls round the back to try to get the homeworkers to join us and then we tried to block the way of the man coming to collect the work. Eliza went first, pushing him backwards, clawing his face, and when he managed to grab her and drag her off to one side, another girl blocked his way, and then another and another.

I had stood in the yard surrounded by girls so many times but now I was part of them, one pulsing, quivering mass. I didn't see Eliza go. But when she came back, with the abattoir girls, carrying tin buckets, I felt a new dark power run through us all. We moved towards the building. The crowd got tighter. I saw fronds of hair escaped from hats, cheeks shiny with sweat, lines etched under eyes. A fist curled round a brick. I was pushed into the front of the crowd and I saw that the buckets were filled with dark, glistening liquid. Eliza lifted one up and splashed the factory door with blood, and then another and another. Mr Simpson came out and she soaked him too. Everyone cheered. Another window went.

And then Eliza took something from her pocket. My whole body jolted when I saw it. I can still see it now: the rough, splintered wooden handle, the great silver blade like a giant tooth. I watched her hold out her forearm, and I turned away. When I looked back, her arm was a mess of scarlet. She started smearing her own blood on the factory windows. The girl next to her took the knife and did the same, girl after girl, dripping, smearing their own insides on the windows and doors, until the police were called.

The following week was awful and wonderful. Eliza and the abattoir girls were arrested, but the rest of us formed a picket line every day. Three of the cutters joined us – Edward, who was friends with Mags's brother, and two of his mates he persuaded to come with him. We could still make it difficult for the rest of them to pass, even as one girl got pushed against a wall and another elbowed in the stomach. But in the end, there was no one to make up the boxes with their card. On Thursday, Mr Simpson closed the factory and that was when we started marching.

We marched up and down the high street and over the marshes, in the cold and the sleet and occasional late autumn sun. Mary said that we needed to look our best for marching – 'show them we're serious'. She'd found a fur tippet from somewhere and she wore it with her best hat. Lou showed me how to do my hair again and I wore my Sunday dress and jacket and my best boots. In the end, the newspapers mocked us for what we wore, going on about our hats and our hair, but we didn't stop. It made a difference to us.

Mary persuaded more of the cutters to join us, and local grocers to support the strike with food on tick. She organised loans for girls who needed the wage most. She went to speak to Mr Simpson to negotiate a pay settlement. The girls in a candle factory on the high street walked out too. Newspapers spoke about a strike fever spreading, and how families would starve.

I woke before four most days and sat in the easy chair with a blanket round my knees, waiting for light, my thoughts breeding and incomplete. I had altered too quickly, like a forced plant or an overfed animal – I was terrible, gargantuan, unrecognisable. My body ached in unfamiliar places from the walking. There were seeping blisters on my feet. I felt one thing and then I felt its opposite. I wanted more than anything for Mary to reach a settlement so we could get back to work, and I wouldn't have to worry about the rooms or the money in the cash box or the girls I recognised queuing at the pawn shop. And then the thought of going back to ordinary life, after all this, was appalling.

The following Thursday, we took a day off marching and met in Victoria Park. It felt like a Sunday afternoon or a bank holiday; it was cold but sunny and a street vendor gave us hot cocoa and warm meat pies: 'For the cause, girls!' We danced and sang. I saw Mr Clifford walking with his wife and a young girl. His wife was pushing a baby in a pram. They were not speaking. She looked sober and stared straight ahead, but it was his face I thought about at four in the morning: sunken, lined, haunted.

When I got home, I found a small parcel of newspaper outside our parlour door. I unwrapped it, not liking the light, soft feeling of what was inside, and I saw a bundle of fur, grimy string, a glassy eye, delicate feet. It was a parcel of dead mice. Mary had got a dead bird, stomach smashed, entrails slopping out in her passageway.

When we marched on Friday, a man shouted, 'Well done, girls!' And then the other calls started: *whores, suffragettes, when are you girls going to give up?* A woman threw a chamber pot at us. Mary wore her rabbit-skin tippet, Lou had found a fur boa from somewhere. I wore my Hampstead dress underneath my coat. I held Mary's hand and she held Lou's, who held Betty's, and we walked together up and down, and I don't think I had ever been happier.

On Monday, Mary asked me to come with her to see Miss Horner's friend, Gwendoline Hartley, who had written about Mags for the paper. She had asked Miss Morton for her address the previous week and written to her the same day. Miss Hartley had replied asking her to tea.

Miss Hartley's address was a place called Unwin Court, in a suburb of Hampstead. We took the train and walked up to the top of the Heath, still beautiful, even in the cold. The skeletons of the trees were emerging as we went past the field where the fairground had been. The colours were deep and wild, gold and bronze quickening through the green, flecks of flame red like falling sparks.

We did not know where we were going exactly, but we kept moving up, past the fence we'd climbed over to swim, past writhing, leafless trees. Our boots sank in water-logged grass. I had worn my good boots, of course, and now they and my stockings and the edge of my skirt were splashed with mud. By the time we reached the woodland, I gave up trying to keep them smart and we ran over the uneven ground, covered in copper leaves, glinting pools of water in sunken ground.

The wood opened up, and the ground became flatter and calmer again. Mary directed us off the main road, past enormous brown-brick houses, down a quiet lane. We first saw a neat hedge and an entranceway striped black and white like sweets in a jar. A porter gave us a look, but told us to follow the cloister round to the stairs on the left-hand corner. He came out of the lodge and watched us go as we walked through a covered passageway that framed a square of green grass.

There was no noise. In the passageway, we were sur-rounded by white walls and ceilings, and pale-blue doors. Large curved arches were set in the wall, looking out to the stillness of the green. We went up a dark wooden stair-case, and knocked at number ten.

Miss Hartley showed us into a small parlour, with a fire burning in the brick fireplace. There was a sofa covered with coloured blankets, a bookcase, a china vase with fresh flowers in it, and plants with giant leaves. A dresser with blue-and-white crockery. A music stand and a violin. We saw another room through an archway, which had a bed with a patchwork quilt over it.

Miss Hartley pulled a floral curtain across the archway, to hide the bed. 'I'm sorry, girls, I'm not quite ready for you,' she said. 'Let me make you some tea.'

There was a small corner kitchen off the parlour and we stared as she started filling a kettle from a clay sink under the window.

'Do you live here by yourself then?' Mary asked. She walked to the long rectangular windows, to look out at the grass below.

'Oh no, I share it with my friend, Jessica,' she said. 'The violin is hers. I'm tone-deaf, I'm afraid. There's another little bedroom just beside the bathroom.'

'You've got your own bathroom?' Mary asked.

'Well, shared with Jessica, yes. And we share the kitchen. Though communal dining is encouraged. Rather like Girton.'

'It's very nice,' I said.

'Isn't it marvellous! I was enormously pleased with myself when I secured the rooms.'

Mary was still looking out of the window. 'Lots of ladies here,' she said. Miss Hartley laughed.

'Oh, it's all women. That was the idea: housing for single working women. "The spinsters' quadrangle" I believe they call us,' she said, putting the kettle on the grate on the fireplace.

'It's beautiful,' Mary said, and I had never heard her speak so earnestly, with such feeling.

'Well, I believe some of the housing has been set aside for women on a low income . . .' She turned to look at Mary and noted her mud-stained skirt and boots. 'And we have servants, of course. I could always ask the porter if there's any need . . .'

She saw Mary's expression and she didn't finish.

'Now,' she said. 'Tell me about the strike.'

We began to tell her everything we'd done, and she listened carefully and made notes in her notebook, saying things like, 'Gosh, how exciting!' and, 'I must say, I think you're awfully brave.'

'I'm meeting Mr Simpson on Wednesday,' Mary said. 'I was hoping you might help us.'

She put her head on one side. 'How?' she asked.

Mary and I were quiet for a moment. We hadn't thought how she might help us. We had hoped she would know. She kept looking at us and I realised then that she saw us the way Miss Morton did: from behind a pane of glass.

'I can try to write about it, of course,' she said. 'Possibly I can get another piece in one of the nationals. But I don't see how else—'

'I don't know what to say to him on Wednesday,' Mary said.

'Well, what do you want from him?'

'We've asked for more pay. To repair the steps. No fines. Somewhere to eat dinner. But he won't listen and I don't know how much longer we can carry on. The cutters are furious with us. We're all out of work. Some of the girls are barely getting by. It needs to end soon, but I don't know . . . We started it and now I don't know how to end it.'

'I suppose you'll have to come to some sort of settlement with Simpson,' Miss Hartley said, still writing in her notebook.

'But I don't know how to make him agree!'

'Now, I wonder if I have a friend who would know more . . .' She picked up a leather address book.

'I'm seeing him on Wednesday!' Mary said. 'We need to know what to say *now*!'

Miss Hartley put the address book down and looked at us. 'Well, girls, I'm not sure I can help you then.'

When she let us out, there was a lady sitting on a bench on the green, reading. On the other side, there were two ladies standing in one of the arches, talking in low tones and laughing. I tried to linger, knowing I would never come back somewhere like this again, to hold on to the feeling of overwhelming peace, so that I could take some of it away with me, but Mary was walking briskly out. I followed her back down through the woods, until the Heath began to get more crowded. We sat next to each other in silence on the train. I thought about what it had cost to come there – the stamp for the letter, the train fare and the time – when savings were running low and the energy of the original walkout was fading. It was only when we got to Camden that Mary spoke.

'Lucky bitch,' she said. 'Imagine having all that room to yourself.'

'She shares it,' I said.

'Still. All that, just for two ladies.' She sighed. 'It was so . . . still and quiet.'

'No men,' I said.

'I don't think I'd care about that,' Mary said. 'Miss Hartley had her mate, didn't she?'

'Well, maybe we could live somewhere like that, one day.'

I thought she'd tell me to shut up, but she looked down at her hands. 'Don't seem likely, Ellen,' she said, but she was smiling, so I carried on.

'Why not? We could be like Miss Hartley and her mate.'

She turned to me and folded her arms. 'You and me? Oh, just like Miss Hartley and her mate, I'm sure.'

'You and me, Lou and Betty,' I said.

A pulse of sadness passed between us. Remembering Mags now was like a physical pain. Sometimes I thought it was better not to forget, because when I got carried away in the marches, or taken up with playing with Iris, or slept, remembering again felt like an explosion inside me, almost unbearable at its pitch, before it slowly subsided. Mary swallowed and her breath got quick. She turned her face to the window.

'Lou'll marry Jim, you'll see.'

'Do you think?'

She turned back to me. 'They've been walking out a while. She's not going to make a fool of him.'

'What about Betty then?'

'I can't see her somewhere like that,' she said. She looked down. 'Mags would have hated it there. Too quiet. She would have torn the place apart.'

'She would, wouldn't she?'

We pulled in at Hackney, one stop from ours.

'Just you and me then,' I said.

'Did you see that little nook under the window?' she said. 'With the cushions, the view of the green. She could sit there and read every day. When I was younger, I used to pin books to the washing line, so I could read them while I did laundry.'

'Go to the Heath every day.'

'Swim. She had a writing desk. An indoor tap!'

'She had a bath!'

'She didn't!'

'She did! I saw it when I used the water closet.'

The train was coming in to our station. Mary stood up.

'You and me then,' I said. 'Why not? We could.'

'Oh, don't be so fucking daft, Ellen,' Mary said, hanging on to the strap in the carriage. She was still smiling.

On Wednesday, Mary met with Mr Simpson to make a settlement. A group of girls gathered outside the factory anxiously, and cried when she came out and said they hadn't come to an agreement. She told me afterwards that he'd said he'd give her, but only her, a raise of three shillings if she called off the strike. When she refused he called her a little fool.

It was all beginning to unravel. I scraped together the rent for Sunday from the savings that I had, but I didn't know if we would last another week. I didn't know if any of us would. We had a strike fund – Mary took a collecting tin round when we marched – but when I thought about the number of families losing out, I started to feel dizzy. I had not been helping with the housework. Mother was doing more, which made me feel terrible, and despite her efforts the rooms were getting out of hand again. I worried every day that Miss Povey would throw us out for my disreputable behaviour or simply for not keeping a tidy household. I wondered if Miss Clavell would hear and stop bringing us food.

At dinnertime, I walked down Digby Street and saw Miss Morton standing outside our house, holding her bicycle, looking smarter than I'd ever seen her, in a large hat and long coat that looked new. I remembered that I had not come to clean her step since the strike started. It all seemed so long ago.

'Ellen!' she said. 'I've been trying to find you for days.'

'I'm sorry I didn't come to clean but—'

'Oh, I didn't expect you. I heard what was going on.' She smiled. 'You girls make quite the sight walking round Hackney. Would you walk with me to the end of the street, Ellen?' she said, and I supposed this would be the moment we lost the rooms. As we walked down Digby Street, Miss Morton pushing her bicycle, I decided to tell her that we had the rent money for another two weeks, though we would have to pawn something for that, and to ask to stay at least until we found another place. I thought about Penn Street. I thought about packing our belongings into a van again.

When we reached the corner, she turned to me and said, 'I'm going home tomorrow, Ellen. Miss Povey will send a new girl to see you on Sunday.'

'Oh,' I said. 'But she's not chucking us out?'

'I don't suppose so. Not as long as you can keep up with the rent.'

'Well,' I said, 'that's a relief.'

'Miss Povey is sympathetic to you girls. I'm not sure she would quite condone all of your behaviour, but she does believe men like your Mr Simpson should be held to account.' She looked at me kindly. 'She also heard about your mother.'

I started, and Miss Morton looked at me carefully. 'She

386

heard about her helping a slum family in Penn Street,' she said.

'How did she know about that?'

'I believe it's the talk of Digby Street. Your neighbours were rather impressed. As was Miss Povey. A remarkable act of kindness, she called it.'

'Oh,' I said again.

'She does think highly of your family and of course I told her I thought very highly of you. But I'm afraid you will have to keep coming up with the rent. I doubt she would ever allow debts, not even in these circumstances.'

'We can pay,' I said, though I didn't know if it was true.

She was staring at me, expecting something. I had got used to pleasing ladies like Miss Morton – schoolteachers, shopkeepers, inspectors. I learnt what they wanted from me, and the best way to give it to them. But now, for the first time, I couldn't read the expression on her face.

'What are you going to do when you get home?' I asked.

She looked down at her hands holding the handlebars. 'Marry, I suppose.'

'Nice to have a bloke,' I said.

'Yes.' Her voice was small and distant. 'Perhaps . . . Once I have a family and a home, I could always take on some charitable work then . . . As long as I'm not traipsing round the East End.' She gave a sad little laugh. 'Miss Horner's going home too. She said it wouldn't be so much fun without me. I don't know if another girl will join, but perhaps if she does, you could continue to be the step girl there. I recommended you to Miss Dawson, who runs the settlement.'

'Thank you,' I said, though I couldn't imagine going back to whitening someone's step, not now. She was still looking at me. She was still expecting something. She looked like she wanted something I had, like she was trying to suck it out of me, but I was empty, and anyway it wasn't important any more. For the first time since we'd met, it didn't matter what she thought of me. I stared straight back at her, too tired to form words, too tired to walk away.

'It must seem so strange to you,' she said. 'But this — being here . . .' She looked down again. 'I fear it will be the happiest time of my life.'

'Why don't you stay then?' I said impatiently. I wanted to take my boots off, to hold Iris, to start making the boys' tea.

'It's not possible.' She smiled faintly. 'I wish I had your courage.'

I didn't have courage. I hated it all, the dead animals, the stares, the shouts in the street, and the newspapers, calling us shrill, going on about our starving families. I hated waking in the early hours, filled with dread thinking about the girls and the cutters, all out of work because of us. I hated it apart from the times when I was disturbingly, absurdly happy, the happiest time of *my* life. I continued only because, as Mary said, we didn't know how to end it.

'I wish I had your money,' I said. I was sharper than perhaps I meant and it surprised us both.

'Well . . .' She held the bicycle steady with one hand and fumbled in her pockets with the other. 'I had to give you this, before I went.' She handed me my savings cards and an envelope. 'I'm sure whoever runs the club next would save it for you, but, well . . . I thought this might be the time.'

The envelope was heavy. It was not sealed and I lifted

the flap. I looked inside, confused. 'It can't be this much.'

'You must swear you won't tell Miss Povey, but . . . you see . . . I put another five pounds in there. We aren't supposed to help with . . . Well, it hardly matters now.'

I held the envelope in both hands. Five pounds. More than eight weeks' wages.

'It's for the strike fund,' she said. 'I want you to keep going. And I thought you might like this.' She held her bicycle out towards me. 'I won't be needing it any more. I thought you might find it useful.'

I took hold of the handlebars. It felt heavy and unsteady in my hands, but I would not let it go. I thought of the spidery branches on my train map, curling tendrils stretching into the heart of the city, out to the north, over the curving river. Broad Street, Hampstead, Queen's Park, Richmond, Kew – I felt the city rushing inwards, towards me. The bicycle would swallow up the miles and I wouldn't even need a fare.

'Do you know how to ride a bicycle?' Miss Morton asked.

I shook my head and gripped it tighter. I could learn to ride a bicycle. I thought of asking Mags to teach me. Another explosion of pain.

'Well, find someone to show you. It takes a bit of time. But once you have the knack. Nothing more glorious than sailing round London.' She looked down again. 'I shall remember it forever.'

'Thank you,' I said.

'I wanted to believe I'd done one useful thing,' she said, and I watched her walk down Digby Street, the money in my pocket, the bicycle in my hands.

It was cold but crisp; the sun was bright and the sky

pale blue. I saw Mary come out of her front door, in her fur tippet with a new feather in her hat, and she waved at me. The world was new, expanded; it was ours.

14

Frances

1984–5

On Monday night, I came home from work and saw Nick at the top of the stairwell, sitting in the window with Jane, smoking, his legs hanging over the long drop to the yard below. As I walked up the stairs, my hands started shaking and I imagined pushing him, hard, him losing control, falling – but as I passed by, I only waved. I went back into our room and sat on my mattress, angry and frightened.

In that moment, the complicity felt unbearable. I had to tell Jane. Or Naomi. I would have to find a time when we were alone. I would have to leave immediately afterwards. I tried to anticipate how they would react, if they would believe me, and plan where I would go to get away from Nick. Sometimes, when I was untangling these thoughts in the middle of the night, nowhere felt safe. He could probably even track me down in Kent. And then, eventually, the anger and fear subsided into sadness. What came to seem more unbearable was losing everything that I had: the shelter, the friendship, the only adult life I'd ever known. I knew it was already lost, really. But I had nowhere else to go.

I heard Nick and Jane come in and when I pulled back the curtain I saw him start, almost imperceptibly, and for the rest of the evening I was acutely aware of his smallest, subtlest gestures. It was hard to know if I was noticing things that had always been there, but the cavalier way he slung vodka in the mug, the number of times he went to refill it, the edge to his voice – it all started to unnerve me. He didn't eat anything. His hands were shaking. He snapped at Malcolm for no reason. His unsteadiness fright-ened me – I didn't know what he was capable of. But, of course, I didn't know him at all.

The next day, it was quiet at work and Dave suggested I go home early. As I walked up the stairs, I heard voices in the opposite room and I wondered if Jane was holding another meeting – her protest was on Sunday. But as I got closer, I realised that it was only Naomi and Jane. My heart started to beat faster – if I was going to tell them, it ought to be now: they were alone, away from the living space. I could have walked in then and imploded everything we'd built together. But I didn't. I waited outside the door.

'Nick thinks it's a great idea,' Jane said.

Naomi sighed. 'I bet he does. This sort of thing is right up his street.'

'I don't know if I see the point in just turning up with placards again. Marching. Handing out leaflets. No one will care.'

'They will care.'

'We need to do something. We need to have some sort of impact.'

'But does it have to be something like this? Sabotage. A public building. You'll get arrested.'

'I've been arrested before.'

'Not for this sort of thing. You could go to prison.'

My breath was getting shorter and louder. I tried to control it, afraid they would hear me. Still, I didn't move.

'Naomi, sometimes I dream that I'm screaming and screaming and no one can hear me. I'm shouting and raving and grabbing people, but no one's reacting. It's like I'm invisible. That's what it feels like, every day. I'm just invisible. The world is full of shit and no one cares!'

'I care.'

'Not enough. It's not enough.'

They were quiet for a moment.

'Please don't say anything to anyone,' Jane said. 'About what we're planning. Especially to Frankie.'

'I'm not going to say anything to her.'

'Good.'

They were quiet again. When Jane spoke, she sounded different. 'I know you think I'm paranoid about her. I know you don't believe that stuff Nick goes on about, corporate spies or whatever. But I have a bad feeling. I don't feel like I can trust her.'

'She's a nice person, Jane.'

'Yeah, just a nice girl, never talks about herself, never does any activism, doesn't have any friends, hangs around, not saying anything . . . watching us all the time. What's she even doing here? What's in it for her?'

'I think you just don't like her.'

'Maybe I don't. But it's an instinct thing, isn't it? Whether you trust someone. It's all you've got to go on.'

There was another silence. I told myself to walk away, that it would be excruciating to be caught.

'What if you're just jealous?' Naomi said.

'Of what?'

'Because Nick was sleeping with her.'

Jane laughed. 'You think I fancy Nick?'

'I don't know! OK, no, I don't, but I think you care about him more than you let on and you're annoyed that he got close to her. And I think you're annoyed because . . . because you and I aren't so close any more.'

'Oh, for God's *sake*!' Jane said, and the scorn in her voice made me turn my face away. 'Naomi, I am *not* jealous of your cosy little sewing sessions, believe me. That's the sort of stuff I'm talking about. That's the stuff I want to leave behind.'

I did walk away then. I went back down the stairs, trying to hurry and not make too much noise at the same time, until I found myself in the front yard. I sat on the front wall as the light faded, shivering in my jacket and scarf, until it was dark and I began to feel unsafe, imagining strange looks from passers-by. I didn't know what else to do but go back inside.

The next evening, when I came back from my shift, no one was there apart from Nick, sitting on the sofa. He held up a hand when he saw me. I was immediately afraid of being alone with him, and then I saw that the curtain in front of my sleeping area had been pinned back, and the mattress stripped. My clothes, my books, my hairbrush, the shoebox I kept personal things in, were in a pile next to my suitcase. My bedding was in a messy heap next to them. The thought of Nick's fingers on my belongings made me feel sick.

'Why have you been through all my things?'

'You have to go, I'm afraid. Jane's orders.'

'But why—'

'She doesn't like you being here. She's all over the place at the moment, doesn't feel like she trusts anyone, wants to eliminate any risk before Sunday. And I want her to go through with it. So that's it, you have to go.'

'Well, I'll tell them then! I'll tell them I saw you!'

'It won't make a difference. They trust me. Jane got people she knew to run background checks on me and I'm fine. It's all there: I covered my tracks before I even started this job. But I told her I got some mates in the public sector to look for your records and you're not there. And she believes me.'

'What?'

'She's suspicious of you; you're not helping yourself walking round like you've seen a ghost, things are getting more intense, she doesn't want you here. And I don't either.'

'Naomi wants me here,' I said.

'Not any more,' he said. 'Group decision.'

'*Malcolm* wanted me to leave?'

'OK, Malcolm doesn't give a shit. But he wants a quiet life. So he'll go along with it. Anyway,' he said, 'none of that really matters. The bottom line is, I want you to go so you have to go.'

'Can I . . . pack my bags properly?'

'Course. Naomi and Jane are at The Swan. I told them not to come back for a couple of hours.'

I took one of the shared laundry bags, and put my sheets and paperbacks in it. I folded my clothes and put them in the suitcase. I had been making stuffed doves for one of Naomi's banners; I left them on her bed, unfinished, and then I took off Clare's denim jacket, folded it, and placed it next to the doves.

Unwillingly, I took off Naomi's scarf. It felt wrong to leave behind something I'd kept against my neck for so long, something now woven with my skin and sweat. I folded it carefully, and then took off Naomi's jumper. On a box next to her bed, I saw the white plastic clip she sometimes held her hair up in, its triangular teeth meeting in a curved grimace. There were strands of her hair still caught in them. I saw her trainers, white leather with grimy creases snaking across the bridge, the insides grey with the print of her foot.

I went to the bathroom to get my toothbrush, and then to the sink to get the mug I'd bought at a junk shop. It had taken no time at all to remove my presence from the place: I felt insubstantial, close to disappearing. I walked over to the window at the back, watching the roofs and the train track, trying to retain every detail of this place, as if by remembering the colour of the bricks, the shape of the window catches, the light that fell through the glass, I could hold on to it somehow. But I knew these things that I had lived with, had handled, been surrounded by, would soon start to fade from my memory. There was no point in prolonging it. I went to pick up my suitcase.

'Key, please,' Nick said, holding out his hand. I put my hand in my jeans pocket and gave it to him.

'Can I ask you something?' I said.

'Go on then.' He was rolling a cigarette and didn't look at me.

'Why did you lie to me? When you first met me. What was the point? You must have known I wasn't doing anything.'

He struck a match and lit the cigarette. 'I was being Nick Walker when I met you. I spent a *lot* of time on Jake, following him and his posh girlfriend about, and then he fucked off to Australia, so that turned out to be a colossal waste of time. I had to keep it going when I saw you again, didn't I?'

He leant forward and pulled the ashtray towards him. 'I could have stopped going to the pub but I liked it there and . . .' He leant back on the sofa, tipping his head to the ceiling. 'And yeah, maybe you're right. Maybe I like being Nick Walker sometimes.' He closed his eyes. 'I liked being him with you.'

'But you didn't have to involve me in any of it! You *know* I would never have come here if it wasn't for you.'

He opened his eyes and sat up again, taking a drag from his roll-up. 'OK, that's true. But I liked the idea of bringing someone new in . . . I was scared I'd always be the outsider with Naomi and Jane. I was trying to make myself useful, with the van, and at demos, but at the end of the day it's a feminist peace group. I'm always going to be a hanger-on. I did this training session, early on, and the leader said something to us, he said: groups bond over a victim . . . an outsider. You see it everywhere once it's pointed out: training sessions, offices, there's always someone who doesn't fit. And when everyone's worked out who that is, and finally someone says it: "What about that bloke over there then? Don't you think he's a bit . . ." Well, that's when the rest of you get close. I thought if I could make *you* the outsider . . .' He tapped his roll-up on the ashtray. 'I never expected it to work out as well as it did, though. I never expected Jane to put all her energies into worrying about you.'

He finally looked at me and, when he saw my expression, he laughed. 'What's wrong? Did you think I *liked* you?'

Years later I would think of better answers to that question, but in the moment I only said, 'Yes.'

'Good. I wanted you to think that. I won't say there weren't . . . perks to the job.'

My face was hot and all the words I could find came from an earlier time; I was a child again, consumed by frustration and anger. 'Shut up! You're a liar! I was happy until you ruined everything!'

He stood up and came to face me. He put his hand out and I recoiled, not knowing what the gesture would contain: violence, tenderness, a threat of either of those things. When he placed his palm on my cheek, it was gentle, and my skin burnt, and in a second I was back behind the bar again, young, open, enthralled, looking at him and seeing all the possibilities, all the different ways of living, he could lead me towards.

He took his hand away. 'You'll keep your fucking mouth shut, won't you, sweetheart?' he said.

I nodded. There was no one left to tell; I was completely shut out now. As I walked down the stairs, carrying my possessions, it was more frightening than when I'd left home in the summer, because then, at least, I'd had somewhere to go. I thought I'd grown up but I hadn't. The others had found the squat, Nick had led me there, Naomi had looked after me. Now I was on my own.

It was dark outside and cold, and I had no coat over my paisley shirt. Tinsel glinted behind the grilles of shop windows and when I turned down a residential street, the bay windows were starting to glow. Some of the houses had their trees up, wonky stars on the top, coloured fairy lights flickering. Curtains were being drawn. I went to Digby Street, to find the house with the phone in it, but when I picked it up, it was silent. Someone must have cut it off. I searched in my pocket for coins; I had one ten-pence piece left. I thought about going back to the telephone box, the awful smell, the cards with drawings of prostitutes sello-taped on, calling my mother, getting the train to Kent.

Instead, I walked down the terrace to the house with the red front door. I rang the bell tentatively. I was expecting to see Clare, but Susie answered instead.

'Shit, are you OK?' she said, and I started to cry.

I couldn't stop. I wasn't making much sense, so Susie told me to go straight up to the bath. The water came out of the hot tap thick and fast, fanning out into a triangle before it hit the enamel. I took my clothes off too early and sat in the bath when it had only filled an inch, letting the water slowly rise up around me.

There was a tap on the door and Susie called, 'Everything all right? I brought you a cup of tea and a flapjack.'

'Oh, thanks . . .' I said.

'Can I bring it in?'

I said, 'Yes,' and felt my body seize up when she opened the door, suddenly self-conscious. But she didn't seem to mind me being naked – she put the cup of tea and flapjack down on the corner of the bath and sat down on the loo next to me.

'Just wanted to check you weren't drowning yourself in here.'

'Thanks,' I said, and I started to cry again.

'What happened? I mean, you don't have to say, but—'

I took the mug of tea in my hands. It was so hot I could barely taste it, but the sensation was distracting, at least.

'They chucked me out. Of the factory.'

'Oh God! Why? Did you fall out about something?'

I didn't know how to explain it. I took another sip of burning tea.

Then she said, 'Hey, don't worry about me. They've always been Clare's mates, not mine.'

'They wanted me to leave. They thought I was . . . infiltrating them.'

'What?'

'They thought I was a spy.'

Susie laughed, and then I laughed too, with relief, breathily, gasping, touched with hysteria.

'I'm sorry, Frankie, I don't want to offend you – I mean, I suppose you could be – but it just seems a bit paranoid?'

'I know! But—' I couldn't stop laughing now.

'Was that something Nick came up with? Jesus, he's jumpy. The first time I met him, I thought he was on drugs before I realised it was just what he was like. What would you have been spying *on*, anyway?'

I didn't say anything. I stretched out in the water and leant my head on the back. I didn't care about being naked any more.

'Look, surely it's a misunderstanding. Can't you talk to the others?'

'It's other things.' I didn't know how to talk about what had happened with Nick, without making it sound melodramatic, like I was making too much of it. Eventually I said, 'Nick and I fell out. We were sort of seeing each other and we fell out.'

'What about?'

It was going too far down the wrong path now; I didn't have the energy to sustain the story. I tried to say that he had wanted to have sex with me and I hadn't wanted to, as if it had been a misunderstanding, but I remembered the feeling of the floor on my back and I couldn't speak. I started to cry again.

'Oh God,' Susie said. She hesitated a moment and then sat on the side of the bath and held my head against her jumper; I suppose she couldn't hug me properly, wet and naked. It was clumsy and uncomfortable; her jumper was rough and smelt of cigarettes.

'Do you need to stay here for a bit?' she asked.

Clare had already moved in with her fiancé and Susie was staying there on her own. I called in sick at the pub for two days and then finally I told them I wasn't coming back at all.

I slept a lot. I would wake up late, after Susie had left for the bookshop, and get up in my dressing gown. I made myself a cup of tea and I wandered round the house, unable to stop thinking about Nick, and Jane and Naomi. I felt guilty that I'd betrayed them, and then angry that they'd betrayed me, until I became exhausted and went back to sleep. Sometimes I composed anonymous letters to Jane in my head, warning her, and I was on the verge of writing it all down, until I thought about delivering it, having to go back to the factory, find a way through the gate without being seen. I wondered if she would go to prison, and how long for. After the weekend, I scanned the local papers for mention of the protest, or Jane's arrest, but I didn't find anything. And then I would go back to sleep again.

Susie said that she wanted to go home for Christmas but she didn't like leaving the squat empty for too long and I was happy to have the excuse to go to Kent just for the day. It was a strange lunch – a turkey crown and two crackers, looking over the sea, the solid absence of my father obstructing any joy. I got back to the empty house in Digby Street and went straight to sleep again.

January came and I began to taste the meals Susie cooked for me. I laughed when she told me stories about the eccentric people who came into the bookshop. I still had my last wage packet and some of my savings and I offered her money for the time I'd been staying, but she refused – 'It's a squat!' – so I started to make myself useful in other ways. I went to the shop to get washing-up liquid. I changed the lightbulb in the hall. Then I began to cook.

There were a few things that I'd seen Naomi make so many times, I felt that I could recreate them. There was a book on the shelf, battered and dog-eared, with the spine coming off, called *The Reader's Digest Cookery Year*, and I opened it tentatively. Then I began to read it every day – coronation chicken, lemon mousse, Eton mess, pork chops, green beans. I read about searing, mixing, kneading, crumbling, and eventually I began to try to do some of it myself, in between sleeping. Some attempts were successful and some less so, but Susie was always encouraging. 'It's just so nice not to have to think about what to make when I get in,' she said.

Once, I got salmon fillets at the fishmonger's and I told Susie about Violet stealing the side of salmon from the party. She laughed a lot more than I expected, so I started telling her other things about the Maxwells' parties: that Angela called Gloucestershire 'Glossie-Possie' and the family had a framed photograph of their dog. That I didn't know how to hold a cigarette. She seemed to like all my stories, and sometimes, after I'd gone to bed, I found myself thinking of new things I could tell her or I'd carry on conversations with her in my head.

When Susie asked about my family, I said my dad was dead. It was late and she'd bought a cheap bottle of wine at the corner shop, so I ended up telling her everything about the night he'd died, the shock and confusion. I told her about the shoebox and I liked how compelling she found the story, gasping and putting her hand over her mouth and saying, 'Oh my God, *no!*' and laughing when I described seeing my dad's reading glasses in the background. I felt lighter when I'd finished, and she held my hand. She told me that she knew her father had had affairs, and she thought her mum did too, and about the daughter of a family friend, who she sometimes suspected was her half-sister.

I began to stay awake for longer, and I started to notice things again. I noticed it was getting lighter in the mornings and in the evenings. I noticed that Susie had a little scar on the side of her face, running between her left eye and hairline, and the fair hair on her arms was unusually long and fine. I noticed that the young Indian woman next door, who said hello to me if she saw me on the street, was pregnant, stomach protruding under her navy coat, and that her blue eyeshadow exactly matched her silk headscarf. It reminded me of the time my body had had life in it, and how that life had gone, but the feelings were not as sharp and overwhelming as they used to be. When I was boiling the kettle in the mornings, I heard a woman on the other side of the house singing to herself in the garden.

I noticed that the box that Susie kept spare keys and screwdrivers, Allen keys and bicycle lights in was familiar. I asked her if it was the box that had belonged to Ellen, the girl with the letters, and she looked sheepish and said yes.

'Clare got rid of a lot of stuff before she left,' she said. 'But she thought this was too nice to chuck.' I didn't ask her where the letters were, and whenever I reached for the spare keys, or the key to the gas meter, I felt a discomfort that, when I interrogated it, I realised was sadness.

In February, I found I could get through most days without sleeping. They were having new windows put in next door and the pregnant woman came round with honeyed pastries on a paper plate. She introduced herself as Asma and apologised for the noise the builders were making. I said it hadn't bothered us. Our other neighbour, a Caribbean woman in a printed dress and a long pink cardigan, her hair greying at the temples, was tending to the plants outside her front door. She introduced herself as Ivy, and gave me some rosemary from the pots by her front door. She said the lavender would be out soon.

I began to feel things again, things outside anger and confusion and sadness. I started dreaming again, dreams that ended in an explosion of sensation and tension and shaking, and sometimes, during the day, I'd think about those dreams and touch myself. I thought about running my finger along Susie's scar or touching the hair on her arms. I liked watching her pick the last bits of meat off a carcass or smash garlic, the heel of her hand on the back of a knife. I liked watching her fix the bracket on a cupboard, the way her body was full, almost plump, but strong and muscular at the same time. Once, I had a splinter and I sat back on the sofa while she knelt beside it, my bare foot in her lap, and she carefully tried to work the splinter out with her fingers. I was mesmerised by the expression of concentration on her face, the gentle way she held my foot, and though it was painful, I wanted it to go on forever.

One evening, I'd made us a chickpea stew and what I'd called 'funny chocolate mousse', which had somehow turned solid.

Susie carved out a small spoonful. 'God, F, you said "funny" not "inedible".'

'Is it that bad?' I said. 'Oh. Maybe it is. I tried halving the recipe.'

'Yeah, I don't think that works. The chickpeas were great, though.'

'It's Naomi's recipe,' I said. 'She's an amazing cook.'

Susie looked down with a strange expression on her face. After we'd eaten, we went into the front room and Susie drew the curtains and started laying the fire. I took our hot-water bottles and went to fill them in the kitchen. We read on the sofa for a bit and then I said something about Naomi again and she made the same expression. Finally, she looked at me and said, 'You and Naomi – were you together?'

'No. *No!*' I said. I didn't know where the tone of alarm in my voice had come from and wished I could take it back, but it was too late: Susie looked hurt.

'I was only asking. You talk about her a lot, that's all.'

'We were really close. But she was just my friend.'

Susie was looking down again. She spoke hesitantly at first and then very quickly, not looking at me the entire time. 'You didn't . . . have a crush on her then?'

'No,' I said, because I didn't know how else to answer. Susie looked at me for a moment, unsure whether to say anything else, and I knew that the conversation hadn't unfolded the way either of us wanted it to. But I didn't know how to undo it.

★

At the start of March, after we'd eaten cottage pie in the dining room, we went into the front room and sat together on the sofa, as we always did. I noticed Susie kept looking up from her book. Finally, she said, 'Clare came into the shop today.'

I stiffened. 'Oh. How is she? Does she want her old room back?'

'No, no, she's still totally loved up, don't worry. She says she was sick every day at the start, which sounded hideous. But you could tell how happy she was. She's got a little bump and everything. She looked fantastic.'

'Good for her,' I said. I felt a brief sadness, but pleasure too: I was surprised by how happy I was for Clare.

'We had a coffee together in my lunch break, and she filled me in on some . . . gossip, I suppose. About the factory gang.'

'Oh,' I said.

'I didn't know whether you'd— You seem so much happier than when you came here, but it feels weird not telling you. I mean, it's not a big thing—'

'That's OK. You can tell me,' I said, but my heart was already beating faster and I couldn't look at her.

'Well, Clare met up with Jane before she saw me. Apparently it all fell apart just after you left. Nick had some kind of breakdown – he was having panic attacks in the night – and then the Friday before Jane's protest he . . . took an overdose.'

'God,' I said, fiddling with the edge of the cushion.

'Yeah. So Jane was the one who found him and took him to hospital. She cancelled the protest and ended up looking after him. He said he didn't want his family to know about the suicide attempt – fair enough, I guess – but that meant it was just her, hospital visits, medication, cooking for him. She really helped get him back on his feet. And after a week of all this, he just disappeared. She got back one day and he wasn't there. She didn't have an address for him or anything. A few weeks later, she got a postcard saying he was going travelling for a bit and he'd get in contact when he got back.'

I held the hot-water bottle closer.

'Clare said Jane was still really bitter about it. Kept saying stuff like, "You think it's this great community, but no one actually gives a shit about you." So she moved in with her parents, Naomi went off to Greenham. It's empty again.'

'Did Clare say anything else about Jane? How she was?' I had thought every day about Nick saying that he would get her for something – 'conspiracy at least'.

'You'll like this – she's applied for teacher training.'

'She hasn't!'

'She has. Starting this September. She wants to teach politics and economics. Secondary.'

'I can sort of see it,' I said. 'Radicalising young minds.'

'She'd be a bloody scary teacher.'

'Wouldn't she?' I felt something lift off me before I'd even understood why. 'So she never got arrested. For the activism stuff.'

'I don't think so. I don't think you can teach if you've got a criminal record.'

I began to cry. It reminded me that, when I first moved in, I'd cried every day, but now I hadn't cried for a long time.

'Oh, love,' Susie said, slightly exasperated now, and she got up to put the kettle on.

★

One morning at the end of March, when it was warm and light, I went to the shops to get things for a new recipe I was trying out. After thinking about it for a long time, I'd finally ordered some dungarees from the magazines that had been lying about – 'with a comfy drawstring waist and slightly tapered legs' – and Susie had lent me a T-shirt to wear underneath them. I liked the way they made me look and I liked going out in them, even if I knew they set me apart in some way.

The magnolia tree in Ivy's front garden was blooming and her brightly coloured hyacinths were out. I saw Asma coming out of her house with a pram and I went over and gazed at the squashed sleeping little face, and we talked for a bit about how tired she was. I usually tried to avoid the little street of shops that led to the factory, but today I walked down it, passing the café where Naomi and Jane had taken me after my miscarriage, and the Black Hart.

The advantage of sleeping for most of the day had been that I didn't have to think about what I was going to do next. Now I was fully awake, it was getting frustrating, haunting the house all day, trying to find little jobs to do, waiting for Susie to get home. But that morning, it didn't seem like such a problem. I had enough experience to get another job in a bar. Or maybe I could apply to university. Start working on my portfolio again.

When I got back to the house, I spoke to Simon, who lived with Michael across the road, about our guttering, and he offered to let me know when they next had some-one in to clear theirs. When I let myself in, I saw a letter addressed to me on the mat. I recognised the handwriting and put it on the mantelpiece without opening it.

I took it down again when Susie had gone to bed. She went to bed earlier than I did, although I knew that she read for about half an hour before going to sleep. I'd hear her get up to go to the loo, and by the time I went up, the line of light under her door would be gone. I sat on the sofa and opened the letter.

Dear Frankie,

I heard from Clare that you'd moved in to her old room with Susie and I was SO happy, Frankie, so relieved, and I just had to write! I feel awful about how things ended. I should have stood up for myself, for you, but I guess we both know I'm not always that good at being brave. Anyway, I wanted to say that I'm sorry.

You're going to laugh, but Clare let me keep the things in the box that belonged to Ellen. She was going to chuck them but I just couldn't bear it. AND it was good that I did because I did some digging about and I ended up having tea with a seventy-year-old man called Harry Parker. He was Ellen's son!!! He still lives in Hackney. He didn't know his mum, but he was close to his aunt, who was called Iris, and his grandma, and he said they were all so proud of her, they talked about her all the time, how amazing and brave she was. He loved having the letters and her bits and pieces. When this happened, you were the only person I wanted to tell.

Come and visit us at the camp!

Love, Naomi x

I held the letter in my hand and I looked at the box on

the mantelpiece. I thought about Ellen from time to time, when I fished in there for something I needed, but it was as if I hadn't understood her story properly till now. She had not lived much longer than I had. She had never known her son.

I had just missed the deadline for applications to art school but it hadn't seemed very important. I could always do it next year, I'd thought, assuming that there would always be more years, there would always be time. But for Ellen, that had not been true. She had had very little time.

It was my nineteenth birthday next month. I imagined only having three years, or less, to live and was suddenly floored with potential regret at the one thing I really cared about going undone. I didn't know if I wanted to go to art school or university or get a job, but there was one thing I wanted, really wanted, one thing that, if it was left unsaid, would crush me with unbearable weight. I wondered if I should think about it, think about what I was risking, but when I looked at my watch, I saw that Susie had gone up-stairs a quarter of an hour ago. There was not much time.

Tomorrow, I decided, I would empty the box of keys and tools, and fill it with the lavender that Ivy had given me. But now, my world was lit with bright, pure clarity, and I was flooded with purpose. I walked up the stairs and saw the line of light under Susie's bedroom door. I knocked and said, 'Can I come in?' When she came to the door, we looked at each other for a moment before I kissed her, and the feel of her lips, her hair, the buttons of her pyjamas in my fingers, it was better than any of my dreams.

15

Amanda

2020

Three days after my nana died, I was back in her living room, standing at an unnatural distance from my mum. It was the first time I'd been indoors with someone who wasn't Lucy for nearly six weeks. I would never have imagined the first person I would see in lockdown wouldn't be Oliver. She went over to the windows and opened them.

The living room was a painful little map of the last things my nana had done before she'd felt so ill she'd called the doctor's surgery, who'd called an ambulance for her. She had declined so rapidly in A&E that they chose not to move her to intensive care. None of us were with her. Oliver had not been working there that day.

The porridge pan was still on the stove; her clothes were in the machine, unwashed. Her reading glasses were on the coffee table next to her book, splayed open. Everywhere I looked, I saw something I didn't know what to do with: should we wash the tea towel hanging on the cooker? When we emptied the bin, should we put a new liner in? Every intervention seemed like tampering. My mum picked up my nana's glasses and put them back in their case. I caught a moment's hesitation before she shut the book, losing her place.

It was also the first time I'd been apart from Iris, since I'd gone back into the office, nearly six months ago. The alternative world, the world I had imagined before the turmoil of the last seven months, was pressing in on me now. I ought to have been back at work, leaving the flat in tailored clothes, Oliver making purées in the kitchen. I had been planning to say blithely: 'Oh, he's a lot better at things like that than me.' It was supposed to be easy. I had thought that messy or complicated feelings about being away from your child showed a lack of resolve, something you could refuse to let in. And yet here I was, longing for the feel of Iris's body, occasionally terrified at the thought of something terrible happening to her in my absence, and at the same time, ecstatic to be alone, half-drunk on freedom. The drive to be with her was exactly as strong as the drive to be away from her; it was impossible to know which to follow.

I was keenly aware of how much harder it would be if it weren't for Lucy, who had offered to take Iris for the afternoon, who had made all the babies' meals, and our meals, who'd told me to go and lie down while Iris napped or between feeds. When the anxiety about not being with her started to pull, I was reassured by all the things that Lucy knew about her, the familiarity of her house, her presence, her world. We hadn't spoken properly since the argument, and I was still annoyed with her, but at the same time I was entirely dependent on her. I was angry that I had to be grateful; I hated needing her. But I couldn't deny that I did.

'Shall I put the kettle on? Before we start?' I said.

'Go on then,' my mum said, and it felt uncanny, lifting the kettle, turning on the tap. My nana would never in a hundred years have let me make my own cup of tea in her flat. I took the mugs into the front room, where my mum was staring out of the window at the balcony. I put hers on the coffee table, rather than hand it to her, so we wouldn't have to risk touching.

'I suppose we'll get a good price for it. One good thing about the place I grew up becoming unrecognisable to me.'

'What do you mean?'

'Well, we'll have to sell it.'

'I didn't know that she owned it.'

'You thought she was still a council tenant? No, she bought it off the council when Granddad was still alive. I actually thought you and Oliver could help me out. Do it up. You know what people round here like.'

I looked down. 'I always said she could sell that sideboard at one of the furniture shops round here and make a killing. Or the cocktail cabinet.'

'That's what I mean. It just looks like a lot of old tat to me.' She shook her head. 'I don't mean that— I just mean—'

'I know what you mean. People round here like old tat.'

'There you go then.'

I thought about me and Oliver sourcing reclaimed wooden flooring, a butcher's sink, artisan tiles, and I couldn't bear it.

'I don't think I can do it. I'm sorry.'

'I understand,' she said. 'We can let someone else do what they want to it.' She walked over to the sideboard and opened the drawer. 'She'll have left anything we need here,' she said.

'I know. She told me every time I came.'

She started taking out manila files with handwritten white labels. 'God, she really was organised,' she said, taking a deep breath. She piled them on the dresser and then she took out a brown A4 envelope. She handed it to me. It said 'For Amanda' in my nana's handwriting.

I took it over to the sofa and opened it. There was a plastic envelope with a newspaper clipping from 1985, an obituary of a woman called Iris Chase, who'd trained as a doctor at the Elizabeth Garrett Anderson Hospital in 1929. I skimmed the article – OBE for services to the war effort, lifelong campaign for maternity care, founding a society for the advancement of women doctors. There was a family tree that my nana had drawn on a piece of lined paper and I guessed from the shakiness of the letters that she had drawn it recently, possibly after we'd last seen each other. There was a photograph, a family portrait taken outside a haberdashery shop. I turned it over. On the back, my grandmother had written: 'Iris Chase, Susan Chase, George Chase, 1931 (?)'.

I handed it to my mum. 'Did you know about this woman?'

'Cousin Iris . . . Yes, my granddad talked about her a lot.' She put the photo down. 'He was so proud of her. And I loved the stories too, you know, someone who made something of herself, made her way out of the East End. It made me think I could do the same. Oh, I wish my granddad could have seen our house in Essex.'

'Is that her with her kids?'

'No, she didn't have children. Let's have a look. She's not the older woman, it's too early for that . . . That must be her mother – Susan, I think – she ran the haberdasher's, which was pretty fancy for a family like my granddad's, in those days, to run a shop. And that's Iris, on the left. The young woman. One of the men is her brother, I think.'

I handed my mum the family tree.

'Oh yes, that's right. My granddad always used to tell me she lost one brother in the First World War and the other in the Second, so this must be between the wars, like it says. And an older sister, who died young, apparently.' She handed it back. 'You'll have to show this to your Iris one day. Inspire her.'

I kept looking at the photograph. 'You said she didn't have children.'

'No. I suppose you couldn't do all that and have children in those days.'

'I was looking through this book someone gave me for Iris, all about remarkable women who changed the world, that sort of thing. Frida Kahlo, Amelia Earhart, Florence Nightingale, Coco Chanel. I don't think any of them had kids.'

'Well, it's not such a surprise, is it? Too busy flying round the world or whatever it was they were doing. Maybe you can't be remarkable and have children.' She saw my face and laughed. 'Not the worst thing in the world, is it, not being remarkable?'

'Do you really think that?'

She shrugged. 'Well, what do you think?'

'I don't know. I want to think that you can, but . . . I don't have anyone to show me how to do it.'

'Well, thanks very much.'

'Oh, Mum, look—'

'Your nana was remarkable. She did her bit. You do yours. You keep on doing your bit, other women do theirs, and then something happens. If you're lucky.' She handed me back the family tree.

When she was sitting at the table, calling the electricity company, I ran my fingers along the fat spines of the photo albums my nana kept on the shelf. She hated digital photographs and made me print them off for her: photographs of Iris and my wedding to David, asking for the names of everyone in them, labelling everything in blue fountain pen. I wondered what would happen to them now.

I took two or three from the early 1980s off the shelf and sat on the sofa with them. There were photos of my mum sitting on the same sofa, pregnant in a giant smock dress. My nana looked younger, but how I remembered her, in her blue coat, set hair and large glasses.

My mum came over and had a look. 'Oh God, this takes me back. I was so anxious. We moved in the nick of time, we really did.' She took the book. 'I know you like it here, but it was horrible, it really was. The lift broken, and most of the lights too, coming up the stairs, not knowing if someone was going to come out of the shadows at you. Stinking of urine all the time. I was mugged on the bus when I was pregnant with you. A man held a knife to my throat. I remember stamping my foot on the floor trying to get the conductor's attention. Squatters next door. I told her to come with me. She could have had our spare room, finally had a garden.'

'Why do you think she didn't?'

'Oh, she liked it, I suppose. She said she liked the community. She liked knowing everyone, Doreen at the Frying Machine, going into Mr Ahmed's and him saying—'

'"Mind the shop for me, Lil, while I say my prayers." I remember.'

'She did care about the area. She protested about the hospital closures, all of that. But honestly, anyone with any sense at that time wanted to get out. We had a garden, clean air, no muggings. And when you were growing up and it was always London London London, wanting to get a job in London, why couldn't we have stayed, but you didn't see what it was really like. You liked coming to visit your nana and having fish and chips, but you didn't see the half of it. And now it's all glamorous and trendy all of a sudden. If you'd had your Iris when it was horrible, you would have done the same thing.'

'Maybe I would.'

I picked up another album and saw photos of me in a pushchair in Victoria Park and another of me chasing ducks. I saw a photo of my nana with three people I didn't recognise: a blonde girl with a nose ring, a man with chin-length hair and a woman in dungarees.

'Who are these people, Mum?'

'Them?' She held the photo album up. 'I don't know . . . Oh God, yes, I do. It's the squatters. I don't know why she had a photo of them. I didn't even know their names.' She put the book down again. 'She was fond of them, I suppose. Particularly that little one with the thing in her nose. She was always bringing round food – it annoyed me, actually, treating your nan like an OAP, when anyone could see that she took care of herself. But your nana did like them. She was always proud of her radical friends.'

Susie at the bookshop had mentioned the squatting scene in the eighties and I wondered, in a half-hearted way, whether there was a story there. That was the part of my job I had loved most. Finding something new, something original, and unearthing the story and turning it into my own line of enquiry. Despite not having used that part of me for what felt like so long, I was still groping around for stories, blindly, clumsily.

I went over to the table and picked up the family tree and newspaper clipping. 'Can I take these?' I said.

'Of course. They're for you.'

I was about to put them back in the envelope when I saw something else in there: another plastic wallet containing a folded sheet of newspaper, this one thinner, yellower and tattered at the edges. I unfolded it carefully. Halfway down the page, the headline read 'Strike Victory for the Boxmaker Girls' and there was a photograph of young women in large hats holding placards. One of the faces was ringed with the name 'Ellen!' written beside it.

'Who's Ellen?' I said.

'Oh, I don't know. The sister?' She took hold of the article. 'I mean, how they can tell who it is from that photograph, I don't know.'

She was right: the photograph was blurred and I couldn't properly make out the face of the woman that had been circled. I fished out the family tree again and saw the name Ellen next to Iris's.

'Didn't you say her sister died young?' I said.

'That's what I remember. Looks like she did something with the time she had, though.' She handed it back to me. 'There you go: maybe Cousin Iris wasn't the only remarkable woman in the family.'

When I got back, the pure delight Iris and I took in each other made it feel as if it had been worthwhile being apart from her just for that. My breasts were starting to feel tender and full, in a way that I hadn't experienced for a while, and Iris feeding felt incredibly satisfying. Just as she was finishing, Oliver rang.

'How was it at your nana's?'

'It was . . . sad. Tiring. I'm exhausted.'

'I bet. Was it all right seeing your mum?'

'Yes. We didn't touch or anything. We kept the windows open.'

'That wasn't what I meant.'

'She was . . . fine, I guess. It still doesn't feel real.'

'I know a lot's happened since we spoke about it. But I still really want you to move back in.'

'What if . . . what if we've made this huge sacrifice, being apart from each other, and then we move back in and you give her Covid anyway? Or me, and then I'm too ill to look after her? Won't that just undo everything we've worked for?'

'I've thought about that. I think about it all the time. But it's clear it's not a risk for Iris any more. It's been clear for a while. If she gets it, or if you do, we'll manage. I just can't do this any more. She's changed so much, in the pictures. I can't miss out on any more.'

'I know, and it seems ridiculous, if I've just spent the morning with my mum, for you not to see Iris, but— I mean, you could come and visit, or we could go for a walk; that might be safer . . .'

His tone changed. 'Do you just not want to come back? Is that it? Because if it is, then you need to tell me and we can work out . . . how we do this, but don't pretend it's about Covid if it isn't.'

'It's not that,' I said, although I wasn't sure if I was telling the truth. 'I just can't seem to get my head around moving, work, childcare, where we're going to live even. Are we going to try to sell the flat again?'

'I'm not working on Wednesday. Why don't you come round in the evening and I'll cook you dinner? You don't have to work all this out by yourself.'

'What about Iris?'

'Could Lucy look after her?'

'I don't know – she's done so much already . . .'

'Just ask her. You said Iris hardly ever wakes up in the evening. She'll be there anyway.'

When I'd put Iris down for her nap, I'd sat on the step at the front of the house. I had noticed people on the street start to socialise in their front gardens, two friends sitting on folding garden chairs or a small crowd gathering with mugs of tea. I liked sitting there – it felt like a way to be outside and connected to others but close to the safety of the indoors. I turned round when Lucy came down the stairs, holding the baby monitor. The sound of Stanley chatting to himself as he fell asleep, mediated by the monitor, had become so familiar to me, it felt peculiar to think it would no longer be part of my day.

I shifted over and asked if she wanted to join me. The doorway was small and we were unusually close, our bodies pressed together, but neither of us suggested moving. I told her that Oliver had suggested he cook me dinner on Wednesday.

'I feel so terrible asking this because you've done so much—'

'You want me to babysit?'

'Would you?'

'Of course. I'd be doing it anyway.'

'I really appreciate it.'

'Don't worry about it. It's a good idea. You guys need to see each other properly.'

We sat together for a while, watching the street. The magnolia tree in the garden next door was a blaze of pink and white and I could smell lavender. We watched a young family with two small children get out of a car and leave Tupperwares of food and children's drawings on the step of the house on the other side. I could see our neighbour who'd given me the fruit and her husband through the windows, waving enthusiastically, while the children jumped up and down, held up their toys to show their grandparents and pressed their hands to the glass. I shuddered, thinking about Oliver and Iris, and how grateful I was that this phase was ending.

'I think I'm going to extend my maternity leave again,' I said. 'I don't think I can face going back with all this, with my nana.'

'That makes sense.'

'I will go back, though. I can't not, even if I wanted to. It feels barely possible financially as it is.'

'You don't have to justify it,' she said. 'Although, to be fair, I can see why you feel you do.'

We were still for a moment.

'Look, I've wanted to say this for a while,' Lucy said, looking straight ahead. 'The reason I was shitty was because I've loved having you here. I hate how much I've loved having you here, actually. I hate feeling like I can't do it on my own. I hate how scared I am of you going. I can't tell you how much I don't want that to be true but it is.' She looked down. 'And maybe I don't like the idea of being left again. I suppose I don't have a great history with it.'

'I would have been totally lost without you,' I said. 'Not just in the pandemic, but before. You taught me how to be a mother.'

'Oh, come on . . .'

'It's true. You were so relaxed and fearless—'

'Fearless? I'm scared of everything! I'm scared of climate change, I'm scared of parabens, I'm scared of non-organic meat. And after everything I said, I'm scared of looking after Stanley alone, with no help, no time to myself. I'm scared of losing my business, my identity. I'm scared of being on my own.' She put her tea down. 'I got a message from Chloe the other day. She's definitely not coming back.'

'No?'

'She's going to try to find her own place near her mum. A fixer-upper, and she's going to post the progress on Instagram. She doesn't think she can cope with the childcare costs in London.'

'I'm sorry,' I said.

She turned her face away from me. 'I just wanted you to know that. I wanted you to know you don't have to go.'

'I do have to, though.'

'OK, but not on my account. You need a house. I've got a house. We could help each other out with childcare, whatever.' She looked straight ahead. 'I've loved having you here. That's all I'm saying.'

'Thank you,' I said.

The next day, when Iris was asleep after lunch and Lucy was in her studio, I tried to have a nap on the sofa. But I found myself getting restless and I sat up and got my nana's envelope off the shelf. I'd had a half-formed idea that I might pitch for a feature about Cousin Iris, how it felt to discover I had a distinguished relative. Gradually, almost without realising it, I had begun to accept that I wasn't going to be able to work in the same way when I went back, that I would have to ask to be moved from my reporting post, that I would lose the thing I'd wanted so much and worked so hard for. I couldn't pay for the childcare I needed to do the job properly and that had remained true throughout my maternity leave. I hadn't found a way to make it work. I was already half-thinking about other things I could do.

I read the obituary over and over again, trying to make myself feel something interesting or noteworthy about it, trying out sentences in my head, but everything sounded wrong. I didn't feel connected to Iris Chase at all – her life felt like it had been a grand adventure from the start, and mine already felt too late for that. Besides, I didn't write this kind of thing. I had never even written a sentence in the first person before. And although I'd never lied about where I came from, I'd tried, so hard, all the time, to fit in, to not draw attention to it. To baldly state in print that I came from a working-class family seemed perverse.

I still got my laptop out and searched in the newspaper archives for any more articles about Iris. I found another obituary, and one line in it kept drawing me back. Iris said that she had been inspired by her older sister, Ellen, who'd taken care of her as a baby and had gone on strike in the factory she'd worked in. She'd died in childbirth at the age of twenty-two. I took out Nana's family tree again. I saw that Ellen had two sons: Harry and Edward. I searched for her name and found nothing, though there were some articles about the strike, and the death of a girl at the factory,

Margaret Card, who was only fourteen. Ellen's life – and Margaret's – had been brutally contracted. I remembered what my nana had said to me: *this is where you come from*.

There was something there, something about the story that got under my skin, but I couldn't entirely see what it was. The feeling of pursuing something, which had once been so quick and natural, was slow and unfamiliar now. I couldn't write like this; I didn't have the time, it wasn't a job, what was the point? I thought about Ellen, whose life had been so limited, in so many ways, but who had still managed to make changes, to grow a family. I got out a notebook and wrote slowly, sluggishly, badly, reaching blindly where my curiosity led.

It felt strange going back to the flat on Wednesday night. It was layered in memory, from misery to happiness and back to misery again. When I let myself in and saw Oliver sitting at the breakfast bar, he stood up and we looked at each other. For a moment, I was afraid to touch him – I had become so conditioned against touch, against closeness. And then when he held me, it was impossible to let go. I hadn't expected it to feel so good; I couldn't believe that I'd lived without this sensation for so long. I kissed him on the cheek, and then the mouth, and then we were upstairs; it was quick and rough, and I felt completely altered afterwards, lying next to him on our old bed.

'It's so good to have you here,' he said, and started to cry. 'It's been so horrible. So lonely.'

'I know,' I said. 'I'm sorry I went.'

'Every day I wondered if we were doing the right thing. And I don't even know if we're doing the right thing now.'

'I just don't think we could carry on,' I said.

'No, I know. Maybe it was a really stupid thing to do in the first place.'

'I don't think there's any point thinking about whether we could have done things differently.'

'I just keep thinking about what we missed out on,' he said, and then he looked at his phone. 'Oh shit,' he said. 'I forgot about the dinner. It was supposed to go in half an hour ago. I guess if I do it now, we could eat in . . . an hour and a half? Are you hungry?'

'I'm actually starving.'

We went downstairs and I put water on for pasta and got out a tin of tomatoes. It was something I often made for Stanley and Iris. Oliver sat on the sofa in shorts and a T-shirt.

'I've got a Zoom with Neil in two weeks,' I said, peeling a clove of garlic. 'Just a catch-up, talking about how it's going to work when I'm back. I'm thinking of asking him to find me a different role.'

'What kind of thing?'

'Something less stressful. An editorial role maybe, regular hours so I can always make nursery pick-up. I can do four days and I won't have to work on the fifth.'

'Would he be able to do that?'

'They'd find me something. It just depends what's available. I don't want to end up on . . . you know, the letters page.'

He smiled. 'Would the letters page be so bad?'

'Yeah, all right, I know it's not getting vomited on in a hospital corridor. To me it would.'

'Look, why don't you just try going back to your old job? It's probably just daunting now because it's been nearly a year. I'm sure you can do it.'

'Everyone says that. "You can do it!" They don't tell you how to do it. The fact is, I can't afford the childcare I'd need to do my job properly. No amount of gumption is going to change that.' I took the scales out and measured the pasta. 'And I want to spend the time with Iris.' It surprised me how ashamed I felt to say that.

'But do you actually want to do something else?'

'Yes, actually. I do want to do something else. Something else would be great. I just don't know what the something else is.'

I tipped the pasta into the water, set a timer on my phone and came and sat down next to him.

'I liked my life when I was away,' I said. 'I don't want it to stay like that but I don't want to go back to the way it was either. And it can't go back to the way it was. And I feel so guilty saying that—'

'I felt guilty too,' he said, 'the whole time you were away. Because sometimes I enjoyed it. I enjoyed the work.'

'Really?'

'Yeah. I mean, it was awful. No one knowing what they were doing, working in half the space you normally have, having to tell someone that their mum was dying and no, they can't go in and see her. But last winter was awful too. And then no one gave a shit. So, yeah, people finally appreciating what you were doing, that was nice. I'm not saying I wanted it to happen, but if it was happening, I wanted to be part of it. I thought I would hate the clapping, but you know, I was in the flat that first night and I leant out of the window and I cried. And I thought maybe you were right. About me being like my dad.'

'I don't think you're like your dad.'

'There are nursing equivalents of what you're planning

to do. You know, nine till five. After this wave is over, I think I should try to do that. I should have just done that in the first place. And then you can do whatever you like.'

'You've been talking about doing that for, what, six years?' I said. 'There must be a reason why you haven't.'

'Because it's terrifying. This is the only thing I know how to do. It's the only thing I'm good at. But you know, all through these last few months, I didn't think about my dad once. I tried to make myself. I worried about my mum, even though she couldn't be less exposed where she is, and she had her neighbours dropping in on her. I worried about my gran, even though I knew she was being careful, and she had her church Zoom sessions and people getting food for her. My dad's elderly now. He's ninety-one and I didn't care if he got Covid. What sort of person does that make me?'

'I don't think it's your fault you're not close.'

'No, it's not my fault, but the reason we're not close is because he wasn't there. And because he's fucking annoying. But mostly because he wasn't there. I don't want that to be me. I don't want to get to the end of my life and Iris doesn't care about me because she never saw me.'

'That's not going to happen. We'll make sure that doesn't happen. And anyway,' I said, 'we're not that old. We can find something else we're good at. Can't we?'

The timer went off and I got up to drain the pasta. We ate it on the sofa, hips touching.

'I should go,' I said when I'd finished. 'I don't think it's fair on Lucy.'

'You should shower.'

'Yeah, I should. Hold on.' I texted Lucy: *all quiet?* She texted back: *yup.*

'We didn't actually decide anything tonight, though, did we?'

'No,' I said. 'We'll have to keep working on it.'

'And you want to . . . keep working on it together?'

I sat back down on the sofa and held his hand. 'Yes,' I said.

Epilogue

Ellen

1911

It was uncanny that the letters should arrive that day, exactly two years after the strike began. One was from Miss Morton, only she called herself Mrs Maxwell now. It was the second letter I'd had from her. In the first letter, she'd congratulated me on the settlement we'd made with Simpson & Fields, and said that she wanted to let me know her new name and address: she'd married a man named Jonathan Maxwell and lived with him in Gloucestershire. She'd enclosed a postal order so I could write back, but I never did. I kept the letter in my tea chest.

This time, she said she didn't know why she'd written. She didn't even know if we were still at the same address, but she had been thinking of me and her time working in Digby Street. Her husband had passed away and she was helping fundraise for the women's suffrage campaign. She had seen Mary at one of the London meetings, she said. She enclosed another postal order, for me to tell her my news.

I sat down at the table in the parlour. Mother had given me some notepaper from the drawer in her dresser, but the words wouldn't come. The truth was, there was no news that I really wanted to tell. The six months after the strike had been the loneliest of my life. Mary's dad had lost his job and the family did a flit to another part of London, owing Miss Povey money. Lou had married Jim – I saw her in Victoria Park six months after with a round belly and a black eye. The candle factory got a better settlement than us after the strikes and Betty had got a job there.

When Mother got a job in a different draper's shop and we didn't need my wage any more, she said I could go back to school if I wanted, but in the end she found me work in a dressmaking factory. It was more skilled work and better paid and I supposed that I could learn to make clothes one day, if I wanted. I hadn't learnt to swim. I hadn't learnt how to ride a bicycle. Mary was the one who'd practised on Miss Morton's bicycle, taking it out every day to Victoria Park, refusing help from the boys who offered to show her, swearing at the ones who laughed when she fell off. Finally, she got the hang of it and she took it with her when she left.

Iris was nearly two and a half now, as stubborn and infuriating as she was enchanting. She was a beauty, full of determined, indistinct words; she wrestled and screamed when she didn't get what she wanted. We were all in thrall to her, especially Davey, who was now her little nurse, racing home from school to take over minding her from Mrs Rose.

I got my tea chest out from under the sofa, unlocked it and folded the letter so I could put it away with the earlier one. I would write to her once I had decided if I was going to get married or not. Edward, one of the cutters from the factory who'd supported the strike, had asked me and

I still didn't know what I would say. I wouldn't have to work again if I did. I wasn't needed at home any more.

I looked out at Digby Street through the bay window, the box on the table next to me. If I was to marry, I would have to leave these things behind: it seemed daft to take these little relics from my childhood to my married home. But as well as leaving my belongings, and my family, and my name, I would leave the purple-and-yellow tiles round the chimneypiece, the oval mirror above it, the window I had cleaned hundreds of times. I would come back and visit, no doubt, but the place would never feel intimate to me again, the way it did now. And anyway, Mother was now talking about looking for new lodgings.

I went out into the passageway to return Mother's note-paper. Outside the doorway to the bedroom, I remembered when it had framed my first sight of Iris, the day she burst into existence. I went over to Mother's dressing table and opened the drawer that she had taken the paper from.

On the dressing table was an open envelope with a folded sheet of newspaper in. I recognised the headline. I slid it out and unfolded it: it was an article about the strike and the settlement from the local paper, with a photograph of us marching. Mother had carefully cut it out, circled my face and written my name with an exclamation mark by it. I put it back in the envelope and turned it over to look at the front; Mother was planning to send it to her sister, my aunt Catherine. I closed the drawer and went back into the parlour, feeling uncommonly light and happy.

I began to get ready to meet Edward. We'd been walking out for a few months – he'd taken me to the Black Hart and the music hall and for ice cream in Victoria Park – and he made me cry laughing. Sometimes, when we went out together, there'd be moments when I couldn't believe what I was doing – walking through the market on a Saturday night with a man from the factory, holding hands – and then I forgot about how strange it was because it felt so natural. On the last bank holiday on the Heath, I'd walked with him the way I'd walked with Mary, up into the forest. Between the trees we'd pushed our mouths and bodies together and I'd felt wild cravings that had only otherwise appeared to me in dreams.

Sometimes I looked at Iris and I remembered when she was a tiny being, melting on my chest as she slept. The connection between her then and her now got thinner every day – it was threadbare, but I could still see it in the right light: the face I'd seen for the first time that night in early June crossing her face now. I wondered what it would be like to grow a baby of my own inside me, whether that baby might stay, as Iris did.

I buttoned my good jacket and picked up my straw hat. I had got to the parlour door when I remembered that two letters had arrived that morning. I went back to the table, picked the other letter up and opened it. When I saw who it was from, I began to laugh, uninvited, uncontrollable gasps. Mary had only written a short note – she had seen Miss Morton at a meeting and thought about me, and how bad she felt about taking the bicycle, but she couldn't do without it now. I folded the letter and pressed it to my chest, squeezing my eyes shut with delight. She had invited me to tea in her new lodgings. The address was Unwin Court.

Frances

1991

We told my mum that Susie had family in Whitstable and we caught the train together for company. When we first started to visit, my mum would ask Susie about her family, and who it was she was visiting that weekend, but she'd stopped doing that now. When I arranged to come and see her, she no longer asked me if Susie was coming too. When we arrived, the table was set for three.

She offered us a glass of sherry and we sat on the skirted wine-red sofa, watching the sea. Last time we'd sat there, a few weeks ago, all we'd seen was shifting tones of greys and browns: the clouds, the pebbles, the water. Now, it was all blue. My mother took the rocking chair and we spoke about London, and the bookshop. Susie told her that she'd been made manager and that we thought we'd be able to afford a mortgage on a small house now. My mum thought we rented our house in Stoke Newington – we'd done so much work on it, you wouldn't be able to tell it was squatted.

We had tomato soup in willow-pattern bowls and my mother apologised for it being out of a tin. And then she said, 'Fiona Maxwell's giving a party at Chester Square next month.'

'Oh, gosh,' I said.

'Antonia's turning twenty-five, I believe, and Fiona and Richard are going to live in the place at Gloucestershire full-time now, so it's the last opportunity for a party at the house. I've been invited and she asked if I'd invite you.'

'It's been such a long time since I saw any of them.'

'Well, they always ask after you.'

'Who's Fiona Maxwell?' Susie said.

'An old school friend of mine. Frances was quite friendly with her children, before . . . Well, I just thought I'd mention it . . . I'd like to go. It's quite rare to get invited to things, you know, when you're a widow. People don't always know what to do with you when you're on your own.'

She said a version of this every time we met. I sighed, but Susie touched her hand. 'That can't be easy,' she said. 'You should definitely go.'

'I'll have a look at my diary when I get home,' I said, but I didn't ask when it was.

After lunch, my mother put the kettle on for tea and Susie took the plates into the kitchen and they argued about whether Susie was allowed to wash them up. I went over to the sofa and looked out at the sea, then flicked through the local newspaper on the coffee table. 'Police Hunt for Broadstairs Stabber', 'Fish Perish in Canal of Death', 'Father-of-Three and Local Policeman Commits Suicide'. I saw the picture and I felt a strange kind of horror.

It was Nick, in between his three boys, the four of them astride their bikes. The article called him Nicholas Hill. I skimmed it: he had jumped in front of a train, leaving his

436

wife and three teenage boys behind. It ended with a sum-
mary of the work he'd done in the community, including
'tireless fundraising for dementia, after his mother died in
1980'.

I closed the paper, and my mum and Susie came back
into the room. We had tea and talked about the sea, and
all the time my stomach was churning. Finally Susie said,
'F, we should probably get going, don't you think? If we
want to get our train.'

'It was so lovely to see you both,' my mother said.
'You'll come again soon, I hope. And let me know about
the party.'

'I will,' I said.

'I'm sure you could come too, Susie, if . . . if you wanted
to.'

'Oh, really?' I said. 'Do you think Fiona would mind?'

'I'm sure she wouldn't.'

'When did you say it was?'

'Twelfth of June.'

'Of course,' I said. 'I remember Antonia's birthday.'

We waited until we were a short distance from the house
before Susie took my hand on the beach, with the un-
spoken understanding that she would let go when we
reached town.

'So are we going to this party then?' she asked.

'No *way*! Honestly, it would be excruciating. I barely
knew her when we were at school.'

'Do you think your mum meant it, though? About in-
viting me.'

'I don't see why not.'

'Would you mind going with me?'

'Of course not,' I said, though I didn't know if that was true. When I was with Susie alone, or with our friends in the pub after seeing something at the Rio, I would look at her and feel an explosion of joy because I thought she was the most incredible person I'd ever met and she got better every day. If she went out without me, I'd lie in bed waiting for her to get home on her bicycle, imagining the telephone call in the middle of the night, and when I heard her key in the door, and the horror of trying to pick our lives apart had passed, I'd still murmur, 'Please don't die, Susie,' and she would kiss me on the forehead and say, 'Oh, you'd be fine without me. You'd call Naomi,' and I'd tell her to shut up and simply feel unbelievably, extraordinarily lucky. And yet, if we got a curious look, some drunken shouting, a threat, I would immediately feel foolish and peculiar all over again. I was scared that if I went back to Fiona Maxwell's giant living room, with Antonia, Felicity and Angela, even Violet, I'd turn back into the person I used to be.

But I could imagine something else as well. I could imagine turning up to Fiona Maxwell's party with Susie, and I knew that, even if we tried not to, our clothes would be wrong, and we'd look out of place, and everyone would talk about us after we left – they might even say cruel and callous things – but I'd only feel unbelievably grateful to be with her. And we'd go to the pub afterwards and make each other laugh, dissecting the food and the outfits. I didn't know if that was possible but perhaps, for now, being able to imagine it was enough.

'I don't understand why you want to go,' I said. 'I hated those parties growing up.'

'I've never been to a party in Belgravia. I don't think

I've ever been to Belgravia, come to that. And I want to see what you were like before you met me.'

'But that wasn't what I was like . . . None of that stuff was me. I never fitted in.'

'It's all part of you,' she said. 'If it made you into who you are now, I'm not complaining.'

I blushed and turned my face away, towards the sea.

'What do you want to do now?'

We always planned on getting the 3.40 p.m., but the trains were every hour and we sometimes stopped in the town for a drink on the beach.

'Shall we just keep walking for a bit?'

We walked through the town towards Tankerton. Then Susie said, 'Oh, look, the spit's out.' A long strip of land had surfaced and snaked all the way from the sea to the land. She looked at me, 'Do you want to paddle?'

'Why not?' I said.

We were both bare-legged, Susie in denim shorts and me in a floral skirt. She pulled off her trainers and running socks, and I undid the buckle on my sandals and we walked into the sea. The water was shallow and it stayed shallow: we walked and walked, and it never rose beyond our knees. When we stopped, we turned round and realised we were standing in the middle of the ocean, and the town was far away.

I had never told anyone about Nick. At first I was afraid of retribution, that if I said something, I'd end up with a knock on my door, a black eye. Even years after I'd left, it could still make me angry, thinking about the lies I'd believed. And then, the anger decreased and I didn't say anything because it seemed to matter less. Other memories had started to surface: him and Jane laughing softly and smoking. The way he cried when he told me about his mother. Some of what he'd shown me, I felt, had been true.

'Beer?' said Susie. 'Or station? I picked up some brochures from the estate agents, by the way. Thought we could have a look at some on the train.'

I looked back at the shore. We were still a long way from the beach. I grabbed her face and I kissed her on the mouth, and I felt the world recede. When I pulled away, her face was pink. 'Let's go home,' I said.

Amanda

2021

I carried my coffee out of the old fish and chip shop, and chose the table where I'd sat with Lucy, the day we'd first met. Lucy was late but I didn't mind this time. At the table next to me, I saw a woman with a baby, probably about three months old, in the same Babygro with tigers on it that Iris had once worn. Just looking at that fabric provoked a wave of unspecific longing, a mixture of loss and regret.

The woman had a coffee, in a takeaway cup, presumably so she could leave at any moment, and her phone and wireless headphones on the table. She lifted the baby up and down, and made faces at her, and then she put her in the pram and dangled a mobile over it with one hand, while she drank coffee with the other. Then she tried to do something with her phone and the baby started complaining. She put her phone and cup down and reached into the pram again. I felt that I knew her – that I had been her, and now I wasn't any more. In that moment, I felt desperately grateful, but also like I'd lost something vital, without knowing when or how it went. I wanted so much to say something to her but the only words that came into my head were the same trite reassurances that used to make me angry and miserable – *enjoy it! it goes by so fast!* – so I looked away instead.

I saw Lucy on the other side of the street and she waved at me before crossing the road. She was in the same rolled-up jeans and sandals she'd worn when I first saw her, but her jumper was new. I was wearing a new white shirt that Lucy had made, which I'd put on just before I left, so that Iris wouldn't get snot or tears or porridge on it. Over the winter, when we couldn't meet indoors, I had only ever seen people in my padded coat and hat, and I began to feel like the clothes and the body underneath it might as well not exist. I was still emerging from that time. Lucy had dyed her hair again. I had put on lipstick.

'How were the kids when you left?' I asked after she'd ordered and sat down next to me.

'Yeah, all good,' she said. 'Oliver and I had lunch with them and they were both asleep when I left.'

'What did you have for lunch?'

'I did this courgette salad. Oliver made a tahini dressing.'

'Did they eat it?'

'Not . . . lots. Iris tried it. They both had a lot of bread. And some yoghurt afterwards.'

'So they had bread and yoghurt for lunch.'

'Yes, but we exposed them to new flavours.'

'Sure, OK. Maybe let's just do pasta for tea, though.'

When they'd announced the stamp duty holiday, Oliver and I were finally able to sell our flat, and when the house we were buying fell through, Lucy said we could live with her temporarily. We'd had dinner together in the summer, and Lucy and Oliver took the piss out of me in a performative way to show they had bonded, and talked about people they both knew from London private schools, who all seemed to live a few streets away. It would have infuriated me in any other situation, but then I was just grateful. We were still living with Lucy when I went back to work in September – I'd been able to change my job, and we shared childcare. Iris and Stanley had a nanny, Nikola, three days a week and Lucy and I did a day each. Before the office reopened, I worked from her spare room.

When Oliver and I found a small house, further east, we kept the arrangement – I would cycle over with Iris in the morning and either Nikola or Lucy would look after her with Stanley while I worked in the bedroom I had slept in during the lockdown. Our lives and needs had meshed together and it felt impossible to extract them. Who was needed and who needed something changed over time – with Oliver's shift patterns, the Covid numbers, the restrictions, the children's ages. Sometimes I would start the day resentful and end it craven. It was uneasy, feeling so dependent on another family, but it was a price that we paid for sanity. Oliver and I still talked about when the pandemic would be over, about what sort of job he'd do next, what I wanted to do long-term, but plans for the future now seemed ornamental. It was nice to have them but they didn't mean very much. I was slowly getting used to this state.

On the days that Nikola came, I spent an hour with Iris and Stanley before she arrived. Lucy finished work an hour early and spent an hour with them after Nikola left. I still remembered what Meera had said about the quality of time with your children being more important than the quantity, and had decided that this hour would be the time

I made count. This was the rewarding time, when I would read to them or teach them about colours or shapes, or do interactive play.

And yet, there I was, lifeless on the sofa, letting them do something that I knew I would regret in less than five minutes – take all of my debit and credit cards out of my wallet, watch a singing video on my phone that I knew Lucy would hear from upstairs and disapprove of. Some terrible bargain for perhaps a minute of respite. Iris would cry because her biscuit broke, and I would say, *oh for fuck's sake*, rather than, *I can see why that's upset you.* Once, I said to Lucy that it felt like being in a room with two alarms that went off every three minutes. 'That would be fine,' she said. 'Three minutes' peace would be great. It's more like every thirty seconds.'

On Friday, the day I spent with both of them, I often finished the day feeling exhausted, empty and ashamed of myself for all the casual failures – anger, screens, sugar – and I'd wonder why I'd given up so much to commit to this endeavour I was so bad at.

'You've kept them alive,' Oliver reminded me, when I complained about not doing anything all day.

'Yeah, but it feels like that should be a baseline. It's not, like, a real achievement.'

'Other stuff's happening, though. They're changing, they're growing, they're learning. You're part of that.'

'It doesn't feel like that. It feels like I'm just watching it. I'm not the one making the change.'

'Maybe it's a bit of both,' he said.

And then one morning when we were waiting for Nikola to arrive, Stanley picked up his coat and Iris banged on the door saying, 'Out, out.' It was warmer now and we didn't all need to wrap up in so many layers of clothes, so I thought, *why not?* And we walked up and down the street, each of them holding my hand. We all wanted to walk in the same direction; the sun was on my face and Iris pointed at the bulbs coming up in the neighbours' front garden and said, 'Look! Flower!' It was the first time I had heard her say that word. Stanley took his coat and hat off and for once I didn't have to hustle him back into them. And I didn't know if it was quality time or not, what they were learning, if we were bonding, what the rewards would be. I only knew that, in that moment, I was happy.

That morning, I'd dropped in to the bookshop and chatted to Frances and Susie, and they gave me a flyer for a sale of Frances's ceramics that they were holding in her garden studio. I got my coffee from the café run by the Turkish sisters. They had started selling gözleme – an elderly woman in a headscarf sat in the window rolling the dough – and they still sold the groceries they'd introduced during lockdown, to survive: shelves of soy sauce, organic baby food and oat milk. And then I walked with my coffee, out onto the high street and past the factory building.

We'd had a few people interested, and in the end we'd had to choose between two offers, both higher than the asking price. One was from a couple in their late twenties and another from a woman in, I guessed, her late thirties. I had wanted her to have it. I made up some reason to Oliver but really I was thinking about how I'd been the same age when I came to the building, and also alone.

I stood in front of the gate, holding my takeaway coffee. I could only just remember what it felt like to be pregnant now – the sensations were beginning to seem almost as foreign as if they'd never happened to me. I could remember much more clearly what it was like before Iris – to come home and feel that utter aloneness and freedom, the joyful absorption in my work.

There were things I liked about my new job – the collaboration, the regularity, the quiet pleasure of improving other people's copy – but at the same time I found myself longing for the unsteadiness and excitement of the old job with a viciousness that astounded me. The last two years had felt like an exercise in modifying ambition, squashing desire, accepting disappointment, and sometimes, without warning, resentment coursed through me, and I felt the weight of all the things I hadn't done.

Despite that, when Lucy or Oliver took the children out at a weekend, when I was pushing Iris on a swing and making notes on my phone, at the end of the day when she fell asleep in my arms and I was finally still and quiet, I kept nurturing ideas. Most of them died from lack of attention, but one of them grew and evolved, painfully slowly. My long feature on women's working lives in Hackney, inspired by finding out about Margaret Card, had run a couple of weeks ago.

Before Iris, I had tried my hardest to be absent from what I wrote – I strived to be measured, emotionless. I prized objectivity and detachment. This was the first time I'd felt truly connected to my subject: I'd spoken to women at the community centre when I'd gone to singing groups, who ran the cafés and the bookshop, who lived on my nana's estate. I was present in the copy: I offered opinions, I took a stance. I was part of the story, part of the multiplicity of women's voices. Before, I'd been proud of how I could steel myself against unpleasant things; now, when I interviewed women in low-wage jobs, in insecure housing, reliant on food banks and baby banks, when I wrote about Margaret Card, I felt a fraction of their vulnerability.

I briefly mentioned my connection to Hackney and, while it felt exposing to write that my grandmother had lived on a council estate, I also knew that nothing could make me feel as stripped bare as the experience of having Iris, and I had survived. 'I mean, not to be crude, but it's a great angle,' my editor said. 'You'll know more about this place than someone who went to Cheltenham Ladies' College. It can be your USP.'

When the feature ran, I had got the congratulatory texts from colleagues, and a brief email from the editor, which I would remember forever. They still made me happy, the greedy little spikes of validation, but it hadn't felt the same as it once had. It was brutal, this rearrangement of desire. I could feel the shifts beneath the surface, see parts of me breaking off and drifting away, not knowing whether they would stay close or be lost forever. I was turning away, or being turned away, from the familiar, and I did not know what I was turning towards. And yet in the centre, something different was forming. I did not know whether it was better or worse, but it was new and I had energy and hope. I looked up at the windows and I thought about the building's new resident. I hoped that her time there would be different, and better.

Lucy and I took the train up to Hampstead together. Mostly we talked about our children and how they combined with our work, but what we were really talking about was time, the way it shrank and expanded, how a meeting or a walk could extinguish a working day, how torturous the hour before tea and bath could be. How many hours did we need to work, how many hours did we need childcare for, what time should we do the children's tea, when should they go to nursery, when should they be out of nappies, when, if ever, should we have more children? But today we didn't talk about any of that. We talked about a new fabric she was excited by, a new idea I'd had for a story, a new café that had just opened up.

The train cut its mad uneven seam through the city, slipping between glass and steel, through and above the rooftops. I watched the jumble unfold through the window – the white turrets, the pastel-blue rendering, the sky-lights, the washing hanging out, the offices, the balconies, the king-size beds in the luxury flats, the drainpipes, the buddleia, cranes, factories, council flats, chimneys.

The sky was bright blue, merging to pale gold at the edges, and the grass was soft beneath our feet, punctuated by bright-yellow wild flowers. We reached the ponds and I'd never seen them so crowded. A girl with pink hair and thick eye make-up, pale breasts slipping out of her black bikini, went one rung down the ladder and screamed and got out. She and her friend clung to each other, laughing. A colossal woman with dimpled thighs and grey hair tucked under a woollen hat looked at them, wryly disdainful. I looked at all the heads in the water, like happy, bobbing seals.

The sun went in as we came out of the changing hut and Lucy stood at the edge of the water in her bikini.

'Oh, I don't know now,' she said. 'The water's still going to be cold, right?'

'You get used to it so quickly, though,' I said.

'Maybe we should just sunbathe for a bit first.'

'No, come on, we've got to,' I said.

I went down the steps and into the water, the iciness still breathtaking, just waiting for the moment when it gave way to pure pleasure. I swam past the black moorhens with a dash of red on their bills, the ducks with sheeny heads and tawny feathers. A heron sat on a ring, neck like a pipe, bluish-grey feathers textured like a waterfall, and a deep-blue V above the eyes. I turned onto my back and dipped my head back into the water. When I looked up, I saw Lucy swimming towards me.

Acknowledgements

The starting point for this novel was Louise Raw's *Striking a Light: The Bryant and May Matchwomen and their Place in History*. I owe a lot to her analysis of the 1888 Matchwomen's Strike. Other very useful books include *Growing Up Poor: Home, School, and Street in London, 1870–1914* by Anna Davin, *Independent Women: Work and Community for Single Women, 1850–1920* by Martha Vicinus and *Love and Toil: Motherhood in Outcast London, 1870–1918* by Ellen Ross. I am grateful to Roxanne Stephen for allowing me access to her oral history of squatting in Hackney, which she compiled for Hackney Museum. The line 'There are so many roots to the tree of anger', which appears in Clare's artwork, is from the poem 'Who Said It was Simple' by Audre Lorde.

I am grateful to the people who agreed to speak to me about, among other things, clothes, pubs, nursing, Waterlow Court and their memories of Hackney: Carol Ackroyd, Tim Donkin, Edwina Gieve, Sophia Hicks, Andrew Howard, Paul Lee, Arnold Linden, Alexandra Rook and Danielle Sprecher.

ACKNOWLEDGEMENTS

Thank you to everyone who provided the necessary conditions to write: Anouchka Grose, Petra Lipenská, Alison Stork, Thomas Stork, Mark Tewfik and Celine Goetz, and Folarin Thompson and her incredible team. I am particularly grateful to my parents, John and Lindsay Murray-Browne, for all kinds of support. I would also like to thank the Society of Authors for an Authors' Foundation grant, the staff at the Women's Library at LSE and Hackney Archives, and the British Library, for having everything and welcoming everyone.

Thank you to my early readers – Robert Williams, Christina Petrie and Laura Kaye – for their kindness and shrewd observations, to Victoria Murray-Browne for her unstinting enthusiasm and support, and to Will Francis and Francesca Main for their dedication, energy and faith in the book. And to Silvia Crompton for her wonderfully attentive and thorough copyedit.

I am grateful to Chris Stork, for wanting me to write and arranging our lives so that I could, for reading it twice and giving invaluable responses, but most of all for our conversations. They were full of insights and observations that shaped the book – and they were so much fun.

This book is dedicated to Florence and Nancy Murray-Browne, the funniest and most determined girls I know. They were inside me, beside me and on my mind as I wrote. I can't wait to see what they begin.

About the Author

Kate Murray-Browne worked in publishing for ten years before becoming a freelance editor. Her first novel, *The Upstairs Room*, was critically acclaimed and selected as a Book of the Year in *The Times*. She lives in Hackney, East London, with her family.